A Detective Chief Inspector Carter Mystery

HIGH-RISE BLOOD

By G.D. Gaherty

[ISBN]: 978-0-6455492-0-1
[ISBN] (e-book): 978-0-6455492-1-8

highriseblood.com

This is a work of fiction. Unless otherwise indicated, all
the names, characters, businesses, places, events and
incidents in this book are either the product of the
author's imagination or used in a fictitious manner. Any
resemblance to actual persons, living or dead, or actual
events is purely coincidental.

For

Mum

Dad among the stars

The Wolfpack & Canoe School

I acknowledge the people of the Woi Wurrung and Boon Wurrung language groups of the eastern Kulin Nation on whose unceded lands this book was written. I respectfully acknowledge their Ancestors and Elders, past and present.

CHAPTER ONE

A soft buzzing sound filled Carter's empty bedroom. His personal mobile in his bedside table rang, beckoning him to answer. The buzzing sound stopped. Silence briefly returned to the sparse bedroom at 4 a.m. Then a chirping sound from on top of his bedside table filled his room. Now his work mobile rang.

He'd missed three calls now and a litany of text messages demanding his attention. He'd lost track of time.

Ice-cold water shot from the showerhead of Carter's ensuite. His hands splayed against the tiled shower; his head hung low. Goosebumps covered his skin, sun-kissed from plenty of summers under the Australian sun. The water cascaded across his broad, muscular shoulders, and down his rising sun Australian military tattoo on his right muscular pec. The golden tattoo had swords and bayonets arranged in a semi-circle with a crown in the middle to show allegiance to the Commonwealth.

Another brash decision for Carter. He enlisted to feel like he belonged. The tattoo faded over the years; the gold dyes had lost their sheen.

The water flowed down his abs and over his flaccid cock. The water pooled on the black and blue tiles. His right foot furiously tapped the ground.

You can't stay in here all day.

Carter stepped out of the shower and towelled himself down. He glanced towards his bedroom. Both his mobiles were ringing.

I'm not ready.

He turned to face the foggy bathroom mirror.

He drew a large rectangle in the condensation at the top of the mirror with his index finger. He wrote 'Thunder

Slot' inside the rectangle and then etched out three square boxes, side by side at eye level. A wave of ecstasy flowed through Carter as he let his imagination create a pokie machine out of mist.

A merman appeared from above, his pale lithe arms draped across the square boxes. Cinched waist with a tail of shimmering green and pink scales moved in rhythm, flicking to and fro.

"Join me for an underwater adventure." His coy voice lured Carter in for a spin.

Carter's fingers tapped the porcelain basin as if they were buttons.

"All right, bet ten dollars." His fingers tapped another part of the basin. "Add a two times multiplier. Why not? I feel lucky." Carter smiled into the mirror. "No, you know what? I *am* lucky."

He turned the cold tap to start the game. The first digital symbol dropped — a golden coin. Cartoon air bubbles floated up as the golden coin settled at the bottom of the digital underwater landscape. The merman winked, encouraging him on. Carter turned the tap to drop the next symbol. Carter grinned. Another treasure chest.

The shimmering merman tail continued to flick to and fro.

"This will be the one, I'll win the jackpot this time." Carter marvelled at the shimmering merman with the smooth muscular arms. "Give me a treasure chest."

"How about I give you something else?" The merman bit down on his lower lip.

Carter felt a bolt of sexual energy strike his cock.

"Not that," said the merman. "We can just stay here and talk. You be the little spoon and I'll be the big listener."

Carter shook his head. "Rather play the pokies."

"Is that really what you want?" asked the merman. The merman smirked as he tilted his head.

2

Carter hesitated for a moment. "Better here than out there," he said as he glanced out a window to the sleeping city of Melbourne.

The merman chuckled as his tail flicked to and fro. "Find out if it's the right choice then."

Carter turned the tap. A cartoon anchor fell. He didn't win the   jackpot. His heart sank.

The merman shook his head at him. "It's always a near miss. You know that." The merman smiled flirtatiously. "One more spin. This time you'll win."

"Hit my limit today, darling."

"You'll be back tomorrow," said the merman.

The silence returned to Carter's ensuite — the fantasy over. He checked himself over: fraying from tip to toe. He ran his fingers through his jet-black hair. The sides and top of his head were crew-cut short. He applied pressure as he pulled his fingers against the grain of the hair. The noise of crunching hair filled the ensuite, silent save for the drips of water from the faucet — drip, drip, drip.

And the relentless chirping from his bedroom, of course.

He finally answered it.

"Leo Carter here."

"It's Davies. Did I wake you?" Superintendent Liz Davies, Carter's boss and mentor at the Major Crimes Division within Metro Police. The daughter of Dutch immigrants, her striking presence at six feet matched her striking wit.

"Not exactly Ma'am, just heading to bed."

"Heading to bed? It's 4 a.m."

Silence filled the air. Carter didn't want to explain himself.

"Don't bother putting on your pyjamas then," she said. "I need you to get to Collingwood pronto, you're Officer in Charge at a scene that's developing."

"Umm, boss, I'm still on holiday."

"That ended on the sixteenth, and we are now four hours into the sixteenth."

Carter shook his head. Davies loathed regulations, red tape, and the general bureaucracy they worked in, but she would not hesitate to break down and enforce a rule if it worked in her favour.

"Yes, boss. Where in Collingwood? And can I request Emily as my 2IC?" Carter asked as he opened his dresser drawer and rummaged through for a pair of underwear. He pulled out a red jockstrap. He dangled the pair in front of his eyes. Not work appropriate, Carter thought to himself as he continued to rummage around.

"She'll be there with bated breath. She can't wait to see you again, I reckon. Told her to skip the welcome back cake and balloons. The crime scene is a laneway next to Vapour. I assume all the gays know where that is?"

"Vapour, or the trendy laneways of Melbourne?" asked Carter. He then pulled out a pair of black briefs that were a size too small. Carter threw the pair across the room into the overflowing rubbish bin.

Those aren't mine, he thought.

"Vapour, I'm not interested in lattes in laneways," said Davies.

"I know of Vapour. One advantage of an inclusive hiring policy, eh, boss?" asked Carter as he pulled out a pair of white briefs. He switched to speaker phone and placed his mobile down on the dresser drawer. Carter stepped into the briefs and pulled them up. He adjusted his package, so his shaft presented front and centre.

"You'd make a terrible florist; you're better off as a cop. And it's time to come back," said Davies.

"Vapour." Carter let the word hang in the air. He knew of that bathhouse. Not from personal experience but through its owner. His first love and one of the current candidates running in the by-election for the federal seat of Melbourne.

"James bloody Hughes," Carter said.

"Know him, do you? Have you visited Vapour recently?"

Carter scoffed. "Sex is the last thing on my mind. I know him from my days as the LGBTQ liaison officer. And before then as well."

"Another reason I need you on point with this. James Hughes might be the federal member for Melbourne by the time this case is closed."

"Has a brother in pink died?"

"In short, yes. We have a deceased Caucasian male, early twenties, left outside a gay bathhouse."

"So, the police bigwigs, PR drones, and a risk-averse government bureaucrat all want to make sure the narrative of this investigation is one of support and understanding for the queer community. They don't want a bull in an China shop leading and being the face of this case."

"Yes, all right, big surprise, you and I know the optics align," Davies said.

"And there's an election," Carter chimed in.

"Yes, and the owner of Vapour is running in that election. I can't have this case getting bungled."

"I'll be there shortly," Carter said.

"Good to have you back on the team," Davies said before she disconnected.

CHAPTER TWO

Hair slicked back, wearing a blue polo shirt and black slacks, Carter stepped out of his flat. Before he closed the door, his eyes glanced down at a black duffle bag. Carter had kept the bag by his door for the last two months. His version of a bug out bag in case he won big at the pokies. He'd grab the bag and hop on a plane at a moment's notice to a tropical destination and never look back at his old life in Melbourne.

As he shut the door, he was instantly drenched in sweat from head to toe. A gusty thirty degrees even though the sun had yet to rise. He lifted his arms and saw sweat stains developing in each armpit.

Melbourne's summers are the worst.

Carter headed for his green Skoda parked outside his flat. He only ever drove Skodas. Some people thought this type of car to be the poor cousin of Audi, but Carter loved them. Efficient, reliable and with a pop of colour; the car of his dreams that never broke down.

The automatic locks switched on the second after he sat down in the driver's seat and closed the door. How he liked it. Locks prevented access. Kept the world out.

He pushed down on the ignition button. His car purred to life. Hands tightened around the wheel. Cool air burst from the vents and hit his face. The radio came to life on Carter's guilty pleasure: talk-back radio.

"Are. You. Listening. People," the radio announcer bellowed out each single word with force. "It's another perfect example of this government gone mad. It's a furphy to think this is a good government," the radio announcer drew out the vowels of government and let them hang in the air like washing on a line. "Corrupt politicians, unions, and lefty activists are steering the agenda, and what do we get" – the announcer paused for effect – "we get a bloated public bureaucracy doing squat and families on the brink of poverty. This by-election let's send a message to the useless Labour party. They are on Goddamn notice."

Carter drove out of his car park onto Rose Street in Fitzroy. The gentrifying suburb included a mix of workers' cottages, townhouses, and warehouses converted into loft-style apartments.

Gnarly branches of Eucalyptus trees intertwined along the length of Rose Street. Colloquially known as gum trees, they had sensed the start of summer. Seed pods and shavings of dead bark rested at the bases of the trees. While the trees' fragrance of mint, pine and a dash of honey filled the air.

Carter's GPS told him it was a ten-minute drive to Vapour, the premier sex-on-premises bathhouse in Melbourne. Located on the border between the Abbotsford and Collingwood suburbs, a short drive from his flat in Fitzroy.

A typical Fitzroy early Monday morning greeted Carter as he drove through the suburb. People partied hard on Sunday night and spilled out early Monday morning from the bars and clubs. The partygoers stumbled over to the junk-food vendors lining the streets soaked in fluorescent lighting from the street lamps. Carter marvelled at their stamina as some continued the party at the clubs that were still open.

Carter parked one block south-east of Vapour in front of a club called Swish. The red-brick club took up an entire block with a set of large oak doors to welcome patrons in. Swish was one of the few queer clubs open till sunrise on the Northside of Melbourne. Rainbow lights pulsed along the length of the building. While techno and pop music mashups pumped out the doors and bouncers checked IDs of incoming patrons.

Never be at Swish when the sun rises. A generation of party animals learned this the hard way and passed this vital intel down to the next generation. At sunrise when the club closes, they switch on the floodlights to move the patrons out.

That light flatters no one; let alone the sticky floors and walls covered in split drinks. The gentle daylight outside from the rising sun, or the dim lighting of bedrooms, were the preferred alternatives.

Vapour was one hundred and fifty metres away. Red and blue flashing lights caught his attention. A small crowd lingered at the mouth of the alleyway, as he expected, but not as big a group as a homicide usually drew. He supposed they don't like loitering in front of a bathhouse.

"Clear a path," said Carter. He started to make his way through the crowd. A couple blocked his path. He had to go through them.

"I wonder what happened?" asked the woman.

"Probably someone from Vapour died. Let's go back to Swish. There's still time for us to pick up," said the man.

"Separately," chimed in the woman.

"Clear a path," repeated Carter with a stern edge to his voice.

"Piss off, we want the best view," said the man.

"I said clear a path. Now," said Carter.

The pair turned around and both took in the towering Carter. Their jaws dropped. "What a hunk of spunk," the man said at a loud drunk whisper that Carter heard. Carter stood at an impressive six foot two inches.

"Or you could come back to Swish with me," said the woman.

"No thanks," said Carter.

"Cuz you'd rather go to Swish with me?" asked the man. A hint of hope and lust carried on his voice.

Carter licked his lips. An enticing offer, he thought.

"I'm on the job," said Carter as he moved past them.

"Hit us up on your break," yelled the couple in unison.

Carter didn't respond but a smile formed as he heard the pair laugh. Still got it, thought Carter.

The laneway nestled itself between Vapour and a red-brick industrial building. High-voltage lights on tripods had been set up in the laneway. These ensured every nook and cranny didn't escape the forensic review by the police for any shred of evidence. Orange plastic evidence markers had already been methodically placed across the pavement. Each one identified a piece of physical evidence to be catalogued. Halfway down the alleyway, a tent had been erected. This concealed the body from curious bystanders with smartphones at the ready.

At the far end of the laneway a second cordon blocked traffic off Punt Road; one of Melbourne's major thoroughfares. Cars and trucks zoomed past, oblivious to the tragedy in the laneway.

Detective Inspector Emily Song and a constable Carter didn't recognise stood by the cordon. Carter moved to cross the police tape. The constable stepped in front of him, blocking his entry. He held a clipboard to track the comings and goings into the crime scene.

"Excuse me, sir, can I get your badge number?"

Guess my reputation doesn't precede me, Carter thought.

"This is the detective I told you about, Zhang," Song said.

Constable Zhang nodded. "Gotcha. Name is Sam Zhang," Zhang smiled and lifted the police tape for Carter to pass under.

Shorter than Carter, Zhang was a compact unit. Rugby player frame with lean muscles, Carter noticed a koi fish tattoo on the constable's bicep. Carter couldn't be certain as the uniform covered the constable's shoulder and back, but he suspected the tattoo continued. Carter wanted to see all of it.

"Do I know you, Constable Zhang?" Carter asked.

"No sir," he said, "I reckon we're neighbours. You live in Fitzroy?"

"Certainly do, right near the markets."

"I live a street over from the markets."

"That must be it. Good to meet you." Carter shook Zhang's hand. He felt a spark from the firm shake that drove straight down to his groin.

"Likewise, Detective," said Zhang.

"Reckon I've also seen you at Railed a few times," Zhang said as he lowered the yellow police tape.

"Used to be my local," Carter said. "You like visiting Railed?"

Carter thought of the mermaid pokies machine at Parlour. "Join me for an underwater adventure," the merman said as he flicked his shimmering tail.

Zhang's smile brought Carter back to reality. "I'm a friend of Dorothy too."

Carter couldn't help but smile. "I'm surprised you know the term."

Zhang smirked. "I grew up watching RuPaul. She taught us a thing or two."

"Come on, Carter, we got work to do," Song said.

Song and Carter walked a few paces past the police tape. She tossed Carter a pair of gloves and plastic shoe coverings. Song motioned towards Zhang as Carter put on his gear.

"Davies is keen to bring in the new guard. Zhang's been supporting our unit, along with a few other constables. He's one of the better ones, approaching the end of his probationary period. Pretty sure he'll apply to join our squad."

The new guard is pretty easy on the eyes, Carter thought. He pulled the plastic shoe covering over his black suede boots.

"Davies got you off holiday for this?" Song asked.

Carter marvelled at Song's composure, 5 a.m., 5 p.m. – it didn't matter. She epitomised composure.

"Was due back today anyways, trial by fire. Brass wants to make sure we seem inclusive."

"Well, it's good to know I'll be Officer in Charge if there are any suspicious deaths in a Thai massage parlour," said Song.

"But you're not Thai," Carter said.

"Brass wouldn't know the difference," Song said dryly.

Carter chuckled and beamed a wide smile. The first smile in a few months. "It'll be your time to shine soon, Song."

"Don't you worry Carter, I know," said Song. She rolled her shoulders back and stood with an air of authority that came from her refined and sophisticated upbringing combined with her status in Metro police.

She'll be Commissioner in no time, thought Carter.

"It's good to see you," Song said.

The pair fist bumped, "You too. Am glad the band is back together," Carter said.

"When do I get a secret handshake?" Zhang asked as he passed the two detectives.

"Pass your probation. Then we'll talk about a secret handshake," Song said.

Zhang nodded, "Welcome back to the jungle, Detective Carter." He appeared to be swapping posts and heading for the second cordon at the bottom of the laneway. Zhang winked as he and Carter made eye contact.

"He's a cheeky bugger," said Carter.

Song let out a laugh, "Runs in the squad."

"Let's see what we have," said Carter.

Carter and Song stood side by side and gazed down the laneway, framed within the crumbling industrial buildings.

He wondered if the victim knew they were approaching their end when they left their home. Death always came faster than anyone cared to admit.

"We have a single Caucasian male victim, mid-twenties. As you see, there are no tyre marks in the alley, but I'm pretty certain the perpetrators dumped the body. May show the location was planned, whole murder orchestrated, rather than a rush, hack job to get rid of the body," Song said.

Jumping to conclusions, but probably right, thought Carter.

Carter and Song began a slow walk on the cobblestone laneway towards the tent. The laneway could have been a trash can; given the volume of discards from the previous night left on the ground. Broken bottles, needles, and ripped-apart takeaway containers littered the cobblestones.

"Middle of Collingwood, bars, and clubs around the corner, there's got to be quieter, safer places to leave a body. If the body was deliberately dumped here, what message are they sending?" Carter asked.

Song nodded, "Lots of potential recipients of such a message. James Hughes, bathhouse users, the general LGBTQI+ community."

"Any evidence so far of a hate crime?" Carter asked.

"There is nothing out of the ordinary here. The victim's body is a different story. There's a single word carved into the victim's chest, and he certainly took a beating," Song said.

"One challenge at a time," Carter said as he stepped around a needle. "We are walking through a bloody sea of needles," Carter said.

"Crystal meth. The bogan drug of choice has surged in Melbourne. Reckon the bikies are cooking it across the regional towns. Funnelling it down to Melbourne. Ruining the regional areas and the city all at once."

"Larger market in the city," Carter said.

"Assuming they don't overdose and die," Song lamented.

Carter nodded. Stats were pretty bad. Even if users wanted help, there are not enough treatment beds. Constables are turning into janitors — finding victims, cold to the touch. He stepped over two needles and a shattered beer bottle.

A lone detective leaned against one of the pillars of the tent. Carter recognised the salt and pepper hair of Detective Perry. A lifer in the Major Crimes unit.

He started out as Song's superior but never climbed the ranks. In under a year the roles changed, and Perry reported up to Song. Perry never expressed a hint of envy or jealousy from the role reversal. He just got on with the job.

"Perry, you know Carter, he'll be OIC," Song said.

Perry extended a hand. "Good to have you back, mate."

Perry reminded Carter of Santa Claus. A jolly heavy-set man, but instead of a sack full of presents, he carried a gun.

"Good to see you too, how's the commute from Geelong going?" asked Carter.

Perry smiled, "Aww, you know, mate, same old, same old."

"Were you the first detective on the scene?" Song queried.

Perry shook his head. He then glanced up and down the length of the laneway. "Nah, he's not around, must be in Vapour."

"Who?" Carter asked.

"Hillier," said Perry

"The golden boy strikes again," Song said.

Perry chuckled, "Very naughty DI Song. We are a collaborative, innovative, and supportive team. At least that's what HR tells us to say."

Carter alternated glances between the two of them, waiting for some explanation about this new detective.

Song picked up on the confusion, "Detective Hillier transferred in as you went on leave. Let's say he has an inflated sense of himself," she said.

"Is that HR-appropriate language DI Song?" Perry asked.

Song shrugged, "I won't snitch to HR if you won't."

Perry motioned that his lips are sealed.

"Why does the name Hillier sound so familiar?" Carter asked.

Song pushed back in the few strands of hair that came loose from her bun. Then she tucked her blouse into her jeans and placed her hands on her hips. She tilted her head towards him – a sign. He should know the name.

"No way, he's related to Assistant Commissioner Hillier?"

Song nodded, "The one and only. Andrew Hillier Jr. Started as a Protective Services Officer with the Metro – personal trainers with guns. Joined the force, and the first non-uniform position he gets is here."

"He got a pretty plum posting off the back of Daddy."

"Pays to know people in high places."

"Not too high, then you're in their pocket," Carter said.

"Where is Hillier now?" Carter asked.

"Taking statements inside the club," Song supplied.

Perry opened one of the tent flaps concealing the body. "Techs have finished up with the body."

"Just to warn you, boss," Song said, glancing around. "Victim shares a similar appearance to" – she paused and made sure no one was within earshot – "Theo. Same age and features."

Carter's heartbeat quickened.

Stay cool mate, he thought. Even though he and Theo had parted on rotten terms, he didn't wish anyone dead in this shitty laneway.

"All white guys look alike," he joked. Then, "He's not though? Is he?"

"That's one of the things I wanted you to confirm."

"Let's see what we got," Carter said.

The two-by-two-metre canopy centred over the victim's body. Harsh fluorescent lights hung along the steel beams that crisscrossed along the top and illuminated the ground. The tent was a stage, the victim was the problem, Carter, the reluctant star.

Carter felt Song and Perry's eyes on him.

Showtime, he thought.

"He shares some traits with Theo, but that's not him," Carter began.

Song's composure broke for a moment as relief crosses her face.

He reached into his back pocket and took out his notebook. Carter scribbled down notes as he walked around the body.

He started at the base of the victim. One bare foot and a single black converse shoe greeted Carter. Where's the other shoe, wrote Carter in his notebook. As Carter scanned the body, he noted the blood-stained blue jeans. The victim lay face up with his empty emerald-green eyes open to the world. A lifeless, lithe body with a single word carved into it.

Carter grimaced momentarily at the sight of the victim's chest. He gulped.

Poof

The bloodied word had been carved across the victim's chest. Just below his pecs.

15

Carter wrote the word poof into his notepad.

"Alright," said Carter as squinted at the word carved into the victim. "The blood is clotted, matted around the incisions."

"Damn, poor lad," said Perry, "Would have hurt."

"Coroner will need to confirm, but it's a safe bet the victim was alive when the word was carved into the body," said Carter.

"They'll be able to determine make and size of the weapon."

"His clothes are pretty casual; he wasn't out clubbing. Doubtful he'd have gotten into any of the clubs around here dressed like that. Might have been to a bar but reckon that is a stretch too. Techs haven't found the other shoe?" asked Carter.

Perry shook his head. "We are checking all the rubbish bins around. May have been tossed in the bin, like the victim tossed out onto the street."

"Not tossed. There's a message behind it," said Carter.

Carter gazed at the bruised and bloodied face staring up at him. The victim's discoloured face stood out the most. Cheeks were dark shades of purple; a thick red line of blood followed the orbital bone's shape. Scrapes and cuts across his forehead; his messy peroxide blonde hair stained a bloody red.

"He took a beating alright," said Carter as he scribbled into his notepad: hate crime.

"His face is swollen. Probably took the beating before he was killed," Song suggested.

Carter nodded. "Agreed, and a beating like this, had to be personal. No one takes out this much anger on someone for nothing."

"I reckon the victim probably knew his attackers given his casual attire," said Perry.

"Or about to get to know them in the biblical sense," said Song.

Carter nodded. "Maybe they lured him for sex and took their anger out on him?" He glanced back down at the word carved into in the victim's chest. "Not here though. This laneway is too busy to lure and murder someone." Carter scanned the cobblestones around the victim. "There also isn't enough blood."

"Maybe the victim and the perpetrators met in Vapour and lured him outside," Perry suggested.

Carter shook his head. "If the murder happened in Vapour there'd have been more commotion. It must have been done somewhere else."

"That means we are looking for two suspects."

"Why two?" asked Perry.

"One to drive, and another to help dump the body. It's a two-person crime," said Song.

"Spot on the money, Song. Unlikely someone risked driving, moving, and dumping a body solo." Carter felt deflated as he processed the crime scene in his head. "I wish we were over this type of crime by now."

Song nodded gravely. "It does make you wonder what sort of world we live in. And what type of message this is meant to be."

"And to whom," Carter said as he lifted the tent curtain. "Let's get him to the morgue. See if we can identify him."

Carter felt his mobile vibrate and thought about the lotto apps on it. The option to buy a lottery ticket enticed him, he salivated at the thought of winning. He had just shoved his hand in his pocket to take out his mobile when he heard footsteps echo down the alleyway.

A plainclothes officer jogged towards Carter, Song, and Perry. The officer had an air to him that Carter immediately disliked. The echo of his shoes sounded too rich.

"Song, who's this?"

The querying detective had the appearance of a Melbourne private-school-boy grownup with a silver spoon tucked in his tailored Jack London suit's pocket. His shoes and watch were more expensive than Carter's entire wardrobe. He carried himself with an authority he never earned, but that comes with the territory when you have blonde hair, blue eyes and a swimmer's build. The impressive square jawline and pinched features made him an impressive specimen of a man.

"This is DCI Carter, Officer in Charge for this investigation," Song said.

"You must be Detective Hillier," Carter said, extending a hand.

"I was the first detective on the scene," Hillier said, ignoring the hand. "Reckon I should be in charge."

Song and Perry exchanged a smirk between each other.

"Well, you're not, and Detective Song is my number two. You can call Davies yourself if you got a problem with it."

Carter shifted his stance so that he and Hillier were staring straight at one another, "Do we have a problem?"

Hillier shook his head, "Nah."

"Good. Give me an update," Carter said.

"Uniforms are in Vapour. A few of the common rabble to interview. The rest of them scattered when the cops were called."

"Rabble," Carter said. His eyes narrowed as Hillier continued talking.

"Building is secure. Should we go inside to interview the ones too stupid to leave before we arrived?" Hillier asked.

A warm gust of wind travelled down the alleyway to rustle Carter from his trance of anger directed towards Hillier.

A piercing siren alarm flooded the alleyway. The detectives' heads turned in unison. Vapour's emergency exit door flung open. A blue light flashed above it.

A group of men poured out the wailing door. Three, four, five men in total stumbled out in tattered clothes with backpacks. They had that frazzled and sleepy appearance like their collective alarm clock had woken them up. Or in this case, a fire alarm.

Carter slowly jogged over to them.

This is dangerous, what if one of them tries a runner Carter thought.

"Whoa gents, stop right there," Carter said. He extended his arms to visually signal to them to stop moving. "Going to get you to head back in and meet the officers at the reception. This area is a crime scene."

A man at the back broke from the pack. Hoodie up, head down, he sped towards Punt Road.

The fleeing figure stood about five feet eight inches. White singlet, jean shorts, ball cap. Male, fit.

Bloody hell, he can run, thought Carter. If he's so keen to get out, why didn't he go before we shut down the club?

"Oi, mate, stop," Carter yelled. "Stop!"

The figure approached the police tape. Zhang, the lone constable stationed there, released a burst of capsicum spray at the target. The fiery orange mist coated the figure's grey jumper.

The figure charged through the misty orange plume. The constable crouched down and moved to tackle him. He sped up. In an arch, he brought his elbow from his side. He slammed it into Zhang's jaw. He hit the ground. The figure darted around the corner. Zhang righted himself and lit out after him.

Carter rushed around the corner onto Hoddle Street to find Zhang hunched over, resting his arms on his legs as he caught his breath — deep frustrated breaths.

"Guy jumped into a white Commodore before I could get to him. So close to tackling him but he jumped into the car. Latin American, I think. That car appeared to be waiting for him."

Carter followed the stream of cars that flowed down Hoddle Street. Half the cars would merge into the various offramps to join the highway. An estuary of roads to the sea that is Melbourne and Victoria.

"Are you all right?" Carter said.

"Yeah I am. Sorry I couldn't catch that dickhead." Tears streamed down his face from the residue of capsicum spray.

"Not your fault. There should always be two officers at the checkpoints."

Zhang shrugged. "You'll have to ask DI Hillier."

Carter nodded. "Have a rest."

After returning to the laneway, Carter slammed Vapour's emergency exit door shut. The alarm still rang in his ears. He saw a CCTV camera hung above the door. "Might get lucky with the camera."

"All the other buildings are unoccupied or don't have any security here. But there are a few traffic cameras on Hoddle Street," Song replied.

"We need all the luck we can muster," said Carter.

A horn from a car zooming past on Hoddle Street echoed through the laneway.

"Make sure highway patrol is on the lookout for the car too."

Song nodded, "On it."

Carter marched towards Hillier, who sheepishly stood in the middle of the laneway with his hands in his pocket.

"Hillier, you were the first detective on the scene, that's your responsibility to make sure the cordon is secure," Carter said. "Where is the other constable?"

Hillier shrugged, testing Carter's patience. The expensive fabric of Hillier's suit tapered across his shoulders as he shrugged again. "Dunno yet, I'll have to check on it."

"Do that, Zhang's injuries are on you."

"I know," Hillier grimaced as he saw Perry who held an ice pack on Zhang's jaw.

"In the meantime, get back into Vapour and properly secure the scene this time, alright. Make sure all those people sit tight till we interview them."

Hillier nodded and walked off towards the main entrance to Vapour, shoulders a little lower.

Song's calm composure split into a wide smile. "Aren't you glad you're back, boss?"

--

The gawkers at the police cordon began to diminish. Too late for the club scene spectators as the sun had risen, but too early for new, office-bound spectators to stop on their morning commute.

Song and Perry departed, and Hillier was still inside Vapour taking statements, leaving Carter alone with the battered Constable Zhang who resumed his position at the mouth of the laneway. Zhang lifted the police tape for the newly arrived coroner's assistants.

Zhang helped the male assistant, whom Carter didn't recognise, roll his gurney under the tape. Then came the female assistant Nicole, a familiar face and a friend. She carried a large bag and had a camera slung across her neck.

Nic, as she preferred to be called, was an Indigenous Australian and had been working with the coroner's service as a pathology assistant for almost two decades. What started out as a temp role doing data entry turned into a career. Now pushing fifty, Nic couldn't see herself doing anything else.

Nic joined Carter by the tent. "How's your mob going, mate?"

Carter snorted. "My mob of one is doing alright. How about you?"

Nic scratched the back of her neck. "My youngest is getting her university offers next week, so I'm treading carefully around the house. The smallest thing sets her off right now. She couldn't find her mobile for twenty minutes, and it spiralled into a tantrum about how she wasn't going to get into her course."

"Yikes Nic, things get dark quick."

Nic nodded, "You don't even know. You look like death warmed over darling."

"Always a charmer Nic."

"I can recommend a good eye cream for those dark circles under your eyes."

Carter, suddenly self-conscious, felt around his hollow eyes. "Sooner you work your magic the sooner I get a nap." Carter lifted one of the tent's curtains.

Inside the tent, Nic circled once around the victim. She made a few notes on her clipboard then took out her camera. Carter squinted as a bright flash of light filled the space. Nic took a few snapshots of the victim. First, a full body-length photo, then she zoomed in around the neck, face and then across the torso.

"They did some nasty work on him," Nic said as she continued photographing all the bruises, cuts, and scrapes. She hung the camera around her neck, felt around the victim's neck and then wrote down some more notes.

Carter struggled to focus on the body while Nic continued her examination. He heard water coming out of a tap. Drip, drip, drip. He moved his head around, eyes fully dilated, peering for the source of the noise. There was nothing in the small tent. A sense of dread grew inside Carter as he turned his head down towards the victim.

The victim and Theo could be twins. A wave of anxiety washed over Carter as the dripping noise returned even louder this time. Carter's chest began to feel tight and constricted. His breathing shallowed. He felt the imprint of his mobile in his pants pocket. Nic took more photos while the waves of anxiety crashed through Carter. He felt a few tremors ripple through his body.

He knew he was losing it. Carter's eyes darted across the tent. I'll step out for a minute, pick up another lotto ticket. That'll calm me down, and it's always good to have a second ticket just in case the first one doesn't win.

"How's Detective Perry been recently?"

The question from Nic was a curveball and threw Carter further off-kilter. "Pardon?"

"Oh, never mind," Nic said as she continued to poke and prod the victim.

Carter couldn't shake off the dread. He clenched his fist. The nails of his fingers dug into the skin of his palm.

Focus, this isn't Theo. He felt his heartbeat returning to a steady beat. Theo is fine. He's gone to live his best life without you. The waves of a panic attack slowly receded. He watched Nic as she continued to feel around the victim's neck. She took out a torch and shone it on the deceased's face and neck. Her light traversed the sides of his bruised and swollen neck. She pulled back the eyelids and shone a light in each eye.

Carter took another deep breath to regain his composure.

"What's your gut feeling, doc?"

Nic wagged a finger. "I'm not a doctor."

"Humour me."

Nic stood up and scribbled a few more notes. "Well, he's dead."

Carter rolled his eyes and gave her a thumbs up. "That joke never gets old."

"That's always the first step. The last scene I attended; the constable assumed the victim was dead. One of the crime techs noticed his chest moved. Had to rush in the paramedics." She shook her head. "If that constable had been more observant then that poor bugger may have lived. So, this guy's dead, that's a good start for us." She combed some of the victim's hair to the side of his head with a gloved hand. "Not for him."

"Anything a bit more illuminating?" queried Carter.

"What's the victim's name?"

"Unknown."

"Well, I reckon strangulation as the cause of death for Mr Unknown. Judging by the bruises on his cheeks and arms, he put up a fight."

"What's your feeling about his chest?"

The two of them tried to avoid staring at the elephant in the room carved into his chest.

"When we get him on the slab Doc Monroe will confirm. But a good bet is that the message across his chest was carved in during the struggle," Nic said.

Nic shone her light across the single word. "You see, there is some dried blood around the incisions of each letter. Doc will need to perform some tests, but yeah, I reckon the poor lad was alive. If we are lucky, there might be some bruises on the victim's legs to confirm. The easiest way to carve that into the chest would be to straddle the victim's lower body."

"Any idea on time of death?"

Nic wagged her finger once more. "That's the doc's responsibility, not mine."

"Humour me. I'll shout you the next coffee."

Nic knelt next to the deceased and moved his legs with ease. She moved towards the head and tried to rotate it from side to side, but it was stiff as a board. "Three to five hours ago, I reckon. Rigour mortis is just setting in."

She lifted the curtain and motioned for her colleague to bring the gurney.

"What time should I let Doc Monroe know you'll be gracing us with your presence?"

Carter glanced at his wristwatch; the time read 5:23 a.m. "Say 1 p.m.? I want to interview some Vapour employees."

"Righteo, I'll see you at the morgue and don't forget the coffees. The boss won't be impressed if there aren't any flat whites," said Nic as she helped position the gurney parallel to the victim.

Nic unzipped the body bag and working with the other pathology assistant, they lifted the victim onto the gurney.

"Poor lad," said Nic as she zipped up the body bag. Concealing the victim until they reached the morgue.

Carter lifted the tent curtain for them to head out. He followed behind them. Carter stopped in the middle of the laneway surrounded by orange evidence markers. He rubbed his temples. The fatigue had settled in. He had a mountain of work ahead of him.

CHAPTER THREE

Where murder is, reporters follow, and it wasn't long before the cameras arrived to this crime scene. A TV news van pulled up to the police cordon. A female reporter stepped out, followed by a cameraman. Carter recognised the reporter as Kris Oke. She worked for the ABC, Australia's public broadcaster. Kris was a mainstay on television, with reporting and news reading roles across most of the major media channels for as long as Carter could remember. He'd had a few run-ins with Kris. He wished they could be on the same side if only to avoid her pointed and no-nonsense lines of questioning. A top-notch interviewer or interrogator depending on the how the interview went.

But they ultimately worked towards different ends. Carter needed to solve crimes and calm the community, whereas Kris delivered spectacle masked as information.

They could never really be friends.

Kris sported her signature hair style, black hair slicked back. A descendant of Greek immigrants, her olive complexion hid her real age behind a youthful glow. Today, she wore white capris and a black sleeveless button-up shirt. Kris ran up to the police tape with her camera operator following behind.

Zhang squared off against the onslaught, not even flinching as he asked them to take a step back. And after getting walloped just an hour prior. He had a bright future in law enforcement.

"Detective Carter," she yelled, "We understand the deceased is the victim of a hate crime, is that correct?"

How in the hell did she already know that? They had a leak. Or else whoever found the body sent a picture to the journos before calling the police?

Carter turned to her. "Ms Oke, always a pleasure, Metro Police have no comment at this time and will be releasing a statement shortly."

Kris persisted, "The victim was found on property belonging to James Hughes, is he involved with this case?"

Carter turned and walked away.

Gossip travelled fast, he supposed. Or the media already had it in for Hughes.

As he entered Vapour, Carter ran down what he needed to know: first the identity of the deceased, then the identity of the runner, third, who had contacted Kris.

A mixture of cheap cologne and mould wafted in the air as Carter walked into the reception area. Is this what sex always smells like, Carter wondered.

There were two sofas covered in a stain-proof and easy to clean fabric. Above them were posters for their upcoming pool party and Under-30 night.

Here a staff member would buzz the customer into the locker area. There, in the locker room, they changed from street clothes to a towel. The towel represented the key to the labyrinth of private rooms, glory holes, a gym, and even a pool — all under cover of dim lighting and house music.

Vapour sold passes and room hires in twelve-hour increments. Any man, whether biologically born or now identifying, who yearned for a release could visit here, buy a pass and head into the lustful raucousness of the labyrinth.

But not today.

Today no customers remained. Three staff sat together on one sofa. Two of them were mid-twenties wearing visors, singlets, and white short shorts with pink stripes across them. The other staff member dressed in jeans and a t-shirt, roughly Carter's age.

Carter didn't recognise any of them, but it had been a while since he'd been a customer.

Spread across the other sofa and on the ground around were the men, and a few others, who had just tested the emergency exit door and Carter's diminishing patience. The group varied in ages, early twenties, late thirties, and forties. What struck Carter were the expressions. Nearly every one of them yawned, and each had a backpack, duffle bag, or suitcase.

They were sleeping, Carter thought. A few rested their heads against each other's shoulders and yawned again. At least they are docile; should make this a bit easier.

The only other two people in the room were Hillier and James Hughes, owner of Vapour, and public office hopeful.

"Look, do you want to be arrested for obstruction?" Hillier asked James. James's reply came in the form of a disdainful and uninterested shrug.

Nothing is ever too easy, Carter thought.

It had been a year or two since James and Carter had been together in the same room. He hadn't changed a bit, still fighting fit at fifty. Probably still did a hundred sit-ups and push-ups each morning.

"Mind your manners," Carter said.

"Darling," James's expression brightened. "Thank you for calling off your attack dog."

"I'm talking to you," Carter gave James a smirk, then tapped Hillier on the shoulder to move him aside. "The media has arrived. Go outside and help Zhang fend them off."

Hillier flipped his notebook closed and complied; lip pushed out in what he probably thought was no-nonsense determination but on Hillier's baby face read as a sulky pout.

"Next time you talk to one of my officers, can you try not being so aloof?" Carter asked as he folded his arms across his broad chest. James mirrored Carter's stance. He didn't intimidate easily.

James, despite running for authority and title, had a strong disregard for authority and titles. If he ever met the King, he'd probably give him a hug instead of a restrained bow. Then he'd go into a monologue about the pitfalls of the monarchy.

James smirked, "Am I that obvious?"

Carter nodded, "Yes, but still, it's good to see you, James."

"It is good to see me darling, I look great," James said.

Carter ignored the self-aggrandising comment, "Keeping out of trouble, clearly."

James's blue eyes set against his scruffy, weathered face had once made Carter's heart flutter. James's gaze didn't waver as he spoke.

"You've been through it. That's a nasty scrape." James placed a hand on Carter's shoulder. The fingers wrapped around the muscle and squeezed. "Has someone examined it?"

Carter shook his head. "It's fine." He moved his shoulder away from that familiar grip. James's hands were Carter's favourite part of him. They emitted a type of heat and force that made Carter want to melt into James's embrace. Carter knew he should pull back. He didn't want to. And yet Carter felt a sensation of leverage being used against him in a very calculated way.

"Stubborn shit." James walked behind reception and pulled out a first aid kit and pushed it toward him. "At least pour some peroxide over it."

"Thanks, Captain." Carter immediately regretted saying that, falling into old patterns.

"You can call me James, you know. I haven't seen you in, or out, of fatigues in what – a few decades now?"

"Less than two decades James. I'm only thirty-six," Carter said.

In his early twenties. His and James's dog tags had once hung on the bedpost of nearly every seedy motel in Toowoomba.

"Captain Hughes," Carter cooed, then immediately flinched as he dabbed his wounds. "Old habits die hard."

"So, I guess you have some questions for me, Detective?"

"Detective Inspector," Carter said.

James smiled as he dabbed Carter's wound.

"Do you know anything about the man found on your property?"

"No, I don't recognise him. And the laneway is not part of Vapour. That's city property," James said.

Carter ignored the semantic clarification. "How many patrons were in tonight?"

James pointed towards the older employee. He had a leathery face and dilated pupils. He was high or coming down off something. James snapped his finger, the employee's eyes fully opened, his attention focused on James.

Still follows the 'command and control' style of leadership with the troops, Carter thought.

"Tom, how many people were in tonight?" James asked.

"We had about twenty guys in. Once the sirens started wailing, the smart ones fled," Tom said.

"And how many employees?"

"Just the three of us."

"And this group stayed behind?"

"This group were all tucked in for a sleep." Tom gestured toward the remaining patrons.

"A sleep?" Carter struggled to understand why anyone would be asleep here.

"Correct." James's voice carried an authoritative tone again.

Carter knew James had something more to say, so he waited. No one said anything.

"You," Carter pointed at the nearest man. He definitely fell into the twink category, early twenties with messy brown hair. Carter noticed a bruise across his cheek, a worrisome sign that he didn't come to Vapour for fun, or trouble met him here. "Tell me where exactly you were sleeping and when you woke up."

He struggled to keep his eyes open as he spoke. "I was sleeping mate, booked out one of the rooms for the night."

"Didn't come to Vapour for some fun?" Carter noticed the overstuffed backpack next to the twink. His whole life is stuffed in that backpack, Carter thought. He's homeless.

"Nah, like I said – sleeping," the man said.

"Thank you, Ty," James said.

"So, you really allow sleeping rough here, in a sauna?" Carter asked James.

"Correct. The younger ones, like Ty, are homeless, others commute in from the country. Cheaper than a motel and you get off. Win-win really." James leaned closer. "I'd appreciate you not telling the city."

James provided protection in the shape of four walls and a roof, as always — a real patron of the community. Carter scanned the group. Their bags stuffed to the edges, a few wearing torn clothes. Running shoes scuffed and dirty, laces tattered. Carter's gaze moved across the older gentlemen. Their bags were less tattered, cleaner, sharper. Each one had a duffle bag, enough to pack a few days' worth of clothes in it.

"Saint James amongst the queers," Carter muttered.

Someone next to Ty was deliberately avoiding Carter's gaze. He was turned halfway to shield his face from Carter. Ty held his hand.

"Ty, who is next to you."

"Who, Bailey?"

Carter rubbed his temples, "What are you doing here Bailey?"

A sheepish Bailey turned to face Carter. Bailey was the same age as Ty, early twenties. He was a fit lad, his body followed in the steps of his dad who was an Australian sporting legend. Bailey was made to play sport with his muscular and athletic build. His life veered off course significantly, struggling to live in his deceased father's shadow.

"Ty and I couldn't find a place to crash tonight," Bailey said.

"You have a home," Carter said.

Bailey shook his head, "Mum and I had a falling out, again."

James chimed in, "Ty and Bailey are regulars. I have a thing for strays."

Carter almost blushed, he knew the subtext was directed to him.

Carter turned to James. "Mr Hughes, the individual who ran from the sauna through the emergency exit and assaulted Constable Zhang wore the uniform of this establishment. Please provide his name and current address."

James glanced at Tom, his staff member, again. Carter saw Tom mouth a word to James. James nodded but didn't say a word.

"Gentlemen, unless you want to all be taken to the station, you talk to me, not each other," Carter said.

"Now DI Carter, here's the problem," James said softly. "One of our staff may not have one hundred per cent legal working rights here in Australia."

Carter took out his notepad and began scribbling the details. "He wore a singlet and jean shorts." Carter glanced over to Tom who wore the same. "Is that Vapour's uniform?"

Tom nodded. "Punters like to see a bit of skin before they enter. Sometimes they leave a tip."

"To clarify, my staff only receive a financial tip occasionally, not the literal tip of any customers," James said.

"One of your staff fled the scene?"

"Correct," James said in an elevated voice that betrayed his nervousness.

"Why?" Carter asked with a deadpan expression.

"He's a refugee. The government released him from detention but denied him legal working rights – it's pretty fucked."

"I'm not interested in his immigration status unless it's relevant to the murder investigation. Gimme a name James."

"Moe, the surname is Bashar, I think. He's from somewhere in the Middle East. I didn't really care where, he's tall and gorgeous – great for business."

Carter simmered with an unexpected peppering of envy. He exhaled heavily. Focus. "Where's Moe living and what's his number?"

"I can give you his mobile number, but that's all we got on the guy. We've been paying him cash in hand."

"Aren't leaders supposed to lead by example? Is paying a staff member cash in hand really appropriate for a political candidate?"

Carter felt morally superior for a moment. He loathed wage theft. Most cash in hand operations were used by employers to avoid paying superannuation and annual leave.

James stood his ground. "How is releasing someone into the community and expecting them to earn an income without working rights?"

Carter sighed. "Let's make something clear. This is a murder investigation; it will not be used by you to advance your political career."

"Murder does make a good soapbox," James said.

"Just give me Moe's number then and let's save the commentary for talkback radio."

James took out his phone, scrolled to a number, showed it to Carter who scribbled it down.

"We will need a copy of your CCTV footage."

James's belly laugh came back in full force, louder this time. "So, umm, funny story, but our CCTV has been busted for about a week. Mostly for show anyways. One average camera in the alleyway doesn't cover much. Most we ever get are ladies and gents going for a slash when the line-up for Swish is too long. Occasionally, the drunken hand job too. You'd be surprised how many people pick up while queuing to enter Swish."

"What about that camera?" Carter pointed to the camera above reception.

"Same mate, and no cameras inside in the locker rooms or beyond. We host a space for perverts, we aren't though."

Carter's patience faded. His willpower to deal with hindrances diplomatically had been chipped away to crumbs. He stepped within centimetres of James and dropped his voice to a whisper.

"Whatever your stature in the community is or will be, a murder has occurred outside your business. A man's life is gone, snuffed out. At the very least your CCTV would have captured this if it had been operational. And the icing on the cake is one of your employees assaulted a police officer. If you're now trying to be a political leader, act like one."

"So, I should embezzle?"

Carter moved in closer. "What are you hiding, James? You don't want me to use a fine-tooth comb here. Don't push me."

James whispered back. "Are you as hard as I am? I never pegged you as the dom top."

"Bailey, you be this hard when I arrest you?"

James relented and took a pace back. "Relax, I'll get you what I can. I know this is a serious issue, and I want whoever did this held accountable as much as you do."

He lowered his voice. "To be honest, I'm really glad you are leading this case. Best detective in Melbourne."

Carter let out a soft chuckle. "Get me what you can ASAP. This detective needs to work."

Carter made his way towards the exit.

"Mate, where does that leave us?" Ty, the youngest of the group, with the bruised cheek asked.

Carter spun around to speak to them, "You're all free to go."

"You don't get it," Ty said, who gave Carter a frustrated look, shaking his head. "Where," Ty dragged out the word, "are we supposed to go?"

"Checkout at Chateau Vapour is around 7 a.m. Showered and fresh as a daisy for the working day," said James.

"Look gents, you'll need to leave the premises. This place won't be open for at least another day. So I'm sorry, but you won't be able to stay here."

"Great, mate, I'll be sleeping on the streets tonight thanks to you. Or maybe you want me to work a trick. Give some old fuck a blowie to sleep for the night," Ty said.

"Why don't you and Bailey go back to his house?" Carter asked.

Bailey shook his head, "Mum is pretty pissed at me."

Ty held Bailey's hand. "It's okay, we always figure it out."

Carter rubbed his temples, searching for solutions. "We can call a social worker, see what emergency accommodation options there are."

CHAPTER FOUR

The number James had given him for Moe went to voicemail.

"This phone number is not set up to receive voicemail messages."

Useless as tits on a bull, Carter thought.

But Nic's examination had turned up a lead he so desperately needed.

"Business card in the victim's pocket." She handed him the battered piece of paper. "There's an appointment reminder on the back. Always check the pockets before you leave a scene."

It was as if the light of heaven shone straight down upon him. "Thank Christ for small favours," Carter said.

"By my count, you owe me a lifetime worth of small favours. I'll collect them in the form of flat whites for life," Nic said.

She hopped into the passenger side of the coroner's van and drove off leaving Carter and Song at the mouth of the laneway.

"Patrick Hoban," Carter read aloud, "Director of Client Services."

Song snatched the card from Carter. "Director at one of the top four consultancy firms in Melbourne. This guy is high up the corporate ladder."

Song held up her mobile, "He's easy on the eyes too."

Her mobile displayed a corporate headshot of Patrick. He sported a thin beard, with medium-length black hair swept to the side.

"He looks too cool to be an accountant," Song said.

Carter let out a short whistle. "Let's give Patrick a visit. He's probably heading into work now and we have time before the post-mortem."

"These corporate drones do more hours than we do," Song said.

"Except their salaries match the trauma," Carter said.

The pair passed Zhang and Hillier. The two were deep in conversation, neither noticed Carter and Song. Hillier had his hand on Zhang's shoulder. Zhang gave a strained and uncomfortable smile.

At least Hillier is trying to make amends, thought Carter. "We'll see you two back at HQ."

Hillier quickly dropped his hand off Zhang's shoulder. "Yes Detective, see you there."

Zhang nodded. "Pleasure meeting you Detective Carter."

Carter and Song passed Kris Oke who faced a camera to give a news report. A bright light projected from the camera illuminated her face. Kris's eyes darted over to Carter and Song, as if ready to pester them for a comment. The pair kept walking down the street towards Carter's car.

"Should we get coffees on the way?" Song asked.

Carter let out a short chuckle, "Detective Song, we are going to one of the top four consultancies in Melbourne. I'm sure they have a barista onsite."

And so they did. After a short drive into the central business district of Melbourne, Carter and Song found themselves in the open-air atrium of a Collins Street office building. Located in the Paris End of Collins Street the luxury hotels and retail outlets call home.

Carter and Song waited for their coffees while a stream of suits entered the building to start the day.

"Detectives?" Patrick asked.

Carter and Song turned around.

Patrick was Carter's height and wore a tight tank top and a pair of shorts. Sweat drenched his shirt and moulded against his defined upper body. The lower body matched his upper body – just as delicious. Patrick had a pair of thick and hairy muscular legs.

"Excuse the look, I try to get a lap around the Tan Track before I start work. My PA told me you need to speak right away."

"Flat whites for Carter," the young barista came out from behind the counter to hand the coffees to him.

"Thank you," Carter said as he passed one coffee to Song.

Song took a sip of her coffee and smiled. Carter held up his badge.

"I'm DI Carter and this is DI Song."

"Good coffee," Song said.

Patrick smiled, "Best in all of Melbourne I reckon. And it's open from 5 a.m."

"Mr Hoban," Song said.

"Please, call me Paddy."

Song nodded, "Paddy, do you know this man?" She showed Paddy a picture of the deceased.

Carter knew the answer before Paddy spoke. A clenched fist, a tightening of the chest, a scrunching of the face. Paddy knew the victim.

"That's Nelson. God damn it." Paddy bit his knuckle. "Is he dead?"

Song nodded, "My condolences for your loss."

Paddy scrunched his face again to regain his composure, "That's Nelson Harris. A good lad."

A wave of sadness crossed Paddy's face at a realisation. "Was a good lad."

"We understand you work in private wealth."

Paddy nodded.

"Yep, I work with C-suite clients and some retail organisations."

Song tilted her head, "Did Nelson work for you? Surely he wasn't a client."

Paddy let out a soft laugh before looking ashamed of the laugh. "No, this is a bit embarrassing, but we met on the apps."

"So, you were in a relationship with Nelson?" Song asked.

Paddy shook his head. "No, we met for a drink six months ago and actually hit it off pretty well as friends. But there wasn't any sexual chemistry between us."

Carter had originally assessed Paddy with his detective hat on. Scanning him from top to bottom for any level of threat. Now, Carter's eyes lingered on Paddy for more carnal reasons. A bead of sweat rolled down Paddy's hairy legs. Paddy caught Carter checking him out. Their eyes hovered on one another until Carter broke the stare.

"I mentored him. He just got a promotion at work. We arranged a catchup this week to discuss how to capitalise on the promotion. You know, develop a wealth and career strategy. He works at the City Council as an urban planner."

Paddy crossed his arms. "Or I mean, worked at the council."

"It's not easy information to hear. Grief hits us all in a different way," Carter said.

"It's standard practice when investigating a murder. Can you account for your whereabouts for the last twenty-four hours?"

"Of course, I understand. I was here at the office till about midnight last night. It's all swipe card entry. Then I took an Uber home and basically passed out. Got up at 5 a.m. to do some work at home before heading for my run around the Tan."

"Thank you. We'll need you to make a formal statement," Song said.

Paddy glanced at his watch. "I hate to do this, but I need to get going. I have a meeting shortly and need to look like I haven't run ten kilometres. You already have my card, please contact me anytime."

"We will," Song said.

"Just one last thing, do you have an address for Nelson?" Carter asked.

Paddy nodded, "Do you have a pen?"

--

The victim, Nelson, lived in St Kilda not far from the city's most degenerate flophouse, The Lodge Hotel. In its final stages of life, the hotel's decaying and crumbling exterior matched with the neglected interior of a former mansion turned rooming house. None of the neon lights spelling out the hotel's name worked anymore, and no one seemed in a hurry to change it judging by the deteriorating facade.

During his tenure as a constable, Carter had been called to The Lodge countless times — so much that it almost aroused a twinge of nostalgia when they passed by en route. He always brought his A-game when he got a callout to The Lodge. Carter never knew what situation he'd encounter. Over the years The Lodge turned into a melting pot for the discarded citizens of Melbourne and Victoria. Released from prison, homeless, suffering from a mental health breakdown, or terminally unemployable. They could all afford a room at The Lodge Hotel.

Two women sat on the front steps, sharing a single cigarette, both in cleaning aprons. They either were finishing up their shift or about to start. Deep lines and wrinkles crisscrossed their faces, straw-like hair pulled back into buns.

"This place has been sold you know." Song gazed out the car window. "Going to be turned into luxury flats. One flat a floor. A TV network is going to have a show focused on the renovation process documenting—" Song said the next words in air quotes. "The design journey."

"I'll give it a miss, I think."

"I wonder where they'll relocate — the residents, I mean."

"One insurmountable challenge at a time," Carter said. "We have a murder to solve."

"Okay. Tell me what you think so far."

"The victim took a beating and judging by his frame, he normally isn't much of a fighter. I'm getting mixed messages here. Being strangled indicates more of a connection with the perpetrators. Still, the carving on his torso indicates more of a hate crime."

Song nodded. "Could be both. Maybe a scorned lover, closet case?"

"His phone hasn't been found yet. Hopefully, it hasn't been destroyed, run over, or thrown into the Yarra River," Carter said.

"Agreed, but I think it is a long shot we will recover his phone. If we follow this line of reasoning, the victim knew his attackers and the victim's murderers are listed in that phone."

"They don't make it easy for us," Carter parked the car in front of a small block of flats. "I give you Mr Nelson Harris's residence."

Nelson's flat was located two streets south of Fitzroy Street in St Kilda. The block of units were one-bedroom apartments made up of two long rectangular brick buildings facing one another with a neglected and derelict courtyard in between. Each unit in the double-storey walk-up had a front door leading out to a shared and covered veranda. The first flat on the second floor belonged to Nelson. Uniformed officers already stood outside the door.

Carter and Song walked up the external staircase to the second-storey landing. Carter felt something scrape his palm. He saw flecks of white paint from the dilapidated staircase dotted his hand. He flicked the flecks of white paint off his hands.

"Owner wasn't too happy getting woken up so early to open up the unit," said a constable guarding the flat.

"Consider it payment for poor upkeep," Carter said with a smile on his face.

"And a bit of karma for the outrageous amount of rent probably charged for this shoebox of a flat," Song said.

Carter checked his watch: 10 a.m. Morning routines were just starting to kick in for those still alive. "Gloves and booties." Song passed Carter a pair and then started to put hers on. Song glanced through the open door to the victim's apartment. "Well, this brings back memories. Advertising this rental as a one-bedroom flat was a bit of an embellishment."

The apartment was split into two separate sections, three square meters each; the first housing the kitchen, dining area, and living room while the second area had a bedroom and ensuite.

Carter knew Song came from money. He wasn't sure how much money, but one thing he did know was that Song picked out her own wedding ring. The diamonds encrusted in the band were big enough to blind a person when angled to reflect sunlight.

"Come on, you've never lived in anything so small," Carter said.

Song shrugged. "True, but I've had friends in small places. We've all been there, ten packed into a tiny flat like this before a girls' night out."

"A long time ago," said Carter as he stepped through the invisible bubble that shrouded this apartment. The bubble burst. This would never again be the flat of Nelson Harris. What wouldn't be catalogued as evidence would soon be boxed up and released to parents and friends.

"No signs of forced entry, nothing disturbed, no signs of blood," Carter said. He picked up the employee badge for the City Council that rested in a ceramic bowl on the dining room table. "We'll have to contact the council to get his next-of-kin details.'

Carter picked up a few betting receipts from the bowl.

"Looks like he's placed a few footy bets recently," Carter said.

Song passed him and moved towards the bedroom.

A glossy red Ikea bookshelf rested against the wall. Along the top shelf were three framed photographs – two with Nelson and what must be his parents, and another with a woman around his age.

Carter lifted the first photo for closer inspection.

"Looks like he's an only child," he called. "No family photos with anyone else."

"Condoms and lube in the bedside table," Song said from the bedroom. "Bed is made, no major sign of a disturbance."

Carter moved into the small nook of a kitchen next to the dining area. He tapped his gloved finger against the laminate countertop. A dish, utensils, and a cup sat in the sink.

"This isn't a crime scene. Nothing is out of place. Looks like he had dinner and went out for the night."

"Never made it home to finish his book," Song said. She held an Australian Rules League (ARL) rules book littered with sticky notes.

"Looks like some studious reading on ARL," Carter said. He glanced along the bookshelf. Lining the shelves were books on history, urban planning, and a series of fitness magazines. "Nothing here tells me he's big into footy."

"But he's been making some bets on the footy," Song answered.

Carter checked the betting receipts again. "He's been earning some serious coin."

Carter flipped through the receipts, "Won a few hundred dollars with each bet."

"Check through his wardrobe, see if he has a jersey for a team."

Song continued to rummage around in the bedroom. "No footy gear."

"Let's get the techs to run through anyway just to be on the safe side."

"Detectives," one of the constables said at the door. He handed Carter a piece of paper. "A young woman came by – an Abby Crosby. Saw the squad car and thought to check in on her friend. Claims she is best friends with the victim. These are her details."

Carter took the paper and walked back into the flat. He picked up the photograph of the victim and a woman.

"Is this her?" Carter asked.

The constable nodded.

Carter carefully placed the frame back on the bookshelf.

"If she doesn't have this photo already, she'll want it and I'm not breaking it."

"You are a bit clumsy," Song yelled.

"Why don't you ask her to wait for us downstairs?" Carter directed his question to the constable.

The constable shrugged. "Said she had to go to work."

Carter nodded, slightly annoyed. "Next time someone connected to an active investigation comes up, make sure they don't leave the scene, okay?"

The constable nodded.

Carter and Song walked down the external staircase to the car. He passed the paper to Song. "Can you arrange a catch-up with Abby?"

Song nodded. "Sure thing."

She turned to face Nelson's flat before turning back to Carter. "I'll stick around here, do another scan of the flat while forensics gets here."

"Do you think we missed something?"

"Dunno, I'll catch a lift with one of the constables."

"Sounds good, I'm going to swing by the pokies spot that Nelson made those bets. See if anyone remembers him. We've got time before we need to head into the office and the autopsy," Carter said.

"I bet Abby is pretty cut-up about her mate's death."

"That's a safe bet," Carter said.

CHAPTER FIVE

I'm not liking where this case is going. Carter thought as he drove down St Kilda Road back into the central business district of Melbourne. The mid-morning traffic was just as dense as the rush hour traffic. Being one of the major arterial roads of Melbourne, traffic never eased along St Kilda Road.

Carter's car slowed down as it got stuck behind a slow-moving silver Range Rover. He turned his head to check his blind spots before switching lanes. He pushed down on the accelerator to pass the Range Rover.

"Bloody Toorak tractors."

Toorak is one of the most affluent suburbs in Melbourne. Acceptance into the suburb was based on holding multiple gold and black credit cards, owning a Range Rover, and having a face filled with at least twenty per cent plastic.

The driver and Carter momentarily glanced at each other. It only took a second to reinforce his perception of Toorak tractor drivers. Hair in a topknot, coffee in a manicured hand, and lips on the verge of bursting with filler.

Carter kept driving in his lane. He felt a bit cheeky and thought of merging back to his original lane and slowing down in front of the Range Rover. But he had other things on his mind.

One body and no suspects. It's a bad combination, he thought. *This case could go cold fast.*

What about Paddy?

A smile formed across Carter's face. He felt his laugh lines form around his mouth and nose. He wondered if Paddy noticed his wrinkles. *Did Paddy think they were sexy.* He knew Paddy wasn't a highly probable suspect.

So, Carter indulged in his fantasy. From mentor to killer? Carter didn't buy it. Paddy didn't seem like a killer type. Maybe a killer in the corporate world.

Carter pictured Paddy in a charcoal three-piece suit tailored to amplify his muscular physique. Paired with a white dress shirt and a red tie to bring out his alabaster skin and blue eyes.

Carter felt that familiar surge in his groin. He'd always wanted to be taken in a boardroom. One of those fantasies that were forever unfulfilled since he wasn't the corporate type. You yearn for the unusual.

What if he and Paddy worked together? Both suits who nailed a presentation and needed to let off some steam.

Paddy sat at the head of a boardroom table. He licked his lips. He and Carter made eye contact. Paddy bites down on his lower lip. Holds the pressure. Teeth dig into lip. Then he releases, his lip flicks towards Carter.

"Come here," Paddy demands.

Carter nods, embracing the fantasy. He places a file down on the boardroom table. Paddy starts to slowly unbutton his shirt. Curly black hairs pepper Paddy's muscular chest. He motions for Carter to come to him as he leans back in his chair.

The Range Rover revved up and refocused Carter to the present. The petrol-guzzling tractor passed Carter and then pulled in front of him on the road. Carter beeped his horn as he pressed his foot down on the brake pedal to slow down. He squinted to see through the tinted window of the Range Rover. The woman raised her middle finger.

Can't make friends on the road. Can't find a lover. Can't hold on to one, Carter thought.

Carter still felt the wrath of Theo's ultimatum when he left. Admit to a gambling addiction or he goes. Carter didn't think he had a problem. Theo followed through. Been months since he'd heard from Theo. He had blocked

Carter's number and blocked him on all socials. He had no idea how he was, or where he was.

So, what if I like a spin? That doesn't mean I'm addicted.

His eyes widen as he approached a twenty-four-hour pokies venue along St Kilda Road. He flicked his indicator to turn into their carpark. This was the pokies venue where Nelson had placed his bets on the footy.

The twenty-four-hour pokies venue was disguised as a friendly local pub. Drink the day or night away while you gambled at the slot machines or bet on any sporting event.

A super centre for all of Carter's vices but designed like a house that gave punters a sense of comfort.

When you come here, you aren't going to the pokies, you're coming home.

Gabled roof, oversized glass doors, and a neon sign for a parma and pot deal beckoned, enticed him to come in.

His hand hovered between the gear shift and the ignition button.

Am I here for myself or the case? If I walk through the door, I can't have a drink or a spin. I need to focus on the case, to find out more about Nelson.

His finger grazed across the Stop text of the ignition button. He tentatively depressed the button.

But first, one spin, he told himself

Carter left his Skoda and walked with purpose across the uneven concrete towards the pokies entrance.

One spin, he thought.

"You want a smoke darling?"

A woman's voice snapped Carter out of his tunnel vision to get into the pokies venue. He saw a Caucasian woman, forties, plump, bleached blonde hair in need of a touch-up sitting on the curb. Her grubby fingers held a rolled cigarette.

He noticed the tell-tale signs of abuse with black and blue bruises across her arms — some new, some old.

Carter glanced towards the pokies venue. He shifted his weight as if to make a move and head inside. Stay, he thought to himself. He squeezed his hand and took a deep breath. "Sure, why not." Carter joined her on the curb.

The woman passed Carter a rolled cigarette and a lighter. Once lit, Carter took a long inhale before blowing the smoke out. He returned the lighter.

"Going to play the pokies?" she asked.

Carter nodded, "Should be elsewhere, but I'm feeling lucky. How about you?"

The woman took a long drag of her cigarette. "Waiting for my man to go to sleep back home. Might try a spin to pass the time, might get lucky too. I'm Rybekkah."

"Rebecca?" Carter asked.

"Nah darling, spelled like Rye the drink. My folks' favourite drink."

Carter nodded, "Gotcha Rybekkah, I'm Leo Carter."

He began to wonder why her best refuge was the twenty-four-hour pokies but shook the idea out of his head. Carter took out his wallet and passed her a twenty-dollar bill.

"Your spins are on me today."

Rybekkah smiled as she took the bill from Carter. "Thanks, darling."

Carter smelled him before he rounded the corner of the building. The stale pungent smell of alcohol assaulted Carter's olfactory receptors. A man rounded the corner — ratty t-shirt, footy shorts, and dirty sneakers. Carter noticed the ankle monitor and knife in his hand simultaneously.

"Oi, mate. Get away from my missus," the man roared.

Rybekkah visibly cowered as if to try and make herself invisible. "Oh shit. I thought he'd sleep off the gear."

Carter's police training kicked into high gear along with his heart rate. He grabbed Rybekkah's arm and pulled her up. "Rybekkah, get inside the pokies. Tell security to lock the door and call the cops."

She heisted as the man stumbled towards them.

"What's his name?" he asked.

Rybekkah stood motionless.

"What's his name?" Carter yelled.

"Jack," she murmured before running inside the pokies.

"Don't run away from me," Jack screamed.

He walked a few more steps towards the entrance of the pokies. Carter stepped towards Jack with hands open to seem disarming and friendly.

"Hey Jack, you've got an ankle monitor on — means you are violating probation being out, hey? It's time to head home."

Jack and Carter were the same height, but Jack sported a bulging beer belly. He swayed and didn't seem entirely confident his two feet would follow the impulses from his drug-ravaged mind to walk. Despite the sway, he had a strong grip on that knife in his hand. Carter noticed old and new scars along Jack's arms. He's a fighter and high as a kite. Not a great combo, thought Carter.

"Get out of my way — I gotta talk to Rybekkah."

Jack moved to the left to pass Carter. Carter matched Jack's moves to block his path.

"That's not going to happen today."

Jack's knife glinted with the neon lights of the pokies as he lunged at Carter. Carter quickly side-stepped the attack and he gripped Jack's wrist. He twisted hard.

"Let go of me," Jack screamed.

Carter twisted harder. Jack wailed as he dropped the knife. Carter kicked the back of Jack's knees to pin him to the ground.

"I just wanted to talk to my missus," Jack yelled.

"Not tonight, or tomorrow I reckon. You're off to jail mate." Carter saw two police cruisers turn into the carpark. He flagged them down, identified himself and packed Jack into the first one.

Unfortunately, the second pair decided to check Rybekkah's name in the police database.

Carter found himself faced off against a stern-looking Constable Dan Coates who twirled Rybekkah's ID card in his hand. Carter guessed Coates to be a lifer as a senior constable. A lifer for all the wrong reasons.

"You're shitting me," Carter said.

"Nah," Coates replied.

"She was trying to escape a bad situation at home," Carter pleaded.

Coates said nothing.

"Who's your supervisor?"

Coates chuckled at Carter, "You're not a Karen, you know how this works. Rybekkah is on probation, and part of her conditions include not going near a pokies venue. Heading to the pokies for a spin is a violation of her probation so she's off to jail."

"Come on, you and me both know she'd have been beaten if she stayed home. This isn't justice, she's a victim."

Coates let out a chuckle, "Justice."

"Remember justice, helping those who need it. Being driven to jail is not the justice Rybekkah deserves from us."

"I don't need a lecture on how to do my job. She violates parole, she goes to jail."

"You're enjoying this, aren't you?" Carter quipped.

Coates smiled, "I do love an election. It flicks a switch. Everybody suddenly gets tough on crime. Helps my stats."

"I'll ask again, who is your supervisor?" Carter asked.

Coates placed his hands on his hips, a classic power stance. "Why are you here, Detective? Going for a spin yourself?"

Shit, Carter thought to himself. "I was on my way to an autopsy when I saw these two get into an altercation."

"Well Detective, as I said before, we have this situation under control." Coates nodded to his partner who handcuffed Rybekkah. "So, you can just get back to it."

"You coppers are all the same. Bloody dogs." Rybekkah started to sob.

"I'll see what I can do for you, Rybekkah."

"Not much, I reckon," Coates said drily.

"All bloody dogs," Rybekkah screamed as an officer led her away.

"Some of us can learn new tricks," Carter said.

Carter went into the pokies venue to ask about Nelson. No one recognised Nelson. He left in defeat but avoided the lure of going for a spin on the pokies. He still had two hours before the autopsy. He got in his car, leaned the car seat back, set an alarm and fell immediately asleep. He dreamed of nothing but spinning pokie machine images tumbling into line over and over. He never once won, though the merman kept telling him it would be next time for sure.

CHAPTER SIX

Carter checked his mobile as soon as he woke up. He opened a text message from Nic: don't be late to the autopsy. Bring flat whites.

He decided he had time to check in with HQ before the autopsy. The major investigations team inhabited the third level of the Docklands police headquarters. Level four had a mezzanine, the floor split in half. Major crimes took the west side of the floor, general administration took the east. The security door's key scanner turned from red to green as Carter swiped his access card.

The team worked in an open-plan office with the floor's centre comprising several whiteboards and television screens on trolleys. Desks spiralled from the centre in groups of two to six. All the staff hot-desked depending on the case to which they were assigned. Superintendent Davies had the only office on the floor, next to the meeting room.

The cluster of two desks towards the windows were allocated to Carter and Song. The next bunch of five desks had Perry and Hillier and spare seats for uniform staff. Perry and Hillier sat at their desk. Each drank a jumbo coffee. Bags under Perry's eyes indicated how they all felt, and the day had just begun.

Song had a puzzled look to her. "Took a while to get here."

"Interviewed a few punters and staff, no luck," Carter said as he slumped down in his chair.

Song nodded, "Don't enjoy the seat for long. Davies wants to see you as soon as you get it."

"No rest for the wicked," he said, standing up again.

--

"Close the door." Davies's gaze hadn't shifted from her computer monitor. Her valleys of crow's feet were illuminated by the blue glow of the screen. She owned glasses but never wore them; instead, she squinted frequently.

Superintendent Davies had led Major Crimes for over a decade now. Carter didn't know how to feel about her plans to retire. It would make sense for him to apply for the superintendent position. The next logical step in his career, if he's ready. Carter leaned against the door, wondering about her imminent retirement. How imminent is imminent. Is today one of the last times he'd do this. Standing at her door while Davies's fingers furiously typed away. Each keystroke echoed in her fishbowl office.

"Do you really need an invitation? Just sit down."

Blunt candour, that's what Carter liked about Davies and why they worked so well together. The 'bespreekbaarheid' of her family's approach to conversations – roughly translated in Carter's mind to blunt candour – had worn off on Davies as the daughter of immigrant parents from the Netherlands.

"Righteo, boss," Carter said as he took a seat opposite Davies. He glanced back. The outer office was abuzz, officers crisscrossing the room to talk to the detectives. The detectives – Carter realised that wasn't correct. They were his detectives; he had the reins of this investigation.

"What's the point of a door when your office is a fishbowl?"

"Don't start redecorating just yet Carter. I'd have preferred a one-way window instead of this fishbowl I call home. Keep an eye on the troops without them keeping an eye on me." Davies then pushed a button to close the blinds. "Beggars can't be choosers when it comes to bureaucratic interior design decisions. It took six months for infrastructure services to arrange blinds. Besides I won't need them much longer." From her desk drawer, she pulled out Carter's service weapon, a matte black .40 Smith and Wesson semi-automatic pistol and placed it on her desk.

"Welcome back. As you have just come back from extended leave, I am to remind you that you can visit any one of our professional mental health workers. Doctor Lynch has confidential drop-in appointments."

"Thanks boss," Carter said as he holstered his weapon and tucked his badge in his pocket. "Did HR give you a script to repeat?"

Davies nodded.

"Well, I still appreciate your help oiling the wheels to get me back up and running."

"Like I said, time is ticking on my bank of favours to call in. And don't make me regret it, I need someone I can trust on this. Someone with tact."

"Someone queer," Carter interjected. "Optics look good if a professional homosexual is investigating the murder of another, especially if it looks like this was a hate crime, eh boss?"

Davies ignored the comment. "Bring me up to speed."

Carter flipped open his notebook. "Deceased is a Nelson Harris, resident in St Kilda, employed at Melbourne City Council. Evidence at the scene and unofficial confirmation by the coroner assistant suggests the body was dumped there. Cause of death – unconfirmed – is strangulation. The victim took a beating beforehand and had the word poof carved into his torso, while alive – most likely."

"Looks like a hate crime to me, and the media's narrative will be the same I reckon," Davies said. Her 'bespreekbaarheid' reared itself, past the pleasantries – it was time for business.

Carter nodded in agreement. "I'm not discounting any motivations yet, but this could turn into a pretty big shitshow boss."

Davies's blinking mobile caught her attention as another ten emails related to the case popped up on her screen. "Witnesses?"

"One viable witness fled the scene," Carter said.

"What do you mean by fled?" Davies's tone changed slightly, and she grabbed her blue stress ball.

"Detective Hillier secured the scene and stationed a single officer at the south end of the alley. There might have been two, details are fuzzy. The suspect flew like a bat out of hell from the bathhouse, struck the officer in the jaw and fled in a car."

Davies squeezed her ball, the contents moved like wet sand, forming different shapes and moulds from the pressure she exerted.

"You know, Hillier seemed very put off by my presence. He expected to be OIC," said Carter.

"Assistant Commissioner Hillier applied some downward pressure on me to make him OIC before I brought in a more senior officer with local experience."

"You mean queer?" Carter asked.

"Yes," Davies said bluntly.

"Don't know if I should be flattered or not," Carter said.

Davies shrugged. "He's keen, that Hillier, in my eyes, though, he's too inexperienced – and expecting too much. I didn't have enough favours in the book to keep him out of my unit. The media team is going to release a statement once all the ducks are in a row. What's your take? Gay-bashing turned wrong?"

"I reckon the victim is gay, but the attack wasn't hate-crime focused. It feels personal," Carter said.

"Carving a homophobic slur into someone's chest is sadistic. A reasonable assumption is the perpetrator has a grudge against queer people. Maybe is queer themselves?"

"I don't know boss. I want to approach this case from a personal angle. The level of trauma against the victim points to an emotional connection, in my opinion."

"How did Detective Song get back to HQ before you?"

Carter shifted in his chair.

"Got held up."

"Why?" Davies's blunt candour presented itself again.

"Saw an assault in progress. Aided until uniformed officers arrived," Carter said.

Davies nodded, about to press further before Carter interrupted.

"Assuming Doc Monroe agrees, strangulation as the cause of death, it shows a personal angle."

Davies smirked. "As my son says: you do you. I've got four different cases under my supervision that I'm looking to tie up soon."

"How soon is soon?" Carter asked.

"Nearly time to start packing up the office."

"You're not looking for an assistant commissioner role?"

"Nope, just retirement. I'm going off into the sunset."

Carter's eye caught the awards against the back wall of Davies's office. The effect Davies had on the department could not be underestimated. It wasn't just the awards. The shelves were stacked with medals, commendations, and qualifications. They all hinted at her impact across the force and her life. All were arranged around a family portrait: two daughters, one son and her wife, Marie. Carter had attended their marriage once the marriage equality legislation passed in Australia.

He thought to himself, what'll be on the shelves of my office? Do I even want an office here?

Davies noticed Carter looking at her commendations. "How are you feeling being back?"

Carter closed his notepad, perked up and smiled "Good boss. You know what they say about idle hands."

"I want this case wrapped up. If it becomes too much to handle, you'll let me know," Davies said.

"Won't be boss."

Davies turned back to the blue glow from her monitor. "Welcome back then. What's that tagline that the TV drag queen always says before an elimination?"

"RuPaul? She says, don't fuck it up."

"She's a wise lady," Davies said.

--

Carter wrote the name Nelson Harris across the top of a whiteboard.

Game time mate, first impressions count.

"Alright ladies, gents and my non-binary officers. Our victim's name is Nelson Harris." Carter clapped his hands. The uniformed and plain-clothed officers gathered around the whiteboard. Carter tossed the whiteboard marker to Constable Zhang. "What do we know and what are we doing?"

"I've arranged a meeting with the City of Melbourne planning department and HR to explore his work life," Hillier said.

"Alright, thanks, good work to arrange that so quickly," Carter said. He assumed Hillier put on his team player cap to make up for this morning's mistake. "Zhang, you'll note that please."

Officer Zhang nodded and started scribbling down Hillier's task. Major Crimes followed an Agile project management methodology for each case. The officer wrote each staff member's name along the board's side and then detailed their particular task on a cue card. As each officer progressed the task, they'd move the cue card along the board's different columns. The columns were 'Backlog' to 'Doing' and then 'Complete.' The dreaded 'Blocked' column on the board was where a cue card went if the task couldn't be completed.

Carter shook his head as he watched Zhang detail Hillier's cue card. How much money did the department spend on this lean, flexible, Agile whiteboard stuff? Carter remembered the overly enthusiastic training manager who explained that the process mirrored the software development process to streamline activities and find innovation. As if innovation were buried treasure about to be seen by writing tasks on cue cards. With a broad grin, the training manager revealed with much fanfare the real value of the process: transparency and accountability. Carter suspected the real reason she exuded perkiness was that her consultancy fee easily surpassed the combined salaries of the unit.

"Parents are in Perth. They are catching a flight to Melbourne tomorrow. Ran a quick check on them. Both have drug possession charges, heroin mostly. The last charge is dated a decade and a bit ago. I spoke with the mum. She mentioned that she's been talking to Nelson a lot recently. More so than in the past. She was about to tell me what they'd been talking about, but her husband woke up. She hung up to break the news to him," Perry said.

"That's alright, we can speak to them both once they ID the body. The time difference between Melbourne and Perth is what, four hours?" Carter asked.

"Three," Perry said.

"Damn, that means the Harrises got the call that their son is dead at 6 a.m."

Perry nodded. "They sounded pretty shocked on the phone."

"And former heroin addicts." Carter struggled to think about how any teenager could handle their parents being drug addicts. "Alright, that means the victim was a young teenager when his parents were charged. We didn't find any drug paraphernalia in the house. Toxicology reports will confirm if he's a user."

Carter glanced at the whiteboards, the timeline section completely blank. "What was the victim doing? Most likely he clocked off work around 5 p.m. on Friday. That means we have almost thirty-six hours unaccounted for before Nelson landed up in that alleyway. Suppose the cause of death turns out to be strangulation. In that case, we are looking at a personal connection – a close friend, lover or acquaintance."

"What about an assault or bashing gone wrong?" Hillier queried.

"I'm not ruling anything out, but we are going with the personal angle right now," Carter reiterated.

Hillier persisted with his reasoning. "Carving on his chest: probably a hate crime gone too far, to the extreme. Maybe the perpetrators didn't realise how much anger they had. Nelson meets them in the gay bathhouse, it gets out of hand, and he winds up dead outside the gay bathhouse."

Don't let it show, Carter thought as he kept his shoulders from raising in annoyance. You don't need to say 'gay bathhouse,' just 'bathhouse,' twat.

"The first sweep of the Vapour doesn't indicate the victim was there before his death. And none of the gents staying in Vapour on the night saw him either," said Song.

Hillier continued. "Okay, but the techs are still combing Vapour. The guy who fled the scene, maybe he stomped the shit out of the victim, strangled him, all part of some sexual/homophobic fantasy."

A slight smirk crossed Hillier's face as he savoured the first jab. Carter returned the gaze with a deadpan glare. "Shame he vacated the crime scene with such ease then."

Hillier sheepishly avoided eye contact by staring at his own shoes. "That wasn't entirely my fault."

Carter shrugged. "What's done is done. We are missing a crime scene, and as the techs are combing through Vapour as we speak, they'll be able to confirm if the murder took place there. I doubt it. Too many witnesses."

Hillier nodded and glanced down at his phone.

Probably giving Hillier Senior an unofficial update, Carter thought. "How's CCTV coming along?"

Song spoke up. "CCTV captured the car fleeing. Looking for a white Commodore. The licence plate numbers were fake. They belong to a silver Audi SUV in Port Melbourne reported stolen a month ago. No other footage around the alleyway. We have an approximate time of death between midnight and 2 a.m. We are getting CCTV footage of the area to identify other cars. Assuming the victim was murdered offsite and dropped off, we are unsure if the white Commodore is connected. So there is a lot of footage before and after to go through."

"Great everyone. Let's get cracking. Perry will divide the divisions of labour," Carter said before pausing. A scheme formed in Carter's mind as he pointed to Perry, who had devoured half a bacon and egg roll. "Actually, Detective Perry, how do you feel about a trip to the morgue?"

Perry tossed his half-eaten roll in the bin. "Count me in boss, just can't handle the smells on a full stomach."

"Great, Hillier will assign duties and Song, Perry and I will be over at the morgue for the autopsy."

CHAPTER SEVEN

Before a body arrived on Doctor Monroe's stainless-steel autopsy tables, the entire theatre was cleaned with a disinfected solution of 0.5% hypochlorite. The sickly-sweet smell of disinfectant always lingered in the room. As a new victim entered the theatre, its scents accompanied it. The aromas of its life from the grand to banal all remained – mothballs, perfumes, cooked garlic and onions. The theatre's disinfectant always won against any smell, bleaching it out of existence and off the victim.

Post-autopsy the victim's body is bathed in a disinfectant solution, dissolving the last vestiges of a victim's life and humanity — its smell.

Nelson Harris lay on one of the three autopsy tables. Before each autopsy, Nic prepared her tools of the trade and placed them on the moveable stainless-steel workbench. The common tools Nic brought out were scalpels, scissors and rib cutters. Non-stick mats surrounded the table. Above it, an incandescent light globe emitted harsh fluorescent light — a lonely place for a body.

Inside the theatre, Detective Perry stood next to Nic. The two were dressed in scrubs, gloves, masks and goggles — a poor man's disposable space suit.

Detective Perry had been planning a post-retirement cruise with his wife when she suddenly died from cancer. The doctors discovered melanoma on her back, it had metastasised and spread through the bloodstream. She passed away in hospice only a month after diagnosis. Perry's kids were fully grown and living overseas, he didn't know what to do. So, he stayed with the familiar and kept working and pushing back his retirement date — better a workaholic than aimless.

Nic and Perry bagged and tagged Nelson's clothes. At the same time, Song, Carter and Doctor Monroe put on the disposable gear in the anteroom.

"No coffee, Carter?" Doctor Monroe asked.

"I told him you'd be mad if he didn't bring you and Nic a coffee," Song said as she entered the theatre while Carter and Doctor Monroe finished putting on their masks.

"Sorry doc, been one of those days," Carter said.

Doctor Patricia Monroe, truly a chameleon with long snow-white hair, as much in her element with a scalpel as with ladies who lunch in the posh suburbs of Melbourne. She'd been one of the top coroners with the service for longer than Carter had been with the force.

"It's good to see you back at the job after your holiday."

Carter snorted, "Thanks doc. Just needed some personal time."

"You know, when I lost my Walter, nearly a decade ago now, I took six months off for personal time. Spent two months in Bali by myself. Read some good books and had cocktails by the pool."

"Sorry to hear about your loss."

Doctor Monroe shrugged. "Don't be. He turned into a cheater, a drunk and by fifty a miserable husk of a man. I think love clouded my vision when we first met. The most liberating thing happened to me when he had that heart attack in our house."

"None of your medical knowledge could have saved him?"

Her ocean blue eyes avoided eye contact with Carter. She tilted her head and half-smiled.

"Depends what hat you have on. I certainly wasn't medically negligent. His time was just up; he passed his used by date. If our children hadn't been adults when it happened, it might have had a different ending."

"Different story for Theo and me. We were just planning our lives together. Then he up and left. Didn't realise how hard it hurt," Carter said.

Doctor Monroe peered through the anteroom window into the theatre. "Be grateful for any time; some of us don't even have that."

"True, but I still wish Theo and I had more time. We didn't exactly end things on a high note."

"No one ever does. There is always something outstanding."

Carter started to grow uncomfortable with the discussion and tried to change the direction.

"Have you tried dating again?"

Doctor Monroe nodded. "I did, but most men who were interested in me were, in fact, looking for a nurse with a purse. Or their inflated sense of ego meant they assumed they should be dating a woman twenty years younger than them and believed they were gracing me with their presence."

"That's ambitious of these men," Carter said.

Doctor Monroe snorted. "Darling, it is beyond delusional."

"The kids these days say, ok boomer," Carter said.

Doctor Monroe flicked on the recording device that hung above the steel slab.

"This commences the autopsy of a presumed Nelson Harris, yet to be identified by a relative."

Doctor Monroe circled the body. After death, blood sinks to the lower extremities and with it, so does the colour of the body. Nelson's skin had turned a sickly grey. She picked up Nelson's left hand and examined it. She closely inspected the fingernails.

"Nelson Harris presents as a twenty-six-year-old Caucasian Australian male. Unlikely to be a smoker, evidence he bit his nails. Perhaps a bit stressed?"

"Now you're a detective," Carter chuckled.

"Scrapings across the nails have been taken, along with swabs from all passageways and abrasions. Fibre samples were taken from abrasions on his knees at the scene," Nic mentioned as she continued to take notes on her clipboard.

Doctor Monroe nodded. "Thank you, Nic. There are no obvious signs of trauma along the top of the feet, or along the calves."

Doctor Monroe shook her head as she gazed along the victim's upper legs and torso. "Abrasions on his knees with significant parallel bruising along his upper thighs."

Carter interrupted. "Someone crouched or kneeled on his legs?"

"Most likely, while they carved that into his chest." She pointed a scalpel to the word engraved in the victim's torso. "Evidence of abrasions along the torso and chest, with one word carved into the chest. I'll be able to estimate when that occurred once we crack the chest."

Doctor Monroe continued walking around the body towards the victim's head. "Significant striations along the neck. Evidence of bruising along the head as well." She moved back some of the victim's hair. "Hmm, an elongated bruise on the back of the head. This may have been the first assault. The force would have been enough to throw him to the ground. While on the ground, he received a volley of kicks." Monroe opened Nelson's eyelids. Dead, green, bloodshot eyes stared back. "And then, strangled. He had beautiful green eyes, like emeralds."

Theo had green eyes too, Carter thought.

The hairs on Carter's arms stood on end again. He imagined Theo lying on the steel autopsy table.

"Do you miss me?" Theo asked.

"I do." Carter answered aloud.

"Someone proposing to you?" Doctor Monroe stared at him. Covered in glasses and a surgical mask, she could still convey her sense of puzzlement with a slight turn of the head.

Carter clenched his hand behind his back. Theo's body disappeared. Nelson lay on the steel autopsy table. Focus, he thought to himself. "Sorry. Please continue."

"Judging by these initial indicators, the victim had been severely beaten. While dazed, his attackers strangled him."

Carter glanced over to Nic, who met his gaze and winked.

She is always on the money, thought Carter.

"You mention attackers Doc – in the plural?" Song asked.

"I'll need to assess this further. If you notice the bruising across the chest. It looks like the victim has been stomped on. The bruising pattern near the left pectoral has horizontal lines, while the bruising along the abdomen has a diamond pattern. The bruising along the thighs is blunter, less defined, most likely from one of the attacker's knees. I'll need to confirm, but you are looking at an size eleven shoe for both attackers."

Doctor Monroe moved her scalpel between the two parallel bruises on the victim's upper thigh. "One of the attackers sat on him, most likely while carving that into his chest." Her scalpel moved between the letters carved into the victim's chest.

Doctor Monroe shook her head. "The victim took quite the beating. His last minutes of consciousness were not pleasant."

Numb the pain with a spin at the pokies, the merman's voice said inside Carter's head. "For fuck's sake." Carter let out an exaggerated sigh.

Clang. Monroe dropped her scalpel. She, Song, Nic and Perry all stared at Carter.

"Sorry, realised we should get going. When do you think you'll have the report ready by?"

"Tomorrow morning at the latest," Monroe replied.

"Great. Thank you. Perry will stay to observe and assist."

Detective Perry nodded. "Spending the day with two lovely ladies – my treat."

Monroe picked up a scalpel from her surgical tray. She pierced the victim's skin and commenced a v-incision across the chest. She slowly peeled back the skin of the chest to reveal the ribcage. Nic then handed her what Carter could only describe as the equivalent of surgical garden shears.

"When's the last time you sat in on an autopsy?" Nic asked Perry. He had sat down on a stool and focused on the ground, wall – anywhere other than the surgical table.

"Been a while. Shouldn't have eaten that egg and bacon roll, I reckon."

"Hun, the bucket is to your left," Nic said.

"Stay strong Perry," Carter said as he and Song left the theatre.

Under her breath Song said to Carter, "Nic usually doesn't tell people where the bucket is."

"Are we witnessing the first blush of love?" Carter mused.

"Or is she tired of mopping up sick?" Song asked.

The pair entered the anteroom and took off their masks and gloves. They started to wash their hands as Carter continued to observe the autopsy through the window. He saw Nic pat Perry on the shoulder. Her pat lingered on Perry's shoulder.

It caused Carter to smile.

Everyone is a moment away from hitting that jackpot of True Love, he thought.

His smile disappeared as he looked deep inside himself.

Did I squander the True Love from my jackpot with Theo? He thought.

Carter watched Nic return to the autopsy table where Nelson lay.

That's next for all of us, death, he thought.

Nic took a pair of forceps to assist Doctor Monroe as she continued to pry open Nelson's chest.

And it's pretty lonely. No worse than how I feel now, he thought.

Carter almost laughed at the realisation. He's the walking dead, with no one to love.

"Do you see any abrasions on Nelson's hands or forearms?" Carter asked.

"Not a scratch," Song said as she grabbed some paper towels to dry her hands.

"He knew, probably trusted, his attackers until it was too late. Might be looking at a lover," Carter said.

"Agreed," Song said. She shook her head, "Terrible way to go. Thinking you know someone and then they turn on you."

"We need to know who that someone is. Let's hope Nelson's friend will give us some clues," Carter said.

"The bestie always knows who you're shagging," Song said.

CHAPTER EIGHT

Song had arranged a meeting with Abby Crosby at the cafe she worked at in South Yarra. Song stood at the counter ordering coffees. While Carter sat at a high-top table at the back end of a concrete shoebox café.

Green ivy snaked across a steel lattice that lined the cafe walls. The espresso machine had more staff operating it than were in the kitchen. One staff member measured out the coffee grind. Another tamped the grind and pulled the espresso shot using the hot water pushed out from the machine. The final one steamed the milk in all its various forms, from low fat, almond, soy to lactose-free, and mixed it with the espresso to create coffee artwork to be consumed in about as long as it took to craft.

"What happened in there?" Song asked as she took a seat.

"What do you mean?" Carter said.

"During the autopsy, you seemed distracted, to say the least, having a few conversations running in your mind."

"I'm alright, just thinking, pondering."

That's all I do now, isn't? Think and then dwell. On James, Theo and the pokies. Should have done things differently.

Song snapped her fingers.

"Ahem. You're trailing off again. Thinking about anything in particular?"

"Nah, just this interview. We are not making enough progress. No real leads yet. I keep getting the feeling we are missing something," said Carter.

"We can only do what we can. Focus on today. You know what they say."

Carter and Song smiled and in unison said, "With one foot in the past, one in the future; you're pissing on today."

"I'm glad you're back," Song said. "You know I'm here if you want to chat. I'm much friendlier than Doctor Lynch."

Carter smiled. "Thanks, but I'm doing alright. How are Aaron and the kiddies?"

Song poured water for her and Carter from a repurposed tequila bottle. Each table had a different type of spirits bottle as a water jug. The table next to Carter and Song had a Southern Comfort bottle that made Carter salivate for a Southern Comfort and Coke.

"Pretty good. Aaron is away on a business trip for a week or so. I've got Umma staying with us to do the after-school pickup."

"Your mum is a bloody saint," Carter said.

"She is. I think she likes being a grandmother more than being a mother. Less pressure, being second office in charge," Song said.

Carter smirked, "How are you feeling being 2IC?"

"To your officer in charge?" Song asked. "If Perry or Hillier had been OIC over me, I'd have lit my desk on fire and finally taken up my father's offer to join him at his company."

When Song's parents moved back to Australia, they established an import–export business between Australia and South Korea. Her family always has the pulse of the industry. Song had told Carter this once, and even then, only in bits and pieces. The story remained blurred to him under a cloud of Soju and fried chicken.

Carter smiled, "That's my concern."

"Don't worry Carter, I'm happy where I am. Aaron and I spoke about this, and we've decided to not have any more kids. He's going to get the snip when he's back. Three kids, two rounds of maternity leave, that is enough for me. I got a promotion in my sights as my next step," said Song.

"Good to have a five-year plan," Carter chuckled.

"A third round of maternity doesn't fit into that," Carter said.

"That's a shit trade-off," Carter lamented.

"It is what it is. Besides, I wouldn't want a third pregnancy, it'll ruin the yummy mummy vibe I have going."

Carter blushed, "In a few years I'll be reporting to you?"

"If I work my magic, it'll be sooner than that."

Carter and Song shared a laugh.

A waiter placed a flat white in front of Carter and a long black in front of Song.

"Enjoy the coffees." The waiter wore a chic Fitzroy hospitality uniform of military boots, forest green shorts and a Hawaiian short-sleeved shirt. The waiter studied Song, then Carter. "Youse the coppers, aye?"

Song nodded.

"We are," Carter said as he spooned a teaspoon of sugar into his coffee. His teaspoon puncturing the caramel crema.

"Abby told us about her mate. Right old shame," the waiter said before leaving.

Song's eyes darted around the cafe. A slow grin formed. "Think about this Carter. Everyone who works here has at least one tattoo."

Carter noticed that the waiter who brought them their coffees had a single line tattoo going along each of his fingers. "Sleeve tattoos get you a promotion."

His eyes followed the waiter as he took a staircase up to the mezzanine level, where he stepped inside an office. Moments later, a woman stepped out of the office and fixed her gaze on Carter and Song. She had applied thick red lipstick and wore black-rimmed glasses. A cream-coloured headband kept her lush black hair out of her face. As she walked down the stairs towards them, Carter noticed her mascara had run.

Carter motioned to Abby and Song glanced up at her before looking at Carter.

"She's been crying," Song said.

"I reckon it's the first time she's lost a close friend," Carter said.

"Won't be the last, age can be cruel," Song said.

Song and Carter stood up as Abby walked over.

"Hi Abby, I'm DI Emily Song, this is DCI Leo Carter. Is there somewhere private we could chat?"

Abby shook her head, her styled hair with more pins than Carter could count did not move an inch. More helmet than hair. She took a seat on the other bar stool.

"No, this is fine, thank you. The afternoon rush is already done. I wasn't going to come in, but these guys are like my family; didn't know where else I should be."

The three sat down, and Song took out her iPad and opened it to Nelson Harris's picture.

"Abby, do you know this person?" Song asked.

Abby's lower lip quivered. Carter never liked this part of the job – forcing people to accept the truth that a friend is dead before they are ready to accept it. He knew he should comfort Abby, but he leaned back and let Song take point.

"That's Nelson, Nelson Harris. We've been best mates since we were kids. We lived right next door to each other in Perth and came over from there together," Abby said.

Song switched off her iPad, "Thank you, Abby, I know how difficult this is."

"How did you two end up coming to Melbourne?" Carter asked.

Abby shakily poured herself a glass of water. She then tried to grasp the glass, her fingers not quite working. Abby shook her hands as tears rolled down her face.

"Take your time Abby, there is no rush," Song said.

Abby smiled and dabbed her eyes. "Let's try this again." She picked up the glass and took a long sip of water. She held the glass in her hand. "You know what I miss from Perth the most?"

"What?" Song asked.

"The pools, everyone had a pool in Perth. Well except Nelson. But he always came over to my parents' house in Claremont, and we'd like literally live in the pool. Best way to beat the heat is with a pool. You can't really do that here, you know," Abby said.

"Did you two move over from Perth together?" Song asked.

Abby placed down her glass. "Nelson got this job working for the City Council in their planning department. He couldn't contain his excitement for the job and moving to Melbourne. But he didn't know anyone here. I needed a break from Perth. It's a great city but you know, it can feel small. So, it seemed like the right time to make a move. We've been here maybe just over a year." Abby's eyes shot wide open. "Oh God, his parents. Do they know? This is going to kill them." As soon as the word kill left her mouth, she immediately regretted it. Another tear rolled down her cheek.

Carter marvelled to himself as Song placed a hand on top of Abby's. Abby immediately began to calm down, her breaths slowing. A small act of compassion helped so much.

Why can't I do that, he thought to himself.

Song continued to question Abby, "Nelson's parents are on their way. You don't need to worry about that. You can help by answering a few of our questions."

"Aside from you, does Nelson have any close friends?" asked Carter.

Abby swayed a bit. She'd never make a spy: her face contorted through the various trains of thought as she processed the question. Carter knew the answer before she said no.

"No, not really. Nelson mostly tagged on to mine. I mean he wasn't a loner. It was just a bit easier for me to make some connections in Melbourne from working hospo. His co-workers were all a bit old and, you know, stuffy. It happens when you have kids and go all corporate, I guess."

Carter smirked ever so, as he and Song made eye contact.

"What about a partner, a casual fling or a friend with benefits?" Carter asked.

"Hard to say, I know he had a guy in rotation. But I got the feeling Nelson was a bit cagey about it."

"You never met the guy?" Carter asked.

Abby shook her head, "I think the guy was in the closet, famous or cheating on their partner."

"What makes you think that?" Carter asked.

"I dunno. If Nelson saw a guy with no strings, he would have been open to the guys I tried to set him up with. But he never took the bait. He seemed really interested in this guy; you know?"

"How long do you think he's been seeing him?"

"Let's say six months. Whenever Nelson had a one-night stand, he'd share his mobile's location with me. He always joked it was so they'd know where the body was."

Abby started twisting and turning her hands; she'd been downtrodden by her own words.

"Nelson must have had a good sense of humour," Song said.

Abby dabbed another tear from her face. "He did. And he kept up such a positive vibe despite everything that happened to him. He had a rough childhood."

Carter's ears just pricked up, "Abby, you just said Nelson used to share his mobile's location with you when he hooked up with guys. When's the last time he did this?"

"Ages ago. Maybe when he first started seeing this guy. I don't know how he did it, part of his Gmail account maybe. When he shared his location, it'd appear on Google Maps."

Carter smiled. "That's great information. We might be able to check his records and get a location of this mystery man – assuming they met at his address."

"Guess there are some benefits from Big Brother," Abby said.

Song and Carter exchanged a smile. Carter tried not to get too excited, but he knew what a significant clue this could be. Abby's mobile buzzed. Head craned down she became oblivious to Carter and Song as her fingers flew across the screen, texting back.

"When do Nelson's parents arrive?" she asked without looking up from her mobile.

"Tomorrow morning," Song replied.

"Good," Abby placed her mobile down. "I got a call from James Hughes. You know, he's that politician. He's organised a few people in the main LGBTQI groups, and they suggested doing a candlelight vigil. They were thinking of doing it tomorrow. It would be nice if Nelson's parents were there. They literally will see how much love there is for him out here. I think he struggled to get some mates in Melbourne, once you get past those dragons at the doors; it's a great city. But it's that first hurdle that is pretty rough. If I didn't have my mates here, I don't know. May have thrown in the towel and headed back to Perth."

A second of irritation crossed Carter's face, "James Hughes has arranged all this?"

Abby nodded, "Yeah, and with Nelson's parents, there is one thing you should know." Abby fiddled with her fingers as she spoke. "They had a pretty bad drug habit when we were kids. They were doing a lot of smack. We thought we had it all as kids, in a weird sense. Nelson would have me over, and we could play the music as loud as possible, his parents wouldn't care. They'd be passed out in the bedroom. Child Services eventually came. They didn't have any family to take on Nelson. So he lived with us for a few years while his parents cleaned up. They did well. His mum got a cleaning job at a hospital, his dad drives trucks in the mines. Nelson gushed about how proud he was of them for kicking the drug. Definitely a hard slog at first for them to kick the drug and build a relationship with Nelson as a teen."

Carter smiled. "Thank you. When you're up to it, we will need you to come in to make a formal statement. But what you've given us so far is really useful."

"Anything to help; he was a brother to me."

"Oh, I nearly forgot to ask. Was Nelson a gambling man? Did you two visit the pokies often?"

Abby looked taken aback, "Nelson doesn't gamble. He strictly avoids anything that could turn into an addiction because of his parents."

"Of course, my mistake." Carter passed her a card. "Give us a buzz if you remember anything else, day or night."

"Thanks. And I'll text you those details of the memorial," Abby said.

Once Abby left, Carter shook his head. "Nelson is betting on the down low."

"A new behaviour or a long-held secret pastime," Song asked.

"One problem at a time, and first up is James-fucking-Hughes," Carter said.

"He's a smooth operator. He's got my vote," Song said.

"Assuming he isn't the killer trying to hide behind the optics of the earnest political candidate and community leader."

"You're a glass half-full kind of guy when it comes to Hughes."

"Tasted that drink, left a bad taste in my mouth," Carter said. "If James finds me his South American employee, then I'll consider changing my tune."

CHAPTER NINE

After all the extensive talk of pools in Perth, Carter decided he needed a swim to process what he had just learned. He headed to the Fitzroy Baths. The baths were one of the leading gyms in Fitzroy. With a full gym, fifty-metre outdoor pool and a locally renowned cafe, it was a mainstay of the suburb. Entry to the cafe went through the gym for an extra sense of exclusivity.

"Surprised I don't need to dust it off," Jim O'Brien joked. He had scanned Carter's gym pass. Jim had an ageless presence to him. Fifty, sixty, seventy, Carter couldn't tell.

The former triathlete swam two kilometres after every shift he did at the pool. Scanning gym passes, handing out towels seemed to be a social bonus to him. As he told Carter over coffee once, he really didn't need to work. He just enjoyed this breezy, stress-free kind of role that gave him some regular connection with the community and the chance to keep up with his swimming.

"I'll grab a pair of speedos, a towel and goggles," Carter said.

"Hopefully, we have your size," Jim said with a cheeky smile.

"Thanks mate. Guess you missed out on the customer-service training module this year," Carter said with a smile forming across his face.

After changing, he walked out to the outdoor area of the public baths. Shaped in a large rectangle, the fifty-metre pool was in the centre. The far side of the outdoor area had concrete benches with the cafe and green space at the bottom quarter of the area.

House beats from speakers greeted him. Every evening during summer a DJ played music for the swimmers. Carter felt a bit like David Attenborough on expedition, observing the local wildlife in heat. Men and women were sprawled across the bleachers, soaking up the evening sun. Instead of parading around to showcase their bright feathers, they all wore the least amount of clothing possible without breaking the law. They lounged around in shorts, speedos and bikinis that cost a fortnight in wages.

Carter stood in front of one of the empty medium-speed lanes.

Why drop Nelson's body at the bathhouse? It must have been a statement, Carter thought.

He dipped a toe into the pool. Carter shivered slightly at the cooling sensation – an odd feeling with the sun beating down and sweat dripping off his body. Carter adjusted his goggles, so they were a snug fit over his eyes. Carter wrapped his toes around the edge of the pool. Each vertebra of his spine cracked as he bent down to reach his toes. God, it has been a while, he thought as his hands gripped the edge of the pool beside his feet.

No one leaves a body at a bathhouse, Carter thought.

He bent his knees and pushed off from the edge of the pool. Carter raised his hands to form an arrow over his head. He sailed through the air until his hands pierced the water, followed by his body.

The first minute underwater is the calmest. The vibrations from the DJ's speakers were his only companion, aside from his thoughts. For a minute, though, even his mind entered a zen-like state as the water enveloped him. Hands outstretched, body streamlined, Carter continued to dolphin-kick under the water to propel himself along. He glided through the water with the back of his body reaching the surface of the water. As he broke the surface, he rotated his head for a quick breath — his ear exposed to the outside world, the noise. House beats, chattering, a kaleidoscope of noise. His mind returned to registered reality.

No one leaves a body at a bathhouse without reason. It's not a dumping ground. With a quick breath, he started to do front stroke. His hands pulled water along and behind him. Feet kicked to build momentum. He began to build pace.

What's the connection the perpetrators have to Vapour?

Carter turned his head again to take a breath. He took an extended breath. He scanned the surrounding area. There were more people in the bleachers in swim gear than swimmers swimming. He plunged his head back into the water and built up his stroke, one stroke, then another. He turned his head to the side to grab a breath again.

This had to have been planned ahead of time.

Carter did a flip turn at the end of the lane. His feet pushed off the end of the pool, which propelled him down the lane. He kept his body streamlined, arms out front, and dolphin-kicked along the pool. The beats from the DJ changed; the vibrations followed suit.

With his face down, his eyes followed the blue tiles at the bottom of the pool as he increased pace.

Is James Hughes behind it all? Did he orchestrate all this to build his profile? He has connections. But the timelines don't work, and he knows easier ways to dispose of a body I reckon.

Carter remembered one of James's favourite sayings – don't shit where you eat.

With one last flip turn to stop, Carter stood up at the end of the pool. Breathing heavily, he leaned his body against the pool wall to catch his breath.

"Detective?"

Carter removed his tinted goggles to see Paddy. He had swapped corporate finance attire for activewear. It made Carter smile. Paddy wore a dark blue workout singlet and a pair of black shorts from which his thick muscular thighs emerged. Carter salivated.

"You work out here?" Carter asked.

Paddy shrugged. "When I can. Usually, use the gym near my work, but this is my local, and the beats are pretty good. Or sick as the kids say, I think."

The two glanced over towards the DJ. There were two of them, a man and a woman, each equally attractive and each wearing a pair of headphones and twirling dials and pushing buttons.

"What does a DJ really do?" Carter asked.

"You got me. I think they just press play on a Spotify track," Paddy said.

"You finished your workout?" Carter asked.

Paddy smiled, his white teeth beaming. "Yeah, back and biceps today." Paddy rotated his forearm and flexed his bicep. "Like turning on a light."

Carter got out of the pool and began to dry himself off with a towel.

"Impressive light," Carter said.

The two caught each other looking at each other. Paddy at the droplets of water beading off Carter's body. Carter looking at Paddy's impressive biceps.

"Thanks for verifying your whereabouts and making a statement so quickly."

Paddy smiled, "No worries, my assistant needed some busy work, gathering all the documents gave him something to do."

Carter wrapped the towel around his waist. "You got plans?"

Paddy shook his head. "Thinking of getting some sun out here for a bit."

"How about you come over? Nearly dinner time, I'll make us some pasta," Carter said.

Paddy smacked his stomach. "All those carbs: gotta love it. You got any beer?"

Carter thought back to the last bottle of wine in the house, tipped out in the bathroom sink. "I've got a few beers at home," Carter said.

"Let's go," Paddy said.

Carter eyed Jim still working over at the counter.

"Let's head out the back door. I don't want Jim's look of disapproval for my short and expensive swim," Carter said.

--

Chlorine coated Carter's skin; the chemical scent turned into a musk. He had slipped out of his bathers and into a pair of shorts, no underwear, and a singlet.

Carter glanced at his bug out bag by the door of his flat. Paddy hadn't paid any attention to it, which Carter was thankful for. He sat on a stool at the kitchen island while sipping on a beer.

"Pure Blonde beers are the best. They are low-calorie, means I can save my calories for good foods," Paddy said.

Oil sizzled in the frypan Carter had on the stove. He dropped in some chopped onions, garlic and chilli. He stirred the ingredients around with a wooden spoon.

"You didn't have to cook. We could have got some takeaway," Paddy said.

Carter stirred the mixture some more before adding some paprika to the mix.

"It's no problem, I'm a half-decent cook," Carter said.

Paddy took another sip of beer. "Probably better than me. I basically poach chicken and bake sweet potatoes in the oven. Sometimes steam some broccoli. Great foods for building muscle."

"Seems to be working. You're a lean unit," Carter said with a hint of lust in his voice.

"Thanks. Hard to keep growing though. I try to do a five-day split, but with morning cardio, work, volunteer work and trying to date. It can be a bit of a nightmare," Paddy said.

"Try doing anything when you do shift work for a living," Carter said.

"How do you balance it?" Paddy asked.

"Poorly, I think." Carter said as he felt Paddy's eyes on him, trying to peel back the layers of his psyche. Carter changed the subject quickly. "I do have a tip on cooking. It's time to enter flavour country. I'll give you the easiest piece of cooking advice you'll ever need. Always start with frying up some onion and garlic to season any food you're cooking. The bonus is the aromas always fill the room, putting people at ease."

Paddy winked. "The beer helps too."

Paddy drank the last of the beer and got two out of the fridge. He passed one to Carter. Their hands touched. Carter felt a familiar surge in his crotch.

Paddy took out a glass and poured in half his beer. The golden ale shone in the glass below a frothy head.

Carter tipped in the chopped olives and bacon.

"What are you making?"

"A variation of a Puttanesca."

"Isn't that a pretty old-school Italian dish?"

Carter nodded. "It is. That's why I add bacon, gives it a modern flare. And because I'm swine."

"Everyone wants to be a pig. They just don't admit it," Paddy said.

Carter tipped in the diced tomatoes, some water and increased the heat. Carter clinked Paddy's beer bottle. "Much like us." He stirred the pot one more time and scooped a small amount into the ladle. "Here taste this."

"Delicious," Paddy said as he took a taste.

A small dab of tomato sauce landed on Paddy's lower lip.

"You've got some sauce on your lip," Carter said.

Paddy wiped his lips but missed the sauce. "Did I get it," he asked.

"Here," Carter said as he wiped the sauce with his finger. Carter licked the sauce off his finger. "It is delicious. It'll need ten more minutes to be just right."

Paddy gripped Carter's arms, "I'm going to need more than ten minutes with you."

"I don't know," Carter said as he stepped back from Paddy.

"What's wrong," Paddy asked.

"I've questioned you in relation to my case," Carter said.

Paddy let out a loud laugh. He planted a kiss on Carter's cheek. "So, I'm a suspect?"

Carter turned off the burner.

"Everyone is a suspect. Don't take it personally."

Paddy placed a hand along the rim of Carter's shorts. He hooked a thumb under the band and pulled at Carter's shorts to get a sneaky peek at Carter's cock.

"Patience is a virtue. And crime is a cockblock."

Carter wrapped his arms around Paddy. He kissed Paddy's neck before letting go.

Carter and Paddy sat down to dinner. They ate in silence, demolishing their meals.

"Bloody delicious mate. But I should go before I want dessert," Paddy said.

Carter smiled. "I have a lot to work through on this case. But I'd like to see you again."

"Once you've made an arrest?" Paddy asked, laughing.

"Maybe even before."

CHAPTER TEN

Carter swiped his access card to the Major Investigations Office. He glanced down at his watch to check the time. The hour hand approached 7 a.m. Carter held a triple-shot flat white in his hand to combat the restless sleep he had last night. Paddy and the case swirled around in his mind; a good night's sleep had been just out of reach.

The key card reader flashed green, and the doors unlocked. "They really still want me," he marvelled under his breath. As he walked through the doorway, two uniformed officers passed him and nodded to him on their way out. I even command a bit of respect, he thought.

Carter stopped at Hillier and Perry's workstations. Perry wasn't at his desk; Carter assumed he took the later train from Geelong and was on his way in.

Hillier's back faced Carter. His fingers flew across the keyboard, coding data into the police database. Carter peered closer to the other tabs opened in the web browser: Facebook, YouTube, and a real estate site.

A genuinely committed officer, thought Carter as he tapped Hillier on the shoulder. Hillier slowly turned his chair around. He took out one of his earbuds and cocked his head. Carter knew Hillier enjoyed baiting him, hoping to provoke a reaction.

"Yeah what?" Hillier asked.

"Excuse me, Detective? Sir, boss or Carter are more than reasonable ways to address me."

"Yeah what, boss?" Hillier said with one of his earbuds still in.

Carter took the bait. "See that wasn't too hard and take the other earbud out when I'm talking to you."

Hillier slowly placed his thumb and forefinger on the cord of his earbud and tugged it gently. He examined the limp earbud before looking up at Carter with a deadpan expression as he let it fall to his desk.

"Song and I interviewed the victim's friend, Abby. She mentioned that the victim used to share with her his location through his mobile when he'd arrange a casual sex date."

Hillier nodded, almost smirking. "Not really a date, is it? And not the safest way to get laid either."

Carter almost shuddered thinking of what Hillier did to get a date. Carter imagined Hillier rolling up to a bar, flashing his pearly-white smile, mentioning he's a copper? If the first woman wasn't interested, he'd call her a slut and move on to the next. Or maybe he skips the bars and clubs entirely. Straight to the strip clubs with his wolf-pack of steroid-abusing lads, each one throwing more bills at the strippers while simultaneously trying to impress one another in how denigrating towards the strippers they can be.

"Regardless, that means his location has been tracked and stored. So, get the techs and legal involved to access that data. I want timelines and locations."

Hillier nodded. "I'll get on it," he said, taking out a cue card to write the activity before sticking it to the whiteboard.

"Thanks. Let me know the victim's movements and locations for the last six months when they become available," Carter said.

Hillier nodded, "You know Davies's boss is speaking to her right now."

"Who? Your daddy?" Carter sneered.

"You can address him as Assistant Commissioner Hillier, or you know, boss. He earns the big bucks to tell Davies and you what to do."

"Just get to work Hillier, or I might tell Daddy what a bad boy you are for failing to secure the crime scene.

86

Resulting in a suspect assaulting an officer and fleeing the scene."

Hillier looked down at the ground.

"Have you checked in with Zhang? Reckon you owe him."

Carter walked off before Hillier Jr could say anything.

Fucking prick, thought Carter as he walked to his desk. God though, Hillier is right about one thing. His dad is earning the big bucks. Must easily be on five hundred thousand a year, he thought as he sat down at his desk.

Carter took out his mobile and fired off a text message to James Hughes.

'Still waiting on Moe coming to the station. Have you made contact?'

Carter placed his mobile down and drummed his fingers on the edge of his desk. Imagine the luxury, the freedom of a salary like that. Property investments, a share portfolio, first-class holidays every year for life; I'd have it all. I'm never going to earn that kind of salary. But the lotto is my ticket to that lifestyle, he thought.

Carter scrutinised Hillier who typed away at his computer. With a lotto win, I'd have it all and I could punch Hillier right in his smug mouth.

Song sat at her desk and pointed to Carter's computer monitor as he approached.

"You have a fan," Song said.

A yellow post-it note stuck to Carter's computer monitor greeted him.

My office NOW, it read.

Davies could have called or texted me, he thought as his phone buzzed. A text message from Davies lit up his mobile screen.

'Now means now.'

"Bet you a round of coffees Davies already knows about the memorial plans for Nelson arranged by James and Abby," Song said.

Carter shook his head. "Pretty high odds of me losing that one. Better chance of me winning the lotto."

"House always wins," Song said.

Carter's mobile buzzed again. A message from James Hughes.

'No word from Moe.'

"Damn it," Carter said as he closed the text message from James.

"What's wrong?" Song asked.

"James Hughes can't find Moe."

"That's not good. We really need to interview him. And the driver of the car he fled in," Song said.

Carter nodded as he closed the message. The main screen of his mobile returned. A smattering of lotto apps appeared. The multicoloured apps drew Carter in. He felt compelled to buy. He opened the app. A rainbow with a pot of gold at one end appeared as the app loaded.

That's a bit on the nose, Carter thought. An image of tonight's jackpot of ten million dollars replaced the rainbow.

That's my pot of gold.

Carter suddenly remembered where he stood. At work, in the middle of the office.

He turned his phone into his chest and walked over to the windows overlooking Spencer Street. A tram stopped at the corner of La Trobe and Spencer Streets. A group of travellers slowly spilled out. Further along Spencer Street, he spotted the bright red double-decker shuttle bus to the airport. He turned and leaned against the window. His glow from his mobile captured his attention.

With my pot of gold, I'll be able to go on a trip. Maybe Tahiti – who cares as long as it's away from here.

His lotto app had loaded. His balance jumped out at him with a staggering number: $7,840.32. Carter's pulse began to rise. Holy shit, he bloody won!

His free hand clenched into a fist before quickly releasing.

But it's not enough? I can't do shit with seven grand.

Carter glanced up from his mobile. The officers and staff continued on with their day while others were streaming in to start theirs. Song scrolled through her mobile at her desk. Hillier sat at his desk, his eyes on Zhang, who walked the length of the whiteboard, updating different elements. Shades of dark blues and purples covered Zhang's lower jaw where Moe's elbow connected to it.

If Hillier feels guilty for his mistake, why is he still such a dick? Doesn't matter, tonight's the night. I'll win the ten-million-dollar lotto pot, solve this case, and afterwards just relax.

The idea of winning gripped him, infecting his mind. His thumb moved across the screen, a familiar pattern. He selected that night's game, the number of games and purchased them. A pop-up sign appeared asking him to confirm the purchase. Are you sure you want to proceed? Carter didn't think twice at the amount he had chosen. The equivalent of seven grand's worth of games. He clicked the Yes button.

A wave of calm flowed across his body.

"Carter," Song said.

Carter glanced up from his phone and saw Song pointing towards Davies's office. Davies opened the door and yelled across the office.

"Now!" The force of her voice sent a piercing wave through the office. The murmurs and chats went silent. Everyone froze. A lone telephone ringing cut through the stark silence on the floor.

"Sorry boss," Carter said as he put his phone in a pocket and strode towards her office. Carter's words released the office from its snap freeze.

Carter walked into Davies's office. He immediately felt the steely gaze of Assistant Commissioner Hillier while Davies squinted at her computer monitor. Either staring at the small text or willing the monitor to combust.

"A vigil?" Assistant Commissioner Hillier asked.

Hillier Sr and Jr really were related, Carter thought.

They were spitting images of each other. Except Hillier Sr had the years of being on the force weather his body down. That youthful glow that Hillier Jr still had was stripped from his father years ago.

What hair, he had left, had migrated from the top of his head to his neck and, Carter assumed, shoulders and back.

"DCI Carter, this is Assistant Commissioner Hillier," said Davies, as she shifted her focus from the monitor to Carter and Assistant Commissioner Hillier.

"Yes, Nelson's friend, Abby, is organising a vigil for him. It's going to be held in the Fitzroy Gardens. A stone's throw away from Vapour," Carter said.

"She's a puppet here. It is really spearheaded by James Hughes." Assistant Commissioner Hillier shook his head and didn't acknowledge Carter as he continued to vent. "The puppet master. You know how much I hate surprises. The commissioner and, from what I understand, some senior parliamentary figures are rumbling about this. They are not impressed he is capitalising off a tragic murder. I understand he's invited all the major political party candidates but forbidden them from having booths. Only charities, NGOs and community organisations are allowed a booth."

"Pretty clever," Davies said.

"He's a smooth operator, sir," Carter said.

"Clever and smooth operator is a recipe for surprises." Assistant Commissioner Hillier stood up. "I expect no other surprises from this vigil and the clock is ticking.

This case is getting media traction, so it needs to be resolved."

"That's why I have my best detective leading the case," Davies said.

Assistant Commissioner Hillier flashed a judgemental gaze on Carter and said "Hmm," before leaving Davies's office.

Davies moved to sit behind her desk and gestured for Carter to take a seat.

"Charming guy," Carter said. "Do you think I should tell him about how his son failed to secure the perimeter last night?"

"Only if you want to also tell him about how you let a suspect run right by you and assault a constable under your command," Davies said.

Carter scowled in contrition. "I haven't had any luck finding Moe."

"He's the one that fled the scene?" Davies asked.

Carter nodded.

"We need witnesses to progress this investigation. Assistant Commissioner Hillier is applying some downward pressure on me to resolve this case, asap," Davies said.

"Did he volunteer to help out?" Carter asked with a smirk across his face.

Davies let out a small chuckle. "You know, he and I moved through the ranks together and did the academy together. Similar to you and Song," said Davies. "Except his career is still going up. Rumour mill says he has his eyes on the commissioner role."

"What a prick though," Carter said.

"A prick with a point."

A small smile formed from the corner of Carter's mouth. For a second, Carter thought he saw Davies smile before her Dutch sensibilities kicked in.

"Keep it PG, Detective. Pull your head out of your arse. He's our superior officer."

"Noted," Carter said.

"Is it? He has the ear of the current commissioner, and his son works for you. Don't get sassy with either Hillier. They could have you in a pincer movement faster than you can blink."

Carter raised his hands in defeat, "Noted boss."

Davies nodded, "Good. We have other problems to handle. The PR team is frothing at the mouth. The optics are bad. As our 'esteemed colleagues' have told me numerous times. We've already pushed forward our media statement, confirming that Nelson's death is being treated as a homicide. And we are including a line that we are pursuing whether the crime is hate-based or not. At this point, we are not drawing any conclusions."

Davies picked up the blue stress ball on her desk and squeezed it a few times. "We are holding off from mentioning the carving on the victim's chest. I'm aiming to have that sealed. The public doesn't need to know that. Friends and family of the victim especially don't need to know the finer details."

Carter nodded in agreement; Davies had followed his advice. "Did you get any pushback from the PR drones about watering down the hate-crime angle?"

Davies placed her stress ball down. "Depends. For once the drones and I agreed on one thing. It is important to keep a lid on that angle as the only link that this crime may be motivated by hate is the carvings on the victim's body."

"But."

There's always the stick with the carrot, thought Carter.

"If the carvings on the victim's chest are leaked to the press, we are in deep shit. The public would not be too happy or trusting of the police if they learned we were hiding information about a hate crime. Whether or not it turns out to be that, the public will assume that it was." Davies released the stress ball and offered it to Carter. "I'm retiring. You have to think about your career. You were on a career track before your leave. Dropping out of leadership training and taking two months off with little to no notice isn't a good look."

"I had long-service leave, approved by you as I recall."

"I didn't have much of a choice," Davies said.

Carter thought about it. If Davies had denied his leave when he called her, he would have quit then and there.

Don't need a career when I win the lotto. Shit, did I really just spend seven grand on the lotto?

"Do you think upper-middle management is still calling my name?" Carter asked. He leaned over and almost took the stress ball from Davies.

Davies moved her stress ball just out of reach from Carter.

"It doesn't add up. Yes, Nelson identified as gay. No, this crime isn't homophobic."

"Edify me." Davies checked her mobile. Carter saw a dozen messages were waiting, if not more. "You have three minutes," she said.

"If he had been targeted because of his sexuality, the assailants would have just kicked and stomped him. But strangulation is the cause of death in the preliminary findings by the coroner. You don't strangle a stranger to death."

"Lots of serial killers strangle their victims. Who are often not known to them," Davies said.

"We aren't dealing with a serial killer. We are dealing with someone trying to distract us by making it look like a homophobic attack. There's something deeper here."

Davies nodded in agreement. "You now have five minutes, go on."

"This seems personal. A targeted murder for a different reason, something else. A bunch of hoons aren't responsible for this."

"How many perpetrators are we looking for?"

"Doc Monroe reckons there were at least two assailants."

"And these two assailants beat the victim before strangling him?" Davies queried.

"They did."

"Stomped?"

"Kicked once or twice," said Carter.

Carter could see the wheels turning behind Davies's eyes.

He knew where this line of questions would explore the semantical difference between kicked and stomped that the public and press wouldn't distinguish. He felt there must be a dozen academic criminology papers doing a deep dive on this issue ad nauseam.

"Stomping is often associated with young males, an overdose of hormones, peppered with questions about their sexuality. That can make for a few bad decisions. Moe who fled the scene." Davies paused as she checked a file on her desk.

"What about him?" Carter asked.

"He could fit the demographic of a hoon," Davies said. She mulled it over as she squeezed the stress ball. "What if Moe and Nelson were in a relationship, hooking up, whatever. Moe struggles with his sexual identity. Nelson triggers Moe. Maybe Moe is with a friend who doesn't know Moe isn't straight. This sets Moe off. He recruits that friend to help beat him up. It goes too far, and Nelson ends up tossed in a laneway."

Carter shook his head. "Doesn't align. Moe worked at the bathhouse. This place isn't like a straight guy working at a strip club. He didn't work for tips."

Davies's eyebrowed raised.

"Not that type of tip. Keep it PG, Superintendent," Carter said.

"If the victim wasn't strangled, I'd agree that we should be exploring the homophobe–hoon angle. But this is too personal for a bunch of lads on the piss," Carter said.

Davies's mobile vibrated. Her attention split between Carter and the mobile. "It's your case, Carter. You know the risks. Pursue whichever line of enquiry you think best. We need to keep a lid on the carving on the victim's chest. No leaks to the media. I'm handling all media and press for this case."

"Including for the memorial vigil?" Carter asked.

Davies opened her web browser to the event listing on Facebook.

"Oh that," she said dryly. "Look, already three hundred indicated they are attending. They've only been promoting it for a few hours. Stonington City Council fast-tracked the permits to host the event." Davies squeezed her stress-ball again. "You know it took that council eight months to approve the granny flat we built in our backyard. Eight bloody months of paperwork passing from one desk to another in that bloody council."

"Expecting a guest?" Carter asked.

"Reckon my youngest is moving back in with us," Davies said as she squeezed her stress-ball again.

"Sofia? She'd be in her twenties now?"

"Twenty-four," Davies lamented and squeezed her ball.

There's more to this. Early retirement, daughter moving in: there is family drama at home. Carter watched Davies destroy her stress ball with an iron grip. How I can help is by solving this case for her. "I know three hundred people say they are coming, but that doesn't mean bums on seats, or feet standing in a park. Might be a lot of hot air. The victim wasn't well known around town."

"That's the point, Carter. This will be big. His story is everyone's story when they left home, moved interstate, overseas – you name it. Everyone at one point or another has been victim Nelson. This will be a big event. In between pics of smashed avocado, these kids know how to organise themselves."

"What's my budget for surveillance?"

"How long is a piece of rope? If this murder is personal, the perpetrator or someone who knows what happened will be there. I want eyes tracking it."

"That's good then. I'll get Perry to take point."

Davies smiled. "It'll bring back fond memories from his time on the counter-surveillance teams. Now, media has asked if the Officer in Charge will be making a statement. We've been allocated ten minutes. You know the spiel. Thank everyone for attending, advise them to look after their mates, call crime-stoppers or talk to an officer tonight if they have any relevant information. Drop in a few mentions that you're queer. It'll be a rousing call to action while alleviating fears that this crime is going to be ignored by the cops."

Carter shifted in his chair. Public speaking drew some of the deepest parts of his anxiety to the surface because he had so little experience in it. It was a conscious decision. He'd much prefer being an operator behind the scenes.

"Dunno boss. Haven't done much media in a while. Prefer to stay under the radar. Have Song and me on the ground."

"Guess I can rope in Hillier Sr or Jr to rouse the masses – I'm sure they undertook media training in their youth at Melbourne Grammar."

Don't take the bait, he thought.

Davies raised an eyebrow. "What does every queer sports club have?" she asked with a smirk.

"A cool, calm and collected lesbian to inspire and organise the gays," Carter said.

"The balance sheets for all the queer sports club in Melbourne would be in the red from extravagant purchase of glitter and vodka sodas without a lesbian to steer them."

"And what would the Major Crimes squad do without their lesbian? First out-and-proud lesbian superintendent; seems pretty fitting for you to calm the masses at the memorial," Carter said.

"Righteo, guess we will bring out the big guns," Davies said.

"Thanks, boss. I know you'll make an inspiring speech to calm the masses. Much better than a gay grunt making the speech," Carter said.

Davies nodded. "But Carter, you know speeches are part of a DCI and Superintendent's roles. I'm giving you some leeway because you are just returning to duty. If you want my chair when I'm gone, you'll need to learn to be comfy being on camera."

Carter sighed. "Yep, I did pass the media relations short course. But while you are still in the chair, I've got some important issues to focus on. And you've got a speech to work on."

"Ha! The media team has already drafted my speech. We are all puppets to someone."

Song knocked on the door before entering in a blur of motion. "Sorry to interrupt. Our friend, Moe, has shown up – in the boot of a car."

Carter stood up, "Duty calls."

"Take Hillier Jr," Davies said.

Carter crossed his arms. "Why?"

Davies waved her hand at him to leave her office. "He's a detective, use him and it'll keep Hillier Sr off my back."

CHAPTER ELEVEN

One hour later, Song, Carter and Hillier were ten kilometres away from Vapour in Ascot Vale. The suburb was essentially divided by its road. On one side of the road was a suburb that exuded affluence, quaint roads with boutique cafes, news agencies and chemists. On the other of the road was the Ascot Vale Estate. A series of cottage and low-rise developments.

When the Ascot Vale Estate first opened it was bright, cheery, and pristine. The builds were freshly painted, and the lawns were neatly trimmed. Now all the buildings were crumbling. The interiors needed a fresh coat of paint. The buildings were all surrounded by patches of parched brown grass.

Carter and Song pulled in just off the main street, Union Road, into a side street cordoned off with police tape and a police cruiser on either side. Hillier had followed behind them in his own car, pulling up as they exited the vehicle.

Inside the cordon, grey screens were erected around a car to allow the technicians privacy to examine both it and the body inside. The same applied for the public, who often think they want a peek but can't handle what's revealed.

"It could be him," Carter said as the three stood looking into the boot of a silver Audi SUV. Two technicians dressed in white coveralls were already there, scouring the car for evidence. A body lay there curled up. He shared similar characteristics to the runner from Vapour. Same build and hair. The critical difference now was the stains of crimson red across the body along with it being cold to the touch. Carter, with blue gloves on, turned the victim's head towards them. A swollen and bruised face greeted them.

"Somebody was angry at him," Song said.

"Seems to be a theme," Carter lamented. "A body stashed in a boot with the car then dumped. Someone is cleaning up. Same build, hair colour and clothes. I didn't see his face, did you?"

Song shook her head, "I didn't. The licence plate numbers match a white Commodore reported stolen from Gippsland. We identified the getaway car from Vapour as a white Commodore. It's a safe bet it is him."

"A bet is not exactly evidence," Hillier said.

Song blinked twice, taken aback by Hillier's forthrightness.

"I know that Detective Hillier. We are working with what we have," Song said.

Carter jumped in to play peacemaker. "We'll get James to confirm it's Moe. He's the best option we have until next of kin can be located."

Song took a photo of Moe. "Poor guy, his family don't even know he's dead."

"Ignorance can be bliss," Carter said. "Unless proven otherwise, this is Moe. That still means we are missing a white Commodore car."

"Someone knows what they are doing," Song said. "What have we got?" Song asked one of the technicians scouring through the car.

The technician shook her head. "The car's been scrubbed clean. We're not going to find any trace here – except for the joyriders."

Carter leaned into the boot and sniffed. "Do you smell that?"

The technician nodded. "That's bleach. Whoever dumped the car scrubbed it. Pretty meticulous. Looks like they bleached all the nooks and crannies before ditching."

"Shit," Carter muttered under his breath.

"Did you say joyriders?" Hillier asked.

"Uniforms spotted the car being driven by a kid. Sirens went on, the car pulled over, and four kids jumped out and ran in all directions. Uniforms popped the boot and found the victim."

"That's pretty presumptuous," Hillier continued. "How do you know the car was ditched in Ascot Vale if the joyriders all scattered? What if they found the car in a different suburb."

The technician shook her head.

"They caught the driver," she pointed a gloved finger at the squad car down the road from the trio. "Officers are holding them in their car."

"I'll never understand guys who think it's a good idea to steal a car and drive around in it. What are they thinking, trying to impress each other, show off who has the bigger dick?" Carter said as they walked towards the squad car holding the driver. Song squinted into the car. "Looks like she has the big-dick energy."

Hillier's jaw dropped. "No way."

A Middle Eastern girl wearing a headscarf sat in the squad car's back seat. Barely a teenager, she funnelled a teenager's rebellious energy. As the three peered into the squad car, she flicked them her middle finger.

"Huh, I stand corrected. Stupidity knows no sex or gender," Carter said.

Officer Crane leaned against his squad car. Carter had worked with him in the past. Crane reminded Carter of Santa Claus after a shave who happened to be a career sergeant. Currently, he worked in the youth liaison unit after nearly two decades working traffic collisions. As Crane told Carter over drinks one night, he had grown tired of helping scrape youths off the side of the road. He thought early intervention might be the trick before he sailed off into retirement in a few years.

"How did you apprehend her?" Hillier jumped straight in with the question, skipping over the pleasantries. A fact not lost on Carter but seemingly ignored by Officer Crane.

Crane let out a hearty belly laugh reinforcing the Santa imagery. "Aliya?" he said while tilting his head towards the girl in the backseat while she plastered her middle finger against the window. "She's too good a driver; obeys the rules cuz she wore her seatbelt. Once she pulled the car over, the others bolted straight away. She fumbled, turning the car off and taking off her seatbelt." Crane let out a slow grin; he could barely contain his laughter. "Seat had been pulled so far forward that she tripped getting out. She nearly fell on my feet as she stumbled out of the car."

The three of them smiled while Aliya's middle finger continued to greet them against the glass window.

"Alright, let's see what she has to say."

Carter sat in the front seat of the squad car, and Song sat next to Aliya. Hillier walked near Crane with his mobile close to his ear. Not really walking, probably sulking — or at least that's what Carter assumed as Hillier kicked a rock.

"I'm Detective Carter, and this is Detective Song."

"Both pigs," Aliya muttered as she stared out the window, refusing to look at Carter or Song.

She has a lot of anger for a kid, Carter thought. But then Carter remembered his childhood.

How many boys did I beat up to hide my feminine side? How many people did I hurt because I didn't know how to admit I was gay?

Carter tried to brush the thought aside with anger that he misdirected towards Aliya. "Aliya." His voice an octave too stern. "Cut the attitude alright? We need to know everything about the car you took."

She let out an exasperated sigh. "Don't be rude, man."

Carter held up his hands as a peace offering. "Fair, please tell us about the car."

She smiled. "Door was open, and the key was here, literally on the seat. I'm going to be a race car driver, so I need some practice, video games don't cut it."

"A race car driver?" Carter said. "What type of car are you going to use to win Formula One?"

Aliya folded her arms. "Not that car for sure. It smelled nasty when we got in."

"Smelled nasty like cleaning products?" Song asked.

"Yeah." She held out her hands that were covered in tiny red dots. "I got all these bumps from holding the steering wheel."

Looks like a chemical rash. The entire car has been bleached. Left outside with the keys and door open. They couldn't have made the vehicle more inviting. Only way to make the car more enticing would have been to place a bow on the bonnet. They were probably hoping someone else would have stolen it. Driven it far away, chopped it up for parts and then discovered the body in the boot. Then Moe would be their problem, Carter thought.

"Why aren't you at school?" Song asked.

"They don't teach you how to drive at school." She stated this as a fact that the detectives should have known.

"You know, that is true, but what school does teach you is math, physics and chemistry. Car engines don't just start up from magic; chemistry makes them work," Song said.

"I know that. Still doesn't mean school isn't boring." Aliya's interest in Song piqued. "What type of car do you drive?"

"Just a boring old Toyota Corolla model. But the police force taught me some pretty cool skills to know when a car is following me and how to evade it," Song said.

"Cool," Aliya said.

Song continued, "The thing is, to be a cop you need to stay in school. To be a race car driver, you need to stay in school. Officer Crane is going to take you to school, and he is going to have words with your mum."

"Oh no. Don't. Please don't, I promise I won't get in trouble ever again." Alia reached into her pocket and pulled out an ID badge. "Here, I'll trade you." She passed Song the ID badge. "I found this in the car when we got in."

Song took the badge and examined it. "City Council ID," Song said before passing it to Carter.

He looked the ID card over and read the name, George Campbell.

"Thank you for giving me this Aliya. But you took a car that wasn't yours for a joyride. You could have got seriously hurt. Your mum knowing is the consequence, and it could have been a lot worse. We could take you to juvenile detention," Song said. "Wait until your feet reach the peddles without having to pull the seat so far forward. No more wagging off from school, alright? We all know school can be lame and boring but just stick with it. Learn what you can about race car driving, and when you're old enough, get your licence and see how you feel."

Aliya let out another long sigh and rolled her eyes.

"This is my card," Carter said. "If you remember anything else that you think could help us find out who killed the man in the car you stole, don't hesitate to reach out."

Song and Carter stepped out of the squad car.

"You can take her to school, Officer Crane," Carter's tone ended the conversation. Hillier stood within earshot but didn't react. Crane nodded before getting in his car. Carter and Song nodded in return; Hillier continued to be absorbed in his phone. Carter continued, "A blessing in disguise that a bunch of kids found the car, didn't look in the boot and got pulled over so quickly. Otherwise, that car and body could have ended up in a chop shop in Ballarat."

Carter glanced behind them. As Crane's car left, the coroner's van took its place. He noticed two men were in the car. Looks like Nic has the day off. Carter didn't have much time for small talk today anyways.

Carter felt Hillier's eyes on him, and it started to get on his nerves. Hillier expected a response about letting Aliya go. Carter kept his cool. "Hillier, you'll supervise this scene."

"I don't want to. My resources could be better used elsewhere," Hillier said.

Song's eyes went wide. "You're talking to your commanding officer, Detective Hillier."

"I'm just saying, all right," Hillier said.

"I decide where resources are allocated, and you're allocated here. It's not a discussion." Carter stated as he folded his arms.

Hillier shrugged and strode off to greet the coroner's staff.

As Hillier walked out of earshot, Carter started to feel more relaxed. His shoulders drew down away from his ears.

"God he's a fucking dickhead."

"Comes with the territory of being school captain at Melbourne Grammar. You know this case just got more complex?" Song asked.

Carter nodded. "Two bodies and the one link is Vapour and Mr Hughes. Let's bring him in for questioning."

"He'll put up a stink about being called in the day before the memorial he's organising," Song said.

Carter glanced at his watch, "It's why I want to question him. If he has any connection, we need to find it out before the memorial. Besides, James has staff to deal with everything. He can spare the time."

Song pulled out an evidence bag and put the ID badge inside it. "I'll get Zhang to arrange it. But, before we bring in Mr Hughes for questioning, I think we need to visit George Campbell. Aliya found his ID badge in the car."

Carter took out his phone and opened an app to access the police database. Carter whistled, "No criminal record at least. But Mr Campbell is the current chief executive officer for the City of Melbourne Council."

"That can't be a coincidence," Song said.

"Let's find out," Carter said.

CHAPTER TWELVE

As a child, Carter always equated noon to being the warmest part of the day during Melbourne summers. It turned out to be 2 in the afternoon. The build-up of solar radiation in the concrete sidewalks and roads reached capacity while the sun stood high in the sky sending more heat down.

The clock struck 2 p.m. as Carter felt the sunscreen applied on his forehead slowly mixing with the sweat and seeping into his eyes.

He and Song stood at the front door of a townhouse in Port Melbourne. Just a few kilometres from the central business district of Melbourne. Port Melbourne had undergone an urban revitalisation project; juxtaposing the industrial port operations with luxury residences, parklands and beaches.

"Is your dad around?" Carter asked. "We are police officers and need to speak to him."

A young girl who resembled a Children of the Corn extra nodded. She turned to face the hallway of their townhouse and screamed: "Daddy!"

Carter's phone buzzed. He checked the text message and smiled. He received confirmation that George Campbell's address turned out to be one of the locations Nelson's mobile had been to when he had shared his location with Abby. Song smiled as Carter showed her the text.

"Did you find our car?" the young girl asked.

"We sure did," Song said. "Do you miss having your car?"

The young girl nodded, "My favourite Lego was in the car, did you find it? I think it was in the backseat."

"What type of Lego was it?" Song asked. She had her best mum voice on.

"A carwash," the girl said.

"In the car, that's meta," Carter said.

Song and the girl shot Carter a look.

"You don't talk to kids much, do you?" Song asked.

"What about my Lego?" stammered the girl.

Carter and Song shared a look between each other – neither one wanted to break the bad news to her.

"Can I help you?" George Campbell opened the screen door. He wore activewear, blue yoga shorts and a grey singlet. The activewear felt more ornamental than practical judging by his protruding pear-shaped body.

Carter and Song took out their badges, "Mr Campbell, I'm DCI Carter, and this is DI Song. Are you the owner of a silver Audi SUV?"

"Yes, and please call me George. Sarah honey, why don't you give Mummy a hand in the kitchen."

"But what if the police found my Lego? We were supposed to build a castle," Sarah said.

"Sarah, go now, please. I'll let you know if they found it," George replied.

Sarah turned and ran down the hallway screaming, "Mummy the police found my Lego!"

George let out a laugh, "Kids aye. You found our car? We had it parked just out front of the house and then one morning we go to get into it, and it wasn't there."

"We believe we have. Unfortunately, a body was also found in it. Do you know a Moe Bashar or a Nelson Harris?" Song asked.

George's eyes darted to the right. Carter prepared for a lie to come from George's mouth.

"Moe? Never heard of him. I believe Nelson is a staff member at the City of Melbourne Council. I'm the CEO there."

"We know," Song said sternly.

George gripped the side of the door frame before looking back down the hallway of his family's home.

"What's your relationship with Nelson?" Carter asked.

"Oh look, I don't have any daily interactions with staff in the planning department."

"So, you know he works in the planning department?" Carter said.

George stammered, "Um, yes I do."

"How often did he visit you at your home?" Song asked.

George's eyes went wide.

"George honey. What's going on?" A woman stood next to George, she too donned activewear: leggings and a tank top.

"This is my wife, Caitlin," George murmured.

Song spoke, "Caitlin, we are detectives, investigating the murder of two individuals. One of them turned up in the boot of your stolen car. The other, a young man, worked at the City of Melbourne Council."

"At the council." Caitlin folded her arms across her chest. "A man, did he identify as gay?"

"As a matter of fact, he did," Song said.

Caitlin's attitude turned ice cold – but not towards the detectives – instead, it veered and did a 180 towards George. "Blonde too?" She asked.

"Yep," Carter said.

Caitlin turned to George. "You said you were done fucking guys." She pushed George. George stumbled back. "Who was he?" she asked.

George stammered, "No one."

"Who. Was. He." Caitlin asked in slow, stern breaths.

"The last one babe, I swear."

"Did you fuck him here, in our bed?" Caitlin's rage reached its boiling point.

"According to our records, the victim Nelson visited this location six months ago," Carter said.

"See," George said, "Ages ago. I haven't been unfaithful since. You have to believe me."

"I don't have to believe anything from your cheating mouth," Caitlin said.

George moved to hug Caitlin. Caitlin stepped back and raised her hands.

"Don't touch me, I swear to God, George."

"You haven't seen or interacted with Nelson since the last time he visited you here?" Carter asked.

George nodded, "That's right, Detective. Sure, the council office is small so once or twice in the hallways, but that's it." George turned to Caitlin, "Honestly, that was it."

"I can't believe I trusted you. Detectives, you know how many times he's done this? Apparently, he likes to be dominated by younger guys. What does that even mean? How does it work?" Caitlin asked.

"The deceased, Nelson Harris, used to dominate you?" Carter asked.

"Don't try to slut shame me," George said.

"You don't feel any shame?" Caitlin asked. If she could, Carter reckoned Caitlin would transform her words into a dagger and plunge it straight into George's heart.

George avoided eye contact with Caitlin by staring at the ground. "That's not what I meant."

Carter asked that question for all the wrong reasons. He guessed that is why Paddy said he and Nelson were sexually incompatible. Paddy didn't enjoy domination, which was great because Carter had in no way any interest in being anybody's Daddy. He had enough problems.

"If you don't leave the house in an hour, I'll rip your balls off for you," said Caitlin through gritted teeth. "How's that for domination?"

Sarah pushed her way between George and Caitlin's legs. Her parents shared a gobsmacked look between each other before looking down at their daughter. Carter didn't know how long Sarah had been there, listening to their conversation.

"Where's my Lego?" Sarah repeated again and again as she tugged on her parents' legs. "Why are you yelling?"

"We aren't yelling sweetie," George said as he picked her up. "We are just having a chat with these detectives who are about to leave."

Caitlin plucked Sarah from George's arms. "That's right sweetie, Mummy and Daddy aren't yelling, and these nice people are leaving."

Carter folded his arms. "We'll leave when you answer our questions."

"Oh God, can you not see we are going through something right now?" George asked.

"Being a CEO of a council is high profile," Carter continued, unperturbed. "Any threats or enemies you can think of?"

"Not really," replied George.

"Can you two account for your whereabouts for the last forty-eight hours?"

Caitlin spoke, "We were on a plane. We just got back from a two-week holiday in America." She paused, "Our last family holiday. We got off a Qantas flight, QF94 this morning. With the time zone changes, we lose two days."

"Do you have any evidence to support this?" Carter asked.

Caitlin passed Sarah back to George's embrace. Carter noted George seemed to hug Sarah as if it was the last time he'd be seeing her in a long time. Caitlin stormed down the hallway and grabbed her purse. With the power of a hurricane, she stormed back to the front door while rummaging through her bag.

"Here." Caitlin handed Carter their crumpled boarding passes. Tears started to stream down her face.

George tentatively placed a hand on her shoulder. She quickly brushed it off and took Sarah back into her arms. Now tears were rolling down Sarah's face too.

George tried to rub Sarah's back, but Caitlin turned away from him.

Carter studied the tickets. The family were high in the sky over the Pacific Ocean on a Qantas flight from Los Angeles back to Melbourne. He noted their seats were in the economy section.

Okay, so he's not financially corrupt at least, Carter thought. In the last financial crimes case he investigated, a local council member had charged first-class international flights for his family on the council's dime. George seemed to be just morally corrupt.

Carter nodded, "Alright then." He handed George and Caitlin his card. "I'll need both of you to come into our office to make a statement."

George took the card with disdain. "Thanks. When will we get our car back?"

"We should be able to release it in a week or two."

"Good," Caitlin said, "You'll have somewhere to sleep." Caitlin slammed the door, which did little to muffle the screams.

Carter and Song walked back to their car.

"So Nelson and the CEO were sleeping together," Carter remarked.

"Been months though since their last encounter. Not much of a reason to kill him," Song said.

"Maybe someone tried to stitch up the CEO?" Carter asked.

"But who? No one cares that much about rates and rubbish," Song said.

"Where does that leave us?" Carter asked.

"With two victims," Song said. She raised her hand to form the number zero with her fingers. "And that many suspects. We know more about the victims at least."

"Victim number one, Nelson Harris. Prior to his murder he worked for the City of Melbourne, under George Campbell the CEO," Carter said.

"Occasionally on top of too," Song said. "They were in a casual relationship."

Carter thought about how vanilla he suddenly felt in the bedroom. Domination, kink, these were things that never appealed to him.

"In any other investigation, learning your husband is cheating would be the golden ticket of motivations for both partners."

"George to silence Nelson. What if Nelson threatened to tell George's wife about his affair? Caitlin on the other hand, taking out her rage of the affair on Nelson," Song said.

Overhead an airplane flew by on its way to Tullamarine airport. The commercial airport for Melbourne. The landing path for airplanes coming into Melbourne had them fly over the city before banking right towards the airport about thirty kilometres from the city.

"No opportunity for George or Caitlin. It's an airtight alibi being stuck in a metal whale flying through the sky while Nelson is murdered," Carter said.

"Rules them out as suspects for now since Nelson's death occurred late evening or early morning. During that time, George and the formerly happy family were over the Pacific Ocean. I'll double check CCTV at the airport to make sure we have a record of them deplaning after the estimated time of death for Nelson, Song said.

"Two accomplices in Nelson's murder and Vapour is where we first meet victim number two, Moe," Carter said.

"In particular Moe's elbow connecting with Zhang's jaw," Song said as she grimaced.

"Moe bolts in a getaway car and ends up dead in it several hours later," Carter said. He folded his arms across his chest. "Can't believe he escaped."

"Do we think the two cases are linked?" Song asked.

"If Moe had just run away, I'd believe they weren't linked. Maybe he thought the cash in hand work at the bathhouse breached his visa regulations or he didn't trust police. But jumping in a car and being murdered. I don't believe in coincidences. These two murders are linked."

"But how are they linked?" Song asked.

Carter pursed his lips before exhaling a long sigh in defeat. He didn't know how they were linked. "What about other suspects that connect Moe and Nelson together?"

"One of the men at Vapour? You recognised one of them, Bailey," Song said.

Carter shook his head. "We are still going through their statements, but it doesn't make sense that Nelson had been inside Vapour before his death. None of the patrons or the staff recognised him."

"What if Bailey is the link between Nelson and Moe?" Song asked.

"It's possible. Bailey is from footy royalty. Maybe Bailey fed Nelson some footy tips. Nelson places the bets and the two share the profit. If Bailey or Nelson got caught up in a gang, they might have been laundering the money. They bring in Moe to help. They start to get greedy and steal from the gang. Gang retaliates with murder."

"Why kill Moe and leave the body in the boot of Nelson's boss? And why kill Nelson offsite and leave his body next to Vapour?" Song asked.

She placed her shoe against the tyre of Carter's car and stretched out her foot. She swayed forwards and backwards. Carter noticed Song had a tendency to sway when she was deep in thought.

"Doesn't make sense," Carter said.

"Next on our list is Paddy," Song said.

Carter thought about Paddy. Should I tell Song I had dinner with him? Carter almost let out a chuckle at the thought. He knew he didn't do anything wrong, compromise the investigation, but it didn't look great.

"That corporate drone? He made a formal statement and we've verified his whereabouts," Carter said.

"A corporate drone that's easy on the eyes," Song said.

Carter didn't make eye contact, "I wouldn't know." He knew he said that too quickly and tersely.

Song picked up on it, "Your long stares when we met him say otherwise."

Carter thought back to the dinner he and Paddy shared. And how Paddy stole a glance at Carter's cock. Paddy patiently waiting for dessert and Carter was keen to provide.

Once this investigation is done, he thought.

"Nelson's friend Abby?" Carter asked to change the subject.

Both detectives shook their head. "She never really made it on the suspect list to begin with," Song said.

"Taking Bailey out of the equation, that brings us back to Vapour as the only common thread between Nelson and Moe," Carter said.

"Vapour and a recalcitrant James Hughes," Song said as she tilted her head. "You know, Nelson, Moe and James are all gay. Abby mentioned Nelson had a famous person in his orbit, maybe not a boyfriend but a regular friends-with-benefits type arrangement. James fits that persona."

Carter nodded, "What if, Nelson and Moe are in a relationship. They are open, poly, or just bored and want to spice things up. They have a three way with James. One thing leads to another and Nelson dies. Maybe by accident during some kink play. That explains the strangulation marks on Nelson's neck. Together, Moe and James dump the body," Carter said.

"He's denied knowing Nelson. Do you really think James then murdered Moe?" Song asked.

Carter shook his head. "On face value, no."

"What if it's a lovers' tiff. Moe thinks he's dating James. Then sees James and Nelson hook-up. That sends Moe into a fury. He kills Nelson, dumps the body, with the help of an accomplice, outside of Vapour to send James a message. James is being coy with us because he's worried about the election," Song said.

That theory resonated with Carter. He could believe that happening and why James had been so reluctant to assist with their investigations.

"Well Song, let's see if Mr Hughes can shed some light on this. Zhang just texted that he's arrived at Docklands HQ for his interview. I'm going to make him volunteer a DNA sample and tell us what he knows."

"Interesting definition of volunteer," Song quipped.

CHAPTER THIRTEEN

The smell of eucalyptus trees filled Carter's nostrils. He felt transported to a time before. Back to a time when he was known as Private Carter and answered to Captain James Hughes. Twigs and grass dug into Carter's knees. James moved between gripping his sweat-drenched camouflage military t-shirt and the back of his head. Sultry lust filled each bead of sweat rolling off Private Carter. The humidity was high with sex in the air. Carter felt a hand gripping the hairs on the back of his head. A sharp pull. He looked up. James looked down at him.

"Thirsty?" James asked as he stroked his cock.

Carter nodded with sultry lust behind his eyes. He'd have done anything for James — then.

A long tone brought Carter back to the present time as he looked at Song and James as they sat in the cramped interview room. Song had just turned on the recording device. Carter and Davies watched in the observation room through the one-way mirror. Davies finished her coffee in a single long gulp. She tossed the cup in the rubbish bin.

"You really should buy a Keep Cup, more sustainable," Carter said.

Davies folded her arms across her grey suit jacket. "Now is not the time to give me a lecture."

"Feeling the pressure from above?" Carter asked.

Davies pointed to James through the one-way mirror. "The only pressure you should be interested in is the pressure you'll be applying on him."

James let out a loud and exaggerated yawn as he leaned back in his chair.

"He looks like he's about to go sailing, and doesn't have a worry in the world," Davies said.

James wore a blue polo shirt, khaki shorts, and Birkenstocks.

"Probably part of his brand to relate to the voters of Melbourne. Set sail with James Hughes," Carter said.

Song's voice rang out through the speakers. "Currently present is Detective Inspector Emily Song and Mr James Hughes."

"Soon to be the federal member for Melbourne. I do hope we have a speedy conversation. I have a round of golf to get to," James said.

Carter and Davies shared an equally unimpressed look between each other.

"Must be some power brokers on the green," Carter said.

"Don't count your chickens before they hatch," Song said. Her voice continued to ring out through the speakers.

James scoffed, "Have you seen the election forecasts? It is looking pretty good." He smiled and caressed a stack of papers in front of him.

Carter suspected this must be James's ammunition with his sassy demeanour being the weapon.

"Mr Hughes has waived his right to an attorney," Song said, ignoring his election prediction.

"I'm smarter than most lawyers anyway."

"Such a dickhead," Carter muttered as he glared at James through the one-way mirror.

"A delusional gay man with masculinity issues who puts up a façade. How original," Davies said.

"I feel very seen," Carter said. "James has always been squeaky clean despite having so many hands in so many pockets, I don't see him doing this. Murdering two people is not his thing. Bribing two people to change liquor laws, that I could believe."

"You understand James might be a member of parliament in a week. And if he's not your prime suspect there could be repercussions if it looks like the police are harassing him," Davies remarked.

Carter shook his head. "He's not my prime suspect, but he knows more than he's letting on. He always knows more than he's letting on."

James looked past Song and directly at the one-way mirror. He smiled and waved.

"He seems pretty confident, and that stack of paper tells me he has his story down pat," Davies observed.

"We'll find out what he knows," Carter said.

"Just remember, Carter, this isn't a fishing expedition. Keep it to the case at hand. Problem with guys like him, you pull the wrong string, and the wrong puzzle pieces come together. And I have enough fires to contend with as it is."

Back in the interview room, James had fully turned on the charm.

"Who's your decorator, darling? Whoever designed this room should be put in jail."

"Hilarious, Mr Hughes. You'll be surprised to learn that room aesthetics are not our primary concern."

"You're missing an opportunity, Detective Song. Might be a whole new business venture for you and your family."

Song's eyes narrowed momentarily.

Carter slammed the door shut as he entered the interrogation room. He didn't immediately sit down next to Song. He preferred to loom over James.

"Ahh, Detective Carter. As I just detailed to your charming associate here. Your room aesthetics are awful. As for the picture," James tapped on a headshot of the second victim in the case, "It sadly looks like Moe."

"But I really can't say anymore," James said with a sad smile.

Carter gripped the back of a steel chair and painstakingly dragged it across the floor. A screeching noise reverberated in the room.

James twitched, before quickly regaining composure.

Carter winked as he sat down.

"Are you flirting with me, Detective?" James asked.

"Can't and won't, Mr Hughes," Carter tapped the badge hanging around his neck. "On duty."

"At least please call me James. We are all friends."

The comment caught Song's attention as she stopped writing in her notepad. "That's an ambitious assumption."

James shrugged. "I aim big." He shifted his gaze to Carter. "Different time, who knows what we could be?"

Carter knew from experience that James would never stop this stream of facetiousness on his own, so he got right to the point.

"Can you detail your location and movements for the last forty-eight hours?"

"These papers detail my movements."

James flipped through the reams of paper he brought. "Today, I've been in the office at Vapour. This little incident has caused a few issues that needed to be resolved."

James smirked and raised his eyebrows as spoke directly to Song. "I can't snap my fingers and have my family solve all my issues."

Song let out a laugh, "I'm sure you have staff to help."

James fanned, "I've personally been on the phone all morning and afternoon. A dead body in an alleyway is a metaphorical boner killer for my clients. And as I own a bathhouse, that is bad news. Plus, I'm organising a memorial for poor Nelson Harris."

Carter rolled his eyes. James saw the eye roll.

"I'm taking it very seriously, Detective Carter. I'm managing all this amid an election, so this is all really a nuisance. Spinning this situation to shine a light on the

119

homeless situation, queer rights, and refugees' plight is taking up a lot of my PR spin skills."

"You're becoming an advocate for everyone," Carter said.

Song shifted her gaze from James over to Carter. "Do you think it's the perfect trifecta to win an election?"

"Did you really bring me in here to discuss my ongoing accomplishments?" James asked as he continued to talk at the detectives. "I'm just a queer businessman trying to support my future constituents. Also, I understand my catering company is supplying a nine-course degustation menu for the annual policing awards ceremony at Melbourne HQ." He projected his voice straight past the two detectives and at the mirror. "Isn't that right, Superintendent Davies?"

Carter let out a chuckle. "Mr Hughes, Superintendent Davies has more important interviews to oversee than this."

"It is refreshing how entitled you feel that your presence deserves such an audience, though. Bravo," Song said.

"There are now two bodies." Carter raised his voice, "Two. With the link right now being you."

"That's incorrect, Detective Carter," James said.

"Detective Inspector Carter," Song cut in.

James exhaled deeply. "It is simply an unfortunate series of events." James pushed the file folder across the table. "Here is an outline of my movements for the last seventy-two hours along with sworn statements, verified by my solicitor, from witnesses who can account for my locations."

James leaned back with a smug look across his face. "One poor sodding bastard gets killed in an alleyway next to my business. And an employee is murdered. That is correlation, not causation. I'll also remind you, every day my business remains closed is affecting my bottom-line –

not to mention the queer homeless population in Melbourne. Your department and masters pulling your strings can't do shit. So, time for both of you," — He pointed an accusatory finger towards Song and Carter — "to be good little Muppets and do your due diligence and find the real killer."

"Then help expedite this for us, James. Provide us with a DNA sample to help eliminate yourself from our enquiries."

James leaned in. His foot grazed Carter's calf.

"Detective Carter, I don't know what type of lad you think I am. I don't just give my DNA to any Tom, Dick or Harry. Unlike some people I know."

James blew Carter a kiss and winked.

"That's way out of line. And stop deflecting the question," Song said.

"Classic sign of defensiveness," Carter told Song.

"Pretty basic?" Song asked.

"You're not basic, are you James?" Carter asked.

"Again, Detectives, I have a tee time to get to. Can we speed this up," James said.

"Are you refusing to give a sample?" Carter asked, his smile continued while he returned the favour and rubbed his foot against James's leg. The heel of Carter's Chelsea boot went up and down the side of James's leg.

James nodded as he said, "Am I under arrest?"

"Of course not. What's stopping you from leaving now? You're free to leave at any time. We just need more information to rule you out of our inquiry."

James wiggled his foot away from Carter.

"I'm simply not comfortable with the government collecting my private and personal information without understanding their collection, use and disposal procedures. After all, the state and federal governments consistently muck up data and privacy procedures. It's one of my other platforms as part of my election campaign. Remember last month when the transportation department released the last four years' worth of 'de-identified' traveller data and a University of Melbourne academic ran a simple algorithm to identify the travellers based on Twitter posts? You can't make this up. This is how incompetent the government is."

Song rolled her eyes. "And you're the wildcard to save Australian politics?"

"You never know," James said.

"Let the record state that James Hughes has declined to provide a DNA sample," Carter spoke into the microphone. He picked up the folder that James had offered, leafed through it briefly then said, "Forgot my reading glasses. Let's just circle back to the beginning. How about you walk us through the last time you saw the deceased."

"Which one? From an outside perspective, it looks like the police are pretty incompetent, there are now two bodies and a killer at large?"

He said killer, Carter observed, not killers. We are looking for killers. James isn't a suspect and he has a point. Carter clenched a fist under the table. But he knows more than he's telling.

"Do you know Nelson Harris?" Song asked.

"No," James said.

"We have a witness that says you and Nelson were a couple," Song said.

"I doubt that." James said.

"Bailey and Ty say you had a sexual relationship with Nelson," Carter said.

He knew it was a gamble to lie. It didn't work.

James let out a laugh, "You don't have anything from those two attesting to that. It is simply false."

"Tell us about Nelson. What did he like to do?" Carter asked.

James shrugged, "I cannot tell you what I do not know."

James leaned towards the recording device, "Because I have never met him."

James beamed a wide smile across his face. His smile goaded Carter to try and push this line of questioning further, knowing how futile it would be.

"What about Moe," Carter spoke with great weariness, as if talking to a senile old man.

"Ahh, I understand." James clapped his hands in a mock celebration. "Last time I saw Moe."

James drummed his fingers on the table.

"Anytime, Mr Hughes," Song said.

"My place. The bedroom in particular, if you are curious on his exact location," James said.

"What you're saying," Song began, "Is you exploited your position of power as his employer to have a sexual relationship with him?"

James scoffed. "That's a bit of a stretch. He's been working at Vapour for a few months. I invited him round to my place. For the first time on Thursday. He came around midnight, and again shortly after that if you catch my drift, and left by 2 a.m."

"Good spirits, disappointed, distant; how did he act?" Carter asked.

"Distracted. I think Moe decided to leave Melbourne. He went on and on about missing his family and why he moved to Melbourne. You know he's a qualified nurse. That's a cruel twist of events. From changing bandages to handing out towels at a bathhouse. Bit of a change of circumstances for him. I think he planned on trying to improve his English in some programme interstate. Or move to Mexico. He mentioned his brother had moved to Mexico, something about money as well. His train of thought didn't exactly line up with the tracks. And he wasn't focusing on me. I invited him to leave."

"All about you, aye?" Carter said.

"Well, I can reciprocate when I'm in the mood." James touched the top of his ear. "As you well know."

"Who were known friends or family of Moe?" Song picked it up again.

"Wouldn't have a clue, darling."

"Take a guess," Carter said.

"Moe handed out towels at the bathhouse and cleaned the rooms. You'll have to ask some of the other twinks there. They hang out, start with Bailey and Ty," James said.

"So," Song said. "Even though you and he were both working at Vapour at the time the body was discovered, the last time you saw or spoke to him had been the previous night?"

"Correct, as the owner, you'd be surprised to learn that I don't hand out the towels. Instead, I do the important work in the back office mostly," James said.

"But you saw him," Carter pressed.

James sighed, "Ok yes, we spoke on the night."

Song took over the reins and pressed him. "About what?"

"Money, he wanted it, I didn't want to provide. I offered him more shifts," James said.

"Did you ask Moe what he needed the money for?" Carter asked.

James shook his head, "Nope, it wasn't my problem."

"That's a bit cold," Carter said.

James let out a chuckle, "It's pragmatic darling."

Carter decided to change approach. "Mr Hughes, you are a well-known man, the election must have stirred up some strong opinions against you. Any threats against you or the establishment recently?"

James shrugged. "Nothing out the ordinary. We receive a dozen or so email threats a week. Mostly from the prudish puritanical type who think a rim job is an ultimate sin." James winked towards Carter.

"What about you, personally?" Carter asked.

"Actually, surprisingly little."

"Really?" Carter and Song asked in unison.

"You two should enter *Australia's Got Talent* as a duet," James retorted.

"Everyone loves me. I'm a pillar of the community. From the federal seat of Melbourne, I'll be prime minister in under a decade." James adjusted the collar of his polo shirt. A sly smile formed across his face. "Maybe I'll have you two as part of my security detail. Wouldn't that be a treat, being responsible for taking a bullet for me!"

"Don't jump too far ahead Mr Hughes. Bathhouse owner is not exactly the best line to appear on a resume for a politician," Song said.

James shrugged. "You make a good point, Detective Song. Originally, my cabal of advisors when I first started vying for pre-selection for the Labor party told me to sell Vapour. So I fired them and replaced them with an equally bland group of faceless advisors, but you know what the difference is?"

"Surprise us," Carter said.

"None of them were career political advisors. Each one had a career before politics, just like me. Besides, look who else is in an elected position. A used car salesman, bouncer, fish-and-chip shop owner and a few psychotic right-wing racists. This is Australia. Everyone gets a fair go. And now it's my turn."

"You considered selling Vapour?" Carter asked.

"There were a few nibbles. It is prime real estate in Collingwood. But no. I'm keeping it to help improve my personal brand as a groovy cool guy rather than yet another boring lawyer or an out-of-touch career political staffer parachuted into a plum seat." James let out an exaggerated yawn. "Are we done here, Detectives?"

Carter nodded. "I reckon that's enough for now, Mr Hughes. We will go through the papers provided. And have a think about submitting a DNA sample: the easiest way to eliminate you from our enquiries."

"I'll think about it. Guess it depends on who is collecting." James gave a suggestive smirk. "And what method you plan to use."

"This interview is complete," Song said as she turned off the recording device. "From the deepest part of my heart, please piss off now, Mr Hughes."

CHAPTER FOURTEEN

Shoes kicked off in the hallway — pants and shirt left at the bedroom door. He texted Bailey as he walked into his bedroom. Carter advised Bailey to get in contact with him asap as he had further questions and to not go back to Vapour. Carter didn't receive a response. He'd texted Bailey's mum asking for his whereabouts. She didn't know but offered a signed football from her deceased husband next time he came over for tea.

Carter flopped face-down on the bed. A kaleidoscope of thoughts ran through his mind. The carving in the first victim's chest, the second victim dumped in the boot of a cleaned-out car. Something isn't right. We aren't working with the full picture. Why dispose of a body outside of Vapour? Who were they sending a message to? What does Nelson, a bureaucrat for the City of Melbourne, and Moe, a refugee, have in common aside from being gay?

Carter rolled over on his back and looked up at the ceiling. He expected the answer to greet him from above. All he saw was dust in the corners. He adjusted his black jocks as he reflected on James.

He's changed a lot, Carter thought as he remembered being sat at a pub.

The type of pub with fake leather coverings that make wiping up spills and vomit a breeze. The smell of sweat and vinegar surrounded him. Deodorant had been a luxury in his military days.

Carter's dog tags hung outside his shirt like the other lads who sat with him. They were all in the midst of their third pint. A group of military babushka dolls, with shaved heads and sand-coloured t-shirts, each one louder and crasser than the next. All of them littered with more tattoos than common sense. Their captain, James Hughes, sat in the middle of the booth, looking over his kingdom of men. Each one trying harder and harder to impress him with a crude joke. Hard to impress a man who smoked, drank for three, and yelled that only women and sissies wear sunscreen. What boorish jokes can you tell him? He's told them all to you before. Despite the gruff and gruesome personality, Carter felt admiration and awe for him. More than that, Carter lusted for him. Not that he willingly admitted that to himself.

Two men walked into the pub and ordered at the bar. One of the men placed his hand on the other's lower back while waiting for their drinks.

James noticed; his eyes narrowed. "Bunch of fags I reckon," he said in a gruff, deep voice.

The troops broke out in laughter, except Carter who skulled his beer and slammed the glass down. The bang captured the attention of his mates.

"You're a fag," Carter said so softly that only the soldiers sitting either side of him heard.

The soldier on Carter's right motioned to James. "Did you hear what Carter thinks of you?" James shook his head.

"Thinks you're a fag," the soldier said.

"He'd be so lucky to get a hunk like me," James said with a dramatic limp wristed gesture.

A roar of laughter erupted from the lads as they cheered their pints.

Carter blushed and sunk back into his seat.

But that was a long time ago. Neither of them was in the closet anymore. Nor had they ended up together.

His hand slowly snaked its way down towards his jocks and massaged the tip of his cock, which swelled, now fully erect. He picked up his mobile. I won't solve the case today, Carter thought as he opened the two essential hook-up apps he used. A deluge of profiles appeared, the closest ones at the top of the screen. Each profile had its own small thumbnail tile, some a black box, others a body part, hardly a face picture in sight.

His index finger hovered over a particular profile. A muscular arm with a koi fish tattoo on his bicep grabbed Carter's attention.

Could be Constable Zhang. The tattoo looks pretty close.

Carter's finger almost pressed on the profile, but he decided against it. Dangerous territory, he thought as he scrolled past the profile.

A drumroll sounded on his phone, indicating he received a tap, a digital doorbell expressing interest in what Carter offered. Carter opened the message.

'Can you host?'

Brevity is the name of the game, Carter thought as he clicked on the sender's profile. A picture appeared of a young, thin man in a polo shirt and shorts with strawberry-blonde hair. His profile read: 22, just moved to Melbourne from the UK, show me the town or your bedroom?

Carter adjusted his jocks again; his thickness grew as his imagination of what to come took hold. He shifted his cock to make it stick out more before taking a photo from the chest down.

I'll give you somewhere to sit, Carter messaged back along with the photo.

'Address?'

Carter typed back: Unit 3 Rose St Lofts.

'I'll be there in five.'

Carter got up to brush his teeth.

--

The guy who'd arrived turned out to be named Elliot. He stayed the night. They fell into a pattern of sex and sleep. Each time Carter had dozed off, Elliot's touch woke him from his slumber. It started softly caressing Carter's hairy legs. Elliot's hands moved up his legs to grab Carter's cock to initiate the sequence of sex and sleep again.

Carter rolled over in his bed to check his mobile.

"6 a.m., damn," he sighed. "Gotta get up," he said to a sleeping Elliot.

Mobile in hand, Carter got up and started to stretch his aching muscles and body. As he leaned his neck to one side cracks and pops peppered the other. He licked his parched lips and lumbered towards the bathroom.

"Time to check my pot of gold," he said.

Carter opened the lotto app he used for his seven-grand wager from yesterday. An animated leprechaun danced around a gold pot as the app loaded. Carter stopped his slow lumber and leaned against the wall of his bedroom.

"Fucking hell," he slammed his mobile into the ground. The screen cracked as the mobile bounced on its side before settling on the floor. Carter's balance read as a single digit, zero.

Carter turned and rested his forehead against the wall.

"It."

He thumped the wall with one fist.

"Is."

He thumped the wall with the other fist.

"Always."

He knocked his head against the wall.

"A near fucking miss!"

Carter's fist punched a hole in the drywall. The pain sent a shock through his system. Full-blown pain and panic set in as he saw his hand buried to the knuckles in the wall.

Elliot stopped in the doorway, "What was that noise?"

Carter glared at Elliot whose jaw dropped at the sight of Carter's hand in the drywall.

"I should go," Elliot said.

"You should," Carter grunted.

Waves of relief flowed through Carter as he heard the door close behind Elliot. He didn't like being so vulnerable in front of anyone. The relief was short-lived and replaced by pain.

"Oh God," Carter said.

He struggled to breathe as he slowly pulled his hand free. Chunks of drywall and blood mixed across his knuckles. He brushed the debris off and flexed then curled his fingers. None of them were broken. He picked up his mobile off the ground. He tapped the cracked screen, and it blinked back to life. The lotto app didn't close. Its bright colours beckoned to Carter. He looked over to his bug out bag in the hallway.

"Can't use it if I don't win," Carter said.

In three successive taps, he purchased another lottery ticket   for   thirty   dollars.

CHAPTER FIFTEEN

"Here for a drop-in appointment?" Doctor Lynch asked as his gaze drifted from a stack of papers in front of him to Carter standing at his doorway.

"What happened to your hand, Detective?" The grey-haired psychiatrist asked.

"I lost seven grand," Carter said as he entered Doctor Lynch's sparse office and closed the door behind him.

"And a not insignificant portion of your epidermis, it seems," Doctor Lynch said as he motioned to Carter to take a seat.

Carter rubbed his bruised and raw red knuckles. "The wall won," he said as he slumped into the plush black chair. Carter squinted at the Birds of Paradise pots in the corners of the office. A thin layer of dust covered all the leaves.

"Your plants are dusty Doctor Lynch."

"Take it up with the cleaning staff. Oh wait, I don't have cleaners anymore, cut in the last budget. Besides, the plants are actually plastic. This office is not conducive for life to thrive." Doctor Lynch said with a deadpan expression.

He took a seat across from Carter. He cracked his arthritic fingers before picking up his notepad and pen. "Take one at counselling. Did you lose or gamble the seven grand?"

"I won seven grand on the lotto and instead of withdrawing it, I bet it all."

"And you rolled snake eyes?"

Carter gulped and quietly said, "Yes."

"A very frustrating situation you've found yourself in," Doctor Lynch said.

"Angry, disappointed, I don't know. I just feel like a fuckwit," Carter said.

"What stopped you withdrawing the money?" Doctor Lynch asked.

Carter shifted in the chair, "I don't know."

Doctor Lynch frowned, "Yes, you do. You made a deliberate choice. Instead of withdrawing the money, you gambled it. Instead of decision A, you did decision B, which led to that bruised hand and ego."

Carter glanced at his watch, it neared 8 a.m. "I need your help to stop. I have a murder investigation to lead."

"Quite a complex case and situation from what I've heard. Tell me about your parents."

"I'm too old to blame my parents."

"We aren't looking to attribute blame here. We need to understand the journey to change the destination."

Carter flung his arms in the air, "I don't have time to give you my autobiography."

"Psychology isn't about band-aid solutions."

"In this case, I need one."

"You know in my private practice I have a waitlist of three months for new patients. Meanwhile, you have the privilege of sauntering in here at a moment's notice."

"I'm sure the hefty pay packet you draw must soften the inconvenience."

Doctor Lynch shook his head. "Very well, unlock and pass me your mobile."

Carter handed Doctor Lynch his unlocked mobile. Carter saw him open the lotto app.

"Are you aware of the concept of delayed gratification?"

"Not really," Carter said.

"Not surprising given your impulsive condition. Well now you will," Doctor Lynch said as he handed back Carter's mobile.

"I've set a weekly limit of fifty dollars for your lottery app. Yes, you could change the limit, but that's an extra step, an additional decision. The extra cognitive step is an opportunity for you to reflect on your actions and stop. I've seen varying degrees of success with this approach. And usually, this is paired with therapy and not a casual drop-in, band-aid session."

Carter tucked his mobile in his jeans pocket. "Thanks."

Doctor Lynch motioned for Carter to leave, "Detective, don't come back here for a band-aid. If you really want to stop gambling, you need to tackle this problem wholeheartedly."

"Noted," Carter said.

"I suspect you're not ready."

Carter stopped at the doorway and gripped the frame. His lower lip trembled slightly. He breathed deeply to centre himself before he turned to face the greying Doctor Lynch. "You're right. Can't I have some faith that I'll win?"

"Faith in yourself will go longer," Doctor Lynch said as he closed his notepad.

--

"You alright, boss?"

Carter slumped into his chair across from Song. He finished off his jumbo latte before putting his Keep Cup in his desk drawer. "Lady Luck didn't have me in her corner last night," Carter said.

"Didn't sleep much?"

"Nah." Carter thought of what really kept him awake and settled with a lie. "Heat kept me up."

"Typical Australian flats, they have air-con in the main rooms but not the bedrooms. You don't want to know how expensive it is to install AC. I had it installed in Aaron and my and the kids' bedrooms. Reckon the tradie that installed it can now buy a mansion. Checked the weather this morning, we are entering a heatwave for the next few days. Might break by end of the week," Song said.

"Lucky us," Carter said as he stood up and headed for the whiteboards.

"Alright. Day two of this enquiry. Where do we stand?"

Perry, Hillier, Song, Zhang, and the other staff gathered around the whiteboards. A sea of multi-coloured cue cards covered the task area of the boards. Each card represented an indicator of what priorities each detective had. Anyone walking by could visually tell the overall case progression by seeing the majority of the cards rested in the 'To Do' and 'Doing' columns. Few cards were in the 'Done' column. Photos of Nelson Harris and the presumed Moe Bashar were taped on the far end of the boards. A stern reminder for Carter that there were two victims. He examined the timeline section of the board, a noticeably bare section – a red flag for Carter.

Perry finished the last morsel of his egg and bacon roll before speaking. "The parents of the first victim, Nelson, arrive into Melbourne in a few hours. I've got some uniforms meeting them at the arrival gate at the domestic terminal of Tullamarine. Uniforms will escort them to their hotel and then to the coroner's office."

"That's good, Perry. Give Nic a buzz. They'll need to arrange the body for viewing," Carter said.

"Already done boss. Spoke to Nic myself."

"Very diligent and professional as always," Song said as she and Carter shared a look.

Carter couldn't help but wonder what else Perry spoke to Nic about or wanted to ask her.

"What about the victim's place of work? We know Nelson had a casual relationship with the CEO of Melbourne City Council, George Campbell," Carter said.

"We'll be taking statements from the CEO and his wife this afternoon," Hillier said as he flicked through his notepad. "Work is a dead end. Nelson got along great with everyone at work. Brought a real youthful vibe to the joint. No disciplinary, behavioural issues reported with his colleagues, manager, or HR."

"Just an inappropriate casual relationship," Song said.

"How is it inappropriate?" Hillier asked.

Song shook her head before responding. "Because of George Campbell's power dynamic being the CEO of the council and Nelson a subordinate."

"Oh right," Hillier said. A dumbfounded look crossed his face momentarily. He then flipped through his notes before finding his train of thought again. "Everyone at work just sung his praise, pegged him as a clever and nice guy. The department has started a collection for his family. They are also attending the memorial tonight. What about George Campbell as a suspect?" Hillier asked.

Song shrugged, "Not looking likely, George and his soon to be ex-wife and daughter were flying into Melbourne at the time of Nelson's death. The timeline doesn't work for him to be a suspect in Moe's escape from Vapour and subsequent murder. It looks like Nelson and George had an affair, but that ended a few months ago."

"Not exactly model behaviour of a CEO," Carter said.

"I hear he's been suspended from the City of Melbourne and a misconduct investigation has commenced. News clearly travels fast," Davies said, as she joined them in the room. A constable offered her his chair, but she declined. She chose to sit at the edge of the desk, like a gargoyle on the edge of a building, seeing and hearing all.

"Sins of the flesh," Carter said. "Alright. Doesn't give us much to go with." Carter picked up the medical report. "Medical examiner confirms cause of death for the first victim, Nelson, as strangulation with an assault beforehand. The coroner has yet to confirm the cause of death for Moe."

Carter pointed to the crime scene photo of Moe's bruised and battered face with a bullet wound between his eyebrows. "We are treating his death as suspicious for obvious reasons. He's on Doc Monroe's table this afternoon. The working assumption is these two deaths are connected, with Moe fleeing Vapour and whoever the driver of the car is responsible for Moe's death. Regarding Moe, we need to establish his involvement. Direct assailant or assistant to the perpetrators of Nelson's death. We need answers."

"What do you know about Moe?" Davies asked from her perch.

Song spoke, "So far, details for Moe are scarce. No next of kin and since he wasn't properly on the books while he worked at Vapour, we are going through Border Security to confirm his identity. The vehicle had zero evidence in it, minus his body."

"What about his movements?" Davies asked.

"At some point, Moe got out of a white Commodore and into the Audi. We are checking CCTV records to determine the route both cars took. Ideally, we need to pin down a location where they switched cars. The cause of death is pretty obvious. I wouldn't be surprised if the victim had been shot while sitting on the edge of the boot and they just pushed him in. Closed the boot, drove off and left the car in Ascot Vale," Song said.

"This could be a lover's murder. Nelson is killed by Moe." Simultaneously, Carter and Song glanced at Hillier. From behind, Davies saw the daggers the two were sending Hillier.

"And what then? Moe kills himself, puts himself in the boot of a car and drives it to Ascot Vale out of remorse?" Carter clenched a fist behind his back.

Hillier continued without looking at Carter. "Moe goes into a jealous rage over something Nelson did. Maybe he cheats on Moe, who knows? So, Moe and a friend beat up Nelson to teach him a lesson. Moe goes into overdrive, strangles him. They realise the stuff-up. Maybe he knows the CCTV is broken at Vapour and dumps the body there. He went in to check something, and that's when we all arrived."

"Any evidence these two lads knew each other?" Carter asked.

"Nothing conclusive yet," Hillier said.

"So no," said Carter with an ounce of venom carried in his words.

Hillier's eyes shifted down to his leather boots. "That's right," he lamented.

"Doesn't seem like we have any links between victim number one, Nelson, and victim number two, Moe," Davies said.

"At this point no," Song said.

"I'm tracking down Bailey to interview him again."

"The footballer's kid?" Song asked.

"The very one. I reckon he's the link between Nelson and Moe. Given the circumstances, we are working on the theory that there is a link. We just need to find it."

"Might be serendipity, because the public thinks there is a link between the victims and James Hughes," Davies said.

Davies held up Melbourne's tabloid newspaper. Seedy Candidate's Secret Sex Business was the headline on the front page. Underneath the headline had a picture of Vapour and James Hughes with the Labor Party logo beside him.

"They almost got the alliteration right," Carter mused.

"Regardless, the press is saying these two murders are linked, and they know that Moe worked at Vapour," Davies said.

"Who knows, James might have leaked the info himself. He told us he called the journalists when we were interviewing him at Vapour," Carter said.

"The commissioner has been fielding calls from the Labor Party elites to understand the link between James Hughes, Vapour and the victims. Are there are any links pointing to guilt?" Davies asked.

"None at this point," Perry said, who brushed a few crumbs from his salt and pepper beard. "His statements and alibis have been vetted, and the tech crew have been through Vapour with a fine-tooth comb. No evidence of any significant amount of blood. Lots of fibres to go through but I reckon it's not our murder site," Perry said.

"The Labor Party will be thrilled," Davies said.

"The opposition party too, both will try and spin this before the election," Song said.

"With the memorial already in the works, looks like James is ahead at the spin game. Vapour can also reopen," Carter said. "Hillier, can you tell him?" A bit of a punishment for his homophobia, thought Carter.

"No problem," Hillier said as he scribbled the task into his notepad.

Carter glanced at one of the whiteboards. A horizontal line broken into thirty-minute segments stretched the length of the whiteboard. It ended at 5:30 a.m. with Nelson's body being transferred to the coroner. In red underneath the times between midnight and 2 a.m. read: victim's death.

"Any luck on the first victim's whereabouts before his death?" Carter asked.

"No luck boss," Perry said. "One of his neighbours saw him around 6 p.m. on Sunday. No one saw him leave.

No reports or complaints by people are around, except for the usual trade in St Kilda."

Zhang, with his trusty whiteboard marker, wrote in the 6 p.m. segment: at home.

"Right now, their only connection is Vapour." Carter pointed to the photo of Vapour on the whiteboard. The grainy image showed the colonial two-storey house with blacked-out windows on the second floor. Along with a simple sign above the entrance that said Vapour.

Carter tapped the image again. "Why here? Carter's question fell on a mute audience. He focused on Hillier, who wore another crisp tailored suit. "Until we know otherwise, these two deaths are linked. Neither one of them is to be treated like a perpetrator. Both are victims."

Davies caught Carter's attention as she shook her head. Then she caught everyone's attention by speaking. "Looks like you are missing a murder scene and Nelson's movements leading to his body being left at Vapour. Don't get me started about Moe's movements. And you have to narrow down the time of death. You've got a lot of work in front of you, along with the first victim's memorial tonight."

"One insurmountable challenge at a time, hey boss." Carter said. "Perry is our main point with the surveillance teams. The briefing is later today."

"Just call me Big Brother," Perry said with a laugh after.

"Alright, ladies and gents: like our leader has said, we have our work cut out for us. Speak to any of the detectives for assignments. Song and I will be at the coroner's office."

"Just one other thing, looping back to the night in question." Hillier pulled out a police arrest record file. "Four blocks away a Craig Dean was arrested for a few summary offences. The offences include vandalising a Vietnamese restaurant and getting into a fisticuffs round before the police arrived. The shop owner apparently knocked Craig to the ground and had him pinned when officers arrived."

"What's the connection here?" Carter asked.

"The Deans are notorious white supremacists with links to Neo-Nazis," Hillier said.

"What's the difference?" Zhang asked.

"Essentially, different levels of control and violence against minorities like you and me," Song said.

"Fair dinkum," Zhang said.

"The Neo-Nazis operate under the Better Times Movement. Think racists, and all the phobias along with confused boomers looking at QAnon posts working under the same confused and muddled umbrella," Davies said. "We arrested a few members a couple years back for the murder of three of their members. The group thought they were police informers. They weren't, they just liked watching *Law & Order*, and the rumour mill went into override. I know the intelligence reports will paint the Better Times Movement differently, but my view is the group is paranoid and idiotic."

"Don't forget wellness influencers too, a huge number of them have been cancelled this year because of racist posts," Zhang said.

Carter raised a hand, "Let's not get too distracted from the case at hand. Can we link Craig Dean to Vapour or Nelson?"

"Not yet, but he said the following to the arresting officer the same night Nelson was murdered. 'Fuck you fag, I'll kick your arse.' Fag is the same word as the epitaph carved into Nelson's chest," Hillier said.

"It's a bit of a stretch, but where's Craig now?" Carter asked.

"Spent the night in custody. He's applying for bail at the magistrate's court, likely to get it as it's his second offence," Hillier said.

"Alright, good catch Hillier. Let's have a chat with this guy," Carter said. "Song, Hillier, and I will go. Speak to Perry for any questions or assignments."

The organised chaos of the office resumed as detectives, and uniformed officers moved about. A choir of mobile phones rang nearly in unison as the trio made their way to the exit.

"Hey boss!" Perry caught up to them. His jolly demeanour seemed a bit jollier today. "When you head to the coroner's office can you give this to Nic? And I guess Doc Monroe." He handed Carter a gift card. "It's for their favourite I near the coroner's office."

Carter took the card and noted the price: fifty dollars. "Quite the present."

"Well, she mentioned how often you forget to bring her a coffee." Carter's face started to turn red while Song let out a chuckle. "Only kidding boss," Perry said as he patted Carter's shoulder.

Carter smirked. "There is some truth in lies. I reckon it's time we find more ways for you to visit the coroner's office."

Perry smiled. "Thanks, boss." He turned around and went back to his desk to prepare for a long day and night.

Song opened the door for Carter. "Playing matchmaker now?"

He shrugged. "Just doing my part. Love strikes at any age."

--

"That's him," Hillier said. He glanced at the police report with a mugshot of Craig Dean. The report listed him as twenty-two, but as the trio advanced on him, Carter would have pegged him as much older given his sun-damaged and scarred skin. Craig blew cigarette smoke in the direction of Hillier, Song and Carter as he leaned against a railing of the magistrates' court building.

"What do youse want," Craig sneered.

"Are you Craig Dean?" Carter asked.

Craig nodded as he took another drag from his cigarette. "Youse coppers?" He asked.

"Yep, we are," Song said as they all flashed their badges. "You know you can't smoke within four metres of any government building."

Craig shrugged, "I just made bail you can't charge me again."

The wilful ignorance momentarily amused Carter. "We can but how about you just answer us some questions instead."

"What do you want to know?" Craig asked.

"On the night of your arrest, you were trying to vandalise a Vietnamese restaurant before getting into a fight. How come?"

"Cuz I don't like Ch..."

"Don't even think about finishing that. You mean Vietnamese," Song said with a glare.

"Whatever. They are running the country mate," Craig said as he rolled up the sleeve on his right side, exposing a Southern Cross constellation tattoo. The constellation features on the Australian flag. "I fight for the country," he said.

"Poorly as your arse was handed to you, wasn't it Craig," Song asked.

Craig took another drag of his cigarette, "What of it, they all know Kung Fu or whatever."

"What do you know about Vapour?" Hillier asked.

Craig's eyes darted, "I ain't a fag."

"You visited Vapour before you tried to vandalise that property."

"Nah," Craig said. He started to light another cigarette as he took the last drag of his current one.

"How do you know Nelson Harris?" Song asked.

"Wrong again, copper. I ain't know him and I ain't been to Vapour."

A car blaring heavy metal screeched to the side of the road. The window rolled down, and a pale, bloated man wearing a bucket hat and rugby t-shirt greeted the detectives.

"Craig," the driver screamed, "Get in the damn car. We're going."

"These coppers are harassing me, Dad," Craig yelled.

"Your dad, I presume," Carter said.

"Craig Sr," Hillier whispered to Carter.

Craig's dad took out his mobile phone, "I'm recording you harassing my son. I'll personally sue the pants off you for harassing Craig. Do you want me to charge you for harassment in the county court and have you pay me sixty-thousand dollars?"

Carter thought about explaining how the legal system worked but bit his tongue. "We were just having a chat. Young Craig here is free to go."

Craig stomped out his cigarette.

"Nice shoes mate," Carter said.

"Fifty bucks and these boots are yours," Craig said as he showed off his black boots.

"What size are you?" Carter asked.

"You got the money or what?" Craig asked.

"What size are you?"

Craig grabbed his crotch, "Too big for you to handle."

"I'll pass," Carter said.

Craig shrugged and got into his dad's car. "It's good Nelson's dead, another fag off this world." Craig slammed the car door shut and the car drove off with heavy metal screeching through its speakers.

"Why'd you let him go?" Hillier asked, "Craig admitted to knowing that Nelson is dead."

"Did you take a look at his shoes? Wearing a pair of boots. The assailants we are looking for were wearing boots too. We need to check the arrest record to make sure he was wearing those shoes he had on at that time."

"You just let him go, what if he destroys the boots? There goes all the evidence," Hillier said.

"We don't have any probable cause to detain him and examine his boots," Carter said. "We need to find out Craig's shoe size and how he knows Nelson. Coroner's report says we are looking for assailants with a shoe size of eleven. Craig's a seven."

"Certainly not a ten in any book," Song said.

"There's someone for everyone Song, you know that. Even for human garbage like him," Carter said. "I dunno about Craig. We need to follow up, but I think he's a dead end. These murders are too calculated for the Dean family, I reckon. The father just threatened to charge us with harassment and force us to pay him sixty grand. They aren't clever enough and are missing a chromosome or two," Carter said.

"I agree," Song said. "We'll alert the counter-terrorism unit to keep an eye out for them, but they aren't our problem."

"Just society's," Hillier said.

"One problem at a time Hillier. We have to head to the coroner's office," Carter said.

"I'll head back to the office to help Perry with setting up surveillance logistics unless you want me there?" Hillier asked.

"Nah, Song and I will be alright, thanks Hillier," Carter said.

CHAPTER SIXTEEN

The coroner's office had a small viewing room for
families to identify a body within. It wasn't a particularly
comforting room with its two-seater sofa, a few
decorative plastic plants, and a window with a curtain.
Coroner staff would bring the body into the cool room
next door. When ready, the curtain would be drawn back,
allowing the family to view and identify the body on the
other side of the window.

Song led in Nelson's grieving parents. Carter knew
the news had hit them hard. Carter had never met them
before but felt they looked like husks of their former
selves. Tattered clothes, grim looks to their faces, they
trudged into the room holding each other's hand for
support.

"Mr and Mrs Harris, I'm DCI Carter. Please, call me
Leo."

Mr Harris extended his hand first. A skinny man with
a growing belly. He had long greasy hair tied in a
ponytail. From Carter's memory, his arrest record pegged
him around fifty. Time had not been gentle on Mr Harris.
Closer to sixty years of age in appearance, blotchy red
face, sagging skin around his neck.

"Call me, Pete." What few teeth he had left were
stained yellow. He motioned to the woman next to him.
"And this is my missus, Diane."

"Thank you for making the trip so quickly." Carter
extended his hand to her. Diane had a rough, dry hand
with nails that were chewed down to the cuticle. She had
a plump physique with greying hair, sun-damaged skin
and wrinkles that turned into caves.

"Reckon I'll get the sack from my cleaning job. I'm
casual there, and my boss is a real prick," Diane said. Her

bloodshot eyes glanced behind Carter to the curtain. "What choice do we have – we need to see him. I can't believe it. The whole flight here, I don't think we can believe it. Reckon we are just taking our first trip to Melbourne to visit Nelson – but really, our baby is dead."

Pete wrapped his arm around her. She leaned into him for support.

"I don't want to believe it either," Pete said.

Carter motioned to the window with the curtain drawn.

How many times now have I given this speech?

"In the other room is the body of a deceased individual. We believe him to be Nelson Harris. I'll draw the curtain back. And if you can indicate if you know the deceased that will help our enquiries into his murder."

The air was sucked out of the room. Pete and Diane took that word as a punch — they both cringed. Murder. It shattered their frail perception of the world. Shattered what safe image they had of their son. Nelson their son, Nelson, the murder victim. If a piece of glass represented their lives, it shattered with a single word, murder.

Carter skated over the misstep with his eye on the prize. "Are you ready?"

The pair reluctantly nodded. Pete gripped Diane's hand and kissed her wedding band. A slight panic set in for Diane. Her breathing grew short as she looked between the curtain and Pete. He kissed her liver-spotted hand. "We can do this, darling."

Diane wiped a tear from her eyes and nodded. Hand-in-hand, they walked up towards the window. "We're ready," she whispered.

Carter flicked the switch. The curtain slowly retracted. Through the window, they saw a gurney with a body on it. Once a human, now pale, lifeless, a shell. The fluorescent lights in the room illuminated Nelson's body wrapped in white towels. His arms rested above the towels along with his face. A towel covered the top part of his head. Carter flicked on the monitor above the window. A close-up shot of Nelson's face filled the screen.

Silence filled the room. Pete and Diane stood silent, motionless. Carter had seen this time and time before. Pete and Diane's bodies knew it. Their minds were still processing the fact that Nelson rested on that gurney.

"I need to sit down," Diane said as she wiped the tears flooding down her face.

Their minds caught up with their bodies as Diane placed a hand on the window.

Song gently guided her to the sofa and gave her a small plastic cup of water. Diane's hands shakily moved the cup to her mouth, but it sat at her lips. Her hand and the cup trembled. Song placed one hand on her back and rubbed it while the other took the cup from her shaking grip.

More tears tumbled down her face.

Pete walked closer to the window. His nose and belly almost against it. "That's my boy."

Carter asked the question he always loathed asking, "Can you confirm you know the deceased?"

"That's our son. That's Nelson," said Pete.

Diane wailed. She drove herself into Song's embrace to try and avoid the truth. Seemingly oblivious to her wails, Pete simply stared at Nelson.

"That's my boy," Pete stammered.

Carter flicked the switch to close the blinds. Black curtains replaced Pete's view of the body. His sense of hearing returned. He moved to take Song's spot consoling Diane on the stiff, mouldy old sofa.

Wiping more tears from her face, Diane spoke to Carter. "May we go in to say goodbye?"

"It's best not to. Once Nelson is released, and a funeral director has seen him, that'll be a more appropriate place to say goodbye. We should be able to release his body shortly."

Pete put his head in his hands. "We were pretty shit parents mate. He still waded through the shit. Got a good council job. More than we ever did. He wouldn't be driving trucks like his old man when he got to my age."

"Who did this to our little boy?" Diane asked as she leaned her head against Pete's shoulder.

"We are investigating the circumstances of Nelson's death. Once we know the cause, you'll know it too."

"Whoever the bloke is that did this, I hope he rots in hell." Pete said in a flash of anger. He made a move to stand up. The strength of his legs left him. He leaned forward and fell back against the sofa. Diane fell against him. The two cried.

Carter and Song started to leave the room.

"We'll give you a few minutes. When you're ready, we have a car upstairs to take you to the Docklands office. We'll need to take a formal statement," Carter said.

"We understand, Detective. Nelson called us last week. He did sound a bit stressed. I just..." Diane struggled to express herself as she buried herself in Pete's chest.

"It's alright, Diane, we can discuss this later. Right now, we'll give you some space," Carter said.

Carter left the door ajar as he and Song leaned against the wall outside the room. Song exhaled loudly and leaned her head against the wall. She mouthed the word rough. Carter nodded as he sat down on the floor. Carter sighed and pushed his head against the cool rough bricks of the wall.

"What's wrong?" Song asked.

"Noth—"

A loud cracking noise, then a shatter, came from the viewing room. Carter and Song rushed in.

Glass covered the floor. Pete had thrown a chair against the glass window. The black curtains swayed, the only thing between them and the body. Pete stood frozen. He didn't comprehend what he had done. The chair on the ground, shards of glass around him. It all appeared alien to him. Carter stepped towards him, crunching and cracking glass as he walked.

"Hey mate, take a step back," Carter said.

Pete moved to pull back the curtains.

"Mate," Carter said again, "There will be time to see your son again. Now isn't that time."

Pete broke off a sharp shard of glass on the window frame.

"Oh Pete, no," Diane screamed.

"We fucked up, darling," Pete said. He winced as he gripped the shard of glass.

Diane shrugged, eyes pleading for forgiveness from the world. "We did the best we could."

"That wasn't good enough," Pete screamed. Blood dripped down the shard of glass as his grip tightened. "It wasn't enough." A drop of blood landed near Pete's foot. "We weren't enough." He squeezed harder, blood started to pour from his gashed hand.

The curtain retracted, Nic's head appeared in the window. "What the hell is going on?" Nic took just a second to survey the situation. "I'll move the body out of here," she said as she pulled the curtain back.

"But I need to see my boy," Pete yelled.

"Pete," Carter bellowed, "Step back."

Nic wheeled the body out, the wheels of the gurney sounding on the linoleum.

Pete waved the glass shard around again. Droplets of blood flew across the room.

"We just weren't good enough."

"Please stop, Petey," Diane said as tears soaked her shirt.

"Listen to her, mate, just stop. Put the shard down. Today you aren't a fuck up. Today you're just Pete, and your job is to help your wife." Carter held his palms open towards Pete and motioned with his head towards Diane. "Your family is hurt enough, Pete."

"We fucked him up so badly. We hurt him. We are just junkies," Pete said.

"You cleaned up, you both got jobs, you two are on the right track," Carter said.

"Doesn't matter no more."

"It does." Carter's eyes pleaded with Pete. "It really does. Today counts. Drop the glass mate."

Pete's teary eyes landed on an inconsolable Diane. He dropped the glass into the fragments of blood and glass spread across the room. As he dropped the glass, specks of blood dripped on the ground from his bloodied hand. "Oh God."

Carter moved swiftly to Pete and pushed him against the wall. A firm hand against his back. Carter reached for his handcuffs.

"What are you doing? He needs help," Diane shrieked.

Song moved to console Diane. "It's only temporary," Song said soothingly to Diane. "We just need to make sure he doesn't hurt himself."

Now they're shattered thought Carter, as he clicked the handcuffs. Carter guided Pete to sit on the sofa. He slumped; his face covered in tears.

Diane rubbed his back, "It'll be okay," she whispered.

--

"You owe me a window," Doctor Monroe said.

Carter sat on the floor, resting his head against the cool brick wall again. He looked up to see Doctor Monroe standing in front of him in blue surgical scrubs and holding a file folder. The pair were just outside the viewing room.

"Add it to my tab," Carter quipped as he stood up. "Sorry, Doc. Things got a bit testy in there."

Doctor Monroe scoffed. "That's an understatement. Did they identify the victim?"

"They did confirm its who we thought. Nelson Harris," Carter said.

"Their only child?" Doctor Monroe asked.

"Afraid so," Carter said. "Song is heading to the hospital with Pete and Diane in an ambulance. Pete cut himself pretty good on your window."

"I keep telling the chief coroner we need stronger glass. But double-thick glass means double the price, and he's always in a cost-cutting mode.

"Management — they are the worst," Carter said.

"They enjoy their ivory tower looking down at the peasants. Can't remember the last time he performed an autopsy," Doctor Monroe said.

"Are we still on for Moe's autopsy?" Carter asked as he stretched his aching body.

Doctor Monroe handed Carter the file in her hands. "I've had to postpone his autopsy to tomorrow morning. I had time to do a preliminary report though, and my notes are in the file. Just one particularly edifying find."

"Which is?" Carter asked.

"You're looking for a revolver as the weapon used to kill the presumed Moe.

"Not a semi-automatic?" Carter asked.

Doctor Monroe shook her head, "Not a semi-automatic weapon. Given the close range, a semi-automatic would have left a substantial exit wound. The bullet entered the victim's skull and is still in there. Highly probable the bullet sliced and diced its way around and is lodged in the grey matter. With any luck, once I dissect the skull, I'll be able to retrieve it. The technicians will be able to confirm make and model for you."

"Thanks Doc. Revolvers aren't too common anymore."

Doctor Monroe nodded, "I thought you'd appreciate some good news."

"Let's not get carried away here, I got a murder weapon, victim, just no location or motive." Carter fished out the gift certificate from his pocket from Perry. "A gift certificate for your local I from Detective Perry, for you and Nic."

Doctor Monroe took the card and turned it over, giving it a close examination, "I assume this is really meant for Nic. Perry really needs to just ask Nic out."

Carter nodded, "He's old school. You know the type, likes to court."

"Let's speed it up. Have Perry supervise the autopsy tomorrow, Nic is assisting me," Doctor Monroe said.

Carter gave a sharp salute, "Yes boss."

"In this domain, you are correct," Doctor Monroe said with a wink.

CHAPTER SEVENTEEN

"How were the parents?" Davies asked as she stared at her computer monitor. She gestured to the chair in front of her desk. Carter slumped in it. He felt a tension headache running from one temple, across the back of his head and connecting to the other temple. It felt like his skin had shrunk and tightened against his head.

"They took it pretty rough. Folks really thought Nelson made it out in the clear. Away from their issues with drugs."

"Aren't they clean now? There aren't any connections between drug use and Nelson's death."

"Yep, but their peak drug use was during Nelson's youth. Those scars remain. They are connecting dots that aren't there," Carter said as he thought of Pete gripping the shard of glass in his hand. A physical scar to match the emotional.

"Doesn't take much to open an old scar," Davies said as her gaze rested on the family photo on her desk.

"Pete, the father, got upset, smashed the viewing room window. They are getting checked out at the Royal Melbourne Hospital. Uniforms will escort them back to their hotel to rest before the memorial tonight."

"It is important for them to attend tonight. Not only for the optics of the investigation. It'll also help them grieve," Davies said.

"How's your speech coming along?" Carter asked.

Davies twirled her hand. "My penultimate speech? The media team is drafting it now."

"Penultimate?" Carter's interest piqued along with his right eyebrow.

"I want this case wrapped up with a bow-tie so I can focus on my last speech which will be at my retirement party." She pointed a finger squarely at Carter. "I'll be expecting a speech from you this time."

Carter smiled in agreement. "Sure thing, boss. In the meantime, though, Doctor Monroe isn't too impressed with us for allowing the window to be smashed. She doesn't happen to owe you any favours?"

Davies shook her head. "Not a single one worth wasting on a broken window. Just get Perry to be primary on all future autopsies."

"You know?" Carter asked.

"The doctor and I play a round of tennis every now and then," Davies said.

"It's a team effort matchmaking mission."

"What is the doctor's assessment of the second victim?" Davies asked.

Carter flipped through the preliminary autopsy report drafted by Doctor Monroe. "Pretty straightforward. Close-range gunshot wound to the head. No real evidence on the victim. Two interesting notes. Moe changed clothes either willingly or by force between our encounter at Vapour and his final resting place in the boot of the Audi."

"So, the perpetrators either wanted to conceal Moe's identify by swapping clothes or removing the evidence from them."

"My thoughts exactly," Carter said.

"What's the second piece of news?" Davies asked.

"Murder weapon is most likely a revolver."

Carter noticed a change in Davies. Her attention seemed laser-focused on him after he said the word revolver.

"Who uses a revolver anymore?" Davies asked.

"Not many, semi-automatics are the weapon of choice for the modern criminal," Carter replied.

"Who used to use revolvers?"

Carter shrugged, "Criminals."

"And us. You know, it wasn't too long ago that the force used revolvers," Davies said.

Carter nodded. "You're right, we all trained with revolvers at the academy. Only swapped them for semis a few years ago. Maybe one of our revolvers fell off the back of a truck during the recall? Ended up on the street. Similar to the US military stationed in Darwin? They lose weapons by accident." Carter used air quotes around the word accident to stress his point. "Magically the lost weapon gets smuggled down to Adelaide and over to the east coast with the bikies."

Davies picked up her stress ball and squeezed. The stretchy blue material morphed into a different bulbous shape as it contoured around her thumb and index finger. "Once the make and model of the murder weapon are confirmed, tell me first, before anyone else."

She turned back to her monitor. "I'll see you at the memorial."

"Thanks, boss."

As Carter put a hand on the doorknob, Davies spoke once more. "I'll be starting my successional planning. Have a think about your next moves."

"One insurmountable challenge at a time."

"You keep saying that Carter – make sure you're ticking off some of those challenges. You still have two bodies and no suspects."

--

The office was abuzz. Song and Perry stood by the whiteboard with the surveillance teams. They had a map of Fitzroy Gardens taped to the board. James Hughes had organised the memorial at the gardens. Carter wondered about the curious choice. There were probably half a dozen public parks closer to Vapour that could accommodate a crowd. Fitzroy Gardens was one of the most prestigious parks in Melbourne, just a few blocks away from Melbourne CBD and next door to the state parliament. Carter couldn't help but wonder how deliberate a choice the Fitzroy Gardens were. James told parliament he was coming for them through the choice of park.

Carter squinted to see the exact location of the memorial in the park on a map. "Good lord, yep, it's a sign," muttered Carter.

He saw the memorial was to be held at the top end of the gardens towards Albert Street near the River of God Fountain. The fountain is made from a statue of a man holding a clamshell.

Fitzroy Gardens was a square-shaped public park exposed to heavy traffic from Wellington Parade at the bottom of the garden, with Lansdowne and Clarendon Streets on either side of the park and Albert Street at the top.

A convenient layout for the team. They would focus their surveillance coverage along the top quarter of the park with Lansdowne and Clarendon Streets closed to traffic. The mobile headquarters would be placed about halfway down the park on Lansdowne Street. Lansdowne, Albert and Clarendon Streets would also have one police van with a team of officers overseeing surveillance. Visible police presence would be high with uniformed officers along all four sides of the park and the remaining grounds.

Perry briefed the team leaders of the surveillance teams as Carter eavesdropped in.

"Anyone exhibiting any unusual behaviours needs to be photographed. Keep the communications clear, very little chatter. We need to be listening for targets from the plainclothes and uniformed officers. We will also have a Crime Stoppers stall set up for anyone to chat with us. This is the best chance we have for someone giving us information about this case. This could be our big win so bring I-game folks."

Big win, Carter thought as he sat down at his desk. He took out his mobile and twirled it between thumb and middle finger. Delayed gratification, Carter thought as he continued to twirl his mobile round and round.

Carter unlocked his phone. His thumb hovered over the lotto app. What does Doc Lynch know anyways? Carter thought as his thumb pushed down on the lotto app. His thumb stayed depressing the icon, pausing the opening of the app.

I suppose this counts as delayed gratification, thought Carter as he lifted his thumb and the app opened.

Carter clicked on the cog icon to open the settings of the app. He scrolled down to the responsible play section. He opened the section and frowned. His weekly limit had come into effect – fifty dollars set by Doctor Lynch.

"Bloody doctor," Carter said as he placed his mobile on his desk. Delayed gratification, I can wait. Show some inner strength mate, he thought to himself.

Carter's fingers tapped his downturned mobile. Gotta be in it to win it though. Carter picked up his mobile again. I have a limit, might as well reach it. In a series of quick automatic movements, devoid of thought, Carter reached his weekly limit in under five seconds.

Carter glanced up and saw Song approaching with two takeaway coffees. He tucked his mobile back in his pocket.

Song handed Carter a coffee.

"Thank you, Detective Song, and don't worry, here's a present for you," Carter said as he handed Song a file folder.

"What's this and it's not even my birthday," Song said.

"It's the coroner's preliminary report on victim number two, Moe. How were Pete and Diane?" Carter asked.

Song casually skimmed through the report, "They are okay. The cut on Pete's hand looks worse than it is thankfully. Just a few stitches were needed. They both were a bit rattled. Reckon some rest at the hotel is what they need. I asked if they wanted some uniformed officers to bring them to the memorial, but they declined. Said they were going to catch up with Abby."

"Strength in numbers, seeing Abby will help them through this," Carter said.

"Got an email from the techs, they confirmed Moe's fingerprints are on the lip of the boot," Song said.

"So, he sat on the edge of the boot when he was shot," Carter said. "And shot with a revolver."

"Not much to go on," Song said.

Carter focused on the timeline section on the whiteboards. He got up and with a red marker blocked off the times for the second victim's estimated time of death, between 6 and 8 a.m., before returning to his desk.

"The car was dumped in Ascot Vale, and that area would have been busy at that time of the morning. All the shift workers and early risers would have been out the door," Carter said.

Song sighed. "The perpetrators would have known we'd be looking for a white Commodore and they wiped the car down pretty damn well, except for Moe's fingerprints on the boot."

Carter's eyes lit up, and he smacked the desk. "You know what. It's a bloody message. They wanted us to know where he was killed. It also means they know what they're doing," Carter said. "Or one of them knows what they're doing."

"What do you mean by one?" Song asked.

Carter rapped his fingers on the table, from pinkie to pointer. "I'm more convinced now there are at least two assailants. We have two different styles of murder. One with passion, the other cold and clinical."

"Two murders, no site," Song said.

"What if both the murders of Nelson and Moe took place at the same site, probably in the Ascot Vale area? Ascot Vale to Collingwood is a twenty-minute drive in the early hours of the morning. They park somewhere in the suburb, kill Moe, wipe down the car and dump it in the same area before walking off. Are these people operating from some type of HQ?"

Song scribbled herself a notice. "It's a start. Still a big area to canvas across CCTV for the cars."

"It's our only lead right now," Carter said.

"I'll get some uniforms to track down any and every CCTV. Traffic, ATM, local stores, we'll get it all," said Song.

"We need to get a hold of that white Commodore. But if they are as smart as we all think, it's probably burned out in some car yard in Werribee," Carter said.

"You still think these two murders are related?" Song asked.

"No way around it. We just need to find the missing link."

"Two murders: only thing tying them together is a seedy bathhouse that the gays use to, um, network."

Carter laughed and threw a pen at Song. "Network. I could think of a better word. Speaking of networking, we have a memorial to prepare for."

"Think Nelson and Moe's killers will show up?" Song asked.

"It's a safe bet. Murderers want to revel in their notoriety. What better place than a memorial," Carter said.

CHAPTER EIGHTEEN

Carter glanced towards the main police contingent outside the park on Albert Street. He spotted Constable Zhang standing with a few other uniformed officers. His hands were looped into his police vest. The koi fish tattoo was visible, travelling up his bicep and triceps. It was definitely the same tattoo he'd seen on his hook-up app; Carter was sure of it.

"Where's your hat, Detective? You know what they say, slip on a shirt, slop on the sunscreen and slap on a hat," Zhang said.

Carter leaned against one of the police cruisers as Zhang approached. Carter wiped the back of his hand along his sweaty forehead to mop up the sweat.

"I got the first two parts right. You don't happen to have a spare hat?" Carter asked.

"No hat that wouldn't ruin your plainclothes outfit, but I've got a spare water." Zhang handed Carter a bottle of water.

"Thanks," Carter said as he took a gulp.

"Good to see so many people coming out for this," Zhang said. He rolled up his shirt sleeve to reveal a half-sleeve tattoo. A watery landscape flowed from his elbow towards his shoulder with shaded blue waves and a bright orange koi fish. The fish's tail wrapped around Zhang's bicep with its body travelling upstream towards his shoulder.

"Is this your first patrol duty for a major event?" Carter asked.

Zhang nodded. "Perry has me assisting him in the mobile HQ." Zhang pointed to a police van with a large satellite dish on the roof.

Carter looked at Zhang, his bruised jawline now a swirl of purples and greens.

"Reckon Perry has made the right choice. The bruise would be a distraction. Part of being on patrol duty is blending into the crowd. Think of yourself as moveable furniture. People will see you but ignore you if you fit their expectation. And that bruise of yours still stands out."

Zhang let out a chuckle. "It doesn't hurt anymore. Hillier wants to take me out for a few pints to apologise." Zhang touched the bruise and winced. "Well, after a few beers it won't hurt as much. But still, I'd rather be out there than in the van watching the action on a monitor."

"It's not watching the action Zhang; it's predicting the action. You, Perry, and the overall surveillance team are our eyes and ears. You see the action coming and steer us towards it and sometimes we steer you too. I can't stress enough how important the intel we gather here is and can push the case forward."

"No pressure," Zhang said.

"Listen to Perry's instructions and you'll be fine," Carter said.

Carter checked his mobile. He saw a text from Paddy asking if he was at the memorial. Paddy dropped a pin and a smile formed across Carter's face.

It turned out that Paddy was just a few metres away from Carter. He was dressed in a cream-coloured business suit. They smiled as they approached each other.

"Just coming off work?" Carter asked.

Paddy moved to hug Carter, but Carter stepped back. There was a moment of awkwardness between the two.

"On-duty professionalism," Carter said as he extended his hand.

"Of course, my bad," Paddy said as they shook hands.

Carter felt that familiar electric surge from his heart to his groin. A surge that turned quickly into an urge.

"I'm still on the clock and I've gotta head back into the office after this. I just wanted to come out, show my support. I'm actually pretty stunned at the turnout."

The pair looked at the huge crowd gathering on the green grass.

Carter nodded in agreement, "It's good to see."

"Doubt any of them knew Nelson, but as community everyone comes together to support each other. Doesn't happen enough."

"If it did, I'd be out of a job. Though that would probably be a good thing," Carter said.

"What do you mean?" Paddy asked.

A bead of sweat formed along Paddy's temple and would eventually roll down his cheek. Carter felt beads of sweat forming on him as well. What Carter really wanted to do was escape the heat with Paddy. Crank the AC in his bedroom and hide under the sheets with Paddy, pants left by the door.

"A lot of my work is sweeping up the mess when society lets people down," Carter said.

"Might not need to do that if we funded social services better," Paddy agreed.

Carter nodded, "But that's not going happen. Well, maybe one day, but until then I'd rather be here trying to help my queer brothers, sisters, and non-binaries when they need the law."

"What about the straights?" Paddy asked in jest.

Carter chuckled, "Them too... I just..."

Carter paused, "I just want everyone to have the justice they deserve despite the adversity they faced while they lived. Victims of crime deserve it, and so do their family and friends."

"You're a good man," Paddy said.

Carter blushed. "I don't know about that."

Paddy shot Carter a quizzical look. He was about to respond when Song sidled up alongside them. She popped in her earpiece. "Ready for a stroll?"

Paddy nodded to Song, "I'd best leave you two, important police business to get to."

Carter smiled, "I'll keep you up to date on the investigation."

Paddy smiled before he walked off, leaving Song and Carter alone.

Song gave Carter a look that said she had questions.

"No comment," Carter said.

Song and Carter navigated their way between the dozen or so media outlets who had set up their news crews. Carter spotted Kris Oke.

"Interesting that Kris Oke is here," Carter said.

"Why's that?" Song asked.

"First on the scene at Vapour too," Carter said.

The pair walked closer to Kris, who faced the camera.

"Join me tonight for an exclusive interview with James Hughes. We'll be discussing the election, his experiences of homophobia in the military and his vision for the future."

Kris stopped talking and looked directly at the camera until a producer motioned to her that they had stopped recording.

"Evening, Detectives," Kris said as Carter and Song passed them. "Superintendent Davies and James Hughes have spoken to me regarding the investigation. Care to make a comment as the lead investigators?"

Carter turned back. "Actually, Kris, I have a question for you. How do you know James Hughes?"

"Pardon, what do you mean?" Kris asked.

"You were the first to break the Vapour story," Carter said. "He tipped you off about the murder, didn't he?"

"My sources are confidential." Kris handed Carter her card. "But I would love to get you and Detective Song both on camera for an insider perspective."

Carter took the card. "We'll have to pass."

Kris shrugged as she pulled out her mobile, "Suit yourself. I hear you don't have many suspects. A media piece might get the public onside, refresh people's memories who might be a witness. "

"We'll take it under consideration," Carter said. Once he and Song were out of earshot from Kris. "Do you think this is a case of 'who doesn't James know,' or that the two of them were striking their own deal?"

"How long is a piece of rope?" Song asked.

Carter noticed Song pulled on the neckline of her blouse momentarily.

"You alright?"

"Yes," Song said abruptly, "Just this heat is getting a bit much."

--

The pair walked around the large stage erected in front of the River of God Fountain in the Fitzroy Gardens. Along either side of the stage were booths and stalls. Carter and Song walked between the rows of stalls on the left side of the stage. All the queer sports teams had set up a booth alongside mental health services and various community services. Melbourne's recreational and support communities were reaching out tonight. From water polo, running clubs to free psychological counselling, anything on offer in Melbourne staked a presence tonight. Crowds drifted between the booths along with Carter and Song who weaved their way in and out of the groups.

The pair were looking for any suspicious behaviour. Carter tended to look at how people walk and the clothes they were wearing. Given the heat today, anyone wearing a puffer jacket got his immediate attention in case they might be carrying a concealed weapon. Thankfully he didn't notice anyone meeting these criteria. The large crowds slowed the pair's pace to a snail's crawl and then eventually to a stop. Carter glanced at the counselling stall beside them. His eyes darted away as he quickly saw the list of counselling services, addiction and gambling high among them.

Won't need to gamble once I win the big one. This isn't my Ahab's white whale, I'll stop after one, Carter thought.

The trifecta of heat, a burning bright sun, and drought turned the once lush, green grass in the gardens into a brown spotted field. A field trampled by the growing crowds who were setting up their picnic spots in front of the stage.

"Holy shit." Carter pulled down his sunglasses as he and Song surveyed the attendees from the stage.

"There must be nearly three hundred people here," Song said.

"At least," Carter said.

Groups of people set out picnic blankets on the park ground and socialised. Nearly every group had a bottle of wine and snacks. Carter and Song started to survey the makeup of the various individual groups.

They were both in plain clothes, but on second glance, it was clear to anyone Carter and Song were officers: earbuds connected them to a walkie talkie on their tactical belts and a no-nonsense look of determination on their faces.

"Pete and Diane must be proud – so many people coming together for Nelson," Song said.

"Hopefully." Carter said as they passed a group of four people on a picnic blanket uncorking a bottle of Australian sparkling wine.

"Or people in Melbourne just enjoy any excuse to drink in a park." Carter glanced back towards the stage. He spotted Davies in her formal police uniform. Even from this distance, he could see the array of commendations pinned to her chest. Next to Davies sat Nelson's friend Abby and a few other people seated on chairs. Carter squinted towards the stage, but Nelson's parents weren't there or to either side.

James Hughes stepped up to the lectern. Next to him stood a sign language interpreter. His voice boomed through the speakers by the stage.

"Before we begin, I would like to acknowledge the people of the Woi Wurrung and Boon Wurrung language groups of the eastern Kulin Nations on whose unceded lands we conduct this memorial. I respectfully acknowledge their Ancestors and Elders, past, present and emerging."

The sound technician adjusted the volume. What started as an ear-piercing boom turned into an elevated dinner voice through the speakers.

"Good evening, ladies and gentlemen. I'm James Hughes. Melbourne lost a member of its community yesterday – Nelson Harris. This evening is about Melbourne coming together. Coming together to remember Nelson. And coming together to be a community. Before everyone leaves tonight, I want you to introduce yourself to someone you don't know. Everyone deserves the support and connections that the most liveable city in the world has to offer."

James gestured to the stalls on either side of the stage. "As you may know, there is a by-election for Melbourne's Federal seat going on, but the focus of tonight's events isn't political. It's about stopping hate. With that said, I am running in the election, and all the major parties have a speaker tonight and a stall set up as well. We have the best clubs, groups and services in Melbourne here tonight.

Take the time to check them out. Join a club. Also present is Crime Stoppers. If you know anything related to Nelson's death, please reach out to them or any of the officers here tonight. On stage with me tonight is Abby Crosby, Nelson's best friend. Also with me is Superintendent Liz Davies who is overseeing the investigation. We will start with a few words from the Superintendent."

Song and Carter turned their backs to the stage and kept walking the grounds. "Fingers in every pie. Do you think one of his companies organised the entire event or he called in a favour to host?"

Carter shrugged. "Either way, the optics look great for him."

The pair walked by a group of people sitting on a picnic blanket. A young man, Nelson's age, stood at the edge of the blanket.

"Mind if I join you?" he said to the seated men and women.

"Of course, sit down," one of the men said.

The group started a round of introductions.

Davies's voice echoed throughout the park. "As a proud and out lesbian, I cannot abide or tolerate any type of violence to the LGBTQI community. When I first started my policing career, I never thought I'd be able to disclose my sexuality to my profession, let alone with an audience. Today is a different time. Despite that, prejudices and hatred continue to be pervasive across the country not least here in Melbourne. I have faith that things will get better. I manage a squad of detectives, some of whom identify with the LGBTQI community. And I'm here to assure you that we will investigate this crime and help bring a prompt and swift resolution. My officers are across the park today. Speak to any one of them if you have information that could assist our enquiry."

"I didn't know that Davies had come out in public," Song said.

"Me neither."

Song let out a slight snort and chuckle at the same time. "Not much of an outing, mate. Your LGBTQIA+ liaison officer profile is still on the police website."

"True. And it's a night of lasts for her. Reckon she is enjoying the soapbox."

"Lasts?"

"She is close to retirement. This is between us, of course."

Song nodded. "I knew that already."

Carter smiled, "What else do you know that I don't?"

"Probably could fill a warehouse," Song said as they walked through the growing crowds. People continued to spill into the park from all roads.

"Getting crowded. Let's do a walk around the perimeter," Carter suggested.

--

Two large eucalyptus trees dotted the south side of the park next to the waist-high fence separating it from the sidewalk. Their long gnarly branches reached high, the green leaves forming a semi-circular canopy. This included the only shade in the entire park. Carter's gaze shifted up, towards the sky. The sun hung low in the sky, its UV rays scorching the dry land. He took out his water bottle and had a sip to quench his thirst.

"Carter, what's the policy on drugs at this event? Noticed a few people smoking joints." Hillier's voice buzzed in Carter's earpiece.

"Like he needs to ask," Carter said to Song before he switched on his radio. "If it's fewer grams than I have dust in my house, we don't care. Tonight, is about being part of a community. Making everyone feel comfortable to speak to us."

"Ten-four," Hillier said.

Song leaned against one of the park's larger eucalyptus trees. Without moving, Song said, "Carter, your four o'clock. Look at that massive unit standing under the tree."

Eyes darted, hidden from scrutiny under his shades, Carter's body froze, in case his movement would startle Song's target. "You're right, he is a massive unit."

A man in his late twenties leaned against the peeling bark of the eucalyptus tree. At least six feet tall and a big rig of a man. He wore white sneakers, rolled up faded black jeans, a white t-shirt and a dark cap and shades. His thick thighs resembled tree trunks. Standing next to the tree, he made it look like a sapling with his broadness.

"He looks out of place, doesn't he?"

Carter nodded as he continued to watch as the man dug his white sneaker into the dirt. The action seemed absent-minded or perhaps the man was trying to avoid thinking as he stirred up the ground and kicked the dirt away with the toe of his sneaker. He then lifted his shades momentarily to wipe his eyes.

"He's been crying," Carter said. "He looks familiar, doesn't he?"

Song shrugged. "All you tall white guys look the same."

Carter laughed as he scanned around for the surveillance teams. Team three on Clarendon Street had the best vantage point. He tapped his radio earpiece. "Carter to team three, require photos of male Caucasian, approximately 198 centimetres, under the second tree from the far wall towards Clarendon Street. I want face pictures."

"Ten-four," a male voice said.

Carter and Song's new target reached into his pocket and glanced at his phone. He put it back in his pocket, wiped his face again and started walking towards Clarendon Street.

"A speedy exit," Carter said.

"Very speedy," Song said.

Carter and Song heard in their earpieces, "Team three unable to get a photo."

Carter tapped his radio again. "Understood. Team five, pursue a person of interest. I want enough photos to identify him. Pursue, do not engage."

"Team five, copy."

Team five comprised a group of plainclothes officers in unmarked cars supporting the prime surveillance teams.

Carter and Song watched their target exit the park. An unmarked police car with tinted windows slowly followed.

"What's your feeling of him?" Carter asked.

"Dunno, could be nothing — just seems like an outlier. Hopefully, we can identify him."

Carter looked towards the stage. The sun nearly set as the speeches were wrapping up. Everyone had moved off the stage and were forming a circle in the central part of the grassy area. Artificial candles were handed out to everyone.

Across the speakers, James's gruff and nasally voice chimed in. "Join us in a moment of silence to remember Nelson Harris."

Song glanced at her watch. She rotated through about half a dozen luxury watches depending on her mood in the morning, all encrusted with diamonds or very good looking cubic zirconias.

"I'm going to head off. Umma's been minding the kiddies. She needs a break."

"Umma Song is a saint. Thank you. I'll see you tomorrow," Carter said.

She nodded and headed towards Clarendon Street.

Silence swept across the park as hundreds of people joined together for the minute of silence. Most heads were down, many people crying as they joined in this moment of reflection.

"Priority alert," Perry's voice rang through Carter's earpiece.

Song had reached Clarendon Street but stopped dead in her tracks and turned to look at Carter.

"What's happening, Perry?" Carter asked through his walkie-talkie.

"Protesters are approaching the memorial from Albert Street, about fifty or so. Mounted unit is approaching," Perry said.

"Protesters? Protesting what?" Carter asked.

"Not sure," Perry said, "They have a huge array of signs and banners."

"It's the Better Times Movement." Hillier's voice chimed in on the radio. "I can see Craig Dean Senior at the front of the protest."

"Have the mounted unit set up a block. All uniforms head there to support them." Carter scanned the park. The attendees were half-way through the minute of silence. He flicked on his radio again, "Hillier, can you see Craig Dean Junior in the protesters, probably near his dad at the front?"

Sweat dripped down Carter's back as his heart rate quickened. His shoulders started to rise. His muscles contracted.

"Hillier, I need an update," Carter said.

Radio silence greeted Carter.

"Mounted squad have boxed in the protesters. The only way for them to go is back into the CBD," Perry said.

"Negative, no sign of Craig Dean," Hillier said.

Where's Craig, Carter thought. Then he caught sight of his target walking, with purpose, hand jammed in his pocket, singularly focused on James Hughes who still stood, head bowed and unaware of the man bearing down on him.

"James Hughes!" Carter bellowed. "Look out!"

Then he and Song both bolted toward the stage.

Heads looking down slowly curled up. Groups of attendees were startled by Carter and Song running during the minute of silence. Waves of fear spread as the pair ran towards the stage. Chaos ensued as attendees started running away from the stage. The crowds grew thick as people began to run.

"Police, stay down," Carter yelled.

No one listened.

Craig Dean had made it to the stage. Carter caught the sight of a knife in his hand.

"Police stay down," Carter yelled as he ran straight for Craig.

He saw James turn around to face Craig. James dropped the mic. A screeching noise came through the speakers. All eyes turned towards the stage.

Craig raised his knife. Carter thought of drawing his weapon, but there were too many people between him and the stage.

Full panic filled the air. Attendees were scattering and screaming. Few stayed on the ground.

James stepped forward. He raised his fists, ready to fight. James threw a punch at Craig. Craig jumped and ducked to the side, avoiding the attack. Craig countered with a slash of his knife against James's leg. James fell clutching it.

"Craig, over here," Davies yelled to distract him from James.

Craig tightened his grip on the knife. His gaze darted between Davies and James on the ground.

"Scared of women?" Davies asked. She tried to goad Craig into attacking her.

It worked.

Craig thrust the knife towards Davies with rage behind his eyes. His gaze locked to her stomach, intent on stabbing her there.

Davies used this to her advantage. She shot her arms out in a cross block. Her wrists landed on top of Craig's, pushing it away from her. Craig tried to slash but only cut the air.

Davies quickly gripped Craig's wrist. She rolled and raised it until he lost his balance.

"Let go," Craig screamed.

She ignored the plea and pulled him forward. He stumbled, then fell. Davies planted her elbow on Craig's arm to secure him. With her hands still wrapped around his wrist, she locked the wrist joint and applied pressure.

"Drop the knife or I break your wrist," Davies said.

"Piss off bitch," Craig screamed.

Davies pushed Craig's wrist back further.

He screamed in pain, "All right, all right." He dropped the knife.

Carter bounded up to the stage.

"Stay down!" Carter bellowed as he kicked the knife out of reach. Craig squirmed but Davies kept the pressure on his wrist.

Carter saw a twisted VIP lanyard around Craig's neck.

"How'd you get the lanyard Craig?" Carter asked.

"Fuck you, pig," Craig said.

Abby ran up beside them, "Craig, stop this!"

Carter was dumbfounded. "You know this man?"

"She's my fucking missus, you pig," Craig yelled.

"You gave him a VIP lanyard?" Carter asked.

Tears streamed down Abby's face. She nodded. "Yes," she stammered.

Song crouched next to James, inspecting the leg wound. "Stay down James, you're going into shock."

"Like Hell I am." James reached for the microphone. "Everyone, calm down, please." James's voice boomed through the park. "Everything is under control, thanks to the swift actions of the Police."

"We love you James," an onlooker from the crowd said.

Davies took the mic from James, "We would like everyone to remain calm and stay seated."

Carter looked at the crowd, half had already fled while a quarter didn't move from their picnic spots, and the remaining quarter filmed the unfolding scene with their mobiles. The ones who stayed all began to cheer and clap. Carter also spotted the camera crews who were filming them and the attendees in various stages of shock. The park soon flooded with paramedics and officers roaming about, providing assistance.

Carter hoisted up a cuffed Craig Dean and beckoned the nearest uniformed officer forward.

"Craig Dean, you're under arrest for assault and attempted murder. Abby, you'll need to go with the officers as well."

"Looks like I'll have another scar to add to the collection," James said. The paramedic had cut off the bottom half of James's khaki pants, exposing a long knife wound along the bottom half of his calf towards his ankle.

Carter squeezed James's shoulder. "You forgot your military training mister."

"What do you mean?" James asked.

"You threw the first punch. Always get the attacker to come to you."

James laughed at the realisation, "I'm a bit rusty and the adrenaline kicked in."

"Glad you're okay." Carter felt a sudden flush of emotions. He squeezed James's shoulder harder for support, afraid he might faint.

James placed his hand on top of Carter's.

"Who was that stupid twat?" James asked.

"Neo-Nazi, shithead" Carter said.

"Shit, I'm on their radar. I'm doing something right," James said.

"Don't hold yourself in too high esteem. We don't know why they targeted you."

"Mr Hughes. Let's get you into an ambulance, alright," the paramedic said.

James nodded. "You'll keep me up to date?"

"No," said Carter in a flat tone. "You leak to the press too easily."

"True. But you'll let me know if they are after me or it is just auspicious timing."

"I will," Carter said.

James pointed towards Kris and her camera operator in the park. "Kris," James yelled, "Do you want to do that interview in the back of an ambulance?"

CHAPTER NINETEEN

A crowd had gathered around the ambulance taking James Hughes to hospital. People wanted to take a selfie with him. James made a quick speech. He reminded everyone to look out for one another, to provide any information on Nelson's death to police and to listen to their instructions.

The ambulance sped off to the hospital. The attendees were directed out of the gardens via the three sides of the garden that didn't face the central business district of Melbourne.

The mounted division were still dealing with the last stragglers of the Better Times Movement in the CBD. They had made a dozen arrests and then most of the protesters had scattered throughout. The officers swept through the city clearing out the stragglers and arresting the ones that refused to move on.

Craig Senior, the leader behind the Better Times Movement, disappeared in the chaos and couldn't be found. While his son sat in the interrogation room with his solicitor.

"That's one angry skinhead," Hillier said.

"Whatever his solicitor is saying, it isn't calming Craig down," Zhang said.

Hillier, Zhang, and Carter stood in the observation room looking through the one-way mirror. Song had to clock out to pick up her kids. Carter brought Hillier in to support. An emotional and handcuffed Craig looked like he was talking a mile a minute. While his solicitor furiously scribbled down notes.

The chain connecting the two cuffs fed through a loop hook secured to the interview table. Every time Craig raised his arms trying to make a point, the cuffs rubbed against his wrists and pulled them back down to the table. Carter saw Craig's wrists were turning red raw. Carter knew he shouldn't, but he smiled at that observation.

"Let's make him suffer a bit more. We already have him for the attempted murder of James Hughes. Find out whether or not he murdered Nelson Harris and Moe Bashar," Carter said.

"Craig's a Neo-Nazi and Nelson is white, so why kill him? Wouldn't that go against whatever code Craig believes in?" Zhang asked.

Carter noticed Zhang fidgeted. He kept flicking his index finger against the thumb of his other hand.

"This is your first interrogation, isn't it?" Hillier asked.

Carter didn't expect Hillier to reach out to Zhang like that.

Zhang nodded.

"It's okay to be nervous. We just can't let Craig, or his solicitor, see it," Hillier said.

"Are you sure Craig should be interviewed by an Asian officer?" Zhang asked

"Absolutely," Hillier and Carter said in unison.

"Craig is already rattled. Just look at him, he's acting like a caged animal, nervous, sweating and swearing up a storm I reckon. Ideally, I would have had Song and you lead the interrogation. But I want to interview him now and not wait till Song clocks in tomorrow," Carter said.

Hillier smiled, "I'm a good runner up and don't worry Zhang," Hillier placed a hand on Zhang's shoulder, "I'm going to lead and what I need you to do in there is just stroke Craig's ego."

"His ego? Seriously?" Zhang asked.

"Yep, his ego. He's expecting an adversarial interrogation. Instead, you are going to shower Craig in praise. But don't go over the top. Just feed him a few breadcrumbs. Make him want more praise from you.

You're going to be his understanding and sympathetic shoulder to confess on," Hillier said.

"Gotcha. Do you really think he's going to want to get praise from me though?" Zhang asked.

"Yes," Carter answered.

Zhang let out a small smile, "You've done this before?"

"The number one lesson I have learned in dozens of interrogations of white supremacists, Neo-Nazis, and the lot is they want to justify their actions to anyone and everyone. If they think you are a sympathetic ear, they'll tell you anything," Carter said.

Carter scrutinised Craig whose head rested on the table. His solicitor leaned back in her chair, appearing calmer too.

"You two are going to find out why he attacked James and what his connection to Vapour and the murders of Nelson and Moe are," Carter said.

"You'll be listening in?" Zhang asked.

"For a bit, then I'm going to have a chat with Abby."

"Come on, Sparkie," Hillier said.

"Can that not be my nickname, please?" Zhang asked.

"It's kinda cute, no?" Hillier asked.

Hillier and Zhang made their way out of the door.

--

A few minutes later, Carter entered a different interview room where Abby waited to be questioned. A lone constable stood in the corner. Carter slumped onto the chair opposite Abby. Neither spoke. Carter took a sip of water and scrolled through his notes. He flicked to the pages of the original interview of Abby at the I she worked at. He remembered the first time he saw Abby standing at the top of the stairs in the cafe. She had been crying before the detectives arrived and similarly today except the tears hadn't stopped.

Carter slid a paper cup filled with water over to her.

Abby cautiously picked up the paper cup and drank all the water in a single gulp.

"Thank you, Constable, you can leave," Carter said.

As requested by Carter for effect, the constable slammed the door shut behind him. Abby jumped in her seat from the startling noise. Her eyes went wide like a nervous possum, sensing danger.

Carter shook his head. "Quite the mess, Abby."

Abby's lower lip started to quiver.

"You are between a rock and a hard place. Best friends with a homosexual and dating a Neo-Nazi. How did that even come to pass?"

"He's not a Neo..." Abby's voice trailed off.

"He's part of a Neo-Nazi group, organised by his father," Carter said. "This is a fact."

"Yeah, but Craig is different, he doesn't think that way," Abby said. "Like look at me, I have brown hair, I'm fat. I don't fit the mould of what a Neo-Nazi should be into."

"That's a bit of a stretch, Abby," Carter said.

"Is that a fat joke?" Abby asked.

Carter shook his head, "How long have you been dating Craig?"

"We met on the Mates for Dates app a few months ago."

Carter mentally scrolled through the rolodex of dating apps in his mind, "That's the one where women initiate the conversation, right?"

Abby nodded.

"That doesn't make him a feminist just to be clear," Carter said.

Abby rubbed her eyes, "He's different, alright."

"He's not different, he's our prime suspect for Nelson's murder. Your best friend."

"He couldn't have done it," Abby said.

"Why not? He was arrested in Collingwood on the night of Nelson's murder. And don't kid yourself, he is filled with hate."

"He didn't kill Nelson. We were together that night until…" Abby trailed off again.

"Come on, Abby, this is your chance to avoid prosecution, tell me what you know, or I can charge you with obstruction."

"We were at a party alright," Abby said. "In Collingwood for a workmate's birthday. She had a few people round for drinks. I'd been talking about Craig for some time. They all wanted to meet him, I wanted to introduce him to my friends. But" Abby said as she clutched the empty paper cup, "can I get more water?"

"No," Carter stated flatly. "Tell me what happened at the party."

"He got drunk, really drunk. You see, my friend is Vietnamese. Well, I mean she is Australian but Vietnamese heritage."

"Ah, I see. Craig didn't take to kindly to you being friends with her?"

"Craig tried to get along," Abby said.

"Did he really?" Carter asked.

"He really did," Abby pleaded with Carter. "It's just when he gets drunk, he gets confused."

"You mean, racist?" Carter asked.

"He really did. He ended up drinking too much. He started saying some shit but passed out in the courtyard. We left him there. I went out to check on him later, and he had gone."

"What time did you go check on him?" Carter asked.

"About 1 a.m. I tried calling his mobile, but he didn't answer. I even checked the laneways around the house for him."

"Do you have any evidence of this?"

Abby nodded; she took out her mobile. "I took a few snaps. I wanted to talk to Craig about his drinking."

Abby slid her phone across the table. Carter picked it up and scrolled through the photos. He scrolled through a series of five pictures of various inebriation levels where Abby and Craig's faces got redder, through to Craig lying down in a courtyard.

"Where were you two before that?" Carter asked.

"At mine. He came over around six," Abby said. "Craig ordered us some UberEATS."

Damn, thought Carter, that rules him out as a suspect for Nelson and Moe's murder.

"Did Nelson know you were dating a Neo-Nazi?"

Abby slammed her hands against the table. "For the last time, Craig isn't a Neo-Nazi."

Carter stood up, "Come with me, Abby."

--

"Fuck you, you're not even from Australia," Craig yelled so loudly that the speakers delivering his voice to the observation room where Carter and Abby stood watching went fuzzy.

"I don't want to hear him," Abby said.

Carter gave Abby a sideways glance. He didn't mute the speakers.

"Craig, please, you can choose not to answer their questions," the solicitor said.

"Fuck em," Craig said.

"Craig, I'm Australian, born and raised. I'm worried about migration and jobs too," Zhang said, his voice carried through the speaker.

182

Carter smiled. Zhang played the sympathetic role well while Hillier played bad cop.

He didn't expect this dynamic to work. Carter knew Hillier's posh upbringing would immediately rile and antagonise Craig. Hillier even used a silver pen to take notes during the interrogation. Not a far stretch from his silver spoon upbringing. Craig knew Hillier was the enemy, and associated Zhang as an ally.

Zhang already had an ocker accent and really dug into it to reach out to Craig. Zhang clipped his words and dragged out the vowels.

"Is your dad a truckie mate?" Zhang asked Craig. Carter had no doubt Craig thought he and Zhang both lived in the same suburb and could be hooning mates. It wasn't a strategy that would always work but Constable Zhang had potential.

"Stop deflecting, why did you try to kill James Hughes?" Hillier asked.

"I get that James is a problem mate," Zhang said. "He's out, he's proud, he's not sending the right message of what Australia is out there, aye?"

"Who put you up to it?" Hillier asked.

"His dad," Abby said, who stood next to Carter in the observation room. She dabbed her eyes with a tissue. "Can you turn it off?"

Carter muted the speakers.

"Craig reminded me of Nelson when we first met," she said.

"How so?" Carter asked.

"A bit of a lost soul. You know if Nelson didn't have me to rely on, he'd have been a mess. It's hard to deal with the type of pain that comes from a parent letting you down when they should be your everything."

"I've met Craig's dad, he isn't great," Carter said.

Abby let out a laugh, "That's true. The more I learned about Craig's dad, the more I wanted to help him. Craig's a good guy at heart. It's just his dad has been his anchor for so long, and he's the real racist, neo-Nazi piece of shit," Abby said.

"Abby, it's a hard lesson to learn, but you can't fix people. They need to want to change. Craig's not ready," Carter said.

Abby hugged herself and swayed as the pair watched the interrogation continue.

"You gotta be cautious, selective on who you give your heart to. Craig chose to attack James today. He's going to face the consequences for that," Carter said.

"I just wish it didn't turn out this way. When Craig asked for a VIP lanyard, I just thought he wanted to talk to James. I wasn't thinking. I wish I could have done more. It's gotta be his dad that put him up to this," she said.

"Unless Craig flips on his dad, it won't matter. Craig had the knife and attacked James. You know, the longer I do this, the more I see this type of generational hurt. Sometimes the hurt gets dulled with the younger generation. Other times it gets magnified," Carter said.

"I'm glad Nelson's parents didn't see this all happen," Abby said.

Carter felt that familiar shot of adrenaline hit his system.

"You had spare lanyards because you were supposed to give them to Nelson's parents?" Carter said.

Abby nodded, "Yeah, but they never texted. I checked my mobile a couple of times, they haven't messaged."

"Shit," Carter said.

"What's wrong?" Abby asked.

"No one's heard from Nelson's parents since this afternoon," Carter said.

--

Carter pounded the door. The obstinate hotel staff member next to him shook her head as she stared intently at her mobile. Carter frowned as looked at her name tag — Mercedes.

Of course, she's named after a car, Carter thought. He nearly had to drag Mercedes from the front desk earlier to assist. Putting down her phone had seemed too significant an ask. She'd already sacrificed enough – she repeatedly reminded him in the lift that she should be on her tea break.

"They are probably out, mate," she said.

"Pete, Diane, it's DCI Carter. Are you in?"

He knocked again, louder.

"Maybe they're not in mate," Mercedes repeated as she scrolled through her Instagram feed on her mobile.

Carter rolled his eyes. He knocked on the door again.

"Pete, Diane, can you open the door?" No answers greeted his queries. "Do you know when they were last seen?" Carter asked.

"Yeah, nah," Mercedes said.

"Alright, open the door then," he said.

She blew a pink bubble with her gum, popped it, and tilted her head slightly.

"Open the door," Carter repeated.

"Where's your warrant, mate? I've seen *Law & Order*," Mercedes said.

"I don't have time for this shit. I don't need a warrant to arrest you for obstruction. And I have sufficient legal rights to enter premises if I believe the occupants are in immediate duress," Carter nearly growled. "Now open the door."

"Sure, whatever. I'm quitting soon. This hotel is shit," Mercedes said.

"Fascinating, don't tell me more," Carter retorted.

Mercedes swiped her card against the room lock. It flashed green.

"Maybe in your next job you should aim for something not involving the public," Carter suggested as he pushed open the door. "And stay there. Don't come in."

Mercedes shrugged as she leaned against the wall, head drawn down to the blue glow coming from her phone.

"Wasn't keen to enter anyways," she muttered under her breath.

"Pete, Diane, it's Carter again, I'm coming in."

The hotel room had a short hallway to the main bedroom painted in warm tones of beige. The blinds were drawn with the only light coming from the corridor where Carter stood. He stepped into the hallway and moved his hand against the wall to flick on the overhead lights to the dimly lit room.

"God damn it."

Carter saw their feet at the edge of the bed.

"Fuck," he rushed over to over the bed. "Pete, Diane?"

He shook the dry, calloused heels of each of them. His breath caught. They were cold to the touch. Stone. Cold. Dead.

The two lay on top of the floral duvet, Diane curled into Pete's embrace. Eyes closed, but not forced shut. Simply released. They had let go. Their deep wrinkles relaxed into death as the two appeared more at peace than they had since they heard the news of their son's death.

Pete's arm was wrapped underneath Diane and held her hand with their wedding bands touching. Carter pulled on a plastic glove and slowly rotated their cold hands to see matching needle marks on their arms.

On the bedside table rested a single syringe and a spoon with droplets of a transparent liquid in the bowl, a lighter and an empty baggie, which held their gear. Heroin, Carter assumed.

A folded picture rested on the table facing the bed. The last image Pete and Diane saw. The grainy, crumpled photo had the two of them standing side by side with Nelson as a child sitting on Pete's shoulders. Nelson stretched out a little reaching for the top of Diane's head.

"Shit." A churning nauseousness hit Carter. One family wiped away. The lot of them erased in just days. Each dry heave Carter did brought up anger and rage. Four dead now, under my watch.

"Fuck it," Carter roared as he kicked the white radiator on the side of the bedroom wall with his black Blundstone boot. A clanging sound filled the room as the tip of his boot smashed the radiator. He kicked it again. Flecks of white paint marked the end of the boot. A shooting pain shot up from his foot. The metal radiator turned out to be stronger than his boot.

Carter slumped down against the wall and stared directly at Pete and Diane's corpses. He tilted his head to the right, then to the left, almost expecting the scene to be different from a different angle. It wasn't.

"Luckier than most? They at least died with someone," he said to no one at all.

One tear rolled down his face along with the hurt.

"Stop it," he said aloud. Another tear rolled down. Carter slapped himself across the face. Tears are for pussies and faggots; his father's voice rang through his head. Carter slapped his face again, each cheek. Each subsequent slap harder than the former. Each slap to rid the tears from his face.

Carter picked himself up, wiping the tears from his face. He inspected the single pristine needle on the table.

Carter wondered. Who injected whom? Did Pete cook up the junk, inject Diane first? As the high kicked in he quickly did himself before putting the needle down? Or did Diane do the cooking and injecting before nuzzling into Pete's embrace? They had better choices.

Carter stepped out of the room and left the door ajar.

"They weren't in?" Mercedes queried, not looking up from the blue glow of her mobile.

"They are deceased. I need you to head downstairs and inform your person in charge that this room is not to be disturbed. Some other officers will be heading here soon."

"Oh," Mercedes nodded, "Sorry mate. Must suck." She gave Carter's shoulder a single pat before she walked down the grubby hallway towards the lifts.

Carter slumped against the wall and slowly slid to the ground.

His phone vibrated. He read the incoming text message: 'Spin and Win at the pokies: $1000 grand prize, at Railed tonight.'

"It's a night of vices and dead loves," he said to the empty hallway.

CHAPTER TWENTY

A pitch-black sky dotted with celestial bodies shone down on Carter as he leaned against a lamp post in the suburb of Richmond. He wiped the back of his hand across his sweat-drenched brow. Suicide rang in his head, with the reality of Nelson's death being too hard to face, Pete and Diane had instead chosen to escape the reality of their situation.

Carter looked up at the sky. His year nine astronomy lesson kicked in. The light from the stars and planets takes hundreds, even thousands of years to reach Earth.

What happened on that star when the light shone, leaving orbit and travelling through the darkness of space to shine into Carter's eyes.

In some strange way Carter felt comforted. Somewhere in the cosmos, Pete, Diane, and Nelson were all together in the past. The light from the flash from their family photo left Earth and launched off into the cosmos. That light travelling through the cosmos carried their life. Down on Earth, Carter struggled to process the fact that all three were dead.

Carter regretted how brisk and cold he acted towards the investigating officer at the hotel. "What do ya reckon," asked the officer, "Deliberate overdose?"

Carter had looked at the picture on the bedside table of Pete, Diane, and Nelson. All three were now together. "Your case, mate. You do the math." Carter left after that.

Carter stood outside a non-descript brownstone in the heart of Richmond. You almost wouldn't peg the building to be a gay bar except for the rainbow pinned to the roof. Well, that and the 'witty' play on words with the name above the door – Railed.

Carter placed a hand on the brass doorknob.

I don't have to have to play on the machines. Just a drink. I deserve this much after this shit day. If I spin it, I won't win it. I'll just lose my money; he thought as he pushed open the door to Railed.

I shouldn't go in, Carter thought again. That fleeting thought in the back of his mind was quickly drowned by a sensory overload.

The stench of stale beer, Abba through the speakers, and the cackle of laughter greeted Carter.

"What's your poison tonight?" Bruno asked as he tossed Carter a coaster.

Carter pulled out a fifty-dollar note and slid it under the coaster.

"Same old, mate. Double Southern Comfort and Coke."

His eyes followed the length of the mahogany bar. Just to the right of the far end of the bar was the pokies room. The doors haven't changed, still there, beckoning punters. What's behind them? Nothing special. They are just doors, he thought. Carter already knew his next moves would include opening those doors.

"Drinks on the house," Bruno said.

Carter's interest piqued.

"When you're in there. You know the rules." Bruno cocked his head towards the pokies lounge. Bruno checked his watch and pointed towards the pokies lounge. "Grand prize draw is happening in a few minutes. Your card needs to be in a machine to win. Not many punters tonight. Reckon you got a good chance of winning."

Carter licked his lips. It's just a door, to just a room, and if I come out with a grand, then I'm in the clear. He grabbed his drink and walked towards the room.

"Why not? About time Lady Luck finds me, just a cheeky spin or two while my card is in the machine."

Bruno smiled, "I'll bring your drink over, take a seat and have a spin."

"Gotta spin it to win it," Carter said.

Carter beelined it straight to the pokies lounge. He felt a brush against his shoulder but was too focused on those pokies lounge doors to notice.

The smell of stale cigarettes and beer-soaked carpets greeted Carter as he pushed open the doors to the pokies room. The low lighting and dim glow of the machines created an eerie otherworld atmosphere. Carter recognised one of the figures cast against a machine. Jill had planted herself at her usual post. Her hairy hands, with manicured tips, fed the machine another twenty-dollar note.

Carter sat down in front of the Mystic Mermaid machine next to Jill, an elderly cross-dresser. She wore heavy pancake makeup, thick eyeliner and a silk scarf across the neck to hide her Adam's apple. A sultry cartoon mermaid with an overly expressive smile and full cheeks swam in between the animated treasure chests. Carter chose to imagine a hunky merman instead of a mermaid.

Ready for an underwater adventure? Cooed the merman in Carter's head.

"Good evening, young man," Jill said in a deep voice with a hint of delicateness shaping each word.

"Evening to you too, darling Jill," Carter said.

"Ain't no zen with that machine. Ate all my money." She tapped the side of her current machine. "Now this one – it has my back."

She hit the spin button. An array of flashing lights danced across the machine. Numbers and symbols dropped. "Oh, come now, you can do better than that." She won back her two-dollar bet.

Carter placed his card in the machine slot. A string of lights illuminated as the machine registered his card. The text at the top of the machine flashed: Welcome back Leo! You have $2.45 in credit.

I'm not going to cash out $2.45, that is just a bit desperate, Carter thought.

Bruno did a round through the pokies floor. "Alright queens and ladies. The grand-prize draw is in two minutes. Two minutes everyone. To win, make sure your card is in your machine."

As Bruno walked by, he laid down a Southern Comfort and Coke for Carter and a white wine next to Jill.

"Enjoy, ladies," Bruno said.

Carter skulled his first drink and started on the new one from Bruno.

"I don't know how you imbibe those putrid concoctions," Jill said.

Carter let out a laugh, "It's a bit fruity and spicy, just like me."

Carter could tell Bruno had made him another double from the pungent sickly-sweet smell of the Southern Comfort.

His finger hovered over the spin button. He pressed down. Might as well clear the ledger, he thought.

The cartoon merman watched along with Carter as numbers and symbols dropped on the screen. The merman flicked his tail and a treasure chest opened.

Carter won three dollars. A smile spread across his face.

He tapped Jill on the shoulder to showcase his win. "I still got the lucky touch," he said as he took another sip of his drink. The sweetness of his drink coated his tongue. He pushed the spin button again.

"Congratulations my dear," Bruno laid down a thousand dollars cash in front of Carter. "You're the winner tonight. Reckon this is better than a meat platter."

Carter picked up the cash and fanned it out. A surge of energy hit him as he counted out the hundred- and fifty-dollar notes. Kiwis and pineapples are what Carter called the denominations as a child.

"Depends on whose meat," Carter laughed.

"Let me know when you two need another drink," Bruno said before he trotted away.

"Good luck darling," Carter passed Jill a fifty-dollar note.

"Thanks," she said. "Trying to win some money for new makeup."

Carter noticed Jill's mascara clumped together across each eyelid, lipstick smeared in certain places. He passed her another fifty, "When you win, buy the top-shelf products."

"Thanks," she said, revealing a gappy smile.

"What about you, what are you going to buy?" Jill asked.

"Don't know." Carter fed a hundred dollar note into the machine without giving it a second thought, let alone even a first. "Just killing time, I guess."

Jill looked past Carter to the man sitting at the pokies machine on his other side. "You all right darling? You're not playing?"

Carter followed Jill's gaze. Carter blushed. He didn't expect to see this man in this context.

"Paddy," Carter stumbled. He was a bit startled and almost embarrassed.

Paddy sat the machine with a pint of beer in his hand. His thick black hair was gelled back. He wore a black linen button up shirt with the top three buttons undone with a pair of white shorts and black sneakers. He wore what would be called a very summer casual look in Melbourne. It also showed off his best assets. Those firm hairy legs made Carter salivate.

"What are you doing here?" Carter asked.

"Always wearing your detective hat?" Paddy raised his beer. "Having a drink with some mates. I saw you in the main. I tapped you on the shoulder when you were walking here. But you didn't notice."

Carter laughed. He didn't realise how powerful his tunnel vision to the pokies had been. "Sorry, just wanted to get my card in the machine."

"I won't take offence, this time," Paddy said.

Carter fanned out his kiwis and pineapples. "Won the house prize tonight."

Paddy nodded, "Impressive haul from just getting your card in the machine. Could set you up with a modest stock range."

"Do you always wear your financial consultant hat?" Carter asked.

The two shared a chuckle and a smile. Carter played with his fingers. He really wanted to kiss Paddy and explore every part of his body with his tongue.

"How's the investigation going?" Paddy asked.

Carter opened his mouth. Nothing came out. He felt his toes ache from when he smashed them against the radiator in Pete and Diane's crummy hotel room. No place for anyone to die, let alone grieving parents.

Carter glanced at the pokies machine from the corner of his eye. The spin button tantalised and drew him in.

"It's ongoing," Carter said.

Paddy nodded, "Saw the scenes at the memorial. Is James Hughes okay?"

Carter nodded, "He'll have some lovely battle wounds to take on the campaign trail."

Paddy took a sip of beer. "Must have been scary."

"You get used to it, working on adrenaline and relying on your training." Carter's heart rate picked up. He really wanted to spin again.

Carter checked the pokies machine Paddy sat at. Paddy didn't have a card in the machine.

"You playing tonight?" Carter asked.

Paddy shook his head. "Not my game, waste enough money on grog."

Carter offered Paddy a hundred-dollar note. "Here, take one. It's free money."

Paddy raised his hand to decline the offer. "That's sweet, but no thanks. House always wins at these games."

"That's true," Carter said.

Paddy cocked his head towards the entrance to the main bar. "I should get going, left some mates in there."

Paddy stood up and placed a hand on Carter's shoulder. "Come join when you're done being scammed."

Carter felt the butterflies come back and a surge in his groin. There was a niggling thought in the back of Carter's mind that Paddy pitied him. That thought was drowned out as he continued to tap the spin button as he got caught up in the stentorian sounds from the pokies that drowned out his despair. He didn't know how much time passed until Jill's voice rang in his ear.

"Darling, you're done," she said.

Carter continued to mindlessly tap the spin button as he stared at the pokies screen. His fantasy cracked; the merman was replaced with a mermaid who swam in between digital treasure chests.

"Honey, you're out of cash," Jill said.

"Huh," Carter said.

Jill's manicured finger snapped him from his reverie as she pointed to his balance of $0.00. Carter stopped tapping the spin button as he realised that he had lost all the money he had won earlier in the evening.

"Damn, this night just gets better and better" Carter said.

"House always wins," Jill said.

Carter looked up at the jackpot for the machine he was playing. The jackpot was $40,000.

"Not tonight, the house wins enough. I need a real win," Carter said.

Carter raised his empty drink glass. "Along with some complimentary drinks." He looked around for Bruno but didn't see him.

"Reckon he's back at the main bar. Quite the crowd tonight," Jill said as she tapped the spin button of her machine.

"I'm going to visit the ATM, grab us some drinks, and then I'm going to win the jackpot," Carter said as he patted Jill on the shoulder.

"Say hi to that charming man if he's around."

Carter paused; he didn't understand what Jill was talking about.

"Oh Paddy," Carter said. "He's probably gone by now."

"Well, if he isn't, send him my way. Don't know what he sees in you."

"Me neither," Carter said under his breath.

Carter didn't realise how drunk he was until he started walking. All the Southern Comfort and Cokes he'd been drinking now circulated through his body as he swayed and weaved his way towards the main bar.

Bruno and another staff member were serving. Carter leaned on the bar and motioned to Bruno who readjusted his tiara.

"One second love," Bruno said as he filled an ice bucket and popped a bottle of Chardonnay in it and moved to the far end of the bar.

"Ready for that drink?"

Carter turned to see Paddy standing next to him. Paddy held an empty pint glass and a welcoming smile.

"I was just about to call it a night. But I can stay for another round," Paddy said.

There was a look of eagerness from the handsome Paddy that Carter did not share.

"I've got to head back to the pokies mate. Just out here to grab some drinks," Carter said, deflating Paddy's eagerness with a few choice words.

"Oh," Paddy said as he combed his thick black hair with his fingers and then scratched the back of his neck.

"Lost my money in there so gotta win it back," Carter said without a second thought of how that made him look.

"That's one strategy," Paddy said. He patted Carter on the back, "Another time then."

"Cheers," Carter said.

Paddy turned to leave but stopped. He turned back to Carter and lightly put his hand on top of Carter's. Carter's senses were so dulled from the alcohol he barely registered the touch.

"I don't know what happened to you today, but I don't think anything in this bar can help you." Paddy looked over to the pokies room. "Or in there. I'll be honest, I'm struggling a bit with Nelson's death. Can we talk?"

Carter bit down on his lip. Paddy caught the flirty insinuation.

"Not like that," Paddy said.

"Can't fault me for thinking it," Carter said as he started to focus on Paddy instead of the pokies.

Bruno stood in front of Carter and Paddy.

"Another Southern Comfort and Coke? I can bring it round to the pokies room in a few minutes."

Carter looked over to the pokies lounge before bringing his gaze back to Paddy and down at his hand over his. Carter flipped his hand round so his palm faced up. He curled his calloused fingers to hold Paddy's hand.

"Just a soda water, I'm done with the pokies tonight."

"Make that two," Paddy said.

Bruno nodded, "For an extra thrill, I'll put some lime in it."

Paddy and Carter found an empty booth at the far end of the bar, away from the booming speaker that was playing remixes of pop songs. Paddy leaned back in the booth and rubbed his temples.

"I've been racking my brains trying to remember anything that might have told me that Nelson was in danger."

Carter took a sip of his soda water. He knew Paddy thought he needed to speak to a detective but what he really needed was someone to listen.

"Ruminations are pretty standard for anyone connected to a murder victim. I know it's hard to stop over-analysing every conversation, catchup, or text message with Nelson. But it won't do you any good. You gotta move on."

Paddy nodded. "I get that, but there was something."

Carter raised an eyebrow. "It's a double edge sword, we don't want you to dwell on the smallest details, but the devil is in the details. Go on."

Paddy took a sip from his glass. "What do you know about escrow?"

"Not much to be honest. I don't deal with financial crimes often," Carter said.

"Most people only know about escrow when they are arranging a house or a flat deposit," Paddy said.

"I've been there, scrimping and saving for that deposit," Carter said.

"Nelson asked me about escrow. And at first, I thought he wanted to save up for a deposit. So, I explained the basics of it but told him the more important thing, given his promotion, was just to save. No point fussing about escrow if you don't have a deposit ready to buy a flat."

"Very sensible advice," Carter said.

"I don't think he took it on," Paddy said. He pulled a grimacing face as if he just ate a lemon. "The more I think about it, he was nowhere near ready with a deposit. But he was really interested in the company structures behind it. Like which company holds onto the deposit."

Carter moved closer to Paddy in the booth. The two were side by side. Paddy leaned his head against Carter.

"I don't know, it might be nothing," Paddy said. "Seemingly out of the blue, he's asking you about escrow?" Carter asked.

Paddy nodded. "It just wasn't in his character for him to ask me about abstract stuff. He's usually more focused on the here and now."

Carter mulled over what Paddy told him.

Nelson came from a poor family. Financial freedom is a big incentive for anyone – especially people who know what true poverty feels like – to commit a crime. If Nelson took a large sum of money in a shady way, he might have been trying to figure out a way to launder the money.

Carter started to sober up as all the different permutations floated around in his mind.

"Thanks for telling me this," Carter said. "But now the dwelling stops. That's an order."

Paddy smirked, "Any other orders, Detective?"

"Come home with me tonight," Carter said.

Paddy sat up and slid away from Carter "I'm going to be on the wrong side of the law and not follow that order. Another time when we both aren't so glum."

"Misery loves company," Carter said hoping Paddy would stay.

Paddy gave Carter a kiss on the cheek. "Take care and I'll see you soon."

Paddy departed, leaving Carter in the booth with his soda water. Carter's eyes followed Paddy as he left the bar. Paddy's shorts hugged his firm arse and Carter imagined all the things he wanted to do to it. Once Paddy left, Carter's eyes darted towards the pokies room as he finished his drink. Carter got up and leaned on the booth's table. He folded his arms as he weighed up his next moves.

Finally, he went home.

CHAPTER TWENTY-ONE

"Alright, ladies, gentlemen and my non-binary colleagues, day three of the investigation," Carter said.

Zhang took out a marker to scribe. Carter didn't envy him the hand cramp he was about to get writing down the shitstorm that happened last night.

"First news of the day. Unfortunately, Nelson's parents passed away yesterday from a suspected drug overdose." Carter paused. Those cold dead feet of Pete and Diane popped into his mind.

"Where did they get the junk from?" Hillier asked.

"Melbourne CBD is a sketchy area, so down any alleyway. You know users are everywhere there," Song said.

Carter frowned, "Ah so, they just willed a hit?"

Song let out a short laugh. "The power of thought."

Carter nodded, "Just think about scoring a hit, and magically you'll manifest a hit." Carter knew there were more important matters at hand, but Pete and Diane's deaths were a scab he wanted to pick at later.

"At the end of the day, their deaths aren't suspicious, and they aren't our case. We need to prioritise the investigation of Nelson and Moe's murders. How is CCTV footage coming along?" Carter asked.

"Not great," Song said. "I've identified about fifty-five cameras each with five or so hours of footage to review. I only have two officers reviewing the footage – almost three hundred hours of it. So, we are getting there, but let's not hold our breath. It'll help if we get some more staff."

"I'll talk to Davies. How about leads from yesterday's memorial," Carter said.

"Is James Hughes still a person of interest?" Hillier raised his voice, drawing everyone's attention.

"Short answer, no. His alibi checks out. Despite owning a bathhouse, being a forthright political candidate and being a bit abrasive doesn't make him a suspect," Carter said.

"But still worth investigating further?" Hillier asked.

"Nah Hillier, he's a dead-end at this point. We need to allocate our resources strategically. We don't have time to cast a net too wide and far. Has George Campbell given his statement?"

Detective Perry finished up his breakfast of choice, an egg and bacon roll. His pudgy hand brushed the crumbs off his dress shirt that fit snugly against his bulging pot belly.

The more Carter worked with Perry; the more Perry reminded Carter of any retired suburban dad. The type of retiree that focused all their energy on watching and commenting on cricket. The type of retiree that attends all five days of test cricket without batting an eye. Perry shunned that retiree life and channelled that energy to the job.

"Got it right here, boss," Perry said as he pulled out a file and began to flip through the pages. "George and Caitlin Campbell gave their statements yesterday afternoon. They were in the air while Nelson was murdered. Boarding passes and the airline records match. George admits to having a casual sexual relationship with Nelson. Like he said to you and Song, their last tryst had been six months ago. Nelson's phone location records corroborate that as well. George has also provided a DNA sample. I reckon it is a safe bet to rule him out as a suspect."

"Gossip travels fast at the City of Melbourne. George has resigned as CEO," Hillier said.

Zhang at the whiteboard had his fingers poised over George's photo to remove him from the suspect section. He glanced over his shoulder at Hillier.

"Are we swiping left with George?" Zhang asked.

"I wouldn't know what you mean," Hillier said with a cheeky smile across his face.

"Save it for the apps, gents. Perry's right," Carter said. "He can't be a suspect for the murder. But something doesn't make sense there. I don't believe in coincidences. His past relationship with Nelson and his car being stolen and used in these crimes – something doesn't add up. Let's keep him in the frame for now."

Zhang's hand returned to his side, as if awaiting further instructions.

"Any leads from Crime Stoppers?" Carter went on.

"We are still sifting through it all. Nothing credible yet, aside from a stack of messages suggesting we hire James Hughes as an officer," Perry replied.

Song smiled. She took an enlarged photo and passed it to Zhang to put on the whiteboard.

"Now, the good news," she said as she pointed to the photo of the gentleman Carter and Song spotted by the tree. "We've had a hit from the memorial surveillance team. During his walk home, this man took off his very expensive and trendy looking sunnies, and our team managed a few snaps." Song waited a few moments as the constables and detectives reviewed the photo. "Now which crack-shot officer here can tell me who this is?"

Song took out a card. "The right guess will win my coffee card for downstairs, which has a free coffee ready to be redeemed." Song tapped on the photo. "Come on, who wants a free coffee? Doesn't anyone watch the footy? This is Melbourne."

"Is that Special K?" Perry asked.

Song handed Perry her card and clapped. "Congratulations, Detective Perry. You are now the proud owner of a free coffee."

"I've actually switched to matcha lattes." Perry said.

"I hope Nic doesn't think this is a red flag," Song teased as she clutched her decolletage, feigning shock.

"You raise a good point, Song. What does our coroner friend Nic have to say about this? Is there another matcha latte session on the horizon?" Carter asked, joining in on the tease.

"Nic introduced me to them. She bought me one after the autopsy as a reward for not puking. And as she likes to remind you, DI Carter, she's a coroner's assistant, not a doc," Perry said as he artfully avoided the real question.

Perry usually had a ruby complexion, but Carter could have sworn it just turned a brighter shade.

Song snapped the card from his hand. "Well let's not waste this on you then." Song pulled another piece of paper from a folder and passed it to the constable to put on the board. "This is Special K."

"Are you sure it's him?" Hillier asked.

Song folded her arms across her chest, and she tapped her foot. "Come on, does anyone barrack for West Melbourne?"

"Nah, I don't barrack for them," Hillier replied.

"Well, I do, and that is Special K. Also known as Sam Kane, twenty-seven, full-forward for the West Melbourne Dingo's football team. I know this is a long shot. Still, he could be Nelson's mystery boyfriend, whom Abby mentioned. Coming out while playing as a professional footy player is probably a career-limiting move. They are still power washed in testosterone and phobias from the oval to the locker rooms," said Song.

"Plus, it would explain the *Footy for Dummies* book in Nelson's flat," Carter said.

Song smiled. "Exactly. And if he is the mystery boyfriend, it would explain why he was at the memorial and tearing up."

"We didn't spot any other sporting celebrities there. No reason for Special K to be there in an official capacity," Perry said.

"Doesn't look like he's a social justice warrior." Zhang piped up as he looked at his mobile. "His Insta profile doesn't exactly give off advocate vibes. More like hot jock with a strong case of the straight vibes."

"Too straight?" Hillier asked.

"Maybe," Zhang said, before freezing like a deer in headlights. He looked to Carter to judge if he'd overstepped his duties by giving an opinion.

Carter smiled, "Go on, the floor is yours. Give us your take."

"Maybe Special K meets the victim, enjoys a romp on the side. They get involved in match fixing. Enjoy the rush of the money coming in. Nelson recruits Moe to help. Nelson feels on top of the world. But he wants more from Special K. Nelson and Special K have a heated argument. One thing leads to another. Nelson threatens to expose the match-fixing scheme. Special K murdering him to keep his mouth shut," Zhang said.

"It's a possibility. I could check into the financials further," Hillier said.

Carter looked at the whiteboard and scanned the images of victims and suspects. "Actually. Pull all the financials for Nelson, his parents, George Campbell, and Moe Bashar. Maybe there is a financial connection between them all. Paddy, Nelson's mentor, mentioned Nelson developed an interest in escrow."

"Did he?" Song asked as she folded her arms.

"He contacted me about it," Carter hastened to add as he realised his mistake. He didn't want to let slip his encounters with Paddy.

"Sure thing, I'll get started on that. It'll be a beast of a task though," Hillier said.

"I'd give you a hand but I'm still going through photos and videos from the protest," Perry said.

"Zhang can assist," Carter said.

Zhang popped a cap back on a whiteboard marker. "Happy to help where I can, but I'm not very familiar with financial crime."

"Don't worry, I'll show you the ropes." Hillier stood and straightened his tie and adjusted his oversized watch encrusted with what Carter assumed were diamonds.

"Nice watch," Carter said.

"Aww thanks, graduation present from Pops. Not the one I wanted but it's okay," Hillier said.

Carter looked deadpan at Hillier and stopped himself from saying something snide. "Get started on that with Zhang. Perry, get us any intel from the protest. Song and I will interview Special K. Do you know his schedule?" Carter asked.

Song smiled. "He's training this morning. Just around the corner in West Melbourne."

Carter felt energised. Their first solid lead. "Let's watch the first bounce."

CHAPTER TWENTY-TWO

Carter and Song leaned against Carter's green Skoda
which he had parked in the footy oval's car park. Another
blustery summer day brought the heat and wind. It didn't
seem to affect the players. Decked out in their brown and
gold kits, the dozen or so passed the football to and fro.
ARL used a slightly smaller and rounder version of a
rugby ball. Other players weaved between pylons
staggered across the area.

Agility is the name of the game for any footy team to
win a match. Spread out across an entire oval, the players
kick, handball and run with a football to move it across
the grounds. Teams score points by getting the ball
through the four posts at each end of the oval.

"Surprised they're back to the pitch already. It's only
January and matches don't start till autumn," Carter said.

"No rest for the wicked after missing out on a spot in
the finals," Song said.

"Who do you think is to blame for their lost chance at
getting into the finals?" Carter asked.

Song tilted her head, "Special K missed some goals,
only scored a few points."

"What's the difference?"

Song let out a small laugh, "You live in Melbourne,
you gotta support footy. Players get six points when they
kick the ball through the two main goal posts. If the ball
touches the posts or goes through the two secondary
posts, they just get a single point. That night, I reckon
Special K scored five points instead of thirty."

"Yikes, bit of a difference," Carter said.

"Game winning difference. If he had made those
goals, the Dingos would have won and gone into the
finals."

The pair surveyed the players on the field, "Special K isn't here."

Carter squinted. "How can you tell?"

"I told you I barrack for the Dingos."

"Never pegged you as a big footy fan," Carter said.

"Whenever West Melbourne has a home game, I take my daughter to it. Just Mae and me. Aaron and Jake stay home and have their father–son bonding time. We all go as a family to see the female ARL West Melbourne games. Umma comes too, Dad is never around," said Song. "Reckon there is a better family atmosphere at the female games. Plus, the tickets are three-quarters the price."

Father–son bonding time. The concept hadn't yet gained popularity during Carter's childhood. He couldn't recall anything he'd actually done with his father. Even the man's image was hazy. He was a blank, save for the image of empty cans of beer in the lounge room corner that Carter Sr built into a castle.

"Special K is an interesting nickname," Carter said.

"No, it's not what you think," Song said. "Zero reports of drugs use. The name started when he was playing at the state level. You know how those nicknames start, bit of a prodigy, something special."

A coach blew a piercing whistle, and a dozen players gathered around.

"That's Courtney Ridge, first female Senior Coach for an ARL team," Song said.

Carter nodded. He didn't keep up with footy news too much but remembered the controversy when she first accepted the coaching role. Talkback radio exploded with comments that always spiralled into male chauvinism. Sometimes they fawned condescending concern.

"Don't get me wrong, she plays a great sport. I'm just worried a lass like her can't handle the men, you know?"

One commentator asked. Other times the commentators didn't hide their disdain.

"Think of all the hard-working male coaches out there who would be doing a better job."

The vitriol seemed to die down once West Melbourne made it to the semi-finals the previous year, the first time in five years.

As the detectives waited, half the players on the field grabbed neon orange singlets and stripped off their shirts. Not an ounce of fat across their midsections. Each of their broad shoulders defined beyond belief. Carter's jaw slightly dropped.

"Calm yourself, mate," Song said.

Carter pulled down his aviator sunglasses. "What? I can look. Don't tell me you don't enjoy the view."

The neon orange-singleted players started to jog across the field. The others began to do high jumps.

Song didn't seem as interested as Carter. "Nah, doesn't do it for me. Not in the slightest. Too muscular I reckon, not enough to hold onto on the sides. I like my men with more meat," Song said.

At that moment, a few bent down to stretch. They treated leg day seriously, with strong muscular lower bodies and thick thighs.

"Plenty of meat there," Carter laughed.

"Close your mouth. I think that goes against some professional code of practice."

Carter gently pushed Song. "Give a brother a break! I can look at the menu, just can't order."

"Can't order, or won't be served?" Song asked.

"Well, if Special K is barracking for my team, you never know. There's hope for an old dog like me."

The tone of the conversation shifted. Song kicked a few pebbles near her foot. "Would be hard though, keeping that type of secret inside, bottled up," she said.

Carter nodded in agreement. "From first-hand experience, it is not great."

"I sometimes worry about Mae and Jack. They're still my little babies but growing up fast. Mae will be a teen in five years. Jack, in seven. What if they don't feel comfortable talking to Aaron or me about their sexuality? I don't want them to bottle it up inside."

"Be the loving and open parents that I know you are, Song. If you make them feel supported, they'll come to talk to you," said Carter. "You know James was the first person I ever told."

"That you are gay?" Song asked.

Carter nodded.

Song's eyebrow arched. "That twat?"

Carter laughed. "I know. Poor choices, right? My first kiss was with James too, when I was in the army. He was my C.O."

He and James decided to do a dusk run through the temperate forest outside the Wagga Wagga military base. The pair followed a running path along a fast-moving river surrounded by Pine and River Red Gum trees that perfumed the air with a sweet, woody eucalyptus scent. Swift parrots sat on the tree branches whistling and squawking with one another.

Halfway through the run, sweat drenched Carter's t-shirt. He stopped and stripped it off, revealing a trim waistline and a furry chest. Carter had just started working out. His chest muscled up and defined thanks to his dedication to a new workout. At thirty-one, James was fitter and spryer than Carter. He hadn't even broken much of a sweat yet.

James pushed the bottle up towards Carter's mouth. "Drink it down, mate. It'll help."

Carter's dog tags clanked against the water bottle.

He heard birds high up in the trees – lorikeets with their bright orange chests and kookaburras chirping and quaking, all looking for a mate. It was springtime, and it wasn't only the birds that were in heat.

The two resumed running, branches cracked under the force of their military boots.

"Keep up," James yelled as he rounded a bend. Carter didn't mind running behind James, he snuck the occasional glance down at his beefy arse.

Carter sped up, planning to overtake him. He flew past James, but a second bend came up quickly. Carter tripped over his feet. He tumbled to the ground, a tornado of twigs and dirt swirling around him. Carter's head slammed against the damp ground.

"Shit, are you alright?" James asked.

Carter sat upright on the ground and brushed off the twigs and dirt. James crouched next to him and gripped his arm and turned it over. A few cuts and scrapes across both. Carter nearly froze as James grabbed Carter. James's thick, calloused hands had a warmth behind them that Carter wanted all over his body.

"Stop, it hurts," Carter said as he surveyed the cuts and bruises across his body.

"Don't be a poofter, mate. A bit of hurt is good for the soul."

Carter bit his lower lip before exhaling. "And if I am?"

"Hurt?" James laughed, "I can tell."

He extended a hand for Carter. Carter gripped the hand and James hoisted him up. Carter curled his lips in as the two shared a look. Carter's gaze wavered along with courage while James's gaze never wavered. Carter found his voice.

"A poofter is what I meant," Carter stammered. He breathed deep, relaxed his shoulders. "What if I'm a poofter."

Carter tensed his shoulders again, expecting a volley of punches from James. It didn't arrive.

"Congratulations. I'm just a regular fag myself," James said. He moved his rough and calloused hand up Carter's body. He gripped the nape of his neck and pulled Carter in for a kiss.

--

"You and he were out in the army?" Song's voice pulled him out of his reverie.

Carter now looked at a much older James through the one-way window.

"God no. That's why being open in the force was never a debate. I hated having to be in the closet in the army and with my family. From day one with the force, I put my pink foot forward," Carter said.

"I remember," said Song. "Reckon that's why I liked you. I always knew where you stood. Clear at work."

And a mess at home, Carter thought.

Song pointed a finger at a car turning into the car park. "There he is."

A black BMW rolled into view. Special K stepped out.

"Definitely the same guy from the memorial. Same hat and sunnies," Carter said.

Dressed in a white singlet, black shorts, and white shoes. Special K took out a duffle bag from the boot. Carter couldn't help but think about the meat under those shorts. He glanced down at his legs, shaved, not a hair in sight. No one is perfect, he thought to himself.

"Sam Kane?" Song asked as the pair walked over to him.

"Um, yeah, mates call me Special K." His voice had a nasal country twang to it. He towered over both Carter and Song. His XXL singlet strained across his chest, barely fitting his muscular frame. He had broad shoulders and was half a head taller than Carter.

Must be something in that country water, Carter thought.

The pair took out their badges.

"We are detectives investigating the murder of Nelson Harris," Carter said.

Special K took a pace backwards and scratched the back of his head.

"Look, I don't know how I can help." He moved to side-step them. "I'm already late for training today."

Carter blocked his path, raising a hand. "This will only take a few minutes of your time and sure beats a conversation down at the station."

Special K sighed, "What do you want?"

"How do you know Nelson Harris?" Carter asked.

Special K folded his arms. "Dunno, never heard of him before."

"Personally, I don't attend memorials for people I don't know. Any particular reason you attended his memorial last night?" Song asked.

Special K shrugged, and quickly said, "Nah."

The two detectives folded their arms in unison.

"I was just in the neighbourhood, didn't know what all the commotion was about. Shame about the lad. Not good to happen to anyone," Special K said, clearly lying. His shifting feet, his clenching hands, all his body language screamed deception but also fear. Carter really didn't want to get into an altercation with an individual who spent all day practising taking body blows if he could avoid it. So, he decided to deescalate.

"Did you know Detective Song barracks for your team?" He uncrossed his arms and stuck his hands in his pockets.

"True." Song kept her arms crossed. "That's why I noticed you at the memorial. I was planning to ask for your autograph, but you took a mobile call and got out of there fast before I could make it over."

"Ah yeah. You know, my coach called. She reminded me I had some stuff to do before today's practice. Had to get out of there quick smart." Special K seemed to relax a little.

"Pretty upsetting to learn about a young guy getting murdered?" Carter asked.

Special K shrugged. "Please, I gotta get to practice, alright?"

Song glanced down and made an attempt to find something in her pockets. "Well, sorry to bother you then. We should probably head off. I'd give you my business card, but we don't have any. Bloody budget cuts. How about you put my number in your phone. Just in case you remember anything."

Special K nodded before taking out his iPhone. "Go for it."

"040555..." Song said.

Special K's mobile suggested a contact already in his phone called Nelson. A common skirting-around-legal-boundaries trick that the detectives liked to use.

Special K froze.

"Oh no wait, those are the digits to Nelson's mobile number," Song popped her head around to catch a glimpse of what she knew was on the screen. "You have Nelson's mobile already saved. Now why would you have Nelson's number if you've never met him?"

Carter maintained his relaxed front, but inside his tension was at a knife point. If Special K was going to run it would be now.

Special K took a step back. "So I knew the guy, so what. Doesn't mean I killed him."

Special K moved to go around the detectives.

Carter blocked Special K's path.

"Now, we are going to have to have that longer conversation at the station," Carter said. "You can come with us quietly, or we can make a big production out of it. Your choice, mate."

"This is bullshit," Special K said.

"Please don't make this any harder. If you've got nothing to hide, then you don't have a thing to worry about," Carter said.

Song escorted Special K; Carter walked in front. He opened one of the rear doors of his Skoda.

"Have a seat." Carter helped Special K into the back seat of the car. As he sat down, his knees pressed up against the seat in front.

"I'll pull the seat forward," Carter said.

Song walked around to the other side of the car to get in but stopped. "Ah shit," she said and pointed.

Half a dozen footy players jumped over the field's fence and ran towards them. If the situation were different, Carter would have savoured the sight of six shirtless footy players running towards him and relished what would happen next.

Instead, Carter swore under his breath and felt the back of his belt for his truncheon and a canister of pepper spray. He didn't want to use force here. He imagined the headlines on the Herald Sun: six footy team members bow out due to police brutality. Or the alternative headline: six footy team members beat up two police officers. Let's try and avoid both situations, he thought.

"Special K, you alright? What's going on?" The pack leader asked the question. He looked like a Nordic god with sunburnt skin. Tall with long locks of blonde hair, who could probably bench press the car and run twenty kilometres afterwards without breaking a sweat. He took out his mobile along with a few of the other players.

"I'm recording this. Don't worry mate."

Mark and the other players stepped forward. The coach came hot on their heels. In footy shorts and West Melbourne polo top. Her hair was tied up in a messy top knot that bounced as she ran. She took off her sunglasses and glared at Carter.

"What's going on," she demanded, "Who are you?"

Great, just our luck, Carter thought. "My name is DCI Leo Carter." He flashed his badge. "Special K here is voluntarily helping us with an investigation."

"What investigation?" The coach stepped forward trying to peer into the car.

"If you'll just let us borrow him for a few minutes, then he'll be back on the pitch by this afternoon."

"Nah," Mark said. "Special K is staying with us. He's not going anywhere with you."

Mark passed his mobile to the closest player, "Keep recording this," he said. He moved a step forward to Carter.

"Stop right there, gents," Carter looked to Courtney.

"Hold up, Mark, lads. Everyone back up," Courtney commanded. "You guys head back to the field, alright? We are already behind on the training."

"They can't do this to Special K," Mark said.

"Turn off the mobiles and head back to the field," she replied.

The players shifted back and forth, grumbling.

"Now," Courtney said with leadership and command carrying her voice.

Slowly the players started to trudge away. Mark spat at Carter. A huge wad of saliva landed centimetres from Carter's boots.

Guess they'll edit that out of the footage they'll post about police being dogs and harassing their star player, he thought.

Courtney yelled towards Special K, "Don't say a word until we get legal down there, alright?"

Special K nodded through the car window.

"Not another word, all right," Courtney said.

"Thank you for helping calm things down," Carter said.

"That's fucked mate," she said, "You should have called ahead. We have a legal team and procedures here to avoid situations like that. What do you think they're going to do with that footage."

"We are within our right to question your player. Those players need to reflect on their behaviour," Song remarked.

Courtney shook her head as Song got into the car.

"Out of curiosity, when's the last time you spoke to Special K before today?" Carter asked. "He says he spoke to you last evening."

Courtney threw a look of disdain towards Carter before she regained her cool, calm composure and raised her middle finger. "Go fuck yourself."

"Know anything about match fixing?" Carter asked.

Courtney turned her back to Carter and walked back to the club.

"Thought so," Carter said. "Don't expect Special K back for training today."

CHAPTER TWENTY-THREE

A media scrum greeted Carter and Song as they brought a handcuffed Special K into Docklands Police HQ. Kris Oke led the pack with journalists, photographers and videographers filming the detectives every step.

"Can you confirm Nelson was targeted because he's gay?"
Kris asked and didn't give the detectives a chance to answer before firing off another question. "Was a homophobic word carved into the victim's chest?"

"No comment," Carter said as they entered HQ, leaving the pack of journalists at the door.

"Lawyer. Now," Special K barked the moment he sat down in the interrogation room.

"He could have requested one in the car," Song bemoaned under her breath as she and Carter left the interrogation room. A constable entered the room to supervise Special K.

In the observation room, Carter watched Special K for a few moments. There was not much to watch. Special K pulled up his hoodie over his head and rested his head on the table.

"Not many body language traits to glean from him," Carter said.

"Not yet," Song said.

"First real lead and already insulated from us by a lawyer. And we have a leak in the department. Someone told the journalists about the word carved into Nelson's chest. We are runners at starting blocks with their shoes untied," Carter said.

"So philosophical," Song remarked.

"Let's get our heads out of the clouds," Carter said as the pair sat down at a small table in the room. A stack of papers in a file folder was on the desk.

"Perry sent down the photos from the memorial," Song said.

"Let's develop a timeline of his movements at the memorial. And note any interactions he had," Carter said.

Thirty minutes passed, and the detectives had little to show. Special K entered the memorial, loitered around the tree, and walked home. There was no smoking gun in his movements.

As Carter was getting restless, Davies walked into the observation room.

"Lawyer's here," Davies said.

Special K furiously scratched his head while his lawyer, Jodie Day, sat next to him, jotting down notes on a pad of paper. She came to Docklands Police HQ as a plump storm wearing a black suit blazer and red high heels.

After the duty sergeant escorted Jodie to Special K's interrogation room, he described Jodie to Carter, Song and Davies. "Good luck, Detectives, I wouldn't last five minutes against her in a ring."

Carter, Song and Davies watched Special K and Jodie through the one-way mirror in the observation room. Jodie appeared to try to calm Special K down. Her body movements were long, slow, and gentle. Whereas his were short, sharp, and fast.

"Mind your Ps and Qs with this one," Davies said.

"You know her?" Carter asked.

"Debate club at university. More recently at Fruit Cup." Davies said.

Carter smirked. That was the queer-networking group. He never attended but knew Davies occasionally did. He knew he failed at networking. He just felt awkward trying to network and promote himself. If he ever got promoted, he'd need to adjust that, and God knows what else.

"A lawyer is a lawyer. They don't get the queer free pass," Carter said.

"I'm not suggesting it. Only providing intel, and you need a lot of it. She is formidable with a retainer to match. She doesn't work for nobodies." Davies patted Carter's shoulder "What's your plan?"

"Get him to open up about the victim. No doubt in my mind, Special K is the secret boyfriend. Nelson wants more from Special K. He refuses. A fight ensues. He strangles Nelson. The strangulation, that type of anger makes sense for a scorned lover. Then he tosses his body outside Vapour. Maybe that's where they first met? One thing still bothers me. Sure, he's a big guy, could have done it all himself. But I doubt it. So does Special K rope in Moe and then kill him? Is there another accomplice?" Carter said.

"You won't find out till you ask," Davies said. "Look at him. He looks like he's regretting something. Focus on that."

Carter looked down at his boots. "Special K just treated Nelson like a boy-toy. Something he got to play with when he felt bored or horny. Maybe got him a gift or two when he wanted Nelson to put out. How much regret could he feel?"

"And it still doesn't explain Moe's involvement," Song said.

Davies placed her finger on the glass. "Whatever happened, he is our best lead. You two need to figure out how he fits into this."

--

Carter closed the door to the interview room. Without exchanging any pleasantries, he and Song took their seats across from Special K and his lawyer.

I'm leading this dance, Carter thought as he breathed in slowly. As he exhaled, he pressed the recording button on the machine. A long chime sounded, indicating that the device started recording.

"Good morning, this is Sam Kane's interview, also known as Special K. Present today are Detective Inspector Leo Carter, Detective Inspector Emily Song, Sam Kane, and Sam's solicitor, Jodie Day. I'll allow them to state their name for voice recognition."

As each person stated his or her name, Carter watched Special K.

"Sam," he said. His brown eyes darted between Carter and the machine as he spoke. His clean-shaven jaw moved slightly. He kept his mouth slightly closed, barely enough for the words to leave.

"Do you have a surname, Sam?" Carter asked. He pitched his voice to match a masculine coach. Firm, assertive and dominating Special K.

Special K had a sheepish look to his face and was about to speak. But Ms Day interjected right away.

"My client is missing a day of practice right now for this inconvenience. Given his income relies on practice and training, we expect this issue to be resolved quickly."

Interesting that she thinks this is an issue, not an interrogation, Carter thought.

"The duration and whether there will be any subsequent interviews really depends on Sam's responses today. Now Sam, will you take us through your activities last Sunday? Day and night, please."

Day leaned into Special K. She held a manicured hand over her mouth while whispering into his ear. Carter could've sworn she dropped some of her fingers, leaving her middle finger extended and directed at them.

"I had my footy training. Did some weights at the gym afterwards. Met up with some mates for dinner. Went home after that."

Ms Day interjected. "We will be providing sworn statements from various upstanding citizens to account for his whereabouts."

Carter let out a slight laugh. Upstanding citizens!

"We look forward to receiving those upstanding statements." Then, to Special K, "After dinner, you went home? What did you then do?"

"Watched some telly."

Song asked the next question, "What did you watch?"

"Dunno. One of the house reno programs Aussie Flips."

Carter kept his eyes on Special K. His mouth did a slight smile.

Song scrolled through her iPad. "Mate, try again. Aussie Flips wasn't on last Sunday night."

When he lies, he says dunno, Carter observed.

"Watched it on demand," Special K said.

"Did you use your phone to stream it?" Carter asked.

"Probably," Special K said.

"Fair assumption if someone messaged you, you'd have answered pretty quickly," Carter said.

"Guess so," Special K said.

"What time did Nelson Harris message you?" Carter asked.

His eyes lit up at the familiar name.

"Dunno," Special K said.

Carter jabbed, "Don't know when he messaged you?"

Ms Day leaned over and whispered in Big Ed's ear.

"My client chooses not to answer that question at this juncture," Ms Day said.

"We can come back to that. Let's start with something simple then," Carter said.

Special K seemed startled by Carter's directness.

"How about you explain your relationship with the deceased," Carter continued.

Special K avoided eye contact and stared down at the table and shrugged, "Dunno, met him a few times, had a few pints."

"Pints? He seems like a vodka soda type of guy," Song said.

"Nah, he didn't like skinny bitch drinks," Special K said.

"You're down with the queer lingo," Carter said.

Special K's eyes darted towards Jodie. Carter smirked; he landed a blow.

Jodie leaned over to Special K and whispered in his ear.

Special K nodded. "No comment."

Nelson meant something to him, Carter thought. "Tell us about the first time you met Nelson?"

"Met for a beer in St Kilda, I reckon."

"This beer a precursor to casual sex?" Song asked. "You used a dating app to connect with him?"

Special K's shoulders hunched up. That terse smile came back — the squinting lines around his temples formed from too many days on the field and too little sunscreen. Ms Day and Special K whispered to each other again.

"Yeah, we fooled around a few times," he said

"How many times did you engage with the victim in a sexual situation before his death?" Carter asked.

"Look, yeah, we had a casual thing going. A few times a week for the last six months," Special K said.

"That sounds like a budding relationship," Song said. "I'm lucky to have sex with my hubby once a month. What do you think DCI Carter?"

Carter nodded his head. "That's a relationship."

There's the loose thread, time to pull, Carter thought.

"Nelson obviously thought the frequency and the duration made a relationship," Carter said.

Song scrolled through her iPad again. "Your Instagram account says otherwise. Not one picture of you and Nelson together."

"If I were Nelson, I'd be pretty upset, thinking I had a boyfriend. But really, in reality, he was in the closet." Carter shook his head, "Such a shame."

"Is there a question in this speculation, Detective?" Ms Day's steely black eyes looked straight at Carter.

"Why were you so scared to admit that you were in a relationship?" Carter kept his eyes on Special K.

"Ask a different question, Detective. You are aware of the precarious situation my client is in given his standing in the football community," Ms Day said. "My client has no further comments on his relationship with the deceased. It was casual in nature."

Song jumped in. "I'd hate to have been in Nelson's shoes. Always home pining for more than a casual fling. He wanted to have more than just the occasional post-sex cuddle."

"Nah," Special K said.

"He wanted more from you," challenged Song. "What happened? Did he threaten to out you?"

"What about match fixing? Was he placing bets for you?" Carter asked. "He wanted more money, he threatened you. Didn't he?"

Special K's eyes went wide. "He'd never do that." His eyes squinted before he wiped a tear from his eyes. "He had a good heart."

"What bullshit," Carter said. "Let's be frank, alright? Nelson was getting upset at you. It had been brewing for some time. Always on the sidelines. Yeah, you came over to his, had a few tender moments. Maybe a drink at your local, but that was it. And look at him, a guy happy with his sexuality."

Carter was well aware of this modus operandi given that he'd himself left a lot of men hoping for more than he could give. He saw his younger self in Special K, and it filled him with contempt.

He continued, "Sunday night, you pull your usual trick – a text message, asking if he's up. He, of course, laps up the chance to see you. But that night something different happened. He had a few drinks, liquid courage. He comes over to your place. You two get a bit frisky, have a root. But then he takes control and says he needs more from you. He doesn't want to be in your shadow anymore. Nelson wants to hold your hand at brunch. Hell, he wants to go to brunch with you! You refuse, of course, callous to his feelings. He threatens to expose you?"

Special K crossed his massive arms.

"Didn't he?" Carter persisted. "Maybe says he has a video or two of you along with a few dick pics? If those hit the internet, there's your career down the drain. A straight-sex video gives you street cred. You eating Nelson's arse makes you the subject of mockery."

Special K's breath grew shallow and sharp. Carter struck his final blow.

"Or was there another reason to kill him? Did you find out he'd been sleeping with his co-worker? You say you loved him. Did you love him too much and in the heat of the moment, you strangle him? A crime of passion. You were cornered, who helped you move the body? One of your footy mates?" Carter asked.

Special K's frypan-like hands slammed the table in a thunderous smack. The reverberations shook the recording machine.

Carter's hand fell to the panic button underneath the table. Song leapt out of her chair, truncheon behind her back, ready to be taken out. Tears streamed down Special K's face.

"Fuck you. I loved him." He jabbed a finger in Carter's direction.

Carter felt the sting of the words.

"I could never kill Nelson; he was the one. He got me. I got him. We just needed some time to sort through it all," Special K said.

"You didn't love him, you used him. He wasn't any better than a cum rag for you. A cum rag that you dumped outside a bathhouse." Carter knew he had gone too far.

"You looking for a smack?" Special K clenched his fists on the table. Ms Day placed a hand on Special K's broad shoulder.

Carter smirked. "Is that what you said to Nelson when he threatened you?"

Special K roared to life. "I said I didn't kill him." He slammed both fists on the table again. "He never threatened me. Are you fucking thick, mate?"

"It's alright, Sam. They've heard." She started to rub his shoulder, calming him down. "Now, I have my own question, Detectives. How did you choose to bring in my client today?" Ms Day asked.

Fuck, she knows, Carter thought.

"We spotted him at the victim's memorial. At this point in the investigation, we are attempting to determine the victim's last movements," Song said.

"So, the police saw him in a park and thought it appropriate to bring him in for questioning?" Ms Day asked.

God damn it. Carter maintained a steady gaze as he and Ms Day continued to spar.

"After denying knowing the victim, my colleague noticed the victim's number listed in your client's phone," said Carter.

"How did you get access to my client's locked phone?" Ms Day asked.

"Your client willingly opened his phone," Carter said.

"Are you aware you need a warrant to search an individual's mobile, Detective?" Jodie asked.

"Not in all circumstances," Carter said.

She held her hand up before Carter could speak. "You provided my client with an inaccurate number. The number that matches the deceased. That is an illegal and circuitous way to access my client's mobile. And no judge will permit my client's mobile into evidence."

"Regardless, your client had every opportunity to speak truthfully to us. He chose not to," Carter said.

"As you see, my client is both grieving and attracts significant public attention. His reluctance to speak publicly shouldn't be punished," she said.

"With or without the mobile evidence, your client's behaviour is suspicious and warrants an explanation. He knows the intimate details and habits, routines, and most likely whereabouts of the deceased. As the victim's lover, he's a prime suspect for Nelson's murder," Carter said.

Ms Day stood up and beckoned Special K. "Unless my client is under arrest, I'm taking him home. The amount of distress you've put him through is distasteful. Come along, Sam."

Carter waved his hand. "He is free to go but needs to stay in Melbourne as we will have follow-up questions."

Special K stood up and wiped another tear from his eyes before giving Carter the finger. "I loved him."

I know, I'm sorry. Is what Carter wanted to say. Instead, all Carter mustered was "We will be in contact."

The door slammed shut as they left.

"Sam Kane and Jodie Day have departed; this concludes this interview." Carter pressed the recording button. He took out his earpiece and threw it against the wall.

"Projecting much?" Song asked. "What happened there? You almost got into a fist fight with him."

"Sorry," Carter said.

A light flicked on in the observation room. Davies, Hillier Jr and Zhang stood in there facing him.

"In my office. Now," said Davies before she flicked off the light.

Song pulled on her collar as she got up. "She's pissed."

Carter nodded. "You go ahead. I'll be there in a minute."

As the interrogation room door closed behind Song. Carter sat still in the uncomfortable hard steel chair in the interrogation room. He let out a heavy sigh as he took out his mobile phone. He opened his lotto app.

Carter saw the gambling limit on the app.

"Fuck."

--

Davies funnelled her frustrations and annoyances into the tiny blue stress ball as she sat behind her desk. The wrinkles in the corners of her eyes became more pronounced with each squeeze of her stress ball and the sweeping glares at the officers in her office.

Carter sat in one seat, Song in the other and Zhang sat on the edge of a table piled high with papers and a moving box. While Hillier just stalked the scene, waiting to pounce and make a kill.

"What the hell happened in there? You lost control in there pretty quick," Davies said.

Carter tried to regain his composure by combing his thick black hair back with his fingers. Resting his hands on the back of his head he looked down and saw sweat stains on his polo shirt. He quickly brought down his arms and nodded. "I did."

"That's an understatement," Hillier chimed in as he tugged down his form-fitting dress shirt. Hillier looked like he fell from a men's fashion magazine. With a paper-thin level of empathy.

"Do you want to tell me how the media learned about the carving on Nelson's chest?"

Hillier glanced over to Zhang. Zhang's brown eyes darted between Hillier and Carter. He didn't say anything. He just stood alongside Hillier with a weird, pitying expression on his face.

"I might have let that slip when we interviewed Craig Jr," Hillier said.

"Thought so, a bit of warning would have been appreciated. Getting harassed by journalists threw me off my game," Carter said.

"That's not an excuse," Davies said.

"Regardless, I don't think Special K is a suspect. We are looking for someone else," Carter said.

"Nah, it's definitely him, Superintendent." Hillier took his case straight to the boss. "This guy," he cocked a thumb in Carter's direction, "Screwed up our chance at getting a confession."

Carter gripped the armchairs. He wished he held Davies's stress ball to slam it into Hillier's smug face.

"My fault, boss," Song said. "I tricked Special K into opening his phone. That's on me."

Carter placed a hand on Song's shoulder. She wore a green silk blouse with a clinched waist. Song gave off that natural allure that she knew it fitted like a glove and she didn't care. Even owning up to a mistake, Song was consistently collected and composed.

Carter shook his head. "Don't try and cover for me."

Davies stood up and picked up a glass behind her and poured herself a whiskey. She drank it down in two gulps. The four of them watched in silence.

"What?" She said. "It's lunchtime. I've been up since 5 a.m. I need a drink to deal with the shitshow you've created."

"That Detective Carter created," Hillier said.

"I don't care who is at fault here. At the end of the day, it's the department and my head. Is Special K our primary suspect?" Davies asked.

"Yes," Hillier said.

"No, he's not," Carter said.

Hillier stood up now, pacing around behind Carter and Song, marking his territory.

"Special K knew the victim, had his number in his phone, which of course we now can't use in court. He meets the profile – closeted man, in fear of reprisals, his career down the toilet – you name it. He had every reason to kill Nelson and more than enough physical strength."

Carter jumped from his seat. He and Hillier were inches from each other. Like two boxers, muscles flexed, adrenaline kicking in — ready to fight.

"And how do you explain Moe then?" Carter said.

Davies poured herself another whiskey and one for Song. The two clinked their glasses while ignoring the testosterone on show in front of them. Carter and Hillier maintained a steely eye-contact waiting for the other one to flinch.

"Why is it necessary to explain him at all?" Hillier asked. "For all we know the two murders are completely unrelated."

Davies tilted her head towards Carter. Song followed suit. Zhang kept his hands folded in front of him. His index and middle fingers tapped his muscular bicep as if the taps were morse code, signalling S.O.S.

"You're the boss, you can stop this," Song said to Davies.

"Not the boss for long" she replied. "But all right. Gents, both of you sit down. Now."

The round ended in a draw. Hillier moved to sit down. His shoulder struck Carter's chest as he moved. Carter clenched his fist. More than anything he wanted to punch the pretensions from him.

Song tugged at Carter's pant leg. "Sit down."

Davies finished her drink. "DCI Carter is still in charge, leading this investigation Detective Hillier, so you'll show him due respect."

Hillier shook his head. "It's the wrong choice, ma'am. He is missing the point. He cannot see what is right in front of his face."

Carter looked up. "Where you can help us is by doing the job that I already tasked you. Start pulling those financial records."

"Righteo," Hillier stomped off, slamming the door behind him.

"Zhang," Carter said.

Zhang formed a terse smile. He reminded Carter of a child of divorce, unsure who to barrack for.

"Can you pull Special K's phone logs? He got a call during the memorial last night. I want to know who called him. After that, give Hillier a hand," Carter said.

"Sure thing," Zhang said as he quickly left the room. He made sure to quietly close the door behind him.

The trio breathed a bit easier with the two junior officers out of the room.

"You're giving Hillier a lot of leeway here," Carter said.

Davies nodded, "That's what happens when you're the assistant commissioner's son. And he's not wrong, in my books, Special K looks like a prime target."

"Mine too," Song said. She looked over to Carter, "Sorry, but he has a motive."

The two sets of eyes rested on Carter. To the outside world, they had his back, but they still needed justification.

"He didn't do it. That grief, it's real, organic. He's not an actor. Nelson's death is a huge shock to him. I'm not saying he's squeaky clean. There is something he's not telling us."

Carter raised his arms; palms open to physically plead with Song and Davies.

"I'll eat my shoe if I'm wrong," Carter said.

Davies nodded. "Keep your shoes on for now. what's the saying – two steps forward, one step backwards?"

Carter nodded. "I get it, but boss, results will follow."

"They better start or else you'll find your chances of promotion slipping away.

Davies finished her whiskey in a single gulp and flicked on her computer. Her signal that this conversation had ended.

CHAPTER TWENTY-FOUR

Carter left HQ, into the windy tunnel that was Spencer Street. The skyscrapers funnelled the breeze down the street creating a wind tunnel that stirred up the dust from a construction site next door. Carter put on his aviators to block out the sun and the debris floating around. He had a choice, walk north into the wind, or south with the wind on his back.

It's what I do isn't, Carter thought. He started walking south along Spencer Street with the wind pushing him along. I just go with the flow and where it takes me. Carter started speed walking along the street, weaving in and out of slow-moving pedestrians. Where am I going, he thought as he passed a slow-walking couple.

Carter stopped and moved to the edge of the sidewalk and looked inside the newsagent that sold the lotto tickets.

Fuck it, Carter thought.

He walked into the newsagent and approached the teenage clerk. The kid munched away on a bag of crisps while he scrolled aimlessly on his mobile.

If he doesn't look up by the count of three, I don't have to do this, I'll just leave, Carter told himself.

One.

The kid's hand went into the bag of chips.

Two.

The kid sighed heavily at something on his phone.

Three.

As if released from a spell, Carter turned on his heel.

The kid looked up "You all right mate?"

Carter didn't answer as he left the shop.

I didn't gamble, he thought to himself.

A wave of sadness suddenly struck Carter, turning his smile into a frown.

He messed up that interrogation of Special K, yes, but that didn't mean he didn't believe him. He seemed so confident, so sure that he loved Nelson. I wish I was that open. But how confident was Special K really, being still in the closet?

Carter stopped in front of a series of shopfronts. Further along, was a barbershop and a 24/7 gym. He stood in front of a shop with black-out windows and a simple sign at the top saying The Stables, another bathhouse.

Thankfully for Carter, this one wasn't owned by an ex-lover of his.

"Different type of bite for lunch," said Carter under his breath as he walked through the door with its overly stylised chrome horseshoes and cowboy hats on heavily tinted black glass.

--

Carter swapped his clothes for a white towel so small it barely covered his arse and cock. He walked down a dimly lit hallway while house music flowed out of the speakers. Along the walls of the hallway were pictures of men in various stages of disrobing. As Carter reached the end of the hallway, the final shot was a naked man wearing a leather cap. His muscular back faced Carter. He was turned slightly to see his profile. He had a thick scruffy bread. One arm was flexed and pointed to the main area of The Stables.

The sex on-premises venue had an open plan lounging area with a long bar on one side, with bar tables and sofas scattered around. On the other side of the room was a door to the movie theatre, which alternated between hardcore porn movies and Disney animated classics. A staircase between them went up to private rooms and down to the showers, spa and darkrooms.

Piece of meat. That was the feeling Carter felt when he walked into the open area. He always hated the feeling of being watched. But today felt different as the lunchtime crowd of men scattered around the floor looked Carter up and down. The group were mostly in their late twenties to early forties. Carter guessed most of them were suits who worked in the CBD. He strutted his way across the floor to the staircase going down to the spa.

The spa's warm bubbles massaged Carter's sore body as he slipped into the empty twelve-seater spa. Letting out a long sigh, he allowed the warmth from the water to relax his entire body.

He wondered if Nelson and George Campbell ever hooked up here. The Stables is less than ten minutes away from Melbourne Council offices at Swanston and Little Collins Streets. Regardless, Nelson and George split up months ago, and Nelson and Special K were together. Probably for the long run if things hadn't turned out the way they did. So why kill Nelson then Moe?

A man slipped into the spot next to Carter in the spa. He was slightly younger. Mid-thirties, clean-shaven with an athletic build. Definitely the corporate type on his lunch break, Carter thought.

"You've got a great bod," the man said as he moved through the water to straddle Carter.

"Thanks," Carter said as gripped the firm arse of the man. "I'm—"

The man cut Carter off before he could finish, "I don't care."

His finger formed circles around Carter's nipple. It spiralled from large to small and small to large. With each rotation, the finger switched between fingertip and nail. Smooth then sharp, around, and around. The circle grew smaller and smaller, before pinching his nipple between forefinger and thumb. Carter was fully erect. The man tilted his arse to and fro as it rubbed against Carter's cock.

"I have a room upstairs," he whispered in Carter's ear, "Or we could hop in the shower."

He doesn't want to get to know me, Carter thought. I'm a masturbation tool to him.

The first tool from the shed for him to use. A means to an end of no specific value. Just sheer convenience based on time and location.

What if Nelson and Moe were never the intended targets but only people who had been used and then discarded in the effort to achieve some greater end? There was only one connection between them: James Hughes. But even that was tenuous. James didn't have any connection to Nelson. Nelson had just been dumped in an alley adjacent to property James owned.

Carter let out a quick grunt as the man pulled on his nipple again. Carter was too deep in his own thoughts to give him anymore.

But could Carter be sure James didn't know Nelson? Could James even be sure? Could they have met like this and just not exchanged names?

Carter felt the man's hands caress his body. His thoughts on the case continued to divide his attention.

And James was a public figure now. Just because you don't remember someone doesn't mean they don't remember you.

Assuming that James had been telling the truth at all.

No, he'd let his fondness for James overshadow the obvious. James was the link and Special K was probably just another dead end. "Come on, let's hop in the shower," the man said.

"I'm sorry, I can't," Carter said.

"Sure you can," the man gripped Carter's throbbing cock.

Carter grabbed the man's hip and moved him to the spa seat next to Carter.

"I gotta go."

"Cock tease," the man said as he crossed his arms and sunk deeper into the spa.

--

"You look flushed, big meal?" Song asked.

Carter took a seat at his desk "My eyes were bigger than my stomach. But my break gave me an idea. What if Nelson and Moe are just pawns? We know Nelson had been asking about escrow, which was out of character for him. What if this isn't a hate crime or a crime of passion? What if both of them were collateral damage from some larger scheme?"

"You think they were part of a criminal conspiracy?" Song furrowed her brow. "Or do you mean that both might have had ties to the same or competing criminal gangs?"

"Either? Both?"

Song nodded, "The links between Special K and Moe are pretty dubious at best, but he's still my top pick for Nelson."

"And if evidence surfaces giving Special K an alibi?" Carter said.

"I'll believe in true love again, I suppose." Song's phone rang. She had a perplexed look on her face and nudged Carter with a pen. "Ok, send her up." She turned towards Carter. "You have a visitor. One Mercedes Lewis, from the hotel where Nelson's parents overdosed."

"Not the most helpful person or even someone I ever wanted to see again," Carter said.

"Apparently, she has something to show you," Song said.

"I'll fetch her, can you get the conference room ready." Carter asked.

Song nodded. "We'll need a laptop, apparently."

Carter arched his eyebrow. "Now I'm interested."

--

"You only got water, no coffee or a cordial?" Mercedes blew a bubble with her gum. It burst. Loudly. She continued noisily chomping on the gum. She sat at the head of the conference room table as she spun a USB in between her French manicured fingernails.

Carter and Song sat at one side of the table.

"Not today, Mercedes. Just water. What can we do for you?" Carter asked.

"More like what can I do for you." She tossed Carter the USB. "You cops are pretty sloppy. Open the video file."

Carter picked up the USB and plugged it into the laptop.

"What are we going to find on this?" Song asked.

"Someone visited Nelson's parents before they died. Like I said, I was quitting. Thought I'd check the CCTV footage before my shift just for shits and giggles. Then I see that, downloaded it for you."

Carter opened the video and projected it onto the primary monitor in the conference room. Mercedes stood up next to the monitor.

"Alright, look. Two cameras one on either end of the hallway of the floor where those people died."

Carter nodded as he drummed the table with his fingers. His patience was wearing thin. "Yes, I was there. I remember."

"Hit the space button," Mercedes commanded.

"Yes, boss," Carter said with a strong hint of sarcasm.

The video on the screen started, time-stamped three hours before Carter arrived to find Pete and Diane's bodies.

"Alright, look," Mercedes said.

The lift door opened, and a man in a grey hoodie, cap and sunnies walked out. "Keep your eyes on him, alright?"

She pointed a finger at the man before blowing a bubble with her gum.

Song wrote a note and passed it to Carter. It read: same clothes.

Carter looked up at the image. The man walking down the hallway looked like he was wearing the same hoodie that Moe had when he fled Vapour. The man kept his head down and slowed his pace before he kneeled down outside a door. The man stood up, knocked on the door and bolted down the hallway.

"That room is where the dead couple was staying," Mercedes said.

Seconds later, the CCTV footage showed Pete opening the door. He was clearly crying and knelt down to pick up what was left at his door. He had a confused look on his face. Then Pete closed the door.

"I reckon, we all know what that guy left at their doorstep," Mercedes said.

Carter grimaced. "You're right. Any video on the guy?"

"Nope, I checked the other cameras. The guy in the grey leaves the lobby. No real video of his face."

"Thanks, Mercedes for bringing this in. Pretty good work. You know, a career in the force might be in your future. Better than working in a hotel. They are recruiting for the next intake. Happy to be a reference for ya."

Mercedes blew another bubble before popping it. "Maybe. Still seems like a pretty shit job."

Carter smiled, "It has its days, good and bad."

"I'll have an officer escort you out of the building," Song said as the pair left the room.

Carter leaned back in the conference room chair. His mind was swirling. Carter scrolled the video back and hit play. He watched the figure walk down the hallway and drop the gear in front of Pete and Diane's hotel room. Carter took out his notebook and began scribbling notes. He observed the man didn't show his face and knew where the video cameras were. The dealer also didn't stick around to get paid. Given the pair were escorted back to the hotel by police, they wouldn't have had the opportunity to purchase gear on the street.

Song came back into the room.

"So, it wasn't an accidental overdose. Someone wanted Nelson's parents out of the picture," Song said.

Carter nodded his head in agreement. "Our murder investigation has jumped from two victims to four. Whoever is behind this is very organised. But they've already made a mistake."

"What's that?" Song asked.

"The clean syringe. Let's check the toxicology report. I bet my badge that gear was high quality, super potent. Guaranteed to give an overdose," Carter said.

"Demonstrates this wasn't a small-time dealer giving a hit," Song said. "Play the footage again."

Carter pressed play. The hotel lift door opened, and the grey figure stepped out once more.

"Could it be Special K?" Song asked.

The pair squinted.

"I reckon no. He's not broad like Special K. This guy is more compact, still fit but not footy fit," Carter said.

"Agree. Someone was worried enough about what Nelson told his parents that he killed them," Song said. "Which might give your conspiracy theory some wings."

"That man is the first solid link between Nelson and Moe we've found," Carter said. "Or at least his hoodie is."

Carter felt his pulse start to quicken. Excitement flowed through his blood.

"We need to confirm if that hoodie is the same one Moe had on," Carter said.

He tried to contain his excitement, but Carter knew that the hoodie connected the four murders together. And some very powerful people were trying to prevent them from finding any links between the murders.

Song gave a terse smile. "That's going to be hard. There are a lot of grey hoodies in Melbourne."

"Not as many black ones," Carter joked.

Song ignored the joke, "You were closest to Moe when he fled Vapour. Do you remember any features or marks?"

Carter pictured himself chasing Moe. Arm within reach of him. He winced as he remembered his tumble at Vapour where he cut his shoulder.

"Moe wore one of those gym bro hoodies at Vapour."

"Gym bro?" Song asked.

"You know that brand all the influencers wear. The one with the infinity circle logo on the sleeves."

"You've fallen for a thirst trap or two, aye? Ever used their discount code?" Song teased.

"Focus please," Carter said with a smile on his face.

Carter played the footage again.

The man in the hoodie walked down the hallway again. Carter paused the footage.

"It's grainy video but there it is." Carter pointed to the man in the hoodie. "You can see the infinity logo on the sleeve."

"If we get our hands on that hoodie and there is DNA evidence of Moe, that's our link to connect these four murders," Song said.

"Until we get concrete evidence, our working theory is a criminal conspiracy," Carter said.

"Agreed," Song said. "But to do what?"

"I wish I knew." A buzzing noise came from Carter's mobile on the table. He'd received a text message from Jodie Day: Meet me at Railed, six pm sharp.

"I've been summoned by Special K's lawyer for a drink this evening."

"What does his lawyer want?" Song asked.

"No idea. Reckon I'll be able to eliminate him from our investigation though," Carter said.

"And we're back to square one." Song folded her hands in her lap. "This time with an even shakier lead."

Another buzzing noise came from the table.

"Popular guy today," Song said.

Carter checked his mobile. This time it was a text message from Paddy.

Carter's face lit up as he opened the message.

'Thanks for the chat last night. Can we do it again? Hectic day for me here. Our IT system has locked everyone out. I'll need a drink tonight. First round on me at Railed? Xx'

Carter was about to respond that he'd love to grab a drink with Paddy but would need to do it on another night when he made another link.

"You know I first met Bailey at Railed?"

"The footy son?" Song asked.

"He was at Vapour on the night of Nelson's murder."

"We've ruled out Vapour and anyone there as suspects," Song said.

"If we have a criminal conspiracy afoot then there might be other collateral players involved, victims, perpetrators and a few pawns. I reckon Bailey wasn't one hundred per cent truthful with us."

CHAPTER TWENTY-FIVE

In Carter's mind, a real sign of a suburb's wealth was the width of its roads. Every time he drove through the affluent suburb of Brighton, he was always amazed by the scale. Not only were the roads wide enough for two-way traffic, a bike lane and car parking, but most roads also had a median strip planted with eucalyptus trees that provided a full, rich green canopy. Concerns of drought and water restrictions skipped this suburb. Carter parked his Skoda in front of a gated mansion then walked up and rang the intercom.

"Hello." A woman's voice came through.

"Gabrielle? It's Detective Carter, I'm here to speak to you and Bailey about an active police investigation."

A buzzing noise sounded as the gate's door slowly swung up.

"You had best come in, Detective. I have heard about Bailey's trip to Vapour."

The plot's footprint afforded room for a three-storey house with pool, conservatorium and tennis court.

As Carter walked along the cobblestone path towards the front door, he thought about the first time he visited Bailey's mother, Gabrielle. It was the Monday after Carter had chased a bunch of teens who robbed a pharmacy. The idiot teens didn't know what prescription drugs to look for and ended up stealing pill bottles of paracetamol. Bailey had dropped his driver's licence during the robbery. Carter found it and decided to stop by that evening.

Bailey was 'detoxing' from all the paracetamol in his room as Gabrielle had so delicately put it when Carter arrived. As Gabrielle and Carter talked more, it became clear to Carter that money doesn't solve any of life's problems. It just provides a softer pillow to recover on.

Gabrielle spoke for Bailey that evening, apologising for his behaviour. Well, the lawyer did the speaking. They were expecting the police and had their script ready. They reinforced that Bailey was just shy of eighteen years and he would liaise with the Crown prosecution on remand alternatives as Bailey was still a minor.

As Carter found out while running a background check, Bailey had a considerable record in his youth. Those records were sealed thanks to the influential and highly paid lawyer.

The lawyers mitigated Bailey's behaviour from his footy career. Too many concussions playing state-level footy and the pressure of being the son of one of the greatest and deceased footy coaches, Mitch Ross.

Or as Gabrielle said, "Sometimes he lashes out when it becomes too much."

Carter pitied Gabrielle and had a soft spot for Bailey, but this case needed to be solved.

A maid escorted Carter through the expansive house into the conservatorium that overlooked Brighton Beach. One part sitting room and two parts greenhouse. The conservatorium was circular in shape with a glass roof that exposed the plants in the room with daily sunlight. The gentle sea breeze came through the louvred windows that wrapped around the conservatory, leaving a salty scent in the air. Carter tried to make small talk with the maid as she escorted him through the house, but the only response he received was a curt smile.

"Madame, Detective Carter for you," the maid said before leaving him and Gabrielle.

Gabrielle stood in the middle of the conservatorium admiring the water lilies in her pond. Below the lilies, Carter spotted a school of fish swimming about and a turtle sunning itself on a half-submerged rock.

Surrounding the pond were all sorts of succulents while at the conservatorium's edge, climbing plants twined around the frames of the louvre windows. Here and there a few dwarf-citrus trees in large cement pots dotted the space. The conservatorium was sparse, but Carter suspected a team of gardeners attended the entire property daily.

"Detective Carter, what an unexpected surprise." She kissed Carter on the cheek and then gripped his hands. "You look well."

Gabrielle was casually dressed in a pair of blue overalls with a black t-shirt underneath. Carter suspected the casual attire was painstakingly selected by a personal shopper for a steep price.

"Thank you, I'm sorry for dropping by unannounced, I just need a few minutes of Bailey's time."

"Of course, darling, won't you join me." She motioned to a table at the far end of the conservatorium facing Brighton Beach. Afternoon tea had already been set up for the two of them.

As Carter sat down, Gabrielle poured him a cup of tea from her Royal Doulton teapot. Carter took the tea and poured in a dash of milk.

"Bailey told me about the recent incident at Vapour. I understand I owe you another thank you for encouraging Bailey to come home. I didn't know he'd gone there. We had another argument about his direction in life. I thought he was getting back on track." Gabrielle shrugged as she finished pouring herself a cup of tea.

"He's been having more good days than bad," she continued as she stirred a teaspoon of sugar into her drink. "One of Bailey's father's friends visited a few weeks ago. He was an assistant footy coach who worked for my husband in his heyday of Carlton in the nineties. He made a joke asking when Bailey was going to come back to the pitch. I was furious at him for suggesting that to Bailey, even in jest."

Gabrielle took a sip of tea, her hand trembled as she brought the teacup and saucer down to the table. "It is just so hard for Bailey, living in the shadow of his father."

"Mitch was a great coach. It's not easy trying to live up to a ghost," Carter said.

"It was the worst timing for that visit. Bailey had just accepted an offer to study IT at TAFE. Not a university, but it is a start. However, we had an argument, Bailey wanted to go back to footy. I told him absolutely not. So, he left. I guess he ended up back at that place. Don't ask me why he'd rather sleep on a plastic mattress there then in his king-size bed here."

"Community? Has he ever talked about his friends from Vapour?" Carter asked.

"He has a few friends who sleep there when they don't have anywhere else to go. He and that Ty boy have become quite close. He's here with Bailey upstairs. But I don't know if that's the crowd to help him get back on track. Ty is the exception, I think. He seems to really care for my Bailey, like you, Detective Carter."

Gabrielle gripped Carter's hand again.

"Thank you for keeping an eye out for him. I dread to think where he might be if you hadn't have given him a rude awakening that night," she said.

Carter smiled and patted Gabrielle's hand. "It's okay, just doing my job."

Gabrielle leaned back, "More than my deceased husband's friends are doing for him."

"Did Bailey accept the college offer?"

Gabrielle nodded, "He's always been really good with computers."

"That's what I thought," Carter said. "May I speak with him?

"You know where his room is," Gabrielle said as she waved

Carter knocked on Bailey's door that was already ajar. "Can I come in Bailey?"

Bailey opened the door, "Sure, Detective." Bailey's hair was messy, and he had bags under his eyes. Carter guessed Bailey hadn't been sleeping well. Ty was lying on the bed scrolling through his mobile. He looked up and nodded in Carter's direction.

Bailey's room was more shrine to his father than a personal bedroom. All the photos on the walls were footy photos. Either him and his dad in footy gear or Carlton victories.

"How's it feeling to be back at home?" Carter asked.

Bailey shrugged as he sat against his bed. "Alright."

He folded his muscular arms across his body. He had inherited his broad, muscular footy frame from his father and his olive complexion from his mother.

Bailey took a football next to his bed and started to throw it up to the ceiling and catch it as it fell back down. Ty moved over, so his head rested against Bailey's shoulder.

Ty was the opposite of Bailey. A lithe and pale frame dotted with freckles. He teased his curly red hair on his head with a finger.

Carter noticed someone had done a number on Ty. There were fresh bruises on his face. Below his right eye was a near black bruise with a deep blue and crimson bruise on his cheek.

"Who did that to your face?" Carter asked. Automatically, his eyes darted to Bailey's hands, but he didn't see any obvious signs of Bailey being the perpetrator.

Ty looked away. Bailey kissed the side of Ty's head.

"Ty's staying here with me," Bailey said.

"When you're ready to talk, you can call me." Carter handed Ty his card. He didn't know if Ty had been beaten by a friend, a stranger, a customer, or Bailey himself during a lapse of temper. "Day or night. Any time."

"Thanks," Ty murmured.

Carter leaned against one of the walls right next to Bailey's photo of him as a child on his dad's shoulders. It was a deliberate move as he folded his arms.

"Bailey, I have got to ask you some questions about Vapour, okay?"

"Do you want me to leave?" Ty asked Bailey.

Bailey shook his head while he kept tossing the ball up in the air. "Am I in trouble?"

"Not at all. Do either of you know of Sam Kane?" Carter asked.

"You mean Special K? He plays for the Dingoes," Bailey said.

"You've never met him or seen him at Vapour?" Carter asked.

Bailey and Ty both shook their heads.

"Is he queer?" Ty asked.

"Don't worry about it," Carter said. "What about Moe. How well did you know Moe who worked there?"

"Moe, me, and Ty would grab a drink sometimes. Go party at Swish," Bailey said.

"With Nelson?" Carter asked.

Bailey shook his head.

"Nelson liked to place a few bets on some matches," Carter let the statement hang in the air to see how Bailey responded.

Bailey grimaced, "Poor sap. Any bet is a losing bet I reckon. Can't predict it. I've seen Nelson out but we never spoke. If he told me he was doing that I'd tell him to stop and save his money. Look at how much trouble my dad got into for match fixing."

Carter nodded, "And you don't think he knew Moe?"

"Don't think so. I've been texting Moe. He hasn't responded."

"We've both been texting him, no response," Ty said.

They don't know he's dead, Carter thought.

"Did Moe ever ask you to help him out?" Carter asked.

Bailey caught the ball. He glanced at Carter and the photo next to Carter's head before looking back to the ceiling.

"What you mean?" Bailey asked.

"Maybe Moe asked you to help him with an IT issue at Vapour?"

"I dunno," Bailey said.

"Come on, be honest with me. I need to know, and you're not in trouble," Carter said. "I'm only concerned with the homicide, not anything else."

"Look, okay. He asked me to switch off the CCTV system at Vapour for a few days. He wanted to skim a bit of cash from the till. Not a lot, just enough to you know, pay rent, buy some beers. You know?" Bailey said.

"You didn't do that, did you?" Ty asked. He sat up in bed and shook his head in disappointment. "James lets us sleep there for free."

Bailey sighed, "I thought I was helping out a mate."

Bailey's glance shifted between Ty and Carter, "I'm really sorry."

Carter nodded, "How'd you do it?"

Bailey chuckled, "Just logged into Vapour's staff wifi network. Their CCTV system is wifi-enabled. Just logged in, deactivated the cameras and switched the user profiles so they couldn't log back in. Wasn't too hard. Their password was cock1."

"Not a very creative password, is it?" Carter asked.

Bailey looked up to Carter. His eyes darted between Carter and the photo of his dad.

"And what day was this?" Carter took out his notebook.

"It was the Thursday before Nelson's body was found at Vapour. I thought Moe was going to skim a bit of the takings from the weekend. Weekends are when they have the most customers."

"You know where Moe is?" Bailey asked.

I should tell him Moe is dead, Carter thought. Then he didn't have the heart. And he didn't want to set Bailey off.

"We are looking for him," Carter said with a hint of regret carried on his voice. "Did Moe seem under pressure or stressed when he asked you to disable the CCTV?"

Bailey shook his head. "Moe is cool as a cucumber. He just asked me to do it to help him out. It didn't seem like he felt bullied to do it."

Carter took out his mobile and showed Bailey and Ty a photo of the suspect wearing the hoodie from the hotel where Nelson's parents overdosed.

"I know this person is wearing a hoodie so you can't see his face, but does he look familiar to you two?" Carter asked.

Bailey took the mobile and examined the photo then handed the mobile to Ty.

"It looks like Moe's hoodie. He always wore a grey one but I dunno. It doesn't look like Moe," Bailey said.

"No idea who that is," Ty said as he returned Carter's mobile.

"Did he have any mates you know of?" Carter asked.

Bailey shook his head, "I don't know. When we went clubbing, it usually was just the three of us."

Carter nodded, he knew Bailey and Ty didn't know anything else.

"Your mum said you got into college. When do you start that?" Carter asked.

"Term starts in the middle of February. Ty is thinking of making a late application to study too," Bailey said.

Ty nodded in agreement. "Not IT, thinking of business or PR."

"You got the street smarts, might as well match it with some business smarts," Carter said.

Ty smiled and the bruise on his face shifted as his cheek lifted.

"The term starts pretty soon. I'll swing by again. We can chat about the study and how to make it stick," said Carter.

Bailey nodded, "Sounds good, Detective."

Carter smiled, "And Ty, I'm serious, give me a call when you're ready to talk about who gave you that bruise."

"I'll think about it," Ty said.

--

Carter returned to his car and took out his notebook. He made a flurry of notes.

So, Moe deliberately arranged for the CCTV to be disabled at Vapour. It wasn't because he was skint; Carter doubted the till had much money in it. Everyone paid with cards these days. So, what had been the real purpose of disabling the cameras? Was it specifically to cover up dumping Nelson's body? And if so, could Moe have been involved in the murder?

No, Moe had been working at Vapour at the time of Nelson's death. However, he could have been one of the conspirators. Or Moe might have just as easily been another pawn.

If he could just find that connection between Nelson and Moe, he knew he could figure out the rest. In the meantime, it was time to go meet Jodie Day.

Special K was not completely out of the frame as far as he was concerned. He could still be involved in match fixing with Courtney, his coach, and have used Nelson to make the bets. Carter was still curious what Jodie was going to say during this special one-on-one meeting.

When he arrived, the bar was near empty. He felt relieved as his regular stool at the bar was free. He had a beeline view of the pokies room, which was open from 11 a.m. till late. Which really meant early, about 3 a.m. or so.

Jodie Day walked in looking like Morticia Addams, Legal Edition. She wore a conservative black jacket and skirt combination with bright red lipstick and high heels to match. Her side bag was jam-packed with files, but she carried only her phone in her hands.

"Evening, Ms Day" Carter said.

"Evening to you too, darling. Call me Jodie." Her tone had changed. It was as if Carter was her gay bestie, and they were about to have a gossip.

Bruno was working in the bar and sauntered over to them.

"A drink?" Bruno asked.

"Yes thanks, I'll have a white wine, maybe a Chardonnay." Jodie rested a hand on Carter's shoulder. "And whatever my esteemed colleague here will have."

An overly friendly move on her part, especially for someone who was his adversary hours ago.

"I'll have soda water, still on the clock," Carter said.

Bruno nodded.

"Go ahead, darling. Get something off the top shelf. You should be celebrating." Jodie sat down on the stool next to Carter.

Carter looked at the bottle of Southern Comfort on the shelf behind Bruno. He shook his head, "Just a soda water."

"Suit yourself, darling," Jodie said.

"Everyone's your darling tonight," Carter said.

"They are when I'm in a good mood," Jodie said.

Jodie dropped a folder in front of Carter. "All the info in this folder clearly demonstrates that my client Sam Kane, aka Special K, had nothing to do with any murder. Phone logs place my client in South Yarra all evening and before that he was at training all day in West Melbourne."

Carter rested his hand on the folder.

"South Yarra is a hop and a skip away from Collingwood," Carter said.

"True. But that's a stretch to think my client covertly got to Vapour somehow. Read the documents, they will put to rest your suspicions of Special K," Jodie said.

Bruno came back with the drinks. "A white wine for the lady and a soda water for the gentleman. I added a lime for that top-shelf vibe."

Jodie took out a hundred-dollar note. "For your trouble and keep the change."

"You can come back any time, darling," Bruno replied as he plucked the note from her hand.

"You are quite the operator," Carter said.

She clinked Carter's glass before taking a sip of her wine. "I'm the best in the business, baby. Which is why on page five, you will see all the text messages between Special K and the victim, Nelson."

Carter took a sip of his drink and flipped open the folder to page five. The messages were there. Carter scanned them. It started with the typical 'you-up?' messages, 'enjoyed our time,' et cetera. Carter flipped to the next page. The message length and depth of conversation grew.

'I love you.'

Carter read the message a few times.

'I'm ready to come out.'

Carter re-read that last line: I'm ready to come out.

Carter skulled his drink. He caught Bruno's eye to get another.

"As you see, my client was in love with Nelson and ready to be more open about his sexuality with the world at large. Special K is experiencing extreme grief. I expect the police department to treat him with respect."

Carter pointed to some redacted texts between Nelson and Special K.

"What about these messages?" Carter asked.

"They aren't relevant to your investigation," Jodie said.

"Wouldn't happen to be some naughty messages about match fixing?" Carter asked.

"As I said, Detective, they aren't relevant to your investigation."

"You could have just sent this over. Why'd you ask me to meet here?" Carter asked.

Jodie had another sip of her wine. "I know your type. This place is home to you. Slightly closeted, slightly open. Still rough around the edges."

"What's your point?"

She turned towards Carter. "I get it, it's an awful situation. No one likes a murder investigation, but I can assure you, you are barking up the wrong tree. Despite what you think, I'm on your side."

"Then can you tell me, are you aware of any connection between Special K and Moe Bashar?"

"The other homicide victim?" Jodie asked. "Not that I'm aware of. Do you think the two cases are related?"

Carter gave a shrug. He watched Jodie's body movements. She was pensive, her thumb and forefingers played with the stem of her wine glass. Carter's phone started to vibrate. It was Song calling him.

"Carter here."

"Carter, you gotta come quick sharp to a flat. There's been an incident." Song's voice sounded stressed. He heard sirens in the background. She must be getting a lift in a squad car.

"What's happened?" Carter asked.

"Sam Kane has been found dead in his apartment. Can't confirm but officers on the scene are saying he has committed suicide. Are you still with the lawyer?"

"I am, why?"

Song gave a heavy sigh. "Please ask her if she has contact information for Mr Kane's next of kin."

"This is my team. They want to know if you have contact information for Special K's next of kin."

"What for?" she asked. "Are you... why do they need that information?"

"To do a death notification," Carter said.

Jodie looked genuinely aghast. Then there was a flicker of rage.

"You and your department are going to be torn apart for this," Jodie said. She took a cocktail napkin and wrote down two names. "His mother and father. You can look up the numbers yourself."

CHAPTER TWENTY-SIX

I fucking loved him.

I'm ready to come out.

Special K's words hammered themselves into Carter's head as he merged onto Flinders Street. Carter cranked the A/C in his car as beads of sweat rolled down his neck.

Traffic was bumper to bumper as he drove along the edge of Melbourne's central business district, where skyscrapers have reigned supreme for decades.

A few skyscrapers had sprung up in the 1950s, swelled in the seventies, and slowed down in the 2000s. As the skyscrapers were built higher and higher, the materials shifted over the years from red brick to steel and finally reinforced concrete. The facades blended the building materials with tinted glass windows to create a sense of opulence in metallic shades of reds, greys, and blues.

Peppered between the skyscrapers were the true landmarks of Melbourne's landscape. The buildings were built in the late 1800s and early 1900s. Carter approached one, Flinders Street Station, at a snail's pace in heavy traffic.

The open-air Edwardian-style building made from red brick spanned two city blocks. Built in 1909, it continues to serve as the city's prime passenger station for local and regional services.

The eclectic building's atrium is framed with a green dome, an arched entrance, and a large clock. Flinders Street Station loosened its stuffy commuter aesthetic at night as the rotating fluorescent light system comes to life and dances across the station. Throngs of people were mingling under the analogue clocks above the entrance to the station as Carter drove past. There was one clock per service leaving the station that listed the departure time. Even though they didn't work anymore, you always met your mates under the clocks.

He left the skyscrapers and the central business district behind him as he travelled across the St Kilda Road bridge with the Yarra River below him. He glanced out his window and spotted the alfresco diners sitting along the edge of the river. Carter longed to be there, watching the night go by with a glass of wine in hand.

A headache grew as he spotted The Convent ahead of him. The complex was a set of luxurious apartments on St Kilda Road, two blocks away from Melbourne's central business district.

--

As he got out of his car, Carter was hit by a wave of dry heat carried on the gusty winds of an early-evening surge in temperature. His lips became parched as the wind whipped dust and sand across his face.

Blue and red flashing lights criss-crossed Carter's face as he walked towards The Convent.

Uniformed officers had already cordoned off the entrance. Two paramedics stood next to their ambulance. It looked as if they were packing up their equipment.

The Convent was made up of one concrete tower with a glossy finish that oozed opulence. As he reached the entry, Carter wondered if Special K would still be alive if they had been called earlier.

The entryway had a large outdoor fountain that ran year-round, even during a drought. The noise of the fountain drew Carter's attention. Three pillars – each with a marble globe on top – stood in the middle of the fountain. Water flowed out from the top of each globe and into three unequally distanced plates. He stared down at the one at the bottom, from which water dripped down.

Carter heard nothing but the sound of the trickling water until a car pulled up noisily behind him. He turned around and noticed a camera crew just outside the cordon.

"Just great," Carter said.

Kris Oke stepped out of the van along with a camera operator and producer. The antenna atop the van slowly rose up and came to life. A camera operator set up a tripod and lifted a camera on top. The producer touched up the make-up for Kris as the camera's leading light lit up. Kris momentarily glanced towards Carter before looking at the camera.

"We are onsite at The Convent," Kris began.

Carter walked out of earshot and into the lobby.

Cold air greeted Carter as he entered the lobby. Vaulted ceilings, tiled marble floors, the entrance had all the pomp and grandiosity that Melbourne's A- and B-listers expected. Carter recalled when The Convent was first built that the starting price for a one-bedroom apartment was a million dollars. And that was for the most basic of floor plans and interiors. Carter flashed his badge at the constable standing guard.

"Make doubly sure no one enters here who doesn't live here," Carter said.

The constable nodded.

A frail concierge looked up at Carter and struggled to stand up from his chair behind the marble front desk as Carter walked towards the lifts. Carter waved his badge. "What floor?" Carter pushed the up arrow. It briefly illuminated. Then went dark.

"Twelve. But lifts aren't working." The concierge pointed a bony finger towards the emergency exit door. "You'll need to take the stairs."

Carter frowned. "Of bloody course. I'll be having more police and equipment brought here soon. I'm not expecting them to carry it all up twelve flights of stairs."

The concierge nodded. "I understand, sir, a technician been called."

"It better be fixed soon." Carter said in a vent of misplaced anger. He bodychecked the emergency exit door. The door swung open.

A blast of hot air hit Carter. Inside the stairwell there was no air-conditioning or air circulation. It was just plain hot. Swoosh. The emergency door slammed shut behind him. The noise echoed up the stairwell.

"For fuck's sake," Carter muttered as he looked up the square spiralling staircase. He felt woozy as he looked up, twelve floors ahead of him.

Carter placed a hand on the warm railing that wrapped the stairs all the way up. He was already sweating as he rounded the fourth floor.

Did I push Special K too far? Maybe I did. He was grieving. He was sad.

Carter wiped the sweat from his brow as he rounded the sixth floor. The twelfth floor, drenched, saturated in sweat, his wet palms barely grasped the railing as he rounded the last staircase.

A constable held the stairwell door blissfully open. A cool breeze from the corridor air conditioning buffeting his face and almost making the whole journey worthwhile. "Long way up."

Carter nodded. He leaned over and looked down the stairwell. "Long way down."

"His flat is just down the hall," the constable said.

"Thanks," Carter said.

--

"I was just about to pick up my kids when I got the call," Song said. She tossed him some gloves and booties.

"Who called it in?" Carter asked.

"Neighbour below Special K called the concierge saying there was water leaking through their ceiling. The concierge knew he had entered recently. The concierge came up. The door ajar, he entered and found Special K in the tub."

"The tub?" Carter heard the dripping sound of water in his mind.

"Techs are on their way. We can take a peek," Song said.

"Alright, let's check it out."

Special K's flat had a massive open-plan living–kitchen area; thirty square meters alone for the kitchen. The living room had a sixty-inch LED screen mounted to the wall and a wraparound balcony with the entire CBD as its backdrop. Down the hallway were three bedrooms.

"He's down the hall in the main bathroom," Song said.

Carter's hands continued to sweat in the blue gloves.

Song placed a hand on Carter's shoulder. "You okay?"

Carter relaxed his tense shoulders, "Yup. Let's take a look."

Carter and Song walked down the hallway. The walls were adorned with football photos including some of Special K in action on the field.

"He's an up-and-coming-star, isn't he," Carter said.

"Was," Song corrected.

The bedroom was made up. The bedsheets were perfectly tucked into the corners of the bed. The room was immaculate.

"What twenty-six-year-old man, living in a place like this, would have such a clean room?" Carter asked.

Song nodded as they both moved towards the ensuite.

"A spotless room isn't a sign of anything sinister," Song said.

The pair came up to the ensuite.

"The concierge said Special K was underwater. He pulled him out of the tub and started CPR. Medics pronounced on the scene. Poor medics had to race up the stairs with their gear," Song said.

She pushed the door open. The pair walked in. Special K lay sprawled out next to the bathtub. The water in the tub was near to the brim. Song and Carter looked down at Special K. His nude body faced them. Carter walked around the body and knelt down next to the head. There were no cuts or abrasions around his face. His hair was still damp from the water.

"Did the concierge say whether Special K was face up or down in the tub?" Carter asked.

"Face up," Song said. "I know with most drowning cases people usually end up facing down. But given the lack of time and size of the tub, it makes sense."

"Agreed," Carter said.

Carter lifted one of Special K's wrinkled hands. He closely examined the wrist.

"No evidence of any cuts. A few bruises on his knuckles, though. If it is a suicide, he must have consumed something orally," Carter said.

Song pointed to a glass on the floor next to the tub. "My guess is toxicology will come back with traces of a strong sedative in the glass."

"Finishes the drink and sits in the tub. Waiting to pass out," Carter said.

"And let the water do its job," Song said glumly.

Song looked at a note on the basin.

"Handwritten note. Looks like a suicide note," she said. "I'll wait for the techs to catalogue it before we review."

"Good call," Carter said.

Carter gently placed Special K's hand back down on the ground. A tear rolled down Carter's face.

Song gripped Carter's shoulder. "What is going on?"

"I'm going to be sick," Carter said.

"Get out. Now!" Song said. Song motioned to the door. "We need to preserve the crime scene."

Carter stumbled into the master bedroom.

"Sit down, mate, catch your breath," Song said.

Carter sat on the edge of the bed. His breath was short, sharp, fast.

Song nudged Carter. He didn't move.

"Carter. We need you out of here. I think the climb might have given you heat stroke."

"I'm going to be sick."

"Do it outside," Song yelled as she pointed to the balcony door.

Carter's stomach was knotted as he turned and stumbled for the door. His cheeks were flushed. He clawed at the door latch and swung it open. Spittle flew from his mouth onto the concrete balcony floor. He ran to the edge of the balcony. Vomit flew from his mouth. Tears followed. Carter looked down; flashes of light greeted him from the TV crew below.

--

Carter passed the next few hours with the pokie machines at Railed. The machines drew him back, like a moth to flames: the lights, sounds and chance of riches. Carter was glued to his mermaid game. He joined the mermaid for an underwater adventure. A treasure chest opened. He really just won his bet back.

I'm on a roll, Carter lied to himself.

You're not on a roll mate. Carter heard a voice in his head, but it was distant.

The glow from the pokie machine refocused him. Seven coins landed in front of his eyes. Animated bubbles floated from the bottom of the screen to the top to signal the start of a bonus round.

I am on a roll.

Carter downed his drink and hit spin. He leaned back and watched the screen run on autopilot. Coins rained down in front of him. His eyes glazed over. The screen was moving too fast for his drunk mind to follow. His eyes darted between the coins and his money tally in the bottom corner of the screen. It kept growing — nearly five hundred dollars.

Carter finished his drink.

"Bruno, mate," Carter slurred the name and snapped his finger.

The way Carter slurred Bruno's name made it sound like Bluce. Jill was at her usual machine and frowned.

"You alright, darling?" Jill wrapped her chipped manicured fingers around her glass of wine. She took the final sip of her white wine and placed her glass down. She readjusted her floral scarf around her leathery and wrinkled neck.

Carter looked at her for a moment. Lost at what to say, he glanced at the machine bonus. He had a credit for $522. Smack. Carter hit the spin button.

"Not in the slightest, love," Carter said. This was the first time Carter had been honest in months.

"I'll trade ya that empty glass for a slice of this," Bruno said.

Carter smiled and handed him the glass. Carter folded the pizza slice in half and ate it in two sloppy bites.

"Oh my, I didn't know you were that good at deep-throating," Bruno said.

Carter smiled again, "I'm a man of many talents. Another drink there."

Bruno smiled. "No problem. I'll bring it around." He motioned to the pizza. "Take another slice."

"Eating is cheating. Too busy, am winning," Carter said.

Bruno put a slice on a paper napkin and left it next to the machine before heading back to the bar.

Carter looked up at the jackpot listed for the game: $56,125. First-class tickets to Bali with a private villa. Buy an investment property with a down payment.

Who the fuck cares, I'll be rich. I can quit this life.

"Fuck it," he muttered under his breath as he selected the maximum bet and multiplier amount to turn out ten dollars a spin.

The spin icon flashed an array of underwater treasure chests as gold coins fell. A rainbow of neon lines created horizontal and diagonal patterns that Carter didn't understand, except that he didn't win.

Ten dollars lost in three seconds.

He pushed the button again. The treasure chests opened, and gold coins fell again. He furiously tapped the spin button in vain to speed the game up. The sequence ended. Carter didn't win again.

Twenty dollars lost in six seconds.

The machine spun again, and Carter's eyes glazed over. Not registering the movement. No win again.

Thirty dollars lost in seconds more.

Carter tapped the spin button again. The tapping noise of Carter's finger sounded louder than the music. It was turning into smacks. He noticed Jill looking at him. He started eating the slice of pizza with his right hand, his other hand still furiously hitting the spin button as quietly as he could.

Carter didn't notice that Bruno had brought him another Southern Comfort and Coke.

A wave of sadness rolled over him.

Carter took a sip of his drink. The ice cubes were now melted. He took out his phone. There were half a dozen messages from Song.

He saw a series of flashes. Nelson dead in the alleyway. Moe dead in the boot of a car. Pete and Diane dead in the bed. Special K dead by his tub. Carter didn't look at the messages, he just replied.

'All good, just a bit crook.'

He stayed until they closed, and Bruno helped him into the cab he'd called.

Carter slumped into the passenger seat. He pulled his seatbelt in a wide arch across his body. He aimed the seatbelt clip into the attachment. He missed. It landed in an empty drink cup.

The cabbie held Carter's hand.

He looked across to him. A plump elderly man was in Carter's blurry view.

"Here, let me give ya a hand." The cabbie buckled in Carter. "Guess we are taking you home?"

Carter bit down on his lower lip. He let the pain bring him back to reality. He stopped biting and focused on the case swirling around in his head. He turned to face the elderly cabbie.

"How much?" Carter asked.

The cabbie tapped the meter, "Depends where."

Carter shook his head, "How much to do whatever I say? I drop a bag of cash in your lap. How much is in the bag to do whatever I want?"

"What do you want done?" the cabbie asked.

Carter wagged a finger, "How much do you need?"

The cabbie let out a long exhale, "Mate, how long is a piece of string? I got what I want. No point risking it. Don't get me wrong, I'd like a bigger house, to retire early, but I'm not going to risk what I have."

"So, if you weren't content, happy, you'd be willing to take a pretty big risk?" Carter asked.

The cabbie shrugged, "Probably."

"Like kill four people?" Carter asked.

"Whoa, I don't want any trouble," the cabbie said as he raised his arms.

Carter showed the cabbie his badge, "I'm a cop, not after trouble. It finds me," Carter lamented.

"Had a rough night, mate?"

Carter nodded. "What about retiring? What would you do?"

"I don't know if retirement is on the cards for me. Maybe switch jobs. Work at a grocery store, something part-time. Reckon I'd get lonely if I retired."

"James Hughes needs a lot of money to change careers," Carter said.

"That lad has my vote," the cabbie said.

Carter shook his head, "Everyone is his fan."

"Mate, you don't know how many trips I've done from the suburbs to Vapour. All in cash too. Lots of gents in the closet out there with a missus and kids."

"You know where Vapour is?" Carter asked.

The cabbie nodded. "Know it like the back of my hand."

Carter slid his hands under his hamstrings. "Take me there. James Hughes has some questions to answer." Carter slurred.

The cabbie turned on the meter and flicked his indicator on and re-joined the traffic.

"There are some breath mints in the glove box," the cabbie said to a drunk Carter on the precipice of passing out.

CHAPTER TWENTY-SEVEN

Carter snorted awake as the cold water hit his face. He gagged. He fluttered his eyes, trying to open them against the stream of cold water. He moved his head to the side and hit a glass wall. He was in a shower stall.

"Wakey, hands off snakey," a familiar voice said.

Carter managed to open his eyes against the stream of water. He saw a mobile shower head that was moving up and down his body. The room spun in the opposite direction of the rotations of the shower head.

Carter's throat felt as dry as sandpaper. His eyes couldn't focus as the room kept spinning.

"Quite the state you've gotten yourself into," the voice said.

Carter steadied himself against the shower walls and looked up. He saw James Hughes holding the shower head. Carter let out a long groan as he struggled to stand up.

"Whoa! Easy. Don't rush. You're safe. You're at my house," James said. "Did you drink a bloody liquor store tonight? Lean back." James moved Carter, so his back rested against one of the shower stalls.

"I'm too hot," Carter murmured. He pulled at his soaked shirt. It snapped back against his skin. He slowly pulled off his shirt. The damp shirt dragged itself up Carter's body until it formed a cone on his head. "Help me."

"Now you ask for help," James said. "I don't know why you fought against me taking your clothes off before. It's not like I haven't seen it all."

James turned off the shower and pulled off Carter's shirt and tossed it in a corner. It thudded to the ground.

"Before," said Carter. "How did I get here?" Carter asked. He was drunker than he'd thought. The room continued to spin. Carter's head snapped back. It struck the shower wall. The noise reverberated around the bathroom.

"Ow," Carter moaned.

"Open wide, I know you're good at that." James rested a cup against Carter's bottom lip and tipped the glass. Liquid poured into Carter's mouth.

"Drink it all," James said.

A sweet concoction flowed down Carter's throat.

"My own recipe. It's a mix of electrolytes and ginger, along with B and C vitamins," James said.

Carter looked up at James. A literal blur of a man, as the room was still spinning, and a blur of a man in Carter's life.

"Hold on. Let's get you dried up and in bed, alright," James said.

James's rough hands undid Carter's jeans' button and lifted out one leg.

"This would have been a lot easier at the beginning," James said.

"How often do you do this at Vapour?" Carter asked.

"Darling, I learned long ago you don't fuck where you work," James said.

"Tell that to the military," Carter said.

James pulled off Carter's soaking wet jeans. "They told me."

"Is that why we never had a proper beginning – or an end?" Carter asked.

"You like having pity parties, don't you? Life isn't fair," James said.

"Tell that to the four murder victims who orbit Vapour and you," Carter said.

James extended an arm which Carter grabbed to hoist himself off the shower floor.

"Vapour is just a safe place for people who identify as lads to embrace their hedonistic tendencies," James said.

Carter leaned on James to stumble out of the shower stall.

"Vapour wasn't a safe place for Moe," Carter said as James wrapped an arm around his waist. "What really happened to him?" Carter asked.

James rolled his eyes, "Fine, look, I gave him his two weeks' notice to find alternative work."

"Because he didn't have working rights?" Carter asked.

"I know I play a big game, but with the election looming I got worried that having an employee without working rights would be the straw that broke the camel's back in the public's eye. Got that one wrong, my image is great. Ahead in the polls by miles. The night Moe died I was going to tell him he could keep his job."

"Misjudged that one," Carter said.

"I know." James said. A hint of remorse trailed his words.

"Moe would have been very desperate for some cash," Carter.

"All ingenue gays are," James said.

"You were my first. Did you know?" Carter asked.

James laughed. "I definitely knew that."

"You just ghosted me," Carter said.

"The military caught up on my sexuality. I was forced to take an 'opportunity' as they phrased it. Meant I had to do a hasty exit from our part of the service," James said.

"You could have written. Anything. I felt so alone again. You opened a door and slammed it back closed," Carter said.

Carter grabbed James's hips and pulled him towards him. Carter leaned in for a kiss. Their lips touched. Carter wrapped his arms around him. James pushed back against Carter's embrace.

"Why not?" Carter stammered.

"Well darling, for starters, your breath smells like a ransacked liquor store," James said.

Carter clumsily peeled off his wet jocks.

"That's not what I meant," Carter said.

"I know, Leo. I can't," James said.

Carter watched as James looked himself over in the mirror.

"You know I love you," James began. "But I'm so close to winning this election and righting some wrongs."

"What does that mean?" Carter asked.

"It means I've been setting a plan in motion since the military. Back then some very dangerous men and women forced me to do some very dangerous things. Some very classified missions where the only record is in my head and the heads of a few others. Most of them are dead. I pissed on their graves. Now I just need to stamp out their legacy. It's a slow-burning fire, mostly embers now, but breathe on those embers and the fire will start up again. In parliament I'll have the resources and clout to bring down their ilk, and their successors," James said.

James slung one of Carter's arms around his shoulder.

"Tell me honestly, is any of what you just told me related to Nelson, his parents or Moe's death?"

James shrugged, "You're the detective."

"Moe disabled Vapour's CCTV," Carter said.

His vision was blurry from the alcohol flowing throughout his body, but Carter could tell the news hurt James. A look of sadness momentarily washed across James before he pulled a brave face.

"No doubt he was desperate for cash," James said.

"What have you done for cash? Running an election is expensive," Carter said.

James smirked. "Expensive and intrusive."

"What if those dangerous men and women know your plan and want you dead?" Carter asked.

"If those powers were trying to kill me, there'd be one body. Not four," James said.

James tilted his head and grimaced to let his statement hang in the air.

"I think. No, I know, you were the real target or else Vapour is," Carter said. "What aren't you telling me? Don't spin me some high tale about faceless and dangerous men and women. Who wants something from you in the here and now that they are willing to kill?"

James let out a sigh. "You're right about the money. Election campaigns are bloody expensive to run. My finances were not looking great. I knew I needed more capital to run a good campaign."

"That champagne lifestyle eating into your coffers, aye," Carter said.

"That's rich coming from you. How much money have you lost at the pokies?" James asked.

Carter diverted his gaze from James. James grabbed a towel, wrapping it around Carter's waist.

"First my problem, then yours," James said.

"There was a bidding war for Vapour? If I lost out, I'd be pissed," Carter said.

James shook his head, "It wasn't a bidding war. I had one very interested party referred to me, but they offered too much."

Carter let out a laugh, "What do you mean, too much?" Carter asked. "And why didn't you tell us this when we interviewed you?"

"Well, to be honest, you were a bit of a dickhead during that interview. You catch more flies with honey darling. And oh right, I'm running for parliament, so I've been a bit busy. Got a few things on my plate."

"Okay, I'm sorry, tell me now," Carter said.

"I calculated the development potential of the site personally. I did the math of boutique luxury accommodation versus turning the building into shitbox one-bedroom apartments. You know, a shoebox with a window," James said.

"A charming addition to Melbourne's landscape," Carter said.

James ignored the comment. "No matter how I did the math their offer didn't make any sense. It was too high; about ten times too high."

"Maybe you're just bad at math," Carter said.

James let a smile show across his hardened face.

"I'm not. I'm amazing at math. What I'm getting at is someone thinks Vapour or the lot is worth way more. It has more potential than I knew about. If that is true, I was missing something. So, I told them to bugger off, the place wasn't for sale. I re-mortgaged my flat and some private donors gave me enough capital to start the ball rolling for my campaign. And overall, I reckon owning the bathhouse gave me some edge in the polls."

"Who was the prospective buyer?" Carter asked as the pair moved to James's bedroom.

"Jade Developments, offshore company. Based in Panama. Not much of a record here," James said.

"Jade Developments," Carter said as James guided him to sit on the edge of the king-size bed.

If Carter's head was a positively charged magnet, the pillow was the negative. Carter's head immediately thudded against it. James then hoisted Carter's legs onto the bed.

"The very one," James said.

Carter struggled to open his eyes. "What was the name?" Carter asked as the need to sleep caught up with him.

"I'll remind you in the morning. Your job is just to sleep right now," James said.

Carter smiled as he felt James pull a blanket over him. "Stay," Carter murmured.

"It's my bloody bed," James said as he climbed under the covers and spooned Carter.

--

Carter peeled his eyes open as the morning sunlight warmed his face. His eyes were bleary; he blinked a few times to restore his vision and get his bearings.

"Ow," Carter said.

He looked down at his arm where he felt a stinging sensation.

"Don't roll over. And don't forget, Jade bloody Developments," James said.

Carter looked down his left arm. A needle stuck out from his inner elbow. A tube ran from the needle along his bicep and up into an IV bag that hung off the bedhead. The near-empty bag contained a neon yellow fluid.

"Relax. This was going to be my next business, but parliament called. A mobile hangover-be-gone service. Just be lucky I'm not charging you. How are you feeling?" James asked.

"Like you injected me without permission," Carter said.

James squeezed the last drops out of the IV bag. "You are welcome. You always liked a prick. I injected you with a mix of saline, electrolytes, pain killers, anti-nausea and caffeine. I was going to have a doctor and a team of nurses to implement this venture. The financial industry, legal services and rich-twat kids of Instagram were going to be my prime market. How are you feeling?" James asked.

"Actually," Carter stretched his limbs, the expected stiffness and headache were missing. "Pretty good. More satisfying than the regular prick you offer."

James moved to undo his bathrobe. "I'll still fuck you if you want."

James winked as he pulled out the needle and replaced it with a sparkly unicorn Band-Aid.

"Pretty butch Band-Aid, right? You should have a hangover stronger than a thousand suns, considering I reckon you drank a bar clean – and probably a few petrol tanks as well," James said.

Carter groaned. "What time is it?"

"Almost six."

Reality sunk in. "Shit, I have to get to work."

James sat at the side of the bed and pointed to some clothes on the bedside table. "Those will fit you. You'd be amazed at what a trick will leave behind. Poor sods, probably hoped I'd call to return them."

"Stealing souls and clothes," Carter said.

"Get dressed and stop moaning," James said. "I have a plan there." James smiled. "Once this case is over, you are checking yourself into rehab, right? I'd say the other way around, but you're a stubborn shit. And from a business perspective, anyone who fucks with my business needs to be fucked harder. Get dressed. You have work to do."

CHAPTER TWENTY-EIGHT

Time to face the music, Carter thought as he swiped his card to enter the Major Crimes unit floor in Docklands Police HQ.

The scanner flashed green. The office was relatively empty – a few staff at desks and Song at hers. She stood up as he approached, pulling him towards the window of the office.

"Carter, what happened last night?"

"Just had an upset stomach. You know how it is. Must have eaten something pretty bad," Carter said.

"Had better have been something pretty bloody bad. I covered for you. Reckon the staff bought it, but the press still got a pic of someone throwing up over a balcony. Are you seriously, okay?"

Carter raised his hand. "We don't need to worry about the picture. James Hughes has got that buried," said Carter.

"Wait, what? How?" Song asked.

"Don't worry about that," Carter said.

"Alright, one tiny problem solved. What about you? Are you alright?" Song asked.

Carter motioned for her to sit down. He sat down at his desk. The two leaned in closely. Carter dropped his voice.

"You know what? I'm not alright," Carter said.

"We are a team. You know I've got your back. Why didn't you come to me earlier?" Song asked.

"I'm stubborn."

"A stubborn shit," Song said.

"I know and I'm sorry. It is okay, I'm getting better," Carter said. "I know I lost it last night, but I'm on the right track now for my mental health," Carter said.

"Maybe some time away will do you well," Song said. "Have you considered taking a break?"

"Nah, first, we solve this case. Together," Carter said.

"We need to look wider. We've been too focused on these murders in isolation," Song said.

"I'm right there with you. Someone, no. A group. Some clandestine group has been working against us. The original target has always been James Hughes and Vapour. Nelson, his parents, Moe, and Special K – they're all collateral damage. Someone has been setting them up as targets," Carter said.

"So, you're claiming that what? A cabal has been after James Hughes or Vapour?" Song asked.

"Maybe both. First two bodies linked to Vapour and then the attack on James at the memorial. He's on the radar of the right-wing. Maybe they were pushed by a more influential source," Carter said.

"That's a lot of conjecture and not a lot of evidence," Song said. "What about the footy angle?"

"How do you mean?"

"Moe and Bailey were friends. Bailey has a lot of connections in the AFL because of his father. While you were getting hammered, I looked at that connection. Special K's coach, Courtney, was mentored by Bailey's father." Song turned her laptop around to show images from an awards banquet. Courtney Ridge and Mitch Ross stood close together, laughing. "What if this doesn't have anything to do with Vapour, but with the AFL. Match fixing perhaps?"

Carter choked back slightly as he struggled to speak. "I've ruled out Bailey as being part of any match fixing."

"Courtney and Special K get in too deep with the match fixing. Maybe they are laundering proceeds of crime. Someone kills Nelson to send Special K a message. I haven't really even considered that."

"It's because you're getting stuck inside your own head and refusing to look around you," Song said.

"Yeah." Carter hung his head.

"I'm not saying there's not a cabal though," Song went on.

"You believe me then? Cuz I still think this is about Vapour," Carter said.

Song smiled, "I'm keeping an open mind. Someone is working against us, but I'm not sure it is a clandestine cabal, secret society or concerned mothers' group."

Carter chuckled at the thought.

"Besides, we have more immediate problems." Song pointed towards Davies's office. "Assistant Commissioner is in there. Seems the Hillier clan is making its presence known and you have been summoned to attend."

--

"Shut the door." Davies's voice carried a wave of fatigue. She sat behind her desk with a large coffee in her hand. She normally had her hair tied in a bun but this morning her long blonde hair was in a Dutch braid.

Carter then noticed the wall behind Davies had been stripped bare of all her commendations and degrees. Her signature stress ball was missing from her desk too.

Davies was getting ready to leave.

"Where's the stress ball?" Carter asked.

Davies pointed to a pile of packing boxes in the corner of her office.

"Packed away, hopefully not too soon," she said.

She clicked a button and the blinds lowered.

"Carter, you remember Assistant Commissioner Hillier," Davies said.

The bald and plump Hillier Sr sat in one of the two chairs in front of Davies's desk.

Carter nodded. "Sir."

"Take a seat," Hillier Sr said. His tone of voice carried his authority in the police hierarchy but underneath it was an edge.

One of his sausage fingers tapped the newspaper on Davies's desk. The headline read: Suicide in Special K's Apartment.

"Lots of mistakes happening in this investigation," Hillier Sr remarked.

"How so? We are making headway. New evidence is coming to light," Carter said.

"New evidence?" Hillier Sr scoffed at the suggestion. "Your murderer killed himself last night. The coroner is finishing up, and the ruling is death by suicide. So, your case is wrapped up. Lover kills boyfriend, can't handle the grief, kills himself. That's the narrative. Follow it."

"We ruled Special K out for the murderer," Carter said.

"You botched the interrogation. Instead of getting a confession from Special K, he killed himself," Hillier Sr said.

"Firstly, I don't think he killed himself," Carter said.

Hillier Sr shook his head, "Mistake after mistake."

"Or, if he did, it isn't for the reasons you think," Carter said.

"The suicide letter makes a very compelling confession," Hillier Sr said in a chastising tone.

Davies took out an evidence bag and placed it on her desk. Carter picked it up. It was the letter he and Song found in Special K's bathroom. He couldn't make out the words because of the bag's logo and evidence collection history details filled in on the plastic.

"The letter is pretty clear. Special K expresses remorse for killing Nelson and Moe. According to the letter, he couldn't stand the pressure of being in the closet, and he apologises to Nelson. He was cheating on him with Moe," Davies said.

"That's rubbish, boss," Carter said. "Have you ever found an actual note at the scene of a suicide? I haven't. Not once. It's an invention of screenwriters. But even if Special K was the outlier, you can't have authenticated the letter in this short a time."

"Show him the other bag," Hillier Sr said.

Davies placed another evidence bag on the desk. The bag contained a single black converse shoe.

"The missing shoe of Nelson Harris, found in Special K's rubbish bin. You will recall Nelson was found at Vapour with just a single shoe," Davies said.

"Yes, boss. I remember. I was there. It could have been planted by the real perpetrators," Carter said. "Hell, this whole thing is so stagey you'd think they hired a props company."

"I disagree," Hillier Sr said.

Carter was about to speak before Davies cut him off.

"Speaking of the scene, though, what happened yesterday?" she asked. "Why are we seeing a photograph of you vomiting off a high-rise patio?"

"Very unprofessional for the lead detective," Hillier Sr said.

"I was sick, that is all. Must have been my lunch. Was just a bug. I'm fine." Carter and Davies met eyes. "Really, boss, I'm fine. Song has found another possible motive within the AFL. There might be a match-fixing conspiracy going on."

"Really?" Hillier Sr asked.

Carter nodded, "Multiple people connected to this investigation have links to the AFL."

"It has happened in rugby league. We've always had rumours it's happening in AFL but nothing credible," Hillier Sr said.

"No matter what there are too many loose ends here. Who killed Nelson's parents?"

"Pete and Diane Harris overdosed on heroin. They had a history of drug use and abuse. Hearing about the death of their son pushed them over the edge. It's a black and white situation. Clear as day," Hillier Sr said.

"We have CCTV footage of a man dropping the gear to Pete and Nelson. He made sure to hide his face from the CCTV in the hotel," Carter said.

Davies nodded, "That is interesting."

"Maybe it was the UberEATS delivery man. Who cares. Two junkies are dead. There is no connection," Hillier Sr said. "You need to stop clutching for connections. The list of your screwups continues. Do you know how much that clusterfuck of a memorial cost us?"

"I can't be blamed for a right-wing protest at the memorial organised by James Hughes," Carter said.

"You can be blamed. What do you think set off Craig Dean and his father? You harassed him outside the court about Nelson's death and ta-da, the Neo-Nazi group associated with them is protesting the memorial," Hillier Sr said.

"We were chasing a lead, raised by your son," Carter said.

"You made a call to bring in additional riot and tactical squads. Do you know much it costs to bring in extra officers?" Hillier Sr asked.

Carter didn't respond.

"Over a hundred grand an hour, your actions cost the department over three hundred thousand dollars. Not to mention a mountain of paperwork," Hillier Sr said.

"It was the right call," Carter said.

"It was, and I back him on that," Davies said.

"One good call too late. I've made my decision. Carter is off the case," Hillier Sr said.

Davies looked at Carter before looking at Hillier Sr. She frowned before nodding.

"There are a bunch of loose ends and paperwork that need to be wrapped up. I don't want to deal with the hassle of bringing another detective up to scratch," Davies said.

"James Hillier is up to date on the case."

Carter interjected, projecting his sassiest self. "You mean your son. The detective with the lowest seniority in the squad? Who also let one of the witnesses escape through sloppy police work? Nepotism runs deep in the Hillier clan."

Davies almost cracked a smile before projecting her best stilted face.

"Yes, Carter, that Hillier. I'd hate to make a report about his errors at the crime scene. It would be a serious blotch on his record." Davies folded her arms across her chest.

"Before you remove me from the case, I think you should check News Breakfast," Carter said.

"News Breakfast? That leftist garbage show," Hillier Sr said.

"Don't like it? Well, Kris Oke filed an interesting report this morning. She interviewed James Hughes and me," Carter said.

"She did?" Davies asked.

"You didn't clear this with the media team," Hillier Sr said.

"I'm a DCI, leading an investigation. I have the discretion to liaise with the media," Carter said.

"What do you and James discuss in the piece?" Davies asked.

"Aside from personally thanking me and the entire police force for their swift action at the memorial. James Hughes, a future member of parliament if the polls are correct, reiterated his faith and support in me leading the investigation of Nelson and Moe's deaths. I kept to script, just discussing the murder investigation is ongoing, call in with any tips. As a queer officer, I am committed to finding the perpetrators of these murders," Carter said. He couldn't help it. He beamed a large gloating smile — a steep contrast to Hillier Sr's expression. "Do you want me to pull up the clip on my mobile?" Carter asked.

"By now, the other channels and papers will be picking up the story. The wrong questions will be asked if we replace Carter now," Davies said.

"You little weasel," Hillier Sr said. He glared at Carter as he paced the room. "I'm a very dangerous man to cross."

"Carter stays as OIC for the case," Davies said.

"Fine. Close this case. The evidence still points to Special K, and I expect the final report to say just that," Hillier Sr said.

"Of course," said Davies. "We are all looking forward to a speedy resolution, aren't we Carter?"

"Absolutely, boss," Carter said.

Hillier didn't respond. Instead, he left Davies's office and slammed the door shut behind him.

Carter let out a sigh of relief.

"That was a close call. If you didn't pull a fast one with James, you'd have been off the case," Davies said.

"I have got to hand it to James, he orchestrated the interview," Carter said.

"He's a smooth operator," Davies said.

"Unlike Hillier Sr. Kinda like father, like son. Special K killing Nelson doesn't make sense. Special K bringing in Moe as a hired goon and then killing him? That is a joke. Special K isn't the ringleader of the gay mafia. It just doesn't make sense," Carter said.

"You're right, Leo," Davies said.

She never calls me Leo, Carter thought. She really believes me.

"I also spoke to one of the regulars at Vapour. Moe got help deactivating the CCTV cameras. Someone is pulling a lot of strings to frame Special K and conceal their actions."

Davies tapped her fingers on the newspaper. "Pretty interesting, how the body was staged. Very similar to a death very close to your heart. If I were trying to gaslight the investigation, I'd try to rattle the lead investigator. Ruin the investigation from the top. Let the effects cascade down like a waterfall," Davies said.

"Are you flushing out a rat?"

"I have some suspicions. There's a rat king or queen. Been wanting to do a final deep clean before I leave."

Carter nodded. "You could have told me."

Davies nodded. "I could have, but I wasn't sure."

"And now?"

"Now, you've got some work ahead of you."

Carter nodded, "First off I'm going to rule out Special K as a suspect."

"Clock is ticking, and the evidence is pretty strong," Davies said.

--

"You're stuck with me," Carter said.

He sat down at his desk with Song next to him.

"The coroner is going to rule Special K's death as a suicide. The higher-ups have him in sight for Nelson and Moe's murder too."

Song turned in her chair to face Carter. She looked exhausted suddenly. Carter reflected on how that was his fault. Doubt she got any sleep thanks to him.

"That doesn't make sense, I know the letter, and the shoe was found at his flat, but it doesn't align with his love for Nelson," Song said.

He nodded. "Yep, I know. Something is missing. I reckon someone was pulling the strings of both Special K and Nelson. Either covertly or overtly. Them falling in love threw a spanner in their plan."

Song tapped her finger on the edge of the desk. "That's the problem; what is their plan? What do Nelson Harris, a bureaucrat working for the City of Melbourne and Special K, a footy player, have in common?" Song asked.

"That's the jackpot. I have no idea. But I'm going to find out," Carter said.

Carter saw that Perry had just entered. Perry waved at them both.

"I'm leaving you in charge of the shop, Song. I want to talk to Special K's coach, get an idea of his state of mind."

"Easy. Always fun being the boss," Song said.

Carter smiled. "Call me with any info. Focus on scouring CCTV and put some pressure on forensics. We need to know the make and model of the weapon used to kill Moe."

Carter got up and started to walk towards Perry, before turning around. "Oh, and let's keep Hillier on a tight leash considering his dad is in his corner," Carter said.

"Don't have to ask me twice to do that."

CHAPTER TWENTY-NINE

Carter parked his Skoda in the car park of the West Melbourne football team's headquarters. The lot was nearly full as a throng of reporters had set up in the car park. Along the fence of the field, a memorial had been established. Fans of the West Melbourne team and of Special K were holding a mini vigil for him.

Photos of Special K taking marks in different games were taped along the fence. Each picture showed him leaping into the air with hands outstretched to catch the ball. At the centre of the photo series was a large picture of Special K kicking the ball through the goalposts. Candles, flowers, and cards were left on the ground surrounding the images — a footy eulogy.

Carter watched two children walk towards the fence. They placed a stuffed Dingo, the mascot of the West Melbourne team, underneath one of the pictures. A throng of photographers took photos of the children as they shared a hug before they ran back to their mum and clutched her legs.

Carter stepped out of his car and was immediately accosted by an elderly woman who was being held upright by a walker frame on wheels.

"Why did you kill him?" she asked.

The woman wore a West Melbourne jersey and hat. The walker was decked out in West Melbourne paraphernalia too. The steel bars were wrapped in blue tape and West Melbourne footy flags were dotted around the walker's basket. A true fan of the team. Probably the oldest one too, Carter thought.

"Pardon me," Carter said.

"I saw the video, you and that woman arrested our dear sweet Special K," she said.

"Ms, it was part of an investigation. An investigation that's still ongoing," Carter said.

Carter moved to sidestep the woman. She pushed her walker in his path.

"Don't Ms me. Special K was going to lead the team to a premiership win this season. You and all the coppers have blood on your hands," she said.

Carter scratched the back of his head, "I understand you, along with the greater fan base, are hurting," he said.

"You understand nothing, dog," said the woman as she started to walk around.

Carter stared at the mass of humanity that lay between him and the entrance. The number of people posed a problem for Carter to get through. Especially if he was recognised again. The sheer volume of noise coming from the crowd was ringing in Carter's ears.

"Detective Carter," Kris yelled as she approached with a camera crew following her.

"Kris, I really need to get inside,".

"I really need you to answer some questions," Kris said.

"How about you help me get through the throng to the front door?" Carter asked.

Kris folded her arms across her chest.

"Forgetting about that early morning interview already?" she asked.

"Never. I do have you to thank for that," Carter said.

"Probably your job too," she said.

"How about you help me again. We walk and talk. And I won't field any questions from other reporters," Carter said.

"Good boy, you learn quickly," Kris said.

She motioned to the camera to begin recording. The camera operator walked backwards, filming Kris and Carter walking together. The producer walked behind the camera operator to make sure he didn't trip. The group made their way for the front door of the clubhouse.

"I'm speaking with DCI Leo Carter again today. Detective, can you give us an update on Special K? He was a star member of the West Melbourne footy team," Kris said.

"At this moment, the investigation is active. As such, I'm limited at what we can discuss," Carter said.

"Can you confirm if Sam Kane, adoringly referred to as Special K, is dead," Kris asked.

"Yes, I can confirm that. The cause of death is under investigation," Carter said.

"What's Special K's connection to Nelson Harris, who was murdered recently?" Kris asked.

"As this is an active investigation, I can't comment on that," Carter said.

Kris and Carter were in the middle of the throng of people. The camera operator and producer were doing their job of filming the interview. More importantly, for Carter, they were acting as a plough, clearing a path.

"Detective, David Arthur from Channel 8, was Special K in the closet?"

The reporter tried to push his way in front of Kris and Carter to force Carter to answer his question.

"No comment," Carter said.

Kris motioned to the camera to step closer. Kris, Carter and the camera formed a tight triangle that pushed out any intruders. That included David Arthur, who looked insulted that Carter ignored his question as he was pushed out.

"We understand, and there is that nasty video, that Special K was taken in for questioning. What was the outcome of that interview? Why were the police heavy-handed in this incident?" Kris asked.

"The police were not heavy-handed in this situation. No complaints have been lodged by Special K's lawyer," Carter said.

Carter was metres away from the front door. It was nearly in reach. And just in the nick of time. Perspiration was forming along Carter's hairline. He needed to get out of the spotlight to do his work. "Who's his lawyer. We will contact them directly," Kris said.

"Jodie Day, isn't she here?" Carter asked.

"No. Only the club reps have spoken," Kris said.

Carter opened the door, "That will be all of my comments for now, thank you."

Where's Jodie, Carter thought. If I was his lawyer, I'd be appearing front and centre calling for the crucifixion of the lead investigator.

Carter waved his badge, and the security guards opened the door to the West Melbourne football team headquarters for him. As the doors closed behind him, the noise from the outside was muffled and then quickly replaced by the buzz of a busy office. The phones were constantly ringing. A very busy and frazzled-looking receptionist sat behind a desk and managed a blinking and ringing switchboard.

A group of footy players loitered around the front desk of the club where the receptionist sat. Carter recognised some of the players, including the Norse god, Mark. He glared at Carter.

"Clearly he remembers me too," Carter said under his breath.

Carter showed his badge to the receptionist. "DCI Carter, I need to speak with Coach Ridge regarding Special K."

Mark nudged Carter.

"You remember me?" Mark asked.

"Hard to forget. Look, I don't want any trouble here, alright. I just need to speak with your coach about Special K," Carter said.

Carter looked up towards the hulking player. Mark had a tattoo that crossed his neck that said 'courage' in cursive. The other footy players stood beside and behind Mark.

Carter remembered standing with three other boys. They were all the schoolyard bullies. He looked down at the boy with glasses. Bits of spaghetti and tomato sauce flew through the air as the child Carter kicked the boy's lunch box, a poor cowardly choice stemming from his own frustrations. So, this is what it's like on the other side – being on the receiving end of intimidation.

"You might not believe it. But I am here to help."

"Was Special K gay?" Mark asked.

"Gay, bi, queer. Special K fell into one of those categories," Carter said.

The football players looked around at each other.

"Clear off," Mark said to the other players.

The other players looked between each other before walking off. Mark motioned to Carter to sit with him at a table out of earshot from reception.

"Why'd he off himself?" Mark asked.

He didn't, he was set-up, murdered, he's a victim. This was what Carter wanted to say.

"Dunno. That's what I'm trying to find out."

"Did you know he was gay?" Carter asked.

Mark shrugged.

"I guess. It makes sense. We'd had a few threesomes, and he always seemed more interested in me than the missus I reckon," Mark said.

Carter nodded, "He never confided in you, though?"

Mark shook his head. "Nah, I wish he had. Would have been shit keeping that to himself. Would do your head in I reckon."

"Yep," Carter said glumly.

Courtney walked in, her trainers squeaking against the tiled floor with each step. "Clear off, Mark. No one should be talking to the cops, let alone him."

Mark stood up.

"He's alright," Mark said, and nodded towards Carter before walking off.

Courtney stood in front of Carter. Legs shoulder-width apart, arms crossed over her chest. She was obviously used to taking down bigger men than Carter with just a stare.

"You may not think it, but I'm here to help Special K. Can we talk somewhere more private?" Carter asked.

"Too little too late, don't you reckon?" Courtney replied as she motioned for Carter to follow her.

--

Carter took a seat across from the couch in the conference room. Behind Courtney was a large, framed photo of Special K.

Right in the middle was a headshot from his draft pick, along with shots of him doing football passing and kicking the ball. In memory, 1998–2020.

"Get to the point. I got a practice to lead in ten," Courtney said.

"Do you think Special K was capable of suicide? Was there a lot going on in his personal or professional life?" Carter asked.

"You know, Special K came to me. Told me he was gay. He wanted to come out. This was early last week. He was nervous but excited, you know. He wanted to be the first open player at the national level. He mentioned he was seeing someone, thought it was real. This is why he wanted to come out now. He wouldn't have killed himself, not when he was so close to…" Courtney said.

She trailed off as she rubbed her eyes. She turned her chair to look at the framed photo.

"I'm trying to prove he didn't commit suicide. I reckon he was stitched up. He had some issues, but I don't think he did what the media is reporting," Carter said.

Courtney's eyes narrowed. "He was a good kid, still wet behind the ears, you know. If anything, he might have been too ambitious. He had a penchant for juggling too many things at once. He wanted to be a business titan after he retired. He was always looking a few steps ahead. Maybe too many," Courtney said.

"I just have one question," Carter said.

"Shoot," Courtney said.

"Why did the club call Jodie Day to represent Special K?"

Courtney looked puzzled.

"Who's that?" Courtney asked.

"Special K's lawyer," Carter said.

"We didn't. ARL bigwigs changed the policy with the recent spate of – well, you know – incidents."

Carter nodded in understanding. From sharing sex videos to getting caught with cocaine, the ARL community had more than a few 'incidents.' We have a streamlined policy when it comes to police interactions – probably a wise move. Courtney continued. "We called ARL bigwigs when you guys took Special K in. The main lawyer the ARL uses is a bloke from one of the top law firms. Mallesons or Clayton, I think. All the legal work is done through them or in-house. Does Jodie work with one of these firms?"

Carter shook his head. "Thanks though. This really helps."

"You know, Special K isn't the only guy on the team or in the ARL who is gay. There are a few I reckon – nah, know. But they won't come out. Too hard, too scary, they're too alone. They don't have anyone, no mentors, no real support. No one to bounce an idea off," said Courtney.

Carter nodded and rubbed his nose. He remembered coming out in the military. By the end of it, a cold pack rested across the bridge of his nose. A fellow soldier broke Carter's nose, so he had broken his arm. That was just before his discharge.

"I get it," Carter said.

Courtney looked straight at Carter. "They need someone who's been in that world. Someone who can show them. They aren't weak for being gay, for having feelings."

Carter repeated himself. "I get it. One challenge at a time. Thank you for your time."

"You owe it to Special K to make it right.

--

Carter's Bluetooth rang as he drove out of the car park. He had to machete his way past the throng of reporters camped outside the door again. He deflected the reporters' questions with a static response: "No comment."

"Carter here."

"It's Nic."

"You okay? How's your mob doing?" Carter asked.

"Our mob is not too impressed," Nic said.

"What do you mean?" Carter asked.

"We had your footy lad, Special K, on the table, ready for the autopsy. Guess what happens?" Nic asked.

Carter glanced in the rear-view mirror at the throng of reporters and mourners standing outside the West Melbourne footy club.

"They're gaslighting you too?" Carter asked.

"The chief coroner comes in with top brass from your mob. They kicked Doc Monroe and me out and then performed the autopsy themselves."

"That's interesting. As I recall Doc Monroe considers the chief coroner a bit of a pencil pusher. Hides mostly behind his desk. Doesn't do many autopsies," Carter said.

"In all my years, I've assisted the chief on one autopsy. Just one," Nic said.

"You said someone from the force was there too," Carter said.

"Yah, an older gent, never seen him before. All you white fellas look the same, to be honest," Nic said.

"Except Perry," Carter said.

Nic let out a long laugh. "I checked out the completed report. They are ruling Special K's death a suicide. Now I'm no conspiracy theorist here, but when we had him on the table, there were signs of a struggle — bruises on his knuckles and across his abdomen. If you asked us in public, we would say how valuable and brilliant the chief coroner is. Something isn't right, mate."

"Thanks Nic. Right as always. I owe you folks."

"You owe us a coffee shop at this point. But I'll settle for you shouting Perry and me a counter meal."

"When are you two going out?" Asked Carter.

"Next week. I'll send you the bill," Nic said before she disconnected.

Carter called Song.

"Pull Special K's phone records and anything and everything you have on Jodie Day."

"No problem. And forensics came back on the weapon that killed Moe. We are looking for a .38 Smith & Wesson," Song said.

"Does Davies know about this?" Carter asked.

"Not yet, and you know what that means?" Song asked.

"Unfortunately. Let Davies know, quietly please," Carter said.

"No problem," Song said.

"Oh, and ask Davies if she has the contact details for Jodie Day," Carter said.

"Special K's lawyer?" Song asked.

"Yes her – not his lawyer according to the ARL," Carter said.

"Where are you going to now?" Song asked.

"I'm going to speak with George Campbell, I reckon he's another puppet in this piece," Carter said.

--

Carter pulled up behind George Campbell's silver Audi in Port Melbourne. The boot of George's car was open, stuffed with suitcases and duffle bags. As Carter stepped out of his car, George walked down the steps of his house with another duffle bag slung across his back.

"I don't have anything to say to you," George said.

Carter lifted his hands in defence, "How about you listen instead?"

George shrugged as he threw the duffle bag into the boot and closed it.

"I reckon you are bisexual, maybe gay – doesn't matter. You noticed Nelson at work, or maybe it was a sheer coincidence, regardless, you hooked up with him."

George nodded. "Sure, I saw Nelson around the office a few times. And then one time at The Stables on our lunch break. There are a few City of Melbourne guys that cruise there."

"Bukkake team building session," Carter said.

"Hardly. What happened at The Stables stayed there. It didn't impact my duties as CEO," George said.

"Until it did," Carter said.

"You and Nelson plan a few more romps at The Stables, he comes over to your house when your wife is away. I'm betting there are some pretty strict policies against the CEO fraternising with an employee."

Carter looked towards the front door of the house. George's daughter stood at the door. She waved to Carter and George. Carter waved back. Carter wondered what their daughter knew or understood about what was happening to her family. Caitlin stood behind her daughter and guided her back inside. Caitlin opened the screen door.

"Was that your last bag?" Caitlin asked.

"It is," George said.

"Good. My lawyer will talk to your lawyer. Don't come back to the house," Caitlin said.

Caitlin closed the screen door and then slammed the door shut.

George leaned against his car and folded his arms, "My marriage is over because of you."

"Your marriage is over because you weren't honest with your wife," Carter said.

George shrugged, "You know I've lost my job now. Council CEO jobs are slim pickings. My reputation is ruined now."

"When did the blackmailing start?" Carter asked.

George's mouth dropped.

"It started with a text message and an image, didn't it?" Carter asked.

George nodded, "They threatened to send the pictures to my wife and the press."

"Who were they?" Carter asked.

George shook his head, "If I knew, I'd tell you."

"What did they want you to do?" Carter asked.

"I think you know what," George said.

"Promote Nelson?"

George nodded, "You got it. I swear, I had cut it off with Nelson, but what could I do."

Carter nodded and walked back to his car.

"Where does that leave me? I'm a blackmail victim here," said George.

Carter shrugged, "Hope your resume is polished?"

CHAPTER THIRTY

Carter walked around the kitchen while he thought. Hillier and then Song were the first ones at Vapour. Hillier brought me Dean Craig, who went on to try to kill James Hughes.

Carter switched on his laptop and opened an email from Song containing Special K's phone logs. He homed in on one particular number and time. He took out his mobile and called Song.

"Yeah," Song said.

"During the memorial Special K received a phone call and then left the memorial quick-smart."

"Yes, and he left immediately after that," Song said.

Carter highlighted the row in the Excel spreadsheet.

"Row forty-one of the sheet you sent me."

"Yep, I see it," Song said.

"That call came in at 6.08 p.m. Can you get the techs to estimate the location of the caller?" Carter asked.

"Got that data already on a different file. Give me a second," Song said.

She disconnected the call.

Carter leaned back in his chair. "I hope the call didn't come from the park," he said to no one.

Minutes later, she called back.

"Guess where the call originated," Song asked.

"Inside the park," Carter said.

"Close enough. We can't pinpoint the exact location, but it was within a radius of one kilometre to Fitzroy Gardens."

"As soon as we put the call out for police surveillance, Special K gets a call and leaves the park," Carter said.

"His solicitor is still in the lurch. No one has been able to contact her. I also did some digging on Jodie Day. She seems to be more of an international law lawyer. Has clients across Asia. And she is a Melbourne-based company director of Jade Developments, along with the now-deceased Special K. Company documents were lodged with the Australian Securities and Investment Commission. Not many details, but guess who countersigned her papers?"

"Nelson Harris?" Carter asked.

"Nope, even better. Andrew Hillier, Junior."

Carter closed his laptop. "I'm heading back to HQ now. We have a rat."

--

"It's Hillier, junior and senior. They are dirty."

Carter could barely contain his excitement at the break, or his fury at the Hilliers. Davies merely nodded. Carter's excitement wasn't contagious.

"Come on, Liz."

"That's Superintendent to you," she said.

"Come on, Superintendent. You know it is true. Hillier Jr has been gaslighting this case from the beginning. You have got to believe me – it is the Hillier clan behind it all."

"There is a pretty wide gap between incompetence to obstruction and criminal behaviour. What evidence do you have?" Davies asked.

"Hillier has been trying to mess up this case from day one. He's the one who set up the cordon at Vapour. Hillier managed to get one of the constables to leave their post. Then he signalled Moe to escape. And used a former police issue weapon to kill Moe. Hillier Sr without a doubt sourced one of the revolvers when the force was changing weapons over to semi-automatics," Carter said.

"If you find the weapon, we can confirm that. And why did Moe disable the CCTV camera?" Davies asked.

"So Hillier, or an accomplice could dump Nelson's body," Carter said.

Davies tapped her fingers on her desk.

"They murdered Nelson to send a message to James. Sell Vapour or else. And Nelson's death was to tie up the loose end that they viewed him as," Carter said.

"That's all very circumstantial. What's the link to Moe? Hillier Jr or Sr don't seem like patrons of Vapour. I do not hear any real evidence yet," Davies said.

"Hillier Jr knows Jodie Day. He co-signed the company registration papers for a company called Jade Developments that Jodie and Special K are directors for," Carter said.

"Now, that is interesting. Hillier never mentioned to us that he knew Jodie Day. At the same time, having a side hustle isn't illegal," Davies said.

Carter started to grow frustrated and irritated.

"Do you want to nail them or not?" Carter asked.

Davies leaned over her desk. A frothy look came over her as her eyes narrowed.

"You don't think I've been trying to nail them for longer than you've been on this one case? My time is running out. I'm being pragmatic. I want to get them, but the case needs to be airtight. Right now, it isn't," Davies said.

Carter nodded, "Okay, so the evidence from the paper trail with Jade Developments shows Hillier and Jodie know each other. And it isn't a stretch to assume that Hillier would know the other director of the company, Special K," Carter said.

"Knowing people isn't a crime," Davies said.

Carter let out a groan.

"This is what the prosecutor and the defence teams will say if we present them with this," Davies said.

"At a bare minimum, Hillier is an accomplice to murder. At the very worst, he may have murdered Nelson, Moe, Nelson's parents, and Special K," Carter said.

"Special K's death was ruled a suicide, and his suicide letter says he killed Nelson and Moe," Davies said.

Carter smacked the table. "That's the whole point. They are pinning this all on Special K. He's their scapegoat."

"Special K is the prime suspect. What you've presented isn't compelling enough for a prosecutor, let alone a jury, to think otherwise," Davies said.

Carter nodded. "Look, I understand. The Hilliers – well Hillier Senior – is a smart operator. And they are a few steps ahead. Just give me twenty-four hours. I know I can prove their complicity. We have at least one dirty cop. And the apple never falls far from the tree. Hillier Junior – he's not smart enough to pull this off. Come on, he witnessed a company registration document. He thinks he's bright, but he's not."

"Hillier Sr and the powers that be are pushing for me to sign off on this case confirming Special K is behind all of this," Davies said.

"Let the clogged wheels of bureaucracy spin for a while before you sign off on the case. Give me twenty-four hours," Carter pleaded.

"You know, every day we delay this case is another day I'm delaying my plane ticket to Bali," Davies said.

"Boss, come on, you know there is a rat. And you want to nail the Hilliers more than me. You should have been at least an assistant commissioner by now. Screw Bali, and screw them," Carter said.

"I have other priorities than getting to Bali and it's a bit late to start career planning for me," Davies said.

"Nothing can be more important than this. Who knows what the Hillier clan has gotten away with?"

Davies leaned back in her chair rubbing her temples.

"Bali can wait," Carter said.

"Jesus, Carter, read the room. I'm not heading to Bali."

"Then why are you so keen to leave?"

"My youngest, Catherine, she's twenty-three now. Not doing well at all. The other two are doing fine, really good actually."

She pointed to the framed family photo. Davies and her wife stood side by side with her three children seated in front of them.

"You know Marcus, still working as a chef in Northcote, co-owner of a cafe there." She then pointed to the next child. "Kira got a new job for an arts council. Catherine though, she's not great," Davies said.

"What are you going to do?" Carter asked.

"Aiming to get her into a private detox programme. Then get her living back home and see how she goes over the next six months," Davies said.

"Does she want to get clean?" Carter asked.

"She wants to. She's tried before by herself with little success. For her, half the battle was doing the paperwork to get a bed. This time it'll be a family activity, wholehearted," Davies said.

Carter had a lightbulb moment. "The council! That bastard. Hillier Jr was responsible for investigating Nelson's employment at the City of Melbourne Council. Nelson worked in the planning department. The former CEO of the council was blackmailed into promoting Nelson within the department. I reckon Special K and Nelson did something criminal there. But then their hearts got in the way. Nelson's death was a message to James to sell but also Special K to keep in line," Davies said.

Davies pulled up Hillier Jr's report on her computer.

"Report is squeaky clean. Looks like Nelson was a model employee at the City of Melbourne Council."

"It can't be a coincidence that Special K is a director of a property development company and Nelson worked in the city's planning unit. Hillier volunteered, no, jumped at the chance to run with that angle, and he omitted something from the report. I just don't know what yet," Carter said.

"You've got twenty-four hours. I'll hold off from releasing any real statements about Special K's death. But that is it – twenty-four hours. After that, the narrative is closeted gay murders his lover at risk of being outed."

"Thanks, boss." Carter walked out.

The office was empty except for Song. Carter walked over to Hillier's desk.

"Fucking prick," Carter said.

He looked at Hillier's drawers.

"Why not," Carter said.

He opened one of the drawers. Nothing interesting was in it. Just pencils, papers, junk. He opened the next drawer down.

"Gotcha, you twat." He hooked a pencil through the handle of a cup – a West Melbourne football coffee mug from 2019. Across the porcelain cup was the 2019 line-up with Special K front and centre.

Carter yelled across the office to Davies. "Hey boss, how's this? When Special K came onto our radar at the first briefing, Hillier said he didn't think it was Special K and that he didn't barrack for West Melbourne."

Carter lifted the mug. "He's dirty, boss."

Davies stood at the edge of her door and rolled her eyes. "Hurry up Carter, time is ticking."

Song joined Carter with an evidence bag in hand.

"We are visiting the City Council first thing tomorrow morning," Carter said.

"What are you doing?" A stern voice from behind them asked.

Carter and Song turned around to see Zhang standing behind them.

"You're going through Hillier's desk."

Carter and Song looked between each other.

"We are," Carter said.

"That's private property," Zhang said.

"It's not," Song said.

"It. It is," Zhang stammered. A look of concern crossed his face as he folded his arms across his body.

"Why are you taking his mug? It's just a mug."

"Look, I understand you and Hillier are a thing."

"Are a thing? This isn't high school. We are in a relationship."

"You're going to need to reassess that. He's dirty," Carter said.

"We're sorry to be the bearers of bad news, but he can't be trusted. For your career, you need to get some distance from him," Song said.

"You two are idiots."

"I beg your pardon. That's way out of line," Carter said.

"He's working for Internal Affairs. He's building a case against his father. He's been trying to get his dad to step down and retire as assistant commissioner."

Carter shook his head, "Lust blinds all."

Zhang moved his hands to his hips. "First off, it's not lust. Secondly, he's on the right side."

"That's not what the evidence shows us Zhang," Song said.

Song moved towards Zhang to console him. He took a step back.

"I'm telling you, he's on our side."

"Where is he then?" Carter asked.

Zhang looked at the ground, "I don't know. He hasn't answered my texts or calls this evening."

"Listen. You know we have your back. So please, get some distance from Hillier. And don't tell him you saw us—"

Zhang cut Carter off, "Snooping?"

"Call it whatever you want. For us, it's further evidence supporting our case that the Hillier clan is corrupt."

"The sins of the father land on the son," Song said.

"In this case, you're both wrong," Zhang said.

Carter rested a hand on Zhang's shoulder. "We'll know tomorrow, cuz I'm taking the Hilliers down."

CHAPTER THIRTY-ONE

The City Council building on Swanston Street had been decommissioned years ago and turned into an arts hub. Council House 2 replaced its predecessor. Just off Swanston Street on Little Collins Street in the heart of Melbourne's CBD.

This building's claim to fame included being amongst the first highest-rated sustainable buildings in the city. From water conservation in the toilets to solar panels on the roof for electricity, and a passive thermal design to support heating, cooling and airflow, Council House 2 had all the features of a picture-perfect sustainable building. The exterior walls were clad in wooden panels designed to weather and age as the building itself aged. As Carter and Song walked into Council House 2, he looked at the ageing wood panels and thought only of rot.

The lobby of the council building spanned the height of the building, with each floor's tearoom jutting out into the atrium along with the lifts. The design allowed natural light to filter in through the atrium and penetrate each floor.

"I don't know if they are in yet," the exasperated receptionist said. He had just finished calling the Planning Department mainline. Judging by the heavy bags under his eyes, the large coffee and the Berocca next to a glass of water, the receptionist, or Kevin as his name tag said, operated at half speed this morning.

Carter checked his watch, it was approaching 8:30 a.m.

"We need to speak to them as a matter of urgency about Nelson Harris's death," said Song.

"Did you make an appointment?" Kevin asked.

"We don't need appointments," Carter said.

"Look, I just sat down, and this is all a bit triggering right now," Kevin said.

"Kevin, you are going to escort Detective Song and myself upstairs to speak with Nelson's managers right now or else I'm going to have every reporter for the major television and newspaper outside your office in ten minutes. If you think we are triggering, you just wait till they're pushing a camera in your face," said Carter.

--

Chilled beams ran the length of each floor of Council House 2. The dark rectangular machines attached to the ceilings, transforming the hot air rising from people and devices back into cold air to fall down.

It wasn't just the chilly air that set the tone to this frigid meeting room.

Carter and Song sat across from the department heads for the council. Sara Ward, the Head of HR, and Todd Torres, Head of Legal Services.

"You really should have made an appointment," Sara said.

Sara had a large ringed binder next to her and a notepad. She wore a grey skirt with a black cardigan and diamond earrings. Hair pulled tight into a bun.

"It would have helped us prepare to fully assist your investigations," Todd said. He wore a pair of black chinos and a white dress shirt with a black blazer. Hair buzzed off, he wore a sterling silver bracelet on his right wrist.

Neither of them is doing it rough, Carter thought.

Carter and Todd shared a quick glance to acknowledge a shared experience. They'd met before, at The Stables. Todd had been the man Carter had a fleeting tryst with over lunch. Neither spoke to confirm the raunchy lunchtime encounter between them, nor did either recuse themselves from the meeting. Carter knew it to be a conflict of interest. But more appealing, he knew it to also be a source of leverage, depending on the outcome.

"Why aren't Nelson's superiors here?" Song asked.

"A bit odd that the council's top guns are here instead of the staff we asked to speak with," Carter said.

"What follow-up questions do you have? We assumed we covered everything with your colleague, Detective Hillier," Todd said.

"We have just a few more questions. What exactly were Nelson's main responsibilities here?" Song asked.

"Nelson's recent transfer meant he had oversight for assessing and approving various permits for the city. This mostly entailed checking client submissions for parking applications for residents and tradespeople in the city's region," Sara said.

"Recent transfer?" Carter asked.

"Yes," said Sara with an air of curtness to it.

"What did Nelson do before his transfer?" Song asked.

Sara and Todd exchanged a quick glance.

"We've been through this with your colleague already," Sara said.

"There really isn't a point in rehashing previous conversations. If your team isn't intent on sharing and discussing information, that is a problem for your department," Todd said.

"It's now your problem. What did Nelson do before his transfer?" Carter said.

"He worked in the building planning applications area," Sara said.

"Can you elaborate on what that entails?" Song asked.

The lawyer interjected. "We've been through this already with your colleague."

Carter responded, "And now we want to hear it."

Sara shrugged, "Essentially, Nelson's responsibility included interpreting rubrics for and against planning applications for high-rise developments."

"That sounds high-risk. A lot of responsibility for one staff member," Song said.

"That is why the City of Melbourne Council has clear assessment rubrics and a collaborative team culture to ensure one staff member is not solely responsible for any decision or advice to the council for voting approval," Todd said.

"Why was Nelson transferred? Seems like a demotion moving from building assessments to parking permits," Carter said.

"He requested the transfer," Sara said. Her eyes darted to the left before focusing on Carter and Song.

"He requested it?" Carter asked.

"You've asked a question, and we've answered," Todd said.

"What project did he work on before he requested a transfer?" Song asked.

"The unit works on applications as the department is an operational unit. After all, we don't construct the buildings. The city's mandate is to make sure it is viable, sound and fits in with community expectations," Todd said.

"Fine, what application did he work on?" Song asked.

"There were a few different applications across Nelson's desk at the time," Todd said.

"How about we help you narrow down the field of applications. Were any of them for a plot in Collingwood?" Carter asked.

"Your colleague, Detective Hillier, didn't enquire about any of this, why the change now?" Sara asked.

"We ask the questions, you provide the information," Song said.

Sara squirmed in her seat, "There was one application for a Collingwood site that came across his desk. There were a few problems with the application."

"Problems? Can you elaborate on that?" Carter asked.

"Usually, a planning officer has a counterpart to sign off on all applications. Nelson's counterpart had been on annual leave, and this application paid a fee to fast-track it. Due to a misinterpretation of the planning bylaws, an application report submitted to the council included incorrect advice for the council to approve the application. The advice should have been for the council to reject," Sara said.

"But in this case, it was approved in error?" Carter asked.

"Correct. The minutes and final documents showed a discrepancy on the number of levels approved for a particular development with the high limit being approved. Essentially the higher limit applied had been based on the development being in the central business district instead of its actual location in Collingwood," Sara said.

"What's the difference? They are only a few kilometres from each other," Song said.

"There is an acceptable height difference. Roughly ten levels for residential buildings are permitted in Collingwood," Sara said.

"And the sky is the limit in the central business district," Carter said.

"That's a bit of an exaggeration," Todd said.

"But the council still approved the higher limit for this Collingwood development," Carter said.

"Correct," Sara said.

"And this wouldn't meet community expectations," Song said.

"Again, correct," Sara said.

"So why not amend the approval?" Carter asked.

"Based on legal precedent and guidance from the state government, we determined there was no need to rock the boat, and the application remained approved. No individual attempted to deceive council. Simply a few admin errors and the way population density and growth is occurring, Collingwood and the surrounding areas will need more units created. Going vertical is a simple solution."

Song interjected, "If no one did anything wrong, why did Nelson apply for a transfer?"

"You'd have to ask him. People are transferred all the time, especially the younger staff. It gives them a scope of the breadth of operations in a council."

"Are transferred. Moments ago, you said it was his suggestion. His request," Carter said.

"A slip of the tongue, Detective, there is nothing sinister here," Todd said.

"Did you know that the former CEO of the council promoted Nelson into the role?" Carter asked.

"As far as our records show, there was a competitive and transparent hiring process for Nelson," Sara said.

"Nepotism isn't part of our hiring policies," Todd said.

"I'll have a statement from George Campbell about that shortly. Also, it's interesting that Nelson made the error but doesn't get any type of reprimand. The council just thought Nelson would enjoy the thrilling aspects of approving parking permits?" Carter asked coldly.

"Indeed, Detective. If that is all, we really need to attend to other business," Sara said.

Carter raised a hand. "One other question. What's the address of the application that caused this trouble?"

"I'm sorry, Detective, that information is confidential," Todd said.

"But council approved the permit," Carter said.

"Correct," Todd said.

"So why can't you tell us the address?" Carter asked.

"Those council records are sealed. The courts will need to be petitioned to open them," Todd said.

"If that is all, we really have to get going with our days. At this rate, I might not be able to have a lunch break," Todd said.

Carter understood the message. Todd wanted to meet Carter at The Stables.

"Thank you two for your time," Carter said.

--

Carter and Song stepped out of Council House 2 and into the Melbourne heat.

"I think we both know the address for that planning application," Song said.

Carter nodded. "Vapour."

"Jodie Day, Special K, Andrew Hillier Senior; all are part of a development company with their eyes on Vapour's location. They've gotta be funded by Day's overseas contacts. Vapour is in a prime location and the last plot to be developed in that area," Carter said.

Carter swiped sweat from his brow as the sun shone brightly in the sky.

"Maybe they rope in the handsome and charismatic Special K to be a spokesperson and they do some digging and know that Nelson would be a malleable planning officer. If they stalked him on Instagram, they'd know he was gay. Then they get Special K to seduce him. Unfortunately, they didn't expect them to fall in love. Add to the drama, James changes his mind about selling Vapour. Keeping Vapour aligned with his political aspirations and thought it'd paint himself as a different kind of politician," Carter said.

"Their proposal and the golden chalice are falling apart, I reckon," said Song. "I don't think Jodie Day and

311

the Hilliers are in retreat. She's been under the radar since Special K's death."

"Shit. She's the connection," Carter said.

"What do you mean?" Song asked.

"At Railed, Jodie knew Moe was Brazilian."

"His nationality hasn't been released to the media," Song said.

Carter took out his mobile and dialled James's number.

"Why hello, stranger. I need your mailing address to send you the bill for my services," James said.

"Listen James, I need to know something. Do you know a woman—" Carter asked.

"A woman?" James cut Carter off, "Are you trying to set me up? I gave up the XY-chromosome breed years ago. Two kids are enough."

Carter's jaw dropped. "Wait, what? You have kids?"

"Two that I know of."

Carter let out a sigh. "Don't distract me, let me finish."

"Do you know a woman named Jodie Day?"

"Oh yeah, Jodie's great, she provides some legal advisory services for me," James said.

"Has she ever been to Vapour?" Carter asked.

"Darling, I know you are going through some things, but you know Vapour is exclusively for men," James said.

"You know what I mean," Carter said.

"Ahh yeah, look yes. She's been in the office once or twice. I had her assisting me with some due diligence when I thought about selling Vapour and some other legal matters with my other businesses," said James.

"Okay, great. Now think very carefully. Has she ever met Moe?" Carter asked.

Silence greeted his enquiry.

The answer Carter wanted.

"Yes. Jodie offered to help Moe with his immigration paperwork," James said.

"You know what that means, James? But don't go crazy, I'll text you. I have a plan."

"Fine," James said as he disconnected the phone.

Carter smiled while Song leaned against a steel pole on the sidewalk.

"Jodie coerced Moe to disable the CCTV cameras at Vapour?" Song asked.

"In exchange for helping him with his immigration application," Carter said.

"Still not enough evidence," Song said.

"We need to get the details of the planning application," Carter said.

"I'll get legal on it, but you know how slow the legal world operates," Song said.

Carter and Song crossed Little Collins Street and started to walk down towards Swanston Street. Out of the corner of his eye, Carter noticed Todd leaving the council. He stopped on the edge of the road and leaned against a concrete wall with a graffitied greyhound racing dog in neon greens and oranges on it. Todd lit a cigarette and deliberately made eye contact with Carter.

"Song, head off. Start work with legal to get those records unsealed. I'm going to approach it from a different angle," said Carter.

"On your back?" said Song.

"On his back, I think," Carter corrected.

"Boss, please don't tell me you're really going to pay for that information with your dick."

Carter shrugged. "It's the cheap and effective solution."

Song shook her head. "I don't like it."

"Are you worried that the information he gives me might be inadmissible?"

"No, I'm worried about you respecting yourself." Song shot him a glare. "If you're going to be a whore, whore for your own sake, not the closure rate... Sir."

"Watch me do both."

--

A few minutes later Carter walked back into The Stables in a tiny towel. He sat in the near-empty main room at one of the bar tables. He straddled the stool. Any passer-by quickly caught an offering of Carter's genitals. There wasn't anyone in The Stables. The only company was the low-volume house music that pumped out from the speakers, until Todd walked in. He strutted in wearing an equally small towel with a file in his hands.

"Did you get a room?" Todd asked.

Carter held up a key, "Let's go."

A single bed with a plastic mattress greeted Carter and Todd as they entered the room. The walls were dark red with a single light in the ceiling emitting dim light, mood lighting. Carter had to pay for half a day. He hoped he'd be out in ten minutes.

Todd sat on the bed with a coy look across his face.

"Do you know where I live, Detective?" Todd asked.

"If I had to guess, Collingwood," Carter said.

"You are a smart cookie," Todd said.

He placed the file on the bed, and his fingers slowly walked up Carter's thick, furry thighs. Carter gripped Todd's hands.

"I'm not here to play games," Carter said.

"You will. I have some documents you'll want to see. Normally, I'm more than happy playing caretaker. Hiding and concealing council mistakes. But my million dollar views will be turned into five hundred thousand if construction ever goes ahead on that garish monstrosity that idiot Nelson approved."

"What's the normal limit for a residential limit in Collingwood?" Carter asked.

"Twelve, and I have a penthouse in a building near Vapour. Who says gentrification is bad," Todd said.

Carter moved to take the file. Todd snatched it before Carter could reach it.

"Drop the towel," Todd said.

Carter gripped his towel. "This is fucked."

Todd shrugged, "I know what I want. I know what you want. The question is, do you want to wait six months for the courts?"

Carter dropped his towel. Todd smiled. He handed Carter the file.

"The approved application to build a thirty-five-storey high-rise development," said Todd. He gently caressed Carter's testicles before he licked his palm and gripped Carter's shaft.

"An error becomes cannon." Carter marvelled at the difference. "The developers will make a killing from this project."

"Not if you do your job," Todd said. He squeezed Carter's shaft. "But first, you owe me."

Todd ripped out a condom packet and placed the condom in his mouth.

Carter gripped the back of Todd's head. Todd went down on Carter and unfurled the condom on Carter's stiffened veiny shaft. Carter grunted before he flipped Todd around and pushed his face into the bed. Carter thought of opening the file on Todd's back, but he decided against trying to multitask.

"Come on, I only get an hour for lunch," Todd said.

"Don't talk," Carter said as he gripped Todd's hips and pulled his arse towards his cock. "This is a one-time deal."

"Don't tell me you are saving yourself for someone," Todd said with a sarcastic tone.

The tip of Carter's hard cock entered Todd. He cooed as he gripped Carter's arse.

"Go deep," Todd moaned.

"Don't you worry. You'll get the full service."

--

Carter sat in his car. The stench of sweaty sex stuck to his skin as he looked over the planning application papers from Todd. He glossed over most of the documents which detailed the design, project plan and costs. His finger landed on a section on the final page. Jade Developments had submitted and had been approved for the application. He scanned for a company address.

"Gotcha," Carter said as he turned on his car.

The company address was listed in Ascot Vale.

CHAPTER THIRTY-TWO

Carter drove to the address in Ascot Vale. It was a red-brick warehouse covered in moss with shrubs along the sides of the building. There was a roller door in front and a door next to it. The lights weren't on; it looked deserted.

Carter's phone buzzed. Song texted that she was ten minutes away.

Carter drummed his steering wheel as he decided how to proceed.

"Should I wait," he said out loud.

He looked at the building again. It still looked just as desolate as before. He imagined what the merman from his favourite pokie machine would do. Gotta be in it to win it, the merman would say as he seductively smiled to entice Carter to take a bet and risk it.

"Fuck it."

Carter undid his seatbelt and got out of the car.

He started to walk around the side of the building. There were a few shipping pallets. The sort that Carter used to climb on as a kid. He looked up. Just to the left of the pallet was a grubby window. He moved two of the pallets underneath the window and stepped up. He squinted through a window to see inside. The only light in the building came through the windows. It was bright enough for him to see a white car in the middle of the warehouse.

"That's our Commodore," Carter said.

"It's not yours," a voice said from behind Carter.

Carter turned around to see Hillier Jr levelling his weapon at him.

"Get down from there, Detective."

"I knew you were corrupt," Carter said as he stepped off the pallets.

Hillier lowered his weapon. "I'm not corrupt."

"Bullshit."

"I'm trying to bring my dad down as quietly and painlessly as possible."

"You signed the development papers with Special K."

Hillier nodded, "Look I did. I didn't realise what Special K was doing with my dad. Special K didn't have a great upbringing or relationship with his parents. He looked up to my dad. He'd follow him straight to hell."

"He did," Carter said.

"And that's why I'm here. I need to stop Dad. I approached IA. They didn't believe me he's corrupt. Still don't, I reckon. If I can get him to stand down then he can retire and head off into the sunset."

"And if he doesn't stand down?" Carter asked.

Hillier took out a pair of handcuffs. "I'm open to suggestions.

--

"Look who I found snooping around outside," Hillier Jr said.

Hillier walked into the warehouse with Carter's hands pinned behind with the handcuffs around his wrists.

Jodie Day turned around.

"Quite the mess you've caused us, darling," Jodie said.

Hillier Jr pushed Carter who stumbled and fell against the white Commodore. Hillier passed Carter's weapon to Jodie.

"So nice of you to join us, Detective," Jodie said as she admired his gun.

"Wasn't a trouble at all, was just in the neighbourhood," Carter said.

Two floodlights turned on above Carter. He squinted at the bright lights that shone down on him.

"That's unlikely," a third voice said.

Carter's eyes adjusted to the harsh light. He was able to make out a third person walking towards them. It was Hillier Sr.

"What do you want to do, Dad?" Hillier Jr asked.

"Nothing for you three to do. You're all under arrest," Carter said.

Hillier Jr, Sr and Jodie all let out a laugh.

"That's cute. I've been working like a dog trying to calm down our overseas investors. You're too late to the game darling," Jodie said.

"For your sake, surrender now, you don't want to be in a shoot-out when tactical arrives," Carter said.

Hillier Sr pistol-whipped Carter across the face. The butt of the gun struck his cheek. Carter winced from the pain as he rubbed his face.

"Fucking fool, we're the police, we use and listen to the same radio frequencies as you. No one is coming to save you," Hillier Sr said.

Carter knew he didn't have much to bluff with.

"If I've figured it out, someone else will, and you three were sloppy. You'll get caught. It is just a matter of time," Carter said.

"What do you mean sloppy?" Jodie asked.

"Don't listen to him," Hillier Sr said.

"What if he's right, Dad?" Hillier Jr asked.

I've caught one of their attention, time to turn their attention to each other, Carter thought.

"Come on, all three of you can be traced back to the planning documents, company structure and Vapour," Carter said.

"That's your silver bullet? This is all circumstantial," Jodie said.

"With you out of the picture, this whole case will be closed and buried. Unlike this case, you won't be buried," said Hillier Sr. He pointed to one of the oil drums in the far corner of the warehouse. "You'll be rotting away in a few of those drums for the next twenty years."

Jodie's phone beeped.

"I wonder who that is," Carter said. "Go on, check your mobile."

The three of them glared at Carter before the Hilliers nodded to Jodie to check her phone. Jodie started to frown as she scrolled through the text. Her face changing from a grin to a grimace as she kept scrolling.

"Shit, this is bad. James Hughes knows." Jodie began to pace around. "He knows everything."

"James Hughes knows nothing. He's going to sell Vapour to us, or we'll kill him," Hillier Sr said.

"I don't know, Dad, this isn't sounding great," Hillier Jr said. He briefly glanced down at Carter.

"With Jodie as the solicitor, it'll make the building process even smoother," Hillier Sr said.

"I can't be his executor and process this sale. We need him to be a willing party," Jodie said.

"There are other ways to make him compliant," Hillier Sr said.

Jodie stopped pacing just in front of Carter. Her mobile was in one hand and Carter's weapon in the other.

"You don't get it."

Carter freed himself from the handcuffs. He jumped up.

"What the—" Jodie said.

Carter tackled Jodie to the ground. His gun flew out of her hand and landed on the ground.

Hillier Sr turned around and raised his weapon.

"Don't do it, Dad." Hillier Jr raised his own weapon and pointed it at his dad. "This has gone too far."

Jodie kicked Carter in the chest, winding him. Jodie crawled towards the gun. She grabbed the gun as Carter jumped on top of her. They wrestled for the weapon as Carter clutched his chest with his spare hand. Jodie kept a firm grip on the gun, even as Carter slammed her hand holding it into the ground.

"Let go," Carter said.

Jodie's hand pulled the trigger in response. A shot rang out into the air.

"You're not going to shoot, son," Hillier Sr said as he turned his gun towards Carter.

Carter saw Hillier Sr pointing his weapon at Carter.

"Run," yelled Hillier Jr.

Bang, bang, bang. Hillier Sr fired a series of quick shots. They missed as Carter and Hillier Jr scurried behind the car. The two breathed deeply. Sweat drenched them. Fear and adrenaline pulsed through Carter's veins.

"That was close," Carter said.

Hillier Jr nodded, "Dad, come on. You need to stop this. Turn yourself in."

"You're on the wrong side and in no position to make this request. Shoot Carter and we can finish this all," Hillier Sr bellowed.

Carter looked over to Hillier Jr. "Your dad's a dick." Carter fired a single shot underneath the vehicle. Hillier Sr and Jodie scuttled back, away from the vehicle.

"This was for you. We would have been set for life. I have no son now. And DCI Carter, don't make this more difficult on yourself," Hillier Sr yelled.

"Yeah, you stupid bastard, do you want to die here?" Jodie asked.

"I'm not dying here," Carter said.

He tensed his grip on his gun and was about to poke his head up to take a shot when another rang out in the warehouse. It shattered one of the front-seat windows of the car as fractured glass shards sprayed across Carter's back. Carter crawled forward and crouched behind the front tyre, glancing up to find his targets.

Hillier Sr was on the right side of the warehouse behind some pallets. Carter saw him pass a gun over to Jodie who was on the left behind the oil drums.

"They both have weapons," Carter said to Hillier Jr.

"Two on two," Hillier Jr said.

"Pretty good odds."

Carter noted that both were carrying revolvers. Between the two of them, they had ten shots against Carter and Hillier Jr's semi-automatic weapons with fifteen rounds each. Two less as he fired at Hillier Sr and Jodie.

"You missed, Carter. Let's make this easy. Just throw your weapon to us and come out. There is still time to cut you in on the deal. Both of you," Hillier Sr yelled.

Carter knew they had them boxed in.

"Dad. Stop this. There's no way you and Jodie won't get arrested."

Hillier Jr's plea was met by two bullets. Both bullets embedding themselves in the car's frame.

Sweat began to run down Carter's neck.

They now have eight bullets between them, thought Carter. He thought of rolling out from behind the car. He'd charge at Hillier Sr and take him out before Jodie could fire. Searching for options, Carter looked up. There were only two lights in the warehouse, and they were both above Hillier Sr and Jodie.

Carter motioned to Hillier Jr to look up at the lights. He nodded in agreement. Carter counted down from three to one, tensing the grip he held on to his service weapon.

They both stood up and aimed for the lights. He squeezed the trigger. Bang. Glass fell to the ground. Hillier Jr aimed his gun at the light over Jodie and released the trigger.

"Lights out," Carter yelled.

Shots were returned and hit the car.

Carter crawled over to the rear end of the car. Two more shots were fired at them. All the car windows were shot out now. Carter looked at his bloodied hands from crawling across the glass. Hillier Jr leaned against the front tyre of the car.

"Any ideas," Carter asked Hillier Jr.

"One," Hillier Jr raised his hands. "Dad, I'm coming out."

Hillier Jr stood up.

"Toss your gun," Hillier Sr yelled.

Hillier Jr nodded as he took his gun and threw it across the warehouse towards his dad and Jodie.

"I just want to talk."

"It's a bit late for talking," Jodie said.

Hillier Sr motioned to Jodie to stand down. She knelt behind an oil drum.

Carter rested his gun on the boot of the car. He was ready to fire.

"There's still time, son."

"I was about to say the same to you. Come on, Dad, you can't get away with this."

"We can. This is our ticket out of here, son. We'll be set for fucking life. This is just the first step. We'll become property barons. Not just Australia but the world. It'll be our oyster."

"Come on, Dad, you have a huge salary. You don't need more wealth."

Hillier Sr glanced towards Jodie. "Not enough. I owe money to some dangerous people."

"Compromise is the name of the game," Jodie said. "Are you with us or against us? We are trying to make everyone here rich."

"At what cost?" Carter yelled.

Hillier Sr aimed his weapon at Carter and fired off a single shot. Carter ducked behind the car.

"Dad! Just focus on me. What type of legacy do you want to leave?"

"One where we are filthy rich."

"At what cost? I can't have a dad who's a criminal." Hillier Sr looked around the warehouse. His gaze rested on the car riddled with bullets before moving to his son.

"Quite the mess I've gotten into."

Hillier Jr nodded, "We can get through it, Dad. Drop your weapon."

"Don't do it," Jodie yelled. "We are so close. Don't drop your weapon. We can let them in on this deal. We'll be set for life, mate. Hell, set for three lives."

"It's over, Jodie," Hillier Sr said.

Bang.

A single shot hit Hillier Sr in the chest. He crumpled to the ground. Jodie's weapon was trained on him. She had fired a killing shot.

"Dad!" Hillier Jr screamed.

Carter stood up and fired at Jodie. "Get behind the car."

Hillier Jr nodded and ran behind it.

Carter ducked down again.

The front and rear windscreens shattered as Jodie fired.

"You piece of shit," Jodie said. "You had to get in the way. We'd been working on this for years."

"Sorry to disappoint you," Carter said.

Hillier Jr curled himself into a ball as tears flowed from his eyes. Carter knew he was in shock and of no further help to him.

Carter snuck a glance. He popped his head up. It was too dark. He couldn't see Jodie.

"There are a bunch of loose ends that need to be tied up. It'll take two. Toss your weapon aside. We can work this out," Jodie said as she fired a bullet into the side of the car. "Or die," Jodie said.

"Carter, are you here?" Song's voice echoed throughout the warehouse.

"Take cover!" Carter yelled.

Carter stood up. He levelled his weapon on the car frame.

Bang.

A shot rang through the warehouse. Jodie fired her weapon towards Song. Carter saw a figure at the door take cover.

The spark from the weapon created enough light for Carter to see Jodie. He aimed his gun at Jodie.

His shot rang out. He knew he had missed when heard Jodie scuttle away. She returned fire at Carter. A bullet hit the car frame.

"Put the weapon down, Jodie," Song yelled. "We have you trapped."

"Go to Hell."

Song switched on her flashlight and shone it on Jodie.

Two shots rang out. Carter and Song had fired their weapon in unison.

Thud. Jodie hit the floor.

CHAPTER THIRTY-THREE

The chief commissioner of the force, Margaret Foster, sat in a boardroom with floor to ceiling windows overlooking Melbourne. She took a sip from a porcelain teacup with a delicate looking matching saucer while Carter, Song and Davies trickled in and took their seats before her. She mostly ignored the trio as she finished her tea while making a few notes on a pad in front of her. She pushed a file in front of each officer.

"Before we proceed, you'll find a non-disclosure agreement you'll need to sign."

"We'll need pens," Carter said.

Margaret sighed, "This mess of a situation and the confidentiality levels mean even my assistants aren't involved. So, forgive the lack of amenities such as pens and no morning tea."

The three looked at her teacup.

"I brought this in myself," Margaret said as she tossed Carter her pen.

Carter, Song and Davies opened their folders. Carter scanned the documents. The headline text provided sufficient detail for him to get the purpose — non-disclosure for life.

"What if we don't sign this?" Carter asked.

"Let's be frank, alright. Hillier Sr was garbage, corrupt, just a plain cunt. His son and you all did a bang-up job getting Hillier Sr out of the system," Margaret said. "It's actually a blessing in disguise that he's dead. As a corpse, he can be hailed as one of the heroes, protectors of police integrity and Victoria. Had you arrested him, Pandora's box would have opened."

Carter opened his mouth to speak before getting cut off.

"I'm aware of the hypocrisies of the situation. But just stop. Think about it. Globally and locally the reputations of policing agencies are not the best right now. The force has managed to skate through it relatively unscathed. I will emphasise the relatively. We have our own cultural issues to work through, prejudices and whatnot. I don't need to give you any harrowing statistics on domestic violence rates for officers or deaths in custody. All our work will be destroyed if the true extent of Assistant Commissioner Hillier's corruption gets out. You know, he was picked as my replacement when I retire for Christ sakes. Just imagine the headlines if the press found out about his corruption. And the protests on the street. My God, the public would be out for blood."

Margaret made eye contact individually with Carter, Song and Davies as she spoke these words. "No one can ever know how corrupt he really was. The narrative is he sadly died in a tragic fire at his Ascot Vale warehouse, along with his dear friend Jodie Day. All associated companies are being wound back. Ladies, gentleman, this incident is buried. Buried so deep not even an archaeologist will find it," Margaret said.

She stared them down with steely eyes. "Hillier Junior has already signed his. Now it's your turn to sign the non-disclosure agreement. Don't worry, there are some plum rewards for your signature."

The three of them signed the documents. The commissioner smiled.

"Wonderful, Superintendent Davies. I understand HR has fixed your pension and superannuation issues. It's now calculated at an assistant commissioner rate."

"Checked this morning; I have a healthier balance in my account," Davies said.

"Brilliant, I'm glad this matter is settled for you. I believe you have a retirement party to attend. And I hear congratulations are in order for your new role," Margaret said.

"New role?" Carter asked.

Davies stood up, "Moving to Canberra as James Hughes' chief of staff."

Carter and Song stared at Davies; their jaws dropped.

Davies smiled, "There are a few big fish he wants to fry. Taking down Hillier Sr has inspired me."

"What about Catherine, your daughter?" Carter asked.

"It's a part-time role. With my new salary and contribution from the force, she'll get the best treatment," said Davies. She squeezed Carter's shoulder. "Keep in touch. Good luck and congratulations, Superintendent," Davies smiled before she left the room.

Carter closed his folder and slid it towards the chief commissioner.

"I don't want that role. I need a few months' break," Carter said.

"I respect ambition, Detective Carter. However, it is misplaced," Margaret said.

Carter flushed with embarrassment. "Ahh, I see." Carter turned to look at Song.

"Congratulations, Ms Song, Superintendent Song now. You have big shoes to fill. Davies was one of a kind," Margaret said.

"Thank you. I know. Reckon I've got a steep learning curve," Song said.

Carter interrupted. "Sorry to suck the energy from the room, but aren't we missing something?"

"Ah, yes. The coroner's report, along with forensic evidence, indicates Mr Sam Kane, warmly remembered as Special K, committed suicide. His letter, phone records and a fibre in a car demonstrate that he murdered Nelson Harris. His associate Moe Bashar assisted. Once his usefulness reached its climax, Mr Kane killed Mr Bashar," Margaret said.

"He could have been a trailblazer. Now he's stitched up for two murders and a suicide," Carter said.

Margaret nodded gravely.

"That's the optics of the situation," Margaret said.

"Optics. Fucking optics. You know he was going to come out of the closet. Be a proper advocate, a leader in the footy world. Make it easier for young guys and gals – to make it easier for them to come out," Carter said. He clenched his fist. "He would have been a role model in Australia." Carter shook his head. "Now what? The optics say he's a murderer, probably pepper it with some mental-health issues as well."

Margaret nodded. "That's what our PR team have advised us to focus on, and how to support the community. We are going to partner with a few footy teams and mental health services to promote LGBTQI issues across sport and service industries. They'll be working on cultivating role models across all these industries. To avoid another such incident," Margaret said.

"God damn it." Carter smacked his hand on the table. "He didn't do that!"

"Maybe not, but he wasn't innocent. He's complicit in fraud and financial deception for advantage. Falling in love with Nelson was not the plan. He participated in the conspiracy for one pure and simple reason – greed. It's a powerful motivator," Margaret said.

"You got that right. Greed makes people do the damnedest thing. Like work for a perverse organisation," Carter said. "What's in this for me?"

"You keep your job. After you take some time off to assess if you want it. I have serious reservations about you. I understand why Davies brought you back to flush out Hillier. Having a senior LGBTQI officer leading the case was a smart move. Kept Hillier Sr off her back. But that is done. I hear the honourable member for Melbourne, James Hughes, has secured you an overseas holiday as a thank you for helping you," Margaret said.

"Has he, now?" Carter asked.

"You'll have your job back when or if you want it after your holiday. Even if you don't, you'll have a full pension, superannuation, the works," Margaret said.

"The department doles out the best hush money, doesn't it?" Carter asked.

The chief commissioner collected the folders. "The very best, Mr Carter. It may not seem it now, but the three of you did some good here. Helped weed out corruption and position the department in a better place. Brought some new voices to the party," Margaret said.

As she stood up, her pristine blue uniform suddenly looked less than pure in Carter's eyes.

"And remember. Role models come in all shapes, sizes. The best ones are damaged. You'll do some great work here," Margaret said.

The Chief Commissioner closed the door behind her, leaving Song and Carter in the boardroom.

"Superintendent Song," Carter said. "It has a nice ring to it."

Song smiled, "It does. The family will be impressed. What about you, boss?"

Carter shook his head. "Not your boss anymore." He looked out the boardroom windows.

"Guess I'm heading overseas for a while. I'll send you a Bintang singlet."

Song stood up and patted his shoulder, "Bring me back one. I expect you back at work. I'm not going to lose my best detective."

Carter placed a hand over Song's. "I'll be back."

Song left the office, leaving Carter alone as he took out his mobile and called Paddy.

"Hello stranger," Paddy said.

"I've got some good news and bad news," Carter said.

"Hit me with the good stuff."

"I'm going to wine and dine your arse… in a few weeks."

END

DCI Carter and the team will return in *Blood Content*.

I hope you enjoyed reading High-Rise Blood as much as I enjoyed writing it. If you could do me a favour, please leave a review on the platform you bought the book from. But, more importantly, reach out to me. I'd love to hear from you. My website has all my social media links: www.highriseblood.com.

ACKNOWLEDGEMENTS

Self-publishing a novel is like peeling an onion, and I'm not talking about all the tears involved. Writing the book is the first layer with successive layers including: editing, rewrites, design, marketing, and promotion. Each layer seems insurmountable.

How did I get through it all? With the support of my family, friends, and the poor souls I pitched my novel to after a few too many margaritas.

Thank you to Aaron, Sabrina, Matt, Christine, Warren and Adrian for your unwavering belief in me and your friendship.

To the wolfpack: Jackie, Nick, Cam, Jamie, Andrew, James, and Luke. Such an insufferable name for my nearest and dearest friends. An Aperol Spritz, a meal and a laugh with you feeds my soul. A special commendation goes to Luke's wine fridge. To John, my unofficial sounding board. To the formatting and styling guru Cam. Your collective talents continue to help shape and guide my craft.

To my workmates who turned into family across the globe. Cat, Jordan, Andrew, Bryan and the larger canoe school family. Downunder: Kat, Bradley, Sara, Hannah, and Liv – the dream team to work with.

To Dad, I'm sorry I missed your final breaths. The wisdom you shared with me during final days continues to breathe life into my art.

Printed in Great Britain
by Amazon

14610703R00195